GODMOTHER'S
FOOTSTEPS

PlaneTree

GODMOTHER'S FOOTSTEPS

Jane Hatton

Published 2004
ISBN 1-84294-154-2

Published by PlaneTree

Old Station Offices,
Llanidloes,
Powys SY18 6EB
United Kingdom

Manufactured in the United Kingdom

AUTHOR'S NOTE

This is a ghost story. I make no apology for it: you, the reader, can believe it or not as you choose. I can only say that the kind of things that happen here, have happened – to me or to others, many of whom I know personally, and I'm not attempting to explain the unexplainable. So far, such things are not susceptible to proof, and like Chel herself, I'm not certain that I believe the evidence, even of my own experience. But then, neither am I sure that I don't believe it. Take water divining, for instance. When Chel points out, in chapter xiii, that more than 40% of people could do this if they tried, she is stating a fact. I should know, I'm one of the 40% - but I don't know how, or why it works, even so. So why should I be sceptical about other mysteries?

The picture exists, although it isn't absolutely identical to that described here. It was painted some twenty-five years ago by my friend, artist Gina Ailes, and its history, though different, is almost as strange. The photograph is – or was, anyway – real. We were never absolutely certain whose face it was.

I

Judy Old roared into the farmyard like a hound of hell, pulled her bike up with a splatter outside the barn, and tooted the horn to tell anyone who hadn't already noticed that she had arrived. Her mother's head poked out of the kitchen door.

'Put the fowls off laying, you will, making all that row!'

Judy removed her helmet to reveal a smiling face, and shook her hair loose.

'I love you, too, Ma,' she said. Dismounting with style, she creaked in black leather across the yard and kissed her mother affectionately. 'I see you're baking. Good.'

'X-ray eyes is it, now?'

'Floury nose,' said Judy. 'So, what's new?'

'Two calves, bull and a heifer. First of the visitors up in the field. Are you coming in, or are you planning to stop out there and freeze us both to death?'

'*I'*m not freezing,' said Judy, but followed her mother into the kitchen.

Millie Jackson picked up her rolling pin and went back to her pastry, deftly lifting it onto the pie dish where steak and kidney already fragrantly nestled.

'You can put the kettle on if all you've to do is stand about like a barn door,' she suggested, crimping.

Judy picked it up, sniffing experimentally.

'What's in the oven? Smells like pasties to me.'

'And if it is, what's that to you? You're a married woman, you make your own pasties.'

'Keith loves your pasties,' said Judy, coaxing. She slid the kettle onto the Aga and returned to the kitchen table. 'You make pasties like nobody else in the world, Ma, ask anyone.'

Her mother smiled, tucking back the corners of her mouth in mock disapproval.

'Give over with the flannel, Judith Old. Fine doctor's wife you make!'

Judy grinned at that.

'It gives the patients something to chat about in the waiting room,' she suggested, and perched herself on the corner of the table. Millie gave her a poke with the end of the rolling pin.

1

'Shift your bottom off my clean table, if you please. If you want something useful to do while that kettle boils, you can take that letter up the field.' She pointed with the pin. 'There, on the dresser. She said she'd come down, but since you're here.'

Judy slid obediently off the table.

'If it's Satan that's supposed to find mischief for idle hands to do, I dread to think what that makes you, Ma.' She picked the letter up, looking at it with interest. 'From estate agents? Are they members of the "Let's retire to lovely Cornwall" brigade?'

'That, my girl, is for them to know and you to wonder. Now be off with you, and let me get those pasties out of the oven without you all over the place. And while you're at it, take that girl a half dozen eggs from out of the scullery.'

'What girl?' asked Judy, who had got as far as the door. Her mother laid down the rolling pin and frowned, but not, it seemed, at her daughter.

'That Mrs. Nankervis, on that letter you're bending,' she said. 'Crazy girl, near as bad as you are. They worry me, them two, though it's no business of mine. *Nor* yours, before you ask.'

Judy looked down at the envelope in her hands. It was addressed, she saw, to *Mr. & Mrs. O.J. Nankervis, c/o Church Farm, Trelewan, Penzance, Cornwall.*

'Nankervis...,' she said, thoughtfully. 'They could be relatives of yours. *Then* it would be your business.'

'They may well be, but that still makes them strangers. I never heard nor saw of them before.'

'Blood,' said Judy, unctuously, 'is thicker than water. They could be descendants of wicked Great Uncle Simon who ran away to get himself a life and never got forgiven.'

'That's one way of putting it, certainly. Now stop jawing, and get off with you. And don't go forgetting those eggs.'

On her way to the door, Judy paused, unable to resist one final tease. 'If you *are* Satan, Ma, what does that make me? Hell's angel?'

'Away with you, devil's child!' said her mother, waving a fork.

Judy laughed, and made her way back to the yard, collecting the eggs on the way. Going out through the gate again, she crossed the lane on foot and turned right, towards the entrance to the caravan park that her father, Jeff Jackson, had opened a dozen or so years earlier to augment the income from the farm. Judy, growing up next door to it, had many happy memories of summers spent playing with visitors' children, being taken on outings, attending parties and impromptu concerts, it was associated in her mind with generally having a ball.

Humming, she swung in her leathers along the lane and turned under the big wrought iron archway that announced CHURCH FARM HOLIDAY PARK. There weren't many happy campers about, she noticed almost automatically, but then it wasn't even Easter yet, and still noticeably chilly, particularly at night. A couple of caravans up to the left; with two whole fields to choose from they had set up house next door to each other as if huddling up for company. One of her father's row of ten newly-installed static vans against the far hedge had teatowels on a line strung outside. And further up the field, all on its own, there was a motor caravan. Useful if her mother had told her which of these four she was heading for.

Just ahead of her, a girl walked on the rutty track that led up through the centre of the site. She walked slower than Judy because she was laden with shopping, and her back view looked young, jeans and a padded jacket, and curling, reddish-gold hair to her shoulders. Judy put on speed. *Crazy girl*, her mother had said, and this one was certainly a girl. And anyone who camped before Easter when it was as early as this year simply had to be crazy.

'Excuse me - 'she called out, and broke into a run.

Chel, hearing her calling, paused and looked round, lowering her bags to the ground as she waited and flexing her arms. Living in their only form of transport presented problems that she had never envisaged when she had planned it. It was difficult just to slip up to the shop with the whole house on her back, like a snail, and right at this moment, she was feeling lonely, a little frightened, and indefinably depressed, caught in a situation that she had created herself, and from which she could see no immediate way out. She wanted something good to happen more than she wanted anything.

It was just about to.

Judy caught up with her.

'Hi,' she said, breathlessly.

They stood for a moment, assessing each other while Judy got her breath back. Chel saw a small, slim girl with a cloud of dark hair, dressed in biking leathers and with a friendly grin; Judy saw a young woman with pale, freckled skin and amazing green-blue eyes with tired shadows beneath them, surely not much older than herself but looking as if she carried the cares of the world.

'Would you be Mrs. O.J. Nankervis?' Judy asked.

'That's me all right.' Oddly, that sounded almost regretful.

'There's a letter for you.' Judy held it out. 'Oh - and half a dozen eggs from Ma.' She paused. 'Ah. Yes. I tell you what, I'll carry them for you, shall I? Or even better, how about I carry one of your bags,

3

too?'

'There's an offer I can't refuse,' said Chel, ruefully. 'My arms feel as if they reach my knees.' She held them out, stretching her fingers. 'Oof! I hate shopping!'

'Depends on the shopping,' Judy suggested. She picked up one of the bags, Chel resumed the other one, and they walked on up the sloping field together.

'I couldn't help noticing,' said Judy, without apology - she had never been backward about coming forward, as her mother frequently remarked. 'The letter's from an estate agent. Are you looking for a house down here? A holiday cottage, or something?'

'Sort of,' said Chel, and paused. Judy said,

'Me and my mouth! We're always rushing in - where even *hell*'s angels fear to tread.' She giggled. 'Tell me to get lost, why don't you?'

But the giggle had disarmed Chel. She had once been a bit of a giggler herself, a long time ago.

'No, please don't get lost. You're the first human being apart from my husband that I've spoken to for what feels like a year.'

'Except for the people in the shop,' said Judy.

'Except for them, of course.'

A silence fell, and Judy ventured,

'They *are* human, you know. Sally and Jim. At the shop.'

Chel said, without quite meaning to,

'We ran away. It's left us... well, friendless, really.'

Judy stopped, and struck an attitude, there in the middle of the track.

'See me - I'm friendly!'

Chel smiled. Her face felt stiff.

'Sorry. I'm talking nonsense.'

Judy wondered if that was true. They fell into step again.

'About the house,' said Chel, feeling that she had been ungracious and wishing to make amends. 'We want to buy one down here, but we're in an awkward position. Our own hasn't sold.'

'Par for the course,' suggested Judy. 'Everything sells in time.'

'We don't have time,' said Chel. She nodded towards the motor caravan ahead of them. 'We're living in that.' She made herself laugh. 'It's a bit of a squash.'

Judy, who was a sensitive person, felt a reticence here that she didn't yet understand, but respected nonetheless. She made a joke of it, to demonstrate she had no wish to pry.

'At least you don't have six children and a dog, like some people.' She paused. '*Have* you got six children and a dog?'

'No,' said Chel. 'No children.' Her throat ached.

4

Judy stopped again.

'It's the bike boots,' she said, apologetically, looking down at her booted feet. 'They clump in everywhere. Why don't you tell me to shut up?'

'No, it's me,' said Chel. She made herself smile. 'Take no notice, it's just that I feel as if I live in a world that's made of glass...' To her horror, she realised that she was on the verge of tears.

Judy realised that she had met with someone with whom, for some as yet unexplained reason, it was impossible to say the right thing. She looked around her for somewhere to sit. The options were limited. The last of the line of big static vans lay to the right.

'We could sit on the step of that van,' she said. 'Nobody's in it.'

Chel, a little to Judy's surprise, followed her across the grass almost as if being told what to do was a relief. They sat together on the narrow step, the shopping at their feet.

'Look,' said Judy, and with wild inaccuracy. 'I'm not a curious person - well, no more than anybody is - and you don't have to tell me anything at all. But if you want to unload onto someone, I'm here, and I promise you, it'll go no further than this step.'

Did she want to unload onto someone? Chel thought about it, and found that she was doing so with what she could only diagnose as *longing*, but could she really confide in someone whose name she didn't even know? So she hesitated.

Judy said,

'I'm Judy. My father owns this camping site, as you will have gathered from the eggs.'

That placed her firmly in context, Chel liked her parents and would trust them, she thought. She said,

'Cheryl. My friends call me Chel.'

'So what do I call you?'

Their eyes met. It happens, sometimes, that friendship is instantaneous, leaping like electricity between strangers.

'How about Chel?' said Chel.

'Hullo, Chel,' said Judy.

A silence fell, strained at first but gradually easing. Chel said, feeling as if she was pushing through a wall,

'If I start telling you, you'll probably find you know most of it already.'

'Then,' said Judy, calmly, 'there's no harm in telling, is there?'

'O is for Oliver,' said Chel. 'I expect you read the newspapers.'

'Sailed round the world,' said Judy.

'That's the one.'

Judy went on, slowly, searching her memory for details, for truth to tell, she hadn't followed the story closely, having had other things on her mind at the time.

'Got himself flattened in some brawl, about a year ago? Found a treasure ship? I'm sorry, I'm a bit hazy on the details. It was last summer I got married.'

Remembering her own impulsive wedding, Chel understood. After all, it probably had been quite small potatoes to most of the world even if it had filled their own horizon from east to west.

'It wasn't exactly a brawl,' she said. 'There was a girl screaming in an alley, and a gang of... well, they were bikers.' She hesitated. Judy made a grimace.

'Tell me about it! It's like football supporters, forty yobs and four hundred and forty carry the can. I blame the media, me. Go on.'

'Not *nice* bikers,' said Chel, thoughtfully.

'There are some not-nice accountants, or civil servants, too. Nobody seems to remember that. It's all those American biker gangs.' Her ill-disciplined sense of humour presented her with a gang of marauding accountants, but she filed the idea for a more seemly moment.

'The girl screamed rape,' said Chel. 'Oliver marched in with all guns blazing, and got beaten up. Later, she took it back. They only got a couple of years for GBH, and some of them even got off. They said Oliver started it.'

'Bit of a bugger,' said Judy, into a pause. Details were coming back now. There had been some sort of Appeal Fund, she remembered. Down here in Cornwall it had made a few minor ripples, Oliver Nankervis had sailed from, and returned to, Falmouth on his epic voyage.

'Yes... well. You know what he says - Oliver? If it had been an accident he could have borne it better... it's the thought that *people* did it to him, deliberately... just for fun, you could almost say. It's ruined his life.'

'He was left disabled, wasn't he?'

'Yes... although, since we got away, he's been a lot better. But where do we go from here? I don't know.'

'You've said that twice,' said Judy. 'Run away, got away. How can you get away from something like that?'

How, indeed?

'It was people,' said Chel, thinking. 'His family, particularly. He has a stepmother who is something else again. They would interfere. And his sister talked me into buying this horrible bungalow, that simply rubbed it in that nothing would ever be the same again.'

'If it was so horrible, why did you let her?' asked Judy, reasonably enough.

Difficult to explain. Chel chewed on her lip, for the bungalow hadn't been horrible to look at, merely dull, she hadn't meant that at all. She hedged.

'You know what some houses are like... they have a nasty atmosphere. I didn't realise until I actually lived in it, it was one of those.' She didn't like to say that the bungalow had nearly killed Oliver, but it had. And it had driven her out, and only a miracle had saved them. But that was in the past, and wasn't something that she could say to someone she had only just met, if she could say it to anyone at all. People at the time had thought she was being silly, refusing to go back, and they were people who had known how unhappy they had been there. Judy, who didn't know, would probably think she was barking.

But there, she misjudged Judy, who would have fully understood.

'This'll be the one that won't sell,' said Judy.

'That's the one. And until it has, we can't afford another. But we can't go on living in the van, either. Oliver was glad to get away at first - we both were - but it's too small, and too cramped, and now the first relief at escaping has worn off, it's getting on our nerves. And it's a nuisance, having to drive such a big vehicle everywhere we want to go.'

Looking back at what they had left behind them, and remembering how grateful they had been to the van to begin with, that sounded harsh. But it was true. The van was a holiday home, they - she, rather, for it had been her initiative - hadn't thought things through properly.

'Could you afford to rent?' Judy asked. Chel looked at her. Oliver had repudiated the Appeal Fund money, saying that he couldn't live on other people's charity, which had left them, not penniless, thanks to insurance and the sunken *Hesperides*, but needing to be careful. Renting temporarily was something they had discussed, but with Oliver still having difficulty in getting about, a lot of places were out of the question, even had there been a lot of places on offer, which, with the holiday season fast approaching, there were not. Anyway, for Oliver's sanity, it had to be somewhere in the country, and preferably near the sea. It was all very well for her sister-in-law, Susan Casson, to say that beggars couldn't afford to be choosers, but people, pavements, and houses were the last things that Oliver had ever wanted, or needed now. Living in a bland, suburban road had been yet another of the factors that had nearly brought them down.

'We've looked,' she said, now. 'It's all holiday lets, anything that

7

might be suitable. We can't keep moving around, and anyway, they're too expensive. If we take a long-term let, it's got to be right. And not cheap, exactly, but certainly inexpensive.'

Judy patted the step on which they sat.

'What about one of these? I know they're not all let before Spring Bank, anyway, with Easter so early, and it would at least give you a breathing space.'

'But it would only be in the short term,' said Chel.

'True, but you needn't get rid of your van, you could just buy a pushbike to get around on if all you wanted was shopping. In fact, there's an old one at the farm that you could borrow.'

Once before, Chel had got so bogged down that it had taken someone outside their problems to straighten her out. The friend who had directed her attention to the van had unlocked the door of a prison - one whose bars were made of interference, of love and of caring in about equal measure. She said,

'It's certainly an idea.'

'They've got proper plumbing, not just chemical loos,' said Judy, tempting. 'And gas fires, and showers, and space to move around in. They're meant for whole families. Think about it.' She changed the subject, thinking that enough had been said for now. 'My mother was a Nankervis.'

'Was she?' Chel looked interested. 'Oliver's grandfather came from somewhere round here, perhaps you're related.'

'Really? Where from.'

'Some place called Higher Vellanzoe,' said Chel. 'We passed it once, when we were down here on holiday... he ran away too, it must run in the family.'

'Great Uncle Simon!' cried Judy. 'Nobody ever knew what happened to him! They thought he must have lied about his age and enlisted, and got killed in the Great War.' They exchanged a look and burst out laughing. Chel looked quite different when she laughed, lively and full of fun.

'His name was Simon, yes.'

'That makes us cousins,' said Judy.

'By marriage, anyway. Oliver is your blood cousin.'

'Wow, fame! This is going to put a crimp into the family album!'

Chel got to her feet.

'You'd better come and meet this cousin of yours, then. He'll be wondering where I've got to.' She glanced at the van as they left, estimating its size. It was certainly a lot bigger than the motor caravan they called home. A temporary respite... if not the full answer, it might serve a turn. Judy caught her eye.

'I could find out which one and bring up the key, if you liked. You could have a look, see what you think.'

There could be no harm in that, Chel agreed. It committed them to nothing. Commitment to anything was something that Oliver seemed to find impossible these days, and she found a heavy burden in the need to take all the decisions herself. Her one attempt to make him share in a plan for the future had been brief and unhelpful.

'We can't do anything until we've got rid of that horrible little house of yours, you know we can't.'

Thanks to him, and his stupid pride that made him reject all help. She would have liked to tell him to stop being childish, but one of the things that they found difficult these days was quarrelling, they had in the recent past done too much of it, too disastrously. When they were able to have a good fight again, Chel concluded, they could consider themselves on the high road to some kind of sensible life together, but that day hadn't yet come, and they were just marking time. He was Oliver, all right, recognisable and familiar now, not the caricature he had been only a few weeks ago, but on the other hand a long way from the tough-minded, independent adventurer of the old days. Something, however, must have shown in her face, for Oliver had given her a sweet, wilful smile, and said,

'What's the matter, are you bored?'

No, she thought now, she wasn't that. Not if he still needed the precious solitude. But surely there had to come a point at which the exclusion of all but herself from his life ceased to be necessity and became an over-indulgence. He was a natural loner, with all his normal retreats closed to him, no sun-washed Mediterranean islands, no great oceans, no wrecks under the deep sea. He could easily become a recluse if she let him, and under the circumstances, a bitter one. The day would surely come when she would have to give him a push and pray that his cruelly clipped wings had grown enough feathers for flying, and she wasn't sure if she had the courage.

Perhaps this was the day? Just a little wobble on the branch?

'When you say you ran away,' said Judy, as they walked together up the field, 'did you mean that literally?'

'Yes,' said Chel, nonchalantly, although the thought of what she had done still brought her out in a cold sweat when she thought about it. Oliver had been in hospital, recovering from the nearest thing to a breakdown she trusted he would ever have, everyone around them, both their families, had been so sure that they knew best what to do, although some with love and some with what could only be described

9

as officiousness and at least one, she suspected, with malice - and she had taken the law into her own hands and gone behind their backs, swept him away in the motor caravan and driven by easy stages to Cornwall and the sea, and what little freedom might remain to him, telling nobody what she had done or where she was going. It had worked - up to a point - but what if it hadn't?

Best not to think about it.

But where next? They had deliberately chopped their lives in half, slid knowingly down the slippery snake of life - but how did they now throw the six that would set them climbing the ladders again?

There was no way she could say this to a stranger, however. There was no way in which she could say it to anyone any more. They had chosen to be alone, and alone was exactly what they were.

'That was brave of you,' Judy was saying.

'Brave, or stupid?' asked Chel, but under her breath, so that Judy said,

'Sorry?'

'Nothing.' *Nothing*?

They had almost reached the motor caravan now, and Oliver, who was sitting in the early spring sunshine in his wheelchair, reading the paper. The wheelchair was an improvement, back "home" in Embridge he had flatly refused to have anything to do with it, here in Cornwall it had turned out to be useful, and Chel was glad that she had insisted on bringing the hated object with them. It was, for one thing, the only seat they had in which he could sit outside comfortably. He still refused to let her push him around in it, but she could forgive that. In any case, he was getting quite handy on crutches these days so it mattered far less than it had done.

She called out,

'Oliver! See what I've found, a relative of yours!'

Oliver jumped, and crumpled the paper in... alarm? Chel wasn't sure. Perhaps that had been a bit tactless, Oliver and his known relatives were in a permanent state of war.

'God, Chel, don't give me shocks like that! I thought you were about to present me with Susan!' He looked at Judy with wary interest, which Judy returned but without the wariness.

'Hi, I'm Judy,' she said. 'We think that your grandfather was my grandfather's brother. I *think* that makes us second cousins, but I'm never sure.'

Oliver looked as if *once removed*, and preferably to somewhere a long way away from here, would suit him better, but good manners made him take Judy's friendly, extended hand.

'Well, hullo,' he said.

'It's Judy's parents down at the farm,' said Chel, helpfully.

Oliver had already suspected that the Jacksons might be relatives, from something said on a previous visit to Trelewan, and had deliberately said nothing. He might have known, though, that he couldn't get away with it for ever, and Judy looked pleasant enough. It occurred to him that Chel might be happier with a friend to do things with; although she had denied it, she must find time hanging heavy on her hands, he knew that he certainly did. So he made himself smile, and Judy's impression of him, as a thin, dark, scowling man, changed in a moment. Like Chel's, the smile lit his face and charmed her. Perhaps they neither of them had that much to smile about and were simply out of practice?

'My - *our*, that is - great uncle William, who is still alive by the way, although knocking on a bit these days, has always told us that his older brother Simon ran away to enlist when he was sixteen years old, but if he's right, he obviously survived.' Oliver made no comment, so Judy continued. 'My grandfather, who is dead now, wasn't born until after 1915, when it all happened, this great family row about yours not wanting to be a farmer - so he never knew him... well, you know what families are. Go back far enough, and you lose your way completely. But that's roughly how it goes. From our side, anyway.' She paused, and Oliver said,

'My grandfather was a solicitor, and a very fly operator if reputation doesn't lie. I don't remember him, he died quite soon after I was born.'

'Fortunes of war,' said Judy, speculating on possibilities. 'It threw all sorts of people together - maybe he was a bit of an opportunist even that far back, and someone gave him a chance after it was all over. I don't suppose we shall ever know now.'

Oliver gave the first indication for weeks that he ever intended to speak to his family again.

'My father may be able to fill in the blanks, if it interests you. You could ask him. But sweeping things under the carpet is a bit of a tradition on our branch of the family tree, and he may not even know.'

Chel took Judy's bag of shopping and prepared to step up into the van.

'I'm going to put the kettle on. Would you like a cup of tea, Judy?'

Judy suddenly remembered the kettle simmering on the Aga in the farm kitchen. Her mother would think she'd been kidnapped.

'I'd better not. Ma's expecting me.' She put the box of eggs and the letter into Chel's outstretched hand. 'I tell you what, though. I'll take a rain check - Keith and I will maybe drop by one evening and get acquainted properly... if that's all right, of course?'

Chel looked at Oliver, leaving him to reply, not wishing to be blamed afterwards if she said the wrong thing. He hesitated, and she held her breath. If he agreed, it would be a big step forward.

'Why not?' said Oliver.

'We'll call it a date then,' said Judy. 'I'll get Dad to drop that key up, Chel. See you both!'

She was gone, running down the field. Oliver raised his eyebrows at Chel, looking guilty in the doorway.

'Key? What have you two been hatching?'

'She suggested we might rent one of the big vans, just for a few weeks,' said Chel. Her expression was so hangdog that Oliver gave a smothered laugh. Chel relaxed. 'It would give us some space,' she said. Oliver held out his hand to her.

'Come here.'

Half-reluctantly, she stepped down to the ground again and came to him. He took her hand, looking up at her.

'Am I so frightening, Chel? Do I bully you? You looked terrified just now.'

'No, of course you don't.' She knew that she spoke too loudly.

'Convince me,' said Oliver.

She sat down on the step, without removing her hand from his.

'It's not you,' she said.

'What is it then?'

Chel bit her lip. His voice was gentle, but she knew, after this past, terrible year, how volatile he could be. She was very afraid of saying the wrong thing.

'Everything...,' she said.

'That's comprehensive! Can you be more specific?'

Chel said, in a rush,

'I can't seem to get past *now*. Where we are, what we're doing. I'm sure it was the right thing to come here, but what's the next step? I don't know.'

They sat silent for a minute or two, touching but not speaking.

'It's all a bit of a muddle, isn't it?' said Oliver, at last. Chel nodded, without speaking. A sudden, shaking anger came over her, familiar and helpless, against the seven young hooligans whose mindless violence had brought them to this place, who had been, in a phrase someone had actually used at the time, *having fun.* And somewhere in the world, she was well aware, were people who would try to excuse them on the grounds of deprivation, broken homes, unemployment, media influence, and plead for mercy and understanding for them, for that very humanity which they had so signally lacked. But Oliver, too, came from a broken home. He was now not simply unemployed, but for the moment at least, unemployable. Probably none of that vast army of do-gooders would think that worth mentioning, after all, he was only the victim, the cause some said, and his father had money. The sheer injustice of it all nearly choked her, ten times a day, and she found it impossible to let it go. Knowing that if she didn't, it was simply conceding violence another point, wasn't enough. Until she - *they*, indeed, for Oliver must surely feel it even more - could resolve it, there was no open road ahead.

'One step at a time,' said Oliver, quietly. He was becoming expert at that, and in more ways than one.

'What step?' asked Chel, in a strangled voice she only barely recognised as her own, because if there had been a step to take it might have been easier to let resentment go.

Oliver gestured down the field.

'Burn another boat. Move into one of those big vans, sell this one, buy a car, make ourselves more mobile. We've got to do it eventually, why not now?'

'But it'd only be for weeks, at the most.'

'Something's got to give, sometime. It may not be much of an opening, but it's something.'

Chel said, fearful,

'We shouldn't jump into selling this van, surely. We might need it again.'

'If we're going to take a gamble, let's make it a good one.'

That sounded so like the Oliver she had married that Chel stared at him in amazement. He gave her a wry smile.

'It's only my legs that have turned stupid on me. My brain still works.'

It occurred to Chel, and for the first time, that Oliver's reluctance to commit to anything was because he had seen nothing to commit to, and perhaps he had been thinking the same about her. If that was so, Judy's offered key to the caravan might prove to be the key to a great deal else. Not a future yet, but a recognisable path down which they might stumble to a place where the viewpoint would be different. As Oliver had said, one step at a time.

'If we do that,' she said, tentatively, because she wasn't yet sure how wide was the opening ahead of them, 'perhaps we ought to let everyone know where we are. Don't you think?'

'Why?' asked Oliver. 'They know we're alive. You ring them on that mobile you insisted on bringing.'

Chel sighed. Oliver sounded less argumentative than she had expected, but it was difficult to preach a gospel in which she didn't wholly believe.

'Because they're worrying. Why else?'

'Your family may be,' conceded Oliver.

'And yours,' said Chel, who was invariably the one who spoke to them.

'Mine?' he asked, derisively. 'Mine are only bothered with how it looks to other people, you know that.'

Chel would have liked to retreat from the tone of his voice, but instinct told her that to let Oliver create a precedent of that kind would be a retrograde step just when things were beginning to show a glimmer of promise. After a short hesitation, she continued, feeling her way and nervous of his reactions, stupidly afraid of precipitating a row and despising herself for it. She hadn't exactly meant to start this particular hare, but having done so, realised that it would give her a chance to say several things that had needed saying for some time. At least one of them weighed very heavily on her conscience. So she took hold of her courage, and went on.

'Not your father,' she said. 'He'd go to the stake rather than tell you, because that's the way he is, but he's so proud of you and the things you've done, he gets all gruff and embarrassed just talking about you.'

He doesn't get *all gruff and embarrassed* talking *to* me,' Oliver told her.

'Because he doesn't know how to handle you, and never has done,' said Chel. 'In his own way, he's always tried to do his best for you, and Helen - '

'You hardly know Helen,' cut in Oliver, swiftly. 'Leave her out of it.'

Chel knew that Oliver's mother was the whole point. She almost backed down and let the moment slip, but there might never be another, and hadn't she already decided not to let Oliver intimidate her?

'It's true I hardly know her,' she said. 'But you can't leave her out. Listen, Oliver - '

'No, *you* listen! She went away to lead her own life, and left me to be brought up as a duty by a righteous, spiteful bore! I don't suppose you've ever been a duty. It's not much fun.'

'She couldn't both take you and leave you, however much she loved you,' retorted Chel, immediately defensive of Helen, whom she deeply pitied. 'She had to make a decision that would be best for you, not her! So, she got talked into the wrong one, just like I did over the bungalow, and you too - '

'And by the same people,' said Oliver, as if that clinched the argument.

'So you should understand,' said Chel.

Oliver said nothing to that, and after a moment, Chel went on,

'Think about it. And while you're doing it, think about this too. You think Helen doesn't love you. You think she ran out on you and only cared about her work. Well, she's an artist, and perhaps in one way she did - but *only* in one way. She loves you and cares what happens to you so little, Oliver Nankervis, that last year when you were so ill, and it looked as if you might be on a dialysis machine for the rest of your life, she was prepared to give you one of her kidneys. So talk your way out of that!'

In the silence, she heard the birds singing in the hedge and the faint rumble of a tractor in a distant field, cars on the road through the village. After what seemed a lifetime, Oliver said,

'I didn't know that. Nobody told me.'

'I know you didn't know it, that's why I *have* told you. Helen just said it didn't matter, once you were safe, and she went back to America, but only because you so obviously didn't want her around. But don't ever say to me again that she puts her work first!'

There seemed nothing more to be said that wouldn't lead to the quarrel she dreaded, and so she flounced back into the van to unpack the shopping. Since Oliver subsequently behaved as if the whole conversation had never taken place, she was left miserably aware that he might feel much as she did. They had a long, long way to go yet before life was anything even approaching normal again.

'What was the letter?' asked Oliver, now, and Chel handed it down to him without speaking. Knowing quite well that he had upset her, he took it, also unspeaking. Chel's family life, he well knew, had been nothing like his own and although he was glad for her, he didn't see, had never seen, that it gave her the right to sit in judgement on him. What Helen might choose to do now made no difference to what she had done before, although, if he was honest, Chel had succeeded in startling him. But Chel had no idea what she was talking about, and that was all there was to it. It wasn't open to argument, it was quite simply graven in stone. He opened the letter, drawing out the sheaf of papers inside and riffling through them.

'Two bungalows on a new estate, no thanks, a terraced cottage in St. Just, where they already know we don't want to live, and Trelewan House which is presently a guest house and has seven bedrooms and self-contained attic accommodation for the owners.'

'Nothing to rent?' asked Chel, making an effort to sound normal.

15

'I think we might be asking in the wrong places for that,' said Oliver, pushing the papers back into the envelope. 'Apart from our flat, I've never rented - and that came by word of mouth.'

'Perhaps we could ask around the village,' suggested Chel, for talking to Judy had brought the village into focus, whereas before it seemed somewhere blurred in the background that was convenient only to buy food. She realised that she had allowed herself to develop a kind of tunnel vision over the last few weeks, directing all her energies onto Oliver and disregarding anything else. Perhaps that had been necessary at first. Listlessly, she piled packets and tins onto the tiny worktop and thought about it. It seemed ironic that they might have run away to learn to live again, and in the process, forgotten how to do it.

The evening was beginning to draw on, and the van felt chilly. She looked through the door at Oliver, who, impervious to the chill, had returned to his newspaper, although she didn't think he was reading it.

'Aren't you cold?' she asked, and was sorry to hear that it came out like a challenge. The word *catalyst* came into her mind. Judy had been a catalyst, bringing the outside world into their quiet little cocoon of healing and peace. Oliver lowered his newspaper.

'You can't want to shut yourself up in a box this early, surely,' he said.

Chel looked at him, feeling her mouth primming into a disapproving line, and just for a moment, a real row hovered in the wings. Then her sense of humour came to her rescue and she found herself, unexpectedly, laughing.

'You are a selfish bastard, Oliver Nankervis!' she exclaimed. 'For someone who's spent so many years living in a tiny space on a yacht, anyone would think you suffered from claustrophobia!'

To her relief, Oliver grinned back at her. He folded the newspaper and started to pull himself out of the chair, while at the same time, apparently giving serious thought to her accusation.

'Do you know, I think you might be right,' he said. He was upright now, steadying himself with one hand against the side of the van, breathing a little fast.

'Not a permanent condition, I hope,' said Chel. Seeing Oliver fight his disability always hurt her, but she knew better, by this time, than to offer help. She kept her voice light. 'I'll turn into an ice maiden!'

'I do, too,' said Oliver. 'But no - I think it's just the effect of spending so long cooped up in hospital.' He didn't mention the bungalow, and neither did Chel. She stood aside from the doorway. There were only two shallow steps to climb, but even so he found it a struggle, and she hated to watch. Two years, they had told them at the hospital. Two years before healing was complete, but one of them was already gone and it didn't seem to Chel that he found it any easier to pick up his feet than he had at the start. Wherever they lived, it couldn't have stairs for him to climb. Laughter gone as quickly as it had come, she began to shove the tins anyhow into the cupboard, the butter and cheese into their tiny fridge.

It was about an hour later that Jeff Jackson knocked on the door. He carried with him a fragrant, newspaper-wrapped package and a key on a tag labelled *No.10*.

'Little present from the wife,' he said. 'She says you're family.' He grinned at Chel, as she stood above him in the doorway. 'Gives you special privileges that does. And here's the key. Have a look when you want, and bring the key down the farm, tell us what you think. We can have it cleaned tomorrow, you could move in when you like. It's this end one, so you won't be bothered.'

'For how long?' asked Chel. Jeff wrinkled up his nose, thinking.

'Four, five weeks, I reckon. Can't do no more, we've bookings. But it might tide you over.' He looked at the motor caravan disparagingly. 'Like sardines in a tin you are, in here. All right for a holiday.'

Chel thanked him, took the package and the key from him and watched him stumping back down the field in the ebbing daylight. She stood there for several minutes.

'Taken root, have you?' asked Oliver, adding, 'Something smells good. What's in the parcel?'

Chel laid it on the worktop and carefully unwrapped two pasties.

'That'll save me cooking tonight,' she observed. 'How kind of her, they look wonderful!' She looked at Oliver, twirling the key on its ring around her finger. 'Shall we have a look? It's not dark yet.'

'Why not? The exercise will do me good.'

Chel had meant to drive down the field, but Oliver was already struggling to his feet, reaching for the crutches on which he was becoming an expert these days. She realised that they had just taken another big step forward, and wondered for a wild moment if their lives were doomed to be always so contradictory. They had fled from Embridge to escape relatives, landed up by chance among different relatives, and apparently fallen through a hole in the clouds into a whole new country. A visit from the Archangel Gabriel could have hardly had more immediate impact than Judy's brief visit. Absurdly, she felt tears choking at the back of her throat, and jumped down off the step onto the ground so that Oliver shouldn't guess. Taking deep breaths of the cool evening air, she got herself under control and when he finally stood beside her, she turned to him an untroubled face.

'Come on then,' said Oliver.

They walked slowly down the field at Oliver's pace, which at present couldn't be described as fast. Hedges and trees cast long shadows, the sun hung low in the sky, a red ball in a puff of pink and orange clouds that lay close to the horizon.. There would be a frost tonight, Chel thought, sniffing the air. A beautiful day tomorrow, with luck. It would be nice to think that it would herald many beautiful days to come, in which the good things would come flooding back to them, but she knew that life seldom worked that way. They had had their golden time, two incredible years of it, nobody got that twice. Living for the moment, doing exactly as they pleased... well, they had always known, hadn't they, that that couldn't go on for ever?

It had turned into a dead end, leading nowhere. The knowledge lay at the bottom of Chel's heart like lees in a bottle of wine.

The caravan was dark inside, but when Chel touched the switch just inside the door, the lights came on. It smelled disused, but not damp. Damp would have been impossible for Oliver. She stepped into a dining area, with stove, sink and worktop under the window to the left of the door, a family-sized fridge, and a door beyond leading into a sitting area with proper chairs and a sofa that probably, she thought, made a double bed. Turning back to explore the other end, she came face to face with Oliver, breathing hard from the effort of negotiating the step.

'Bedrooms,' he said, in answer to her unspoken question. 'One double, one tiny one with bunks, we could even have visitors.' He was smiling. 'I've been in plenty of smaller boats than this. And at least we could get away from each other. Stop getting on each other's nerves so much.'

So he realised that, too. The afternoon had been full of surprises, one way or the other.

'Go for it, then?' asked Chel.

'To hell with it! Why not?'

They had moved together almost without realising it. Oliver leaned one crutch carefully against the kitchen units and put the arm thus freed around Chel. She leaned her head into his shoulder. She felt safe, but whether it was Oliver or the van, she wasn't sure.

'Home, sweet home,' she said.

Oliver bent his head to kiss her, lightly, on the temple. She turned her head, and their lips met. There was more of the love that had once been between them in that kiss than there had been for a long time.

'Right then,' said Chel. 'Decision taken. So let's go get at those pasties.'

II

They moved into the big static the next day, and parked their own motor caravan outside, still undecided as to what was the best thing to do about it. Oliver was all for getting rid of it and thus increasing their mobility, and Chel could see his point. At the back of her mind, though, was always the thought that they might need it again, and she hesitated. Suppose they found nowhere else?

'We can't go on living in it for ever,' Oliver pointed out, reasonably. 'It's a bloody great monster for you to wrestle around these narrow lanes. Be sensible.'

Chel knew that this was true. She also knew, and dared not point out, that there were advantages that offset the disadvantages, such as the fact that wherever they took it, there was always somewhere for Oliver to lie down if he needed to. Although this was becoming less and less essential, it was still a fact of life. They couldn't go out for the day without this facility, and if she said so, he would probably fly into a... well, a tantrum, actually. Oliver had recovered enough now to need an occupation, he hadn't admitted it yet, but time hung heavy on his hands. He carried around with him a distinct aura of unexploded bomb - inherited, had they realised, through the maternal line - and Chel was wary of it. She wished she could think of an answer, but the answers that had flowed so thick and fast during their escape from Embridge seemed to have dried into a stony river-bed in a persistent drought. The - rather daunting - explanation for this, she realised, was that she didn't actually know enough about Oliver and so had no idea how to help him onward. It hardly helped.

Judy brought Keith to meet them on the Saturday, three days after their move into the new van. They came up the field in windy sunshine under a sky of brilliant blue, with patches of grey cloud scudding across and spatters of rain in the wind, a rainbow day. With them came a remarkably pretty golden-brown mongrel with a white chest and paws and an exuberantly friendly disposition. Chel was sitting on the step in the open doorway, peeling apples for a pie, she saw them coming and waved her knife in greeting.

'We've got visitors,' she said. Oliver, who was pottering experimentally in the kitchen, making coffee, said,

'We don't know anybody, do we?'

'Looks like Judy to me,' said Chel, getting to her feet. 'Although without her leathers, I scarcely recognise her. She somehow looks much smaller.'

'Less menacing,' suggested Oliver, with a short bark of laughter that wasn't altogether amused. Chel decided to ignore it. She did, she realised, ignore a lot of things, probably too many. She gathered up her saucepan of apples as Judy and Keith arrived at the step.

'Coffee?' she greeted them.

Keith held out the six-pack he was carrying.

'Got something better than that. You must be Judy's cousin.'

'I'm the *by marriage* half of the partnership. Do come in. It's about to rain again.' She turned to say to Oliver, 'Hold the coffee. They've brought beer.'

Oliver promptly turned off the gas, as Keith and Judy crowded into the van. Rain spattered momentarily on the windows. Keith said,

'So long as you're not on any medication that fights with alcohol, that is.'

'Stop talking like a doctor!' said Judy, pushing him out of the fairway onto one of the bench seats at the table. 'Sit down. Behave yourself. This is my husband, Keith. And our dog, Sheba. Do you mind?'

'Mind Sheba? Certainly not!' Chel bent down to pat the dog and Oliver gave a smothered laugh.

'Keith's another story,' he said.

'I didn't mean that, of course I didn't!'

They all laughed.

Sheba had spotted Oliver, and bounced up at him, making him stagger. Judy grabbed at her.

'*Sheba*! Honestly, this dog has no manners, you have to excuse her!' She didn't add, as nine people out of ten would have done, *did she hurt you*? and Keith said,

'Put her outside, for God's sake!'

Judy tipped her out and closed the door, but the resulting volley of barks proved deafening and she had to come in again. Keith booted her under the table and told her to be quiet, and she laughed up at him with her tongue hanging out.

'Sorry,' said Keith. 'Shall we go out, and come in again?'

It was almost a chemical reaction, thought Chel, fascinated. A moment of confusion, a burst of laughter - and suddenly, there they were, friends. She slid onto the bench beside Keith, and ripped the ring-pull off the can he passed her.

'Cheers!' she said. It seemed appropriate.

Judy and Oliver, pleased with each other, were exchanging family history - or, to be more accurate, Judy was telling Oliver about the Vellanzoe Nankervises, and Oliver was listening. It was interesting watching them, for seen side by side like this they were recognisably related. Judy's eyes were brown, her dark hair curly, but nevertheless, some elusive family resemblance came and went like the fitful sunshine outside.

Keith turned to Chel.

'So, how's your search for a home going?' he asked her.

'Not terribly well. Partly, admittedly, because we haven't any money.'

'Ah. I can see that would be a disadvantage.'

Chel liked Keith. He was a nondescript man, painted in neutral colours, engaging. Moreover, as a local man, he would possibly have inside information. So she said, almost idly repeating the litany of their present life,

'What we really need for the moment is a long-term let. Only most of the good ones seem to be holiday places and only short-term. Like this is.' She gestured round the caravan. 'It's great for now, but it isn't the answer.'

Keith took a leisurely swig at his can, lowering it to the table to say,

'Have you had a look at that place out by Uncle William?'

Judy's quick ear caught the question. She broke off what she was saying to Oliver and made a face.

'Come on, Keithie baby, that's a disaster! Anyway, it's for sale. Not that anyone in their right mind would touch it with a ten foot pole!'

'Why not?' asked Oliver, curiously, but Judy shrugged her shoulders and made no reply.

'I don't know what you've got against the place,' said Keith.

'Ask anyone in the village, and they'll tell you,' said Judy. She turned to Chel. 'I tell you what. Why don't you and I go into town one day next week, and trawl through every estate agent in the place? There's hundreds. One of them must come up with something, surely.'

'Sounds like a good idea,' said Oliver. Chel looked at him quickly. Leaving Oliver on his own, except to walk up to the village, was something she had not yet done. He was unbelievably better since they had come to Cornwall, but the shadow of the awful months recently endured still hung in the back of her mind like black arras. She said,

'Would you mind?'

'Why should I mind?' asked Oliver. It was no answer. Judy said, full of enthusiasm for her idea,

'Tuesday. I can do Tuesday - I could pick you up here about eleven, if you like.'

'On your motor bike?' asked Chel, doubtfully.

'We can't afford to run a second car. Do you have a problem with the bike?'

For herself, the answer was no, but to qualify that there were confused, unformulated thoughts about the vulnerability of motor cyclists and Oliver's need of her, so that her answer came tepidly.

'No. I've ridden pillion before.'

Keith appeared to read her thoughts.

'Borrow your mother's car, Jude, she won't mind if you tell her what it's for. Chel can't afford to take risks.'

'Risks!' exclaimed Judy, affronted. 'I'm perfectly safe, I'll have you know!'

'It's Chel we're worried about,' said Keith. He caught Oliver's eye and grinned. 'Although, having said that, it's small choice in rotten apples really. Judy's driving is awful!'

Judy put her tongue out at him.

'We could have lunch,' she suggested, pointedly directing the remark to Chel.

Chel hesitated.

'Good idea,' said Oliver, encouragingly. 'It's time you had a break.'

'But you...' said Chel. Their eyes met.

'I shall be fine. You go.'

Chel held his gaze for a moment, trying to read behind his expression, but he was giving nothing away. Between them was the memory that once before he had urged her to leave him alone, and when she had gone, had attempted to take his own life. But that was then. They had surely moved on from that. It was only, she realised, that trust had been eroded. That, like so many things, must be rebuilt or they were going nowhere whatever they did.

'All right. I'll leave you a sandwich.'

'Don't bother. I can manage making a sandwich.'

Was that a reproach? Chel didn't know. She backed away.

'Good, then. I'll make sure there's some ham or something.'

Keith had finished his second pint. He put the empty can down on the table.

'Anyone fancy continuing this discussion in the pub?' he asked, but that was going too far for Oliver - quite literally too far, Chel realised. Lacking sensible transport, it would mean the hated wheelchair and the time was not yet when he could come to terms with that. Yesterday, the thought would have depressed her, today, for some reason, felt quite different. She could see - no, *feel*, if that wasn't silly - that the ice was breaking up, the warm sunshine coming. How, or why...? She gave herself a mental shake. Clairvoyance, of which she had more than once been accused, was something in which she couldn't wholly believe, in spite of some strange experiences which she tried very hard to rationalise away. She stood up.

'I've got a better idea. There's a bottle of wine in the cupboard, and a new loaf and some rather good cheese. Why don't you stay and have lunch with us?'

'That sounds wonderfully indigestible,' said Keith. 'Yes please. Don't you think, Jude?'

Judy was happy to agree, and they enjoyed a casual picnic together before Keith and Judy took themselves off, saying that as they had so little time to spend together they were going to walk for miles along Whitesand Bay and Gwenver while the tide was right. When they had gone, Chel swept the debris into a pile and sat down on the end of the bench.

'We ought to register with a doctor,' she said. 'If we're going to stay here. We are, aren't we?'

Oliver looked at her gravely, mildly irritated as he had been over the sandwich.

'I'm all right, you know. Don't fuss.'

'I'm not fussing. I'm trying to be practical.'

Oliver apparently saw the justice of this, for he said,

'All right. Not Keith though. Let's keep business separate from pleasure.'

Don't touch me, don't come too near. Keep away!

Chel sighed, stood up, began gathering up the crumby plates. She could feel depression creeping back unbidden, and turning her back, turned on the tap at the sink. Hot water gushed out obediently. Mains water, one great improvement in their lives. There must be more to come. Oliver said, quietly, behind her,

'We need space, Chel. You as well as me. Go with Judy on Tuesday, and have a good time. Don't take this amiss, please, but I shall enjoy being alone.'

Chel squirted washing-up liquid, concentrating on the green blob it made in the hot water.

'We are all right, aren't we, Oliver?'

'I'm sure we're going to be,' said Oliver.

In both their minds, the wide beach of Whitesand Bay, gleaming at low water, where they could no longer run together, stretched out to infinity.

Looking back on the events of the day much later, Chel thought that the name TUESDAY should have been written in neon lights, because it turned out to be a turning point of huge dimensions, although at the time it seemed fairly ordinary. She walked down to the farm and met Judy, as arranged, at half-past ten, they climbed into Millie's little Renault Clio, and bucketed their way to Penzance. Keith had been right about Judy's driving, it *was* awful. She seemed quite unable to judge the width of a car, and more than once Chel found herself shutting her eyes as a wall or a tree seemed hurtling towards the passenger side.

'I told you we should take the bike,' said Judy, which she hadn't quite, but Chel took the point.

Judy parked the car in a side street.

'Coffee first,' she said. 'Let's make it a real Girl's Day Out. Then we'll work our way down one side of the town and back up the other, taking in lunch on the way. I know a lovely little place on the way down to the Barbican where we can have really imaginative salad and freshly squeezed orange juice that's to die for. Come on!' And she led the way towards the shops.

Perhaps *hundreds* hadn't been quite the word, but there were certainly plenty of estate agents. A few of them even had places to let on their books, but none of them was really suitable and Chel was getting dispirited, although Judy seemed unflagging. Going into the fifth office she still had a spring in her step, and Chel, following behind, found herself thinking, traitorously, how easy it was for her new friend to be cheerful and positive when she wasn't personally involved. Judy, it now appeared, had been at school with the girl behind the desk and launched into a sea of greetings and explanations, and Chel wandered along the wall, trying not to worry about Oliver, and looking enviously at the houses for sale. Some of them looked really nice, she thought, and if only that awful bungalow would sell, but she couldn't imagine anyone even wanting to look at it. It needed to lie fallow for years, and then be filled to bursting with a cheerful family without a sensitive bone in their bodies who would lay the unquiet spirits that had seemed to inhabit it... and then she paused.

The house in the picture was nowhere she could remember seeing before. It stood sideways on to the road, with a neat wrought-iron gate in a stone wall leading to a short path up to an enclosed porch. Windows either side, roses round the door, double gable, no, she had never seen anywhere like that. But there was something about the line of the roof that was familiar, and the shape of the trees that grew behind the house. Chel frowned, and her eyes moved across the picture looking, she realised, for further clues. There were none, but beside the first photograph was another, of the garden. The house seemed to be deep and narrow, with an octagonal conservatory built out over a paved terrace. There was a long, narrow lawn, edged with flower borders. Above the conservatory, two sash windows must command superb views of the surrounding countryside.

MOOR HOUSE, TRELEWAN, read the details beneath the pictures. *Traditionally built cottage conversion with three bedrooms, bath and downstairs shower room. Open-plan ground floor with kitchen and dining area, seating area with wood-burning stove and french doors leading to conservatory. Extensive country views. Double glazing. Oil central heating. Parking off road.* And a price that, until they sold the bungalow, they could only dream about.

Judy had come to stand at her shoulder.

'That's that house,' she said. 'The one Keith was on about on Saturday. You don't like it, do you?'

'It looks rather nice,' said Chel. 'But we can't afford it, it's too big, the bedrooms are upstairs and it isn't to let, so it doesn't matter if I like it or not.'

The girl at the desk said, unexpectedly,

'It might be to let. They're having trouble finding a buyer, they might let it go on, say, a renewable six month rental with an option to purchase. If you were interested.'

'Why won't it sell?' asked Chel. The girl didn't answer directly.

'It's nice and quiet, a lovely position. Hardly anything goes past, but it isn't that far out of the village.'

'It's haunted,' said Judy, firmly. 'Everyone knows that.'

Chel turned away, regretfully but firmly. The last thing they needed was a haunted house - *another* haunted house. No, be sensible, the bungalow wasn't haunted. There was nothing else on offer.

'I could give you the details, if you wanted to think about it,' said the girl, as they turned to leave. 'Of course, I couldn't promise anything.'

On impulse, Chel said yes, although it didn't sound at all what they needed, and left the office pushing the sheets of paper into her shoulder bag.

'You can't want to live in that place!' said Judy.

'I was just interested.'

'I can take you past it on the way home, if you like,' said Judy. 'But don't try to live in it, please! It's creepy!'

They had both of them had enough estate agents for the moment, and Judy led the way to her chosen café for their lunch. They sat at a table in the window where they could watch the street, and when they had ordered their salads, Judy said,

'You look so worried. Don't be, something will turn up.'

25

'I didn't realise I was looking worried.' She had been thinking about Oliver again, wondering if he was all right on his own. There was no obvious reason why he shouldn't be, but the habit had become ingrained over the past year.

'I hadn't fully realised that your requirements were so specific?' said Judy. She made it into a question. Chel rubbed her nose, thoughtfully.

'It's stairs. Oliver can't do stairs yet. He has trouble lifting his feet.'

'But he will?'

'God knows,' said Chel. She rested her elbow on the table, her chin on her hand, and with her free hand picked up a knife and began to trace round the pattern on the table mat. 'Two years, they said. They put a steel rod into his spine, but they said the rest would heal - *in time*. But we've had nearly half the time they gave us already, and...' She tailed off and laid down the knife. 'I don't think there's really much difference,' she said.

'Bugger,' said Judy, sympathetically. Chel frowned.

'I sometimes think... I mean, maybe I'm just being stupid here, you know, shutting things out... but I sometimes think, since we came here to Cornwall particularly, that half the problem is that there's nothing for him to try *for*. All the things he did... well, he can't do them any more. But they made his life. If you have no life... well, where's the use of trying?'

'So what you're saying is, he needs something to do,' said Judy.

'Not quite, no.' Chel thought about it, her frown deepening. 'Not occupational therapy sort of stuff, he was never very good at that. Some... some *direction* to go in. There doesn't seem to be one.'

'And you really think that might help him to pick up his feet?' Judy raised her eyebrows. It did sound far-fetched, when she put it like that. Chel gave a reluctant laugh.

'In his head, anyway. And that might be enough.'

'OK,' said Judy, willing to help. 'So what are his interests apart from sailing and diving and things?'

'I have absolutely no idea,' said Chel. They looked at each other.

'Could you ask him?'

'I think he might bite my head off.'

'Look,' said Judy. 'Maybe I'm speaking out of turn here, but should you let him terrify you like that? Men are awfully quick to take advantage, you know.'

'It's not that,' said Chel. Their salads arrived, and for a moment or two they were busy sorting things out on the table. It gave her time to think, even to decide that she wouldn't continue with that sentence, but Judy forestalled her.

'What is it then?'

Chel sighed.

'Oliver's will is much stronger than mine, he's had more practice. He's been defying everyone, all his life. It's made him tough. He can run rings round me any time he wants.'

'You shouldn't let him.'

'I try not to. It didn't matter when I first met him, I thought he was wonderful anyway and I was happy to do what he wanted... but now, I know he's human like the rest of us, and moreover, I'm not sure he wants anything, and if he does, I'm not sure that it's the right thing... am I making sense?'

'No,' said Judy, cheerfully.

Chel paused, a forkful of pasta twirls suspended in mid-air, and her eyes, unfocussed, on the street outside.

'We've been shunted into a siding,' she said.

'Not the maintenance sheds?'

'No... it was that *bloody* breakdown!' Chel's eyes suddenly re-focussed, and she lowered her fork to her plate.

'Ah... Keith thought there might have been something like that,' said Judy, but Chel wasn't listening. She was staring at something beyond the window as if she had seen the holy grail. Staring so hard, indeed, that Judy instinctively followed the direction of her eyes.

People walking past, parked cars, the pub down the road, the art shop opposite, a man on a bicycle, a wandering dog... Judy turned to look at Chel again, but she seemed to have gone into a trance.

A voice from the recent past - ironically, she thought it was his stepsister Susan's: *Oliver was always rather good at drawing at school.* Chel remembered being surprised at the time, she had never seen Oliver pick up a pencil except to write something down, he was far too physical. But it made sense, she realised now. Helen was an artist - well, a sculptor anyway - and even Oliver, who seemed to dislike her, admitted that she was good. Things like that could be inherited. If Oliver could find something, even if it was only a hobby, that he could still do well, it might put him back on the rails, bring him back to life... out of the siding onto the main line again, if she wanted to carry on the metaphor.

Dared she? She hadn't been entirely joking when she had told Judy he might bite her head off. He was completely unpredictable at the moment, except for a resistance to being pushed around and coerced for his own good. Independence was no good if you had nowhere to plant the flag.

'I think I've had an idea,' she said.

27

She would say no more, not even certain if the idea was a good one, and while they finished their salad, ate home-made nut biscuits with their coffee, and settled the bill, they returned to the vexed question of housing. Out on the street again, Judy turned to Chel.

'Where now? There's a couple more estate agents along past the Green Market we haven't tried.'

'Over the road,' said Chel, coming to a decision.

She had no idea what was needed to start drawing and painting, or even what branch of the discipline Oliver had been so particularly good at, if indeed it wasn't just a Susan-ism in the first place. Judy was little help, finding the project interesting but bewildering.

'He couldn't paint in oils in your little van,' she said. 'It'd stink the place out and it makes a mess.' That was only useful in a negative kind of way. Chel bought pencils, a squashy rubber, a small sketch pad and a larger block of thick, textured paper, and guided by the shopkeeper, a palette, a generous handful of little tubes of artists' watercolours and a fatter one of Titanium White. On impulse, she added a fine-tipped felt pen and then looked, bewildered, at the enormous range of brushes on the rack. They varied in size, shape, quality, and even more significantly, price. She had no idea where to begin.

'Just grab a handful of assorted sizes,' suggested Judy, but cost put a stop to that idea. The shopkeeper asked what kind of work her husband did, and for the second time that day, Chel had to confess to ignorance. There was always the thought, too, that Oliver would never make use of the gift, simply because of the connection with Helen. Chel was acutely aware that she was walking on eggshells down this particular street.

Judy was getting bored.

'Middle price. Large, medium and small,' she said briskly, so that's more or less what Chel chose. The goods were slipped into a big plastic bag and paid for, they stepped out into the street again.

'I thought you didn't know what Oliver was interested in,' said Judy.

'I'm not sure that I do.' Chel hoped she hadn't just spent what represented quite a large sum of money to them on a non-starter. Doing so on Oliver's behalf on the basis of something that Susan, of all people, had said was probably a recipe for complete disaster. The two of them were chalk and cheese, perennially at daggers drawn, and, she had often suspected, on one side at least, violently jealous.

'I think I've just run mad,' she said, awed. Judy seemed unconcerned.

'Best thing to do when you're out of options,' she said. 'Come along now - don't dawdle! There's work to be done!'

28

The plastic bag was heavy - heavy in the hand, heavy on the conscience. Chel followed Judy up the street in a chaos of mixed emotions.

They drew a predictable blank at the last two estate agents, and returned to the car with very little more than Moor House to show for their trouble. Chel dragged it, crumpled, from her bag and looked at it.

'You say you know it?' she asked Judy. Judy gave a disgusted snort.

'Everybody knows it! You're not seriously intending to live in it, are you?'

'I don't know. It's all we've got. We could at least go and look at it.' Judy started the engine. Her face was expressive.

'Well, I'll show it to you, we've got time, but you won't want to live there unless you're loopy.'

'What's actually wrong with it?' asked Chel, for the pictures looked innocent enough. She flipped over the page and began to read the fine print about room sizes and facilities, and Judy didn't reply.

Judy drove out of Penzance along the coast road.

'We'll take the scenic route,' she said. 'No point going back through Trelewan, and it doesn't take much longer. You might as well see the area it's in as well.'

Chel glanced surreptitiously at her watch. Oliver had been on his own for four hours, longer by far than he had been alone since his... accident? She was never entirely sure how to describe what had happened to him, accident hardly seemed to fill the bill. Judy caught the movement.

'He wanted to be alone,' she said. 'You could tell. He really wanted it.'

'I know,' said Chel, unreasonably annoyed to have Judy telling her something so personal that she had already worked out for herself. 'But sometimes, when you get what you want, you find you don't want it after all.'

Judy didn't reply to that, but drove on between Cornish hedges and open fields, heading west along the coast up and down the switchbacks of a rambling country road.

'There's a good pub along there,' she said, once. 'We could all come there for lunch one day, when Keith isn't on call. It's time you both started living again.'

This was so true that Chel didn't make the obvious rejoinder. She was beginning to wonder if Judy hadn't been sent as the answer to a prayer. A relative of Oliver's with whom he would pass the time of day without fighting about it? It had to be a miracle!

After a few miles, Judy branched off along a narrow lane to the right.

'This comes out right opposite that house,' she said. 'Uncle William's farm is next door - actually, it was part of the farm at one time but he flogged it off a few years ago. I don't think he fancied the place after what happened there. He certainly never bothered to repair it.'

'Why, what did happen?' asked Chel, idly, and then something clicked inside her head. Uncle William. *Old William Nankervis, down Vellanzoe...* somebody had used that phrase on their last visit, trying to trace genealogies, if she remembered rightly, and Oliver had, as usual, walked away. She looked at the picture again. Oh God, no! The double gable was right, but the porch was new... the conservatory was where the two front doors would have been...

'It was never called Moor House at all, was it?' she said.

'They changed the name,' said Judy. 'I suppose they hoped it might make people forget, but it didn't, of course, and anyway...' She broke off, resuming casually, 'Do you know it, then?'

'I think we might have explored it when we were last down here,' said Chel, still hoping against conviction that she might be wrong. 'It was derelict then... Vellanzoe Cottages, they called it in the pub.'

'That's the place.' They were approaching the familiar junction now, and Judy slowed for the turn. 'So you know what happened there. Do you still want to stop?'

'We might as well, having come this far.' Chel was curious now. The place had been a mess, it was hard to see how it had metamorphosed into the solidly traditional Moor House. She added, 'They told us someone flew a plane into the roof, and hangs around the place calling for help. Jack - the friend who told us - said it was a load of balls.'

Judy had turned into the main lane now, pulled onto the verge almost exactly where Oliver had stopped on that other occasion. She pulled on the handbrake and switched off. For a moment, she said nothing. Then, 'What did *you* make of it?' she asked. 'Did you think it was a load of balls?'

The experience she had once had at Vellanzoe Cottages, the desperate, calling voice she had imagined she heard on the evening breeze, had been so disquieting that Chel had pushed it right to the back of her mind. *Upsetting.* It had upset her, deeply. She hedged.

'Do you believe in that kind of thing? Spirit voices... ghosts... all that jazz.'

'I don't *dis*believe it,' said Judy.

Chel spoke carefully.

30

'Any particular reason?'

They realised, both of them, that they were circling around each other, trying to avoid some shared belief or knowledge. Judy raised her head, stared out through the windscreen.

'I've had some funny experiences... known things that I couldn't logically have known... Keith says it's my subconscious on overtime, and I *must* have known them, but I didn't. They were about people that in one case at least I'd never heard of before... and as for this place, Uncle William was the first person to be here. He says the things that people say they hear are what he heard.'

'What does Keith have to say about that?'

'He says that as it was all in the papers at the time, it's hardly surprising. But Uncle William says no, some of it wasn't. And Keith just laughs.'

'Coincidence?'

'The very word.'

Chel hesitated.

'You weren't going to tell me, were you? Not until you realised I knew anyway. Why was that?'

Judy's fingers drummed on the wheel. She still didn't look at Chel.

'Someone would have told you in the end. I suppose I hoped you would just take a look and realise it wouldn't do. And if you *didn't...*' She paused. 'Well then, it wouldn't matter, would it? And this house has a way of sorting things out for itself.'

'What on earth do you mean?' demanded Chel, but Judy wouldn't say.

'Shall we go now?' she asked, instead. Chel hesitated. She almost agreed. Then some perverse streak in her that had got her into trouble before this, made her say,

'No. Having come all this way, let's just take a look.' She opened the car door and walked up to the gate. Judy hesitated, then shrugged her shoulders and followed. The slam of her door as she got out made Chel turn round, her hand on the latch. Judy came to stand beside her, they looked up together at the gables above them.'

'He came down smack in the middle,' said Judy.

'I know. I saw the hole.'

'Poor man. It was thick as porridge, Uncle William says, you couldn't see your hand in front of your face, he heard the bang up at the farmhouse, and came out to see, expecting to find a crash on the road, and for a minute he didn't see anything at all... you don't expect to look up above your head... and then he heard the cries...'

'How did it happen?' asked Chel. 'Was it just the fog? Or what?'

31

'I don't think they ever worked that out. The Board of Trade or something held an enquiry at the time, but it's really no use asking me. It's too long ago, I wasn't born.'

Chel unlatched the gate. It moved easily under her hand. They stepped onto the short path. To their left, the wall turned at right angles and met the wall of the house, to their right it did the same, but here there was an arched doorway leading through to the garden. It was closed by a tall gate to match the front one, through it, the grass could be glimpsed, in need of mowing, full of daisies. The windows to either side of the new porch beneath the left-hand gable had curtains drawn across them, it was impossible to see through them, the wall to the right had a chimney-breast running to the tip of the gable where it ended in a sturdy chimney. All four gables, Chel remembered, had been the same. Now, they weren't, that was probably why her recognition of the place hadn't been immediate, that and the porch. The emptiness of the place was all around them, but... nothing else. Chel listened, but there was no voice crying on the early spring breeze. Birds sang in the trees. There was the sound of a distant tractor, and a helicopter buzzing overhead on its way from the Scillies. Nothing more.

Judy walked along to the arched gate and tried the latch. It opened, and they walked through onto the lawn.

Here, the transformation had rendered the place unrecognisable. Where a scrubby field had run uninterrupted to the verge, there was now a new stone wall with shrubs planted against it. The tumbled stone outhouses at the far end had been spruced up, turned into what exploration proved to be a coal shed and a garden store, with new windows and doors and mended roofs. But the biggest change was to the front of the house.

Where two front doors had gaped behind the privet and brambles there was now a handsome modern conservatory, furnished, they could see, with cane chairs and a coffee table. Dead geraniums hung limply in pots on the window sills, and french doors led onto the terrace with a shallow step down to the lawn. Peering through the glass, Judy and Chel could see another set of french doors leading to the house. To either side, the plastic replacement windows, imitating the original sashes, were shuttered on the inside. It was just possible to make out through the distant glass doors that the room beyond appeared to be furnished. Above, the upper windows were as shuttered as they were unreachable.

They stood on the terrace and looked at each other. Judy giggled.

'You can almost see our antennae, reaching out to catch signals from another world,' she said, derisively.

'There's nothing here,' said Chel, wondering if she was right. 'Perhaps mending the roof exorcised it - whatever it was.'

'And perhaps it didn't,' said Judy. Chel turned away, back to the gate, Judy followed her. She suddenly giggled again.

'Oh God - what am I like? I was just about to say that you looked dis-*spirit*ed!'

They both laughed.

The gate clicked shut behind them, and they climbed back into the car, drove away.

Behind them, Moor House that had once been Vellanzoe Cottages seemed to settle into its surrounding trees. The fanciful might have said that it was waiting.

Judy dropped her at the gate leading to the camp site, promising to come by soon and see how things were going, and Chel finished the journey on foot with her artistic burden, once more a prey to terrifying doubts that she had done the right thing. To take such a step on the say-so of Susan, of all people, she thought again, could land her in serious trouble, for Susan's understanding of her stepbrother was seriously flawed. There was also the consideration that a lot of people could draw well without being either brilliant or in any way committed, and it was natural that Oliver should be one of them. The fact that he had never said so could mean no more than that he found painting no substitute for treasure-hunting beneath the sea or sailing single-handed round the world, and, daunting though the conclusion was, nobody would blame him for that.

Something had to be a substitute. A year was long enough in which to lick his wounds. It was true what people said, however annoying Oliver might find it, life had to go on, and what didn't kill you had to be lived with, and if he couldn't go forward, living with it was going to be hell for both of them. Oliver's body was healing by the day now, his mind would have to catch up or they were lost. She thought about it, on and off, all the way up the field.

'You were long enough,' Oliver greeted her, in a tone of voice that had a slight, unidentified edge to it. She looked at him carefully, and dropping the plastic bag to the floor inside the door, came to put her arms round him where he sat. Problems, problems, always problems.

'You told me not to hurry,' she reminded him. 'Were you OK?'

'Of course I was!' He sounded angry that she should have asked, but went on immediately to say, 'I was just beginning to wonder if something had happened to you.'

She heard it properly that time, the grating insecurity that was partly the result of his necessary, if hopefully temporary, dependence on her, partly her own fault, and the hairs stirred on her neck. This could be deadly when he had the quality of his future so comprehensively tied up in her. Not just her own will to stay or go, random chances like accident or illness could sweep the ground from beneath him. She saw it suddenly, clearly through his eyes, and it shook her. To ask what could possibly happen to her would only particularise whatever general fears he might have, and she resisted the temptation. In any case, she thought she knew. It stemmed from what Keith had so lightheartedly said about Judy's driving.

'We got sidetracked,' she said, apologetically. 'One of the estate agents had that house at Vellanzoe - you remember? It was falling apart. It's all tarted up now, and we just went out to have a look. I'm afraid we rather forgot the time.'

Oliver had pulled himself together again, knowing as well as she did that he had almost precipitated them both into a totally untenable situation. He grinned at her, almost naturally.

'Frightening each other with ghost stories? Don't tell me about it!'

'Not exactly, no, although of course it was mentioned. It was Judy's - and your - great-uncle who got to the scene first. But ghosts... I'm not sure about ghosts.'

'Is anyone? Really sure, that's to say.' He looked at her under his eyelashes, not absolutely on balance yet. 'Tell me, Chel. What did happen in the bungalow? You were scared shitless when you left. And every time the subject comes up, you skate round it as if it was going to attack you.'

Chel hesitated.

'Oh... the couple who owned it before us weren't very happy.'

'And?'

Chel swallowed.

'He was an invalid...'

Oliver waited. Finally Chel said, through a tightness in her throat,

'She left him, he was horrible to her. He... he committed suicide.'

Oliver looked down at his hands, examining the nails with close interest.

'How?'

She could say that he put his head in the gas oven, or hanged himself - and Oliver wouldn't believe her. Particularly not right at this moment.

'He took an overdose of her sleeping tablets. She'd left them behind, his carer had charge of his own.'

'Oh?' Oliver continued to study his fingers. 'I used my own,' he added, casually. Chel said, with unexpected, and under the circumstances inappropriate, force,

'You aren't the suicidal type.'

'I didn't think I was.'

She could bear it no longer. It might be the wrong moment, but at least it would change the subject.

'I brought you a present from Penzance,' she said, and picking up the bag, dumped it unceremoniously in his lap. Oliver looked, not so much surprised, as startled.

'Well, it's not a stick of rock, that's for sure,' he said, and half-tipped the contents onto his knees. The little tubes of paint rolled out and two of them fell on the grass. Oliver had gone very still.

'I thought you might like them,' said Chel, lamely. Oliver fingered the things, she thought, as if she had given him fine gold and jewels, but he still didn't say anything and after a moment, she asked,

'Do you mind?' with such anxiety, that to her relief, he laughed at her.

'Healing for the mind, as well as for the body? No, of course I don't mind. I was just a bit... well, taken aback.'

'Why, particularly?' asked Chel, suddenly wanting to know. He smiled at her, but wryly.

'Because... well, because you seem to have got yourself closer to me than I consider absolutely safe, I suppose. Have I any secrets left, I wonder?'

'You don't have to take it too seriously,' said Chel, with a horrible feeling that she had trodden on forbidden ground. 'You can just doodle - strings of sausages, or cats - '

'Strings of cats?' asked Oliver, and they both laughed.

'Idiot!' said Chel.

She made them both a cup of tea and then, later on, took their washing across to the laundry room. She had got away with that, she thought, but what he would do next she couldn't guess.

When she got back, she found out. He had taken the felt-tip pen and drawn her a string of cats.

They were no ordinary cats. They were of every known breed, from haughty Persians to battle-scarred alley cats, kittens to great big doorstop toms, in every pattern from tabby to tortoiseshell, each one individual and all of them very slightly caricatured. It was funny and clever, but not at all what she had expected, and for some reason, took the wind out of her sails. Oliver, however, looked at his handiwork with satisfaction.

'A great cartoonist was lost to the world in me,' he said.

Chel leaned on the back of the chair and peered over his shoulder.

'It's not too late,' she suggested, but Oliver only laughed and tore the cats from the sketch book and handed them to her.

'There you are, you daft girl. One string of cats.'

'You haven't signed it.'

'Good God,' said Oliver, taking it back. 'What do you want, blood?' and wrote *Nankervis* across the corner with a flourish.

This time, Chel accepted the gift and looked at it with interest.

'I'll say this, it may not be great art, but you've got a wickedly clever eye,' she said. 'Do you like cats?'

'I suppose I do. I've never really thought about it.'

'We ought to get one, when we get somewhere to live. I read somewhere that stroking pets is great for reducing tension.'

Which brought them straight back to the head of the great snake. Chel hesitated, discarded the bungalow as a dead subject, in need of instant burial, and plumped for Vellanzoe as the lesser of two evils.

'You'd never believe how that house has changed,' she said. 'Somebody has spent a fortune there. The outside is almost unrecognisable. Look.' She groped in her bag and hauled out the details, now rather crumpled, and put them into Oliver's hand. He looked at them, but only with cursory interest, she saw.

'It wouldn't do for us,' he said. 'Our cat wouldn't like the resident spook.'

'Oh, rubbish!' said Chel, more forcibly than she had meant to.

'Rubbish, animals don't care, or rubbish, there isn't a spook?'

'If there is,' said Chel, and repeated with an emphatic conviction for which she had no possible grounds, '*if* there is, it's nothing like the bungalow.'

'Bloody good thing, too!' said Oliver. He looked at her seriously. 'You do realise, that place nearly had us, don't you?'

'Yes.' Sobered abruptly, Chel slipped her arms around his neck from behind and laid her cheek against his hair. 'We need somewhere different now. Something that will mend us.'

'It'd have it's work cut out to mend me.'

Chel decided to ignore this, and went on,

'I feel closer to you now than I ever did before I ran away and left you, I don't know why. Even in our early days - I loved you madly, but this is... different.' She wasn't sure why she had said that, it had no recognisable connection with Vellanzoe, it had just bubbled out of her like spring water.

'I know what you mean...' said Oliver, thoughtfully. 'I suppose it's the same way I felt about the *Girl* the first time we came through a really bad storm together - and I suppose, for the same reason. If we can come through that, we can afford to start relying on each other.'

Oliver would never change much. Chel suppressed a smile at being bracketed with a boat and continued in the nautical metaphor.

'It was more by luck than judgement. Perhaps our navigation will be better in future.'

Oliver picked up her hands and kissed them.

'Sweet and beautiful Chel, if you think we were *navigating* through that reef full of sharks and overfalls, I'm never going round the world with you!'

Chel withdrew her hands with a gentle caress along his jaw, and picking up her picture, propped it aside out of harm's way. Looking at it, she couldn't help smiling. What had she expected, anyway? She had taken Oliver by surprise, of course he wasn't going to pour his heart and soul onto paper just like that. If he drew cats for the next six months, it was a step forward.

She hadn't thought of it before, but Helen's wonderful animals and birds were caricatures in a way - clever, like Oliver's cats, but more cruelly clever and a lot more subtle, proving once again, if it needed proving, that the female is more deadly than the male. So far, at least up until last year, Oliver had let any quarrel he might have had with life flow outward into physical action, good or bad, not inward into Helen's twisted interpretation of what was beautiful. Chel hoped very much that his cats would always be funny, that the worst was behind them, and that he would continue to stick it out without following his mother's path into bitterness.

III

At Easter, it snowed. Chel woke up on Good Friday, drew back the curtains, and couldn't believe her eyes. Soft, white flakes poured down from a sky the colour of an uncleared grate, to land softly on the grass and melt away to slush. It crusted on the window pane, and slid down, melting, to plop to the ground with a splash. And it was bitterly cold.

'Good God!' she said, in disbelief.

'What's up?' asked Oliver, stirring beside her.

'It's snowing!'

'Never! It's April.'

'It may be, but it's still snowing.'

Oliver sat up. To do this, he needed to use a gadget like a rope-ladder that fastened to the foot of the bed, he went along it hand over hand and peered over Chel's shoulder.

'You're right. It's snowing.'

'Told you.'

'None too warm either, is it?'

Chel began to get up.

'I'll go and get the fire lit, warm the place up a bit. And for God's sake, don't slip on the way over.'

For the weather was only one more problem to add to others. The pretentiously titled No.10 had given them space and better facilities, but it hadn't proved possible to live in it quite as they had planned. The bed, designed for holiday rather than permanent use, had proved impossible for Oliver with his damaged back, and they were still having to use their own van as a bedroom. It had served to keep in both their minds that their situation was impermanent, and far from ideal, and effectively prevented any intention they might have had to rationalise their transport. Perhaps because of this, they had still not got round to letting their respective families know exactly where they were. In fact, not even the friend who had helped orchestrate the details of their escape knew exactly where they had gone, which meant, in effect that nobody knew. There was no particular reason why a snowfall should have made Chel feel that this was undesirable, but it did. She looked at Oliver over the breakfast table and, not for the first time, said,

'We can't go on like this for ever.'

'It works for me,' said Oliver.

Chel knew that they had come to the end of this road. She had known it now for days. The hope for something new and different that Judy had brought with her seemed to have fizzled out down another cul-de-sac. She looked at Oliver helplessly.

'We should at least say where we are. Mum's really hurt, I know she is, because I won't confide in her. She thinks I don't trust her and Dad.'

'They're not the problem,' said Oliver, who had always been more than a match for his in-laws in the past and knew by this time that he would be again. There was nothing to fear there. Chel looked down at her plate of toast.

'Nobody can make us do what we don't want to do,' she said, but Oliver replied simply,

'We can stop them making us, true, but we can't stop them trying. And they will. *She* will.'

'So, are you never going to tell anyone where you are again?'

'I wish,' said Oliver.

'We can't,' said Chel, flatly.

A silence fell between them, a silence filled with the ghosts of words too often spoken. Finally, Chel sighed.

'So what's your suggestion?'

'I haven't one,' said Oliver. 'This is your adventure. I came along for the ride.'

'That's not fair! You can't have it both ways.'

Oliver took a sip of coffee and looked at her over the rim of his mug.

'O.K. Next time you speak to my father, tell him where we are. Then let's just sit back and see what happens, shall we?'

Chel was silenced. She knew, as Oliver was well aware, exactly what would happen. If it achieved anything at all, it would only be grief. The old dilemma, while they had nowhere to live, no game plan for the future, they were vulnerable. She didn't trust Oliver's stepmother an inch further than she could throw her - and she was a big, stout woman. Reluctantly, she also knew that to tell only her own parents would simply serve the same purpose, they were in awe of Oliver's and would crumple at the first hint of interrogation. To mention the one person she felt that they could safely take into their confidence - Helen - would be to precipitate a row that, this morning, seemed to be hovering in the wings ready to make an entrance.

Oliver is cleverer than me, she thought resentfully, but does he have to use that to block every turn? Her mouth primmed together angrily. She might even have struck a match and set light to the tinder, but fortunately, before she could do so, there was a knock on the door.

'Saved by the bell,' murmured Oliver, quietly, into his mug. Chel got to her feet, stepping, she hoped with dignity, across to open the door. Judy's mother stood there, muffled in woolly hat and scarf and beating her hands together against the cold. Flakes of snow powdered her shoulders and thinly lay on the grass behind her.

'Brrr! Right old morning, isn't it?' she asked.

'Come in,' invited Chel, but Millie shook her head, stamping her feet to draw attention to the mud and slush clinging to her boots.

'No thanks, my lover, I've just come to give you a message. That friend of Judy's, you saw her in town, she rang to say that if you was interested, she could arrange for you to see that house you was asking after. She's spoke to the owner, she says, and he might let for a while. Up to you.' She gave a quick nod.

'Oh,' said Chel, to be truthful, startled. She had put Moor House out of her mind as inappropriate in every way, and Judy's contention that *this house has a way of sorting things out for itself* returned eerily to her mind. She could feel her flesh creeping, like spiders on her skin. She shook herself to get rid of the sensation. 'Thank you. I'm sorry you had to come out in all this weather.'

Millie laughed.

'I was out in it anyhow, girl. Hens and calves need seeing to, weather or no weather. It's no trouble.'

She clumped away down the field in her heavy boots, and Chel closed the door, turning to find Oliver looking at her pensively.

'What house was that?' he asked.

'I told you,' said Chel.

'Ah. I rather hoped that you hadn't.'

Chel stood still.

'There's nothing there.'

Oliver laughed.

'It's falling apart.'

'No it's not. Actually, it's rather nice. Lovely conservatory, you could paint in there.'

Oliver sat back, idly playing with a spoon on the table. He almost looked interested, Chel thought, although the word *paint* was so far inappropriate. He had drawn a great deal - rough sketches of nothing in particular, boats and birds and trees all massed together on the paper as if he was testing things out - as, of course, he well may have been - but not making any pictures of anything specific, and certainly not coloured. Like the cats, which although she loved them, she had found strangely disappointing, they seemed to Chel to be simply a way of passing time. She began to pull out drawers, shifting things around, hunting.

'What've you lost?' asked Oliver.

'The details. I had them, I started to show you, but then we got talking - ' She paused, her hands still. 'Well, we got talking, and I put it down somewhere and now I don't know where.'

'It doesn't matter,' said Oliver. 'We can get them again... if you want, that is. Do you?'

Chel straightened up. She stood with her hands at her sides, thinking. The snow had put an end to any last vestiges of pretence, reality was back with a vengeance. Someone had to do something, if it wasn't Oliver, as it wouldn't be, then it had to be her. Only one thing, so far, had offered itself to do.

'We might as well,' she said.

She should have known; once she had shown interest in Moor House, the news ran around Trelewan like the fiery cross. Everyone knew everyone, and although, so far, none of them knew Chel, they knew who she was.

'I didn't know it was to let,' said Jim Tregillis at the shop, when she was paying for her groceries. 'I thought they wanted shut of it.'

'We don't know if it is,' said Chel. 'It was just an idea. Why, do you know who it belongs to?' It was in her mind that she might put in a piece of special pleading... maybe.

Jim looked thoughtful.

'Bloke that rebuilt it, he sold it on smartish to some other bloke down here on holiday, eighteen months back that would be. I don't know why *he* bought it, unless for a holiday cottage, we haven't seen him around.' He raised his voice and called to the back of the shop. 'Sally, do you remember who bought them cottages out to Vellanzoe?'

'That builder from Camborne had it first.' Sally came to the counter, her hands full of tins and her face full of curiosity. 'I don't know who had it from him.'

The customer waiting behind Chel at the till looked interested.

'Glad to get rid, I wouldn't wonder. Stopped work, didn't they, because of the ghosts? Downed tools and left him to finish the job himself.'

'Oh, that's just tales for the tourists!' Sally laughed. 'Everyone knows as he ran out of money to pay them, and that's the truth of it, you ask Jim!' She looked apologetically at Chel. 'People used to say it was haunted, but it was only ever talk.'

'Do you believe in ghosts?' Jim Tregillis asked, with a shamefaced grin, and Chel said she kept an open mind, which was safe and non-committal.

'One of the men out there on the building said as he saw one,' stated

41

the customer, delighted to have generated such interest. 'A man, he said, in one of the upstairs rooms and they all walked out and refused to go back. They tried to hush it up, but there, folks will talk.'

Obviously.

'I've heard about people hearing voices and things out there,' said Chel, cautiously, but nobody seemed able to add to what had already been said, and as she left the shop she heard them all discussing early new potatoes with the same fervour and fascination as they had discussed the putative ghost of Vellanzoe.

It was food for thought, nevertheless.

She paused outside the shop to load her borrowed bicycle. When Judy had described it as *old*, she hadn't been joking, it belonged to the era of sit-up-and-beg, but it did the job. Shopping had become far less of a chore now, although Chel couldn't help thinking, wistfully, that a car would be even better. Now, dumping her bag of shopping into the convenient, but far from trendy, butcher's basket attached to the handlebars, she was startled to hear herself hailed from across the road.

'Cheryl! It *is* Cheryl, isn't it?'

Looking up, she saw a plump young woman hurrying towards her, shoving a pushchair ahead of her with one hand, in which sat a baby of around a year old, with an older child dragging on the other hand. The woman had long flowing blonde hair, long ethnic cotton skirt under a serviceable but unflattering duffle coat, and *long-time-no-see* written all over her. Chel was doubly surprised because she had asked Judy, in an idle moment, if she knew Jack and Maggie Soames, and after a little thought, Judy had replied, as idly,

'Name doesn't seem to ring a bell.'

'Up-country hippie people - lived up on the moor behind Zennor somewhere?'

'Oh, *her*!'   That had rung the bell all right. Judy had pulled an expressive face that said, as clearly as words, that she had little time for Maggie. 'Mother Earth and her never-ending trail of undisciplined brats, didn't anyone ever tell her about the pill? Not to say *know*, no, she's the kind of person I try to avoid. They moved away, thank goodness, two or three years ago - I think they went to Australia. He had ideas of opening a diving school on the Great Barrier Reef, I bet that went down a bundle with the Aussies!'

Chel had herself found Maggie a bit over-enthusiastic when they had met, some years ago now - particularly about Oliver - and annoyingly *arty*, but otherwise pleasant enough. To Judy, she had merely said,

'Jack and Oliver got on pretty well, they both liked diving - '   She had broken off, for that was hardly a recommendation these days. Judy had shrugged her shoulders.

'Gone.' Which was disturbingly ambiguous.

And now here was Maggie, not gone at all, bearing down on her in full cry, as hippie as ever and with - Chel did a quick calculation - at least one more child since they had first met.

There was nothing for it. She was caught bang to rights, but not unpleased to see Maggie, a passing acquaintance from their earlier visit, but one she had, she recalled, half-relied on to ease their arrival, with no friends, no family, in Cornwall. Having taken her name in vain when she had thought herself in need, the least she owed Maggie now was a smile.

'Maggie!' she said. 'I was told you were in Australia!'

'It didn't work out. We got back a couple of weeks ago.' Maggie had reached her, and stood there smiling. The child at her side pulled at her skirt.

'Maggie,' she whined. 'Maggie, who's the lady? *Maggie!*' Tug, tug. Chel remembered Judy's comment and hid a grin. Uninhibited, Jack and Maggie's children, she recalled. This one must be the baby she remembered from happier days, then there had been a male toddler with anarchic tendencies, and two older ones who had, thankfully, mainly been at nursery school or playing with friends. That made five in all, counting the one in the pushchair. Maybe Judy had a point, because on top of that, Maggie was very obviously pregnant again.

'Hush, India,' said Maggie, now. She and Chel smiled at each other, with nothing immediate to say. The silence, broken only by a steady grizzle from the child, India, had time to become noticeable before Maggie said, brightly,

'Have you come down for Easter?'

'To find somewhere to live, actually,' said Chel.

'Oh, great, we'll have to get together sometime. Jack will be pleased, he often wondered what happened to you and Oliver - do you ever see Oliver these days?' Maggie paused, her head cocked to one side, waiting. Oliver was obviously worth hearing about. Chel stood frozen, her mouth open in shock, and the pause went on and on.

'I think...' began Chel, but stopped, at a loss. The one good thing about all the publicity that had followed Oliver's tragic misadventure was that she had never, ever, had to explain. Jack and Maggie must have somehow missed the news of the hasty wedding, and the ultimately tragic history of the marriage had passed them by entirely somewhere in Australia. She had no idea where to begin, even. She simply stood there, feeling stupid, shocked, unreasonably angry with Maggie for her ignorance, and Maggie smiled sympathetically.

'Bit of a sore subject, is it? Well, he was gorgeous, but you have to admit, not for every day really - *yes, what is it, pet?*' This last to the child, whose tugs at the gauzy cotton cloth of her skirt were becoming dangerously determined. 'Jack? Yes, Jack's coming, now hush a moment and let me talk to Cheryl.'

Chel swallowed. She wasn't sure any more if she was propping up the bicycle, or the bicycle was propping her.

'I think I should explain,' she said, knowing the words to be inadequate. 'Oliver and I got married.'

It was Maggie's turn now to be lost for words, to stand open-mouthed and staring like a fool.

'You *what?* Go on, you're kidding me! He wasn't the kind to marry anyone!'

'Not kidding.' Chel shook her head. 'We got married quite soon after we got home.'

'You never said a word!' accused Maggie.

'No. We didn't know ourselves until the night before we left.'

'Tell me about it,' Maggie commanded. 'What are you doing in Trelewan, and are you really coming to live here? Where's Oliver?' She broke off, her eyes narrowing. 'You are still married to him, I take it?'

'Of course I am!' cried Chel, indignantly - the more so since she knew it had been touch and go. She broke off, looking past Maggie with relief. 'Here's Jack now. He hasn't changed a bit!'

Oliver had.

Jack was coming across from the Post Office, the same chunky, balding, friendly figure as always, face split in a wide smile.

'Hey, the face is familiar, but the name escapes me,' he said. 'I seem to connect you with diving somehow, am I on the right lines?' He held out his hand. Chel took it, feeling helplessly overwhelmed by events.

'Think Oliver Nankervis,' prompted Maggie, and went straight on before Chel could speak. 'She's married to him, and they're looking for a place down here to live - '

'Hey, hey, put on the brakes there!' Jack swooped down to pick up his daughter, balancing her on his shoulders where she rattled her fingers on his bald patch as if it was a drum. 'Cheryl, isn't it? Yes, I remember, of course I do! Coming to live here are you? That's good news, perhaps Oliver can give a hand with the cadets down at the diving club...' Something in Chel's face dried up the speech before it was finished. 'Cheryl?' he said, and then, reaching up to still the beating hands on his head. 'Stop it India, easy there.'

Another of those silences, this time pregnant with unspoken pain.

44

Then Maggie said, her voice cold with foreboding,

'He's dead, isn't he?'

'Don't be silly,' said Chel, in a flood of relief, for nothing would sound too bad after that, surely. 'I've already told you we're still married, haven't I?' Then, as Maggie and Jack stood there, waiting for her to go on, she said, 'There was an... incident. He's disabled. He can't walk much.' She closed her eyes momentarily, screwing them up tight against Maggie's expression.

'I *knew*!' cried Maggie, intensely. 'I *knew* there was something dreadfully wrong!'

'Hey, that's bad news,' said Jack, quietly. 'Anything anyone can do?' He meant himself and Maggie, Chel understood, but whoever he meant, the answer was,

'No. Not really. But thank you for asking.'

'Bugger,' said Jack. He looked ludicrous, Chel thought, standing there with his hands on the top of his head and the child India's feet now kicking at his chest, but so kind. She hadn't realised until that moment how much she still dreaded kindness. The Jackson family's help had been practical and straightforward, friendship rather than kind intentions. She began to feel a familiar, panicky breathlessness. Maggie said,

'I can't imagine Oliver, disabled,' as if she was intoning a response in church, but Chel could see her imagining it anyway, and the need to go over all the ground again was wretchedly painful, although she surely should be used to it by now.

Jack, finding his position uncomfortable, swung India down to the ground, where she kicked her feet in the slush left by the melting snowfall and grizzled audibly.

''s cold, I wanna go home, I'm *tired*!'

Chel seconded all of that, but silently inside her head. Jack turned his wrist to look at his watch, the same kind of heavy diver's watch that Oliver had used before it was broken in the back-street attack in Embridge. She could feel the panic progressing into a tight, painful lump behind her breastbone.

'Look, we can't talk here, or now,' said Jack, forestalling Maggie, who had opened her mouth to speak. 'Where are you staying? We'll come over and see you some time, without the children.'

Reprieve, for Chel, time to collect her thoughts, but Maggie looked indignant.

'But I want to know *everything!*' she cried. 'We could have coffee in the Cornish Arms, have a real talk.'

'No,' said Jack, firmly, his eyes on Chel. 'Shut *up*, India, we've heard enough about how cold you are! Tell us where we can find you later, Cheryl.'

Chel sighed. She said,

'We're in one of Jeff Jackson's static vans at present, the one at the far end. Come any time, we don't go far - or you could ring.' She remembered the mobile phone that Oliver despised, their only link with other people. 'Have you got a pen and a bit of paper? I'll give you our mobile number.'

Jack scribbled the number on the back of an old bill from Maggie's purse, and swept his family off in the direction of a battered old minibus parked outside the church, and Chel climbed onto her borrowed bicycle and rode slowly back to the campsite.

It was unreasonable of her, she thought as she rode, to expect everyone there was to know every detail of their abrupt decline from the top of the world to the bottom of the heap, so that there was no valid reason why that encounter should have upset her quite so much as it had. It had something to do, she realised, with the fact that although Judy and Keith and the Jacksons were prepared to respect the privacy and rights of herself and Oliver, Maggie had something of the crusading do-gooder about her, and possibly wouldn't, but it went much further than that. Jack's interests and Oliver's, on their last meeting, had coincided exactly. They had gone diving together, part of a whole crowd of strangers bound together by common interest, immersed in a physical activity that was totally exclusive for those not qualified to join in. That was how Jack and Maggie came to meet Oliver, how they had known him, so how would they react to his present and permanent disablement? Of course, he would get better... of course he would... but not, ever, to the point where he would go diving again. All their other friends and acquaintances, their families, and a good proportion of the British population had learned this a long time ago, but Jack and Maggie? Apparently not. What would their reaction be, when faced with the inescapable fact?

What would Oliver's reaction be when faced with theirs?

The answer to either of these questions, Chel couldn't even begin to guess.

God, that wasn't fair, she accused, in her head, to a deity in whom she hardly believed.

Fair or not, it was going to have to be faced. Short of telling Jack and Maggie that they were unwelcome, which wouldn't have been true, there had been no way out. So why was it, Chel asked both herself and that misty and problematic God, that they had fled to Cornwall believing it held all the answers, and found only more questions that led them deeper and deeper into the mire? Was it themselves, that wouldn't face the answers, or was there no answer?

Up the ladder and down the snakes.

But back at the van, Oliver had a surprise in store for her. He had seated himself at the table so that he could put his new paints within his reach and work in reasonable comfort and had, at last, taken up a brush. So absorbed was he in this new activity that at first he was hardly aware of her return. She put the bag of shopping on the little worktop and came to stand behind him. Which is when she got her surprise.

She had not really envisaged what Oliver might paint when he got around to it, still less *how* he might paint. His crowded sketchbook indicated an understandable preoccupation with merchant shipping, yachts under sail, seabirds, rocks and huge dashing waves, with the odd lighthouse thrown in here and there, and Chel had wondered once or twice how such things would translate into watercolour, which always seemed to her to be a gentle, almost maidenly medium. Her limited knowledge did go so far as to include awareness that there had been famous male watercolourists but she couldn't quite reconcile this with Oliver once her first, impulsive purchase was behind her, and had begun to think that she had made a serious mistake when he merely drew, day after day. She had told herself that she had only bought him watercolours in the first place out of considerations of price and convenience, and a daunting lack of personal know-how on artistic subjects in general, without stopping to wonder if they and Oliver were compatible and thus made a nonsense of what might have been a good idea. Now she had the answer to her fears.

'Oh, my goodness!' she exclaimed, before she could stop herself. 'I've never seen anyone do *that* with watercolours! I always thought of them as pale, transparent things!'

Oliver gave a smothered laugh, and laid his painting flat on the table.

'Fortunately, I never rated you as an art critic, anyway' he said. 'So what do you reckon?'

The picture consisted mainly of a roughly sketched outline, a curving, rocky bay, an anchored yacht, a small boat pulled up on a beach, but where Oliver had laid on the paint, it glowed. There was no other word. A dark, stormy sky heaving with clouds, with a narrow band of light along the horizon that had turned the sea into a pale green flash merging into steely grey as it came nearer to the shore, smooth as polished tin. That was as far as he had got, but the difference between this and other watercolours that Chel had seen was in the depth and richness of the colours. Not for Oliver, obviously, the delicate washes so typical, in Chel's mind, of watercolour painting.

'I like it - I think,' she said, after a pause. 'Have you always painted like that?' She hesitated, on the edge of an uncharted sea. 'Come to that, have you always painted? I really didn't know.'

Oliver gave the block a push further onto the table and swirled his brush clean in a mug of water. He didn't look at her.

'So what made you choose painting as occupational therapy?'

Was there an edge there? Chel wasn't sure, but some instinct bade her to tell the absolute truth and not try to cite Helen as a reference point.

'It was something Susan said,' she said. 'Was she right?'

'Depends what she said,' said Oliver.

'She said...' Chel searched her memory. 'She said something like, *he was always good at painting at school.* Something like that.'

Oliver made no comment on whether this was right or not.

'Since you're back, how about making us some coffee?'

'You're blocking the stove.' But she reached for the kettle and began to fill it. 'Are *you* pleased with it - your painting?'

'I never did admire that wishy stuff, anyway,' said Oliver. He laboured to his feet, shuffling out of her way so that she could light the gas, but stayed standing, leaning on his crutches and looking with eyes that didn't focus on the green field outside. Chel shot a glance at him, and quietly made the coffee. It wasn't until she carried the two steaming mugs through and set them on the low coffee table among the accumulated newspapers and magazines that she said,

'What's wrong, Oliver?' She was afraid that she had somehow done something terribly inept, and beneath the fear was aware of a new anger as unfocussed as Oliver's empty stare. Part of it, she thought, was against Oliver himself for being so moody and difficult, so impossible to help, and as she thought this, she felt it like a sharp stab in the guts, stopping her breath and making her close her eyes against the familiar pain that she had thought left behind in Embridge. After a moment, she opened her eyes and found him looking at her with an awareness that shocked her.

'I've disappointed you again - haven't I?'

'No!' cried Chel, too quickly. 'No - no, of course you haven't. It's just... well, things are difficult... aren't they?'

'I love you, you know,' he said, as if it followed on naturally from her question. 'You do know that?'

'Me too. But not the way we did. Do you?'

'No,' said Oliver. 'No... but anyway, I think two years is about the limit for that sort of thing. We were coming to the end of it anyway... weren't we?'

48

Was that true? Had the magic of their first two years of marriage been doomed to change? And if so, did that happen to everyone?

'You mean,' she said slowly, 'that after the honeymoon period, real life kicks in? But surely, not always with such a bang as we had.'

'Be honest,' said Oliver. 'It had already begun.'

She thought back. Oliver had stormed out of the flat they had shared, to meet his destiny on the heels of a serious quarrel over money - a subject that had never, until then, been raised between them. She had been making a fuss because she was pregnant, and afraid that he would sail away somewhere and leave her. She thought now that their life had been changing before that, their attitudes to each other and their conception of their future... she had never meant to be pregnant, and now she never would be again... not if she stayed. And how could she go?

'Don't cry,' said Oliver, with unexpected gentleness. 'It's not the end of the world, it happens to everyone.'

'It's the end of that world,' said Chel, her eyes squeezed shut to hold back the tears that, even so, were trickling down her face.

'Sit down,' said Oliver. 'Drink your coffee. We need to talk.'

The words struck terror into Chel, although they were true enough. She had been wanting to talk - sensibly - with Oliver for weeks, but now that the moment seemed to have arrived out of nowhere, she dreaded what he might have to say. She sat down obediently and reached for her mug.

Oliver sat opposite, where he could see her. He knew, had known for some time, that he was being too hard on Chel, leaving her with too much responsibility and too many worries, behaving unfairly. It was how to explain *why* that had been too difficult, when he wasn't sure himself.

'We've got problems,' he said, now. 'Nowhere permanent to live, no plans, no prospects. Believe me, I know.'

'You wouldn't talk about it,' said Chel, trying not to sound accusing.

'No... I couldn't think of anything to say, to be honest. And the last thing I wanted was a row with you. But it can't be swept under the carpet for ever.'

'I know that.'

Oliver caught the note of resentment in her voice.

'I wasn't saying you didn't. What I wasn't sure of was, what did you expect me to do about it?'

'Anything, would have been good,' said Chel, past a lump in her throat. 'Oh *shit*, Oliver, I thought I was past all this weeping stuff!' She dashed at her tears, uselessly. A hero of romance would have

49

passed her a perfectly laundered handkerchief, Oliver sat and watched her sniff.

'Don't, Chel. Please.'

'I'm *sorry*!'

'Look at it objectively,' said Oliver. 'All my talents - all my experience - lie in one area, and the door has been slammed in my face.'

'I know, I *know*!'

'I can't do nothing, Chel. I can't sit around for ever, depending on you. I feel... desperate.'

There, it was said. They looked at each other dismally.

'Me too,' said Chel. After a pause, when Oliver said nothing, she went on. 'I thought perhaps, if I gave you something to do... it might lead somewhere. Anywhere. It was the only thing I knew - that you could draw - I'm sorry. I didn't mean to... to upset you.'

'You haven't,' said Oliver. 'Or not in the way you mean.'

'I didn't realise, until this happened, how little I really knew about you,' said Chel, miserably.

'You've given me a few surprises too, if it interests you.'

'What?' asked Chel, bitterly. 'Running away with someone else, when you needed me? Thanks a bunch!'

'Don't be so prickly, I didn't mean that at all. I didn't blame you, if you want to know. No... it was your coming back that surprised me. That, and your understanding... and your courage too... that brought us here. Only, it's time I took some of the load too... and to be honest, Chel, I haven't a clue where to go from here.'

Chel said, hopelessly,

'I suppose I thought, perhaps you could paint, and sell pictures to the tourists.'

'Wishy-washy watercolours for the undiscerning? Thanks a bunch to you, too!'

'I'm sorry,' cried Chel, distressed at his tone. 'I got it wrong again - I always do - '

'Oi, no breast-beating, if you don't mind. I didn't mean that... not quite that, anyway.'

She saw that her distress had rubbed off on him, and took a breath, counted to ten.

'We're going to be quarrelling in a minute,' she said.

'Not us. Let's talk about this painting thing. That's what's suddenly got to you, isn't it?'

Was it? Had something about the dismissive way he put the painting from him finally tipped the scale, for both of them?

'If you want,' said Chel, reluctantly. 'I put my foot in it, didn't I?' With Susan's help - and trust Susan for that! Oliver ignored the query.

'I always have painted - a bit, anyway, when I had time. I didn't realise you didn't know, but I suppose, since I met you, we've been busy doing things together whenever there was a spare moment. I only do it for fun - for my own pleasure. I've given a few away here and there, and binned a great many more... it isn't serious.'

'Do you mean, you don't take it seriously, or it isn't a serious talent?' asked Chel, pertinently.

'Who knows? The first, certainly, and I have my doubts about the second. But the thing is, Chel, apart from art classes at school - and you know what they're worth - I know nothing at all about it. A bit of a natural gift, I suppose. I can't claim it can be put any higher.'

'Surely, that's all you need,' said Chel. She hadn't, when she bought the paints, thought about Oliver selling pictures, but now the idea had entered her head she clung to it. Anything, to make him feel useful, to give him hope - and pride. The idea, she realised now, had come into her head only a few minutes ago, and something inside her seemed to be rising up and opposing his repudiation of it.

'Whatever you do, Chel,' said Oliver, on a dangerous note, 'don't patronise me.'

'I wasn't!' denied Chel, knowing that in her head, perhaps she had been. Oliver had always had the gift of reading her thoughts in the past, she had thought that he had lost it over the past year. Not so, apparently. She must be careful.

'So what do you think we should do?' she asked.

'I have no idea. But I do think we should try to be able to talk about it sensibly, and I do know it's been my fault that we haven't. That's all I wanted to say, really.' He paused, and added, gently, 'Your coffee's getting cold.'

Chel reached for her mug and took a sip.

'This is disgusting,' she said. 'Don't drink it, Oliver - I'll make some fresh - '

Making the fresh coffee restored some balance to the day. She came back with the refilled mugs and said, almost naturally,

'You'll never guess who I ran into outside the shop.'

'You'd better tell me, then,' said Oliver, taking his mug with the glimmer of a smile.

'Jack and Maggie,' said Chel. Oliver blinked, that was the last thing he had expected.

'They're in Australia,' he objected, as if Chel must have been hallucinating.

'Apparently not. They said it didn't work out. They're coming to see us sometime.' She wondered whether to add that Jack and Maggie had needed bringing up to speed on recent events, but decided not to. They knew now, after all.

'Well well... Jack and Maggie. Who'd have thought it?'

'They've got even more children,' said Chel.

'It felt as if they had a dozen or so before.'

Children was a dicey subject between them, since the loss of their own child. Chel said, lightly,

'The baby we knew is a now grizzler called India, there's a tot in a pushchair and another on the way.'

'That'll keep Maggie busy - ' Oliver paused.

'I think she already has been,' said Chel, with a grin. 'Jack, too. What's the matter? You look as if you've seen a ghost.'

'Nothing...' said Oliver, but a moment later Chel, too, remembered something.

The same thing? She wasn't sure, and didn't dare to ask.

Maggie was - had been anyway, an art teacher.

IV

It was as if, Chel thought when she looked back, that snowy day when she met Maggie outside the shop had completed the turn-round in their fortunes begun when she first met Judy, as if the addition of new people to the slow tempo of their life had acted like slow-rising yeast in a dull, flat dough. Even the snow itself had played its part, highlighting their need to stop drifting, to take hold of events and get out of their rut before it claimed them for ever. It was the snow, she suspected, that had jerked Oliver back into the real world. Until then he had been subconsciously believing he would wake up and find it had all gone away, she was sure of it. How this linked with his sudden essay into painting a real picture, she had yet to work out. Ignorance - of art, of Oliver - kept her in the dark, but that it did link she was increasingly certain. Perhaps if he could find some channel for his unsuspected creativity it would lead on to something else that might give him - give them, for she was bound to him by invisible ties as strong as steel, she knew that - some kind of future. She could only hope for it, although what it might eventually be, she couldn't imagine. She only knew, she at last began to feel hope, rising like sap through her heart and mind, promising spring after their long winter.

It was a couple of days before Jack and Maggie came to see them, then they came rattling up the field in their battered old minibus when Oliver had gone to lie down. Better though he had been since their escape to Cornwall, the effort to complete all the exercises he had been instructed to do tired him, and sitting still, even in the wheelchair, made his injured back ache after a while. But he was improving daily, fighting back at last, and seemed finally to have grasped the idea that the advice from surgeon and physiotherapist was designed to help him. It was hard work for Chel, too, who had to play her part and was relieved to be at last permitted to do so without having to fight every inch of the way. She had curled up on the sofa for a quiet hour to herself with a good book, when she heard the sound of a vehicle pulling up outside she was far from delighted.

'Bugger!' said Chel, to the quiet and empty van, and got up and went to the door.

'Hullo, it's us, did you think we weren't coming?' Maggie bounced through the door full of energy, and Chel thought, ungratefully, that they might have bothered to ring first. Jack, following more slowly, gave her a rueful grin.

'Sorry Cheryl, I couldn't hold her back. She was so thrilled to see you again she couldn't wait.'

Chel didn't think it was she who was the attraction. She reached for the kettle.

'Coffee or tea?'

'Do you have herb tea?' asked Maggie, her eyes all over the van. 'I mustn't have caffeine, the baby, you know.'

'No,' said Chel. 'Orange juice? Water? What about you Jack?' She saw, out of the corner of her eye, that Maggie had found Oliver's picture, propped against the window sill.

'Coffee's fine for me. Maggie'll have orange.'

'Go through. Sit down.'

Maggie turned away without making a comment, which Chel found amazing. Finished, the painting had startled her, but that was maybe because she knew nothing about it; as she kept telling herself, she had no idea if it was good or bad. The little yacht sheltered from a storm whose force had blown the sea flat, patterned with vicious catspaws under the lowering sky. Rigging streamed curving in the wind, against the horns of the little bay spray leapt and flew. Shelter from a raging storm... and yet, on the horizon, there was that flash of light. Chel thought that a psychologist might have found it interesting, she found it stunning.

'Do you like it?' she asked, unable to resist.

'I couldn't live with it,' said Maggie. She took the glass of orange juice that Chel handed her and followed Jack to the sofa. 'Oliver out?'

'Having a lie down,' said Chel. She brought coffee and placed it on the table. 'Why couldn't you live with it?'

Maggie didn't even think about it.

'Far too unrestful,' she said. 'Sorry. That's just me.' Chel raised her eyebrows.

'You think pictures should be restful?'

'I don't think they should sock you in the eye like that one does,' said Maggie. 'I'm sorry - that was rude of me. Ignore me.' She smiled, and it occurred to Chel that Maggie thought she had painted it. She sipped at her coffee, thoughtfully. Maggie looked around her, patently wondering where Oliver was. She asked, obliquely,

'The motor caravan outside - is that yours, or does it belong to the people in the next van?'

'It's ours.' She put Maggie out of her misery. 'We use it as a bedroom. I expect Oliver heard you arrive, he'll be over soon.' Maybe. Possibly.

'So tell us,' said Maggie, pretending she didn't care. 'Have you found yourselves a house yet? Where have you been looking?'

'We've an order to view a place tomorrow. I don't know if it'll be any good, mind you, but we have to start somewhere.

'Where is it? Anywhere near us?'

'I don't know where you are,' Chel pointed out, hoping not and feeling guilty. 'It's on that lane that goes through to the coast road - Moor House, it used to be Vellanzoe Cottages.'

Jack gave a long whistle.

'That place! It's derelict, are you planning to rebuild?'

'Someone already has,' said Chel. 'It's rather nice, actually.'

'You don't object to ghosts, then?' Jack grinned at her. Chel shook her head, speaking with more certainty than she felt was strictly justified.

'There's nothing there, not any more. I don't think it's stood the test of being renovated.'

'Nice position,' said Jack, thinking. Maggie objected,

'Ghosts don't just *go*.'

'How d'you know they don't?' asked Chel. Maggie shrugged.

'You don't believe in them, obviously.'

Chel was surprised.

'Do you?'

Jack laid his hand on her knee.

'Cheryl dear, don't start her off. Maggie hunts ghosts with the enthusiasm other folk keep for foxes - in full cry!'

'Don't be silly, Jack!' cried Maggie, sharply. 'I don't at all - just because *you've* never seen one - '

'Why, have you?' Jack interrupted.

It was obviously an old argument, and Chel felt all the discomfort of someone dragged into a long-standing dispute that is nothing to do with them. Maggie hunched her shoulders towards Jack and spoke pointedly to Chel.

'I really believe there is some communication between us and the spirit world,' she said, throwing it out like a challenge, and Chel, thinking of the bungalow, didn't feel disposed to deny it, not absolutely.

'I'm not sure about direct communication,' she hedged.

'Oh God, not you too! I can't bear it!' Jack covered his eyes with his hand that wasn't holding a mug. 'Spare me, please!'

'Quiet, you!' ordered Maggie, and to Chel, 'What are you sure about, then?'

Chel caught Jack's eye, and nearly laughed aloud at his expression.

'Well, not ghosts in the grey lady sense... but feelings left behind, maybe. Like, some houses are unhappy or sad - and Moor House or whatever you like to call it didn't feel like that, at least not from outside. Not any more.'

'So you think it did, once?' said Maggie, swiftly. Chel shrugged.

'It was getting dark... bats and things. It was falling apart too, it feels quite different now.'

'Hardly surprising!' scoffed Jack. 'Any derelict house is a natural for ghost stories, particularly one where there's been a tragedy. What does Oliver make of it all? Don't tell me he believes in ghosts too!'

'We've not discussed it,' said Chel, excusing the evasion by telling herself that they were talking about Moor House, not ghosts in general. And even in connection with the bungalow, the word *ghost* had not been mentioned between them.

'Lucky Oliver,' commented Jack. 'Maggie discusses it *ad nauseam*.'

'One of these fine days, something'll happen to make you laugh on the other side of your face,' Maggie told him, darkly. 'I'd like to see a ghost, but I don't seem to be the kind of person they appear to. But I certainly believe in them - so there!' Seeing Jack raise his eyes to heaven, she then laughed and changed the subject.

'So tell us,' she said. 'How come you both got married in such a rush? Were you pregnant?'

'No.' Not then. 'We just did. Is there a law?'

Maggie laughed again.

'How romantic! Or did you just grab him while the chance was there? I wouldn't blame you if you had.'

'For God's sake, Maggie,' said Jack.

Chel could see, out of the corner of her eye, that the door to the motor home had opened, and Oliver was emerging, curiosity having dragged him from his bed. She said nothing, knowing that he would hate Maggie, and more particularly Jack, to watch his laborious struggle down the step and across the grass. With an effort, she managed to smile at Maggie.

'His idea - not mine.'

'Bet you didn't argue though.'

She had, just a little, Chel remembered. Not so much at the proposal itself, but at the speed of events. She had been apprehensive - rightly as it turned out - about the reactions of her parents and, more particularly, of Oliver's family. Occasionally, when she was feeling depressed, she wondered even now how much of Oliver's impetuousness had been due to a wish to rock the familial boat. She wouldn't say that to Maggie - to Judy perhaps, one day, but Maggie, never. Oliver's family, in particular his disliked stepmother, thought a lot of themselves. Her own father ran a village shop. Maggie grinned at her hesitation, misinterpreting it completely.

'There, you see Jack? She can't deny it!'

'Hullo Maggie,' said Oliver.

Maggie jumped, and turned bright red, wondering how much of that conversation Oliver had heard. It was one thing to tease Chel, she stood a little in awe of Oliver.

Oliver had seen Jack, sitting beyond his wife.

'Jack! Good to see you. How was Australia?'

'Full of kangaroos,' said Jack. He rose to his feet, clasped Oliver's outstretched hand with pleasure. 'Maggie was afraid to lift the lid of the dunny, so we thought we'd better come home.'

'Roos under the seat, were there?'

Both men laughed. There was no way Oliver could handle the sofa or the armchairs, and Chel knew better than to drag out the wheelchair in front of Jack and Maggie. He seated himself, with deceptive casualness, on the bench beside the table, and Jack slid easily into the seat opposite. Chel got to her feet.

'I'll make you some coffee. Anyone else for another cup? More juice, Maggie?'

This, of course, left Maggie alone in the far end, so she followed Chel into the kitchen area.

'Budge up, Jack.' And there she was, sitting opposite to Oliver, with a smile on her face. Magic!

Chel recalled, as she waited for the kettle to boil, that Maggie's attitude had always left her feeling rather cynical. She was about to have justification for this view.

Sitting at the table gave Jack, perhaps for the first time, a full view of Oliver's painting. He picked it up to look at it better.

'I can see what Maggie means,' he observed, consideringly. 'You couldn't relax to it - it's good though, isn't it Mags? Well done, Cheryl!'

Maggie had opened her mouth to make some comment, but Chel forestalled her.

'Oh, I didn't paint it - my painting is limited to window frames. Oliver did it.'

Maggie's already open mouth sagged in surprise, but she recovered herself well, Chel had to give her full marks for that.

'I should have guessed!' she exclaimed. 'It isn't a woman's painting. Silly me!'

Amen to that, thought Chel, uncharitably, and wondered why Maggie was getting on her nerves quite so much. Surely she wasn't so mean-spirited that it was because of her coming baby?

Maggie took the sketch block from Jack and turned it so she could look at the painting full on. Truth to tell, she was a little ashamed of herself, knowing that her immediate first reaction had been from shock - jealousy? - that another woman could paint as well as, or better than herself. Although the comment she had made had been the truth, she knew that it had not been all of the truth, and that she had deliberately belittled work she had thought was Chel's. It made her careful now.

'I never knew you could paint,' she said slowly, buying time. 'Cheryl always told us that you were a philistine.'

'Cheryl has found out that life is full of surprises,' said Chel, dryly. Maggie ignored her.

'Have you done any more? May I see?'

'Not paintings,' said Oliver.

'But you've done all those sketches,' said Chel. 'Can I show her?'

Thus cornered, Oliver said in an offhand way that he supposed she could, and Chel fetched the sketches from the folder in which she had put them - left to Oliver, they would have ended up on the floor or in the bin. Maggie took them and went through them with growing amazement.

'But these are really good!' she exclaimed.

'Said she, with unflattering surprise,' said Oliver, and pulled a face at her.

'No, but really - did you ever go to art college?'

'No.'

'Then you should have,' said Maggie, firmly. 'If you were one of my pupils, I should be over the moon with excitement!'

Chel's heart gave a thump of the same emotion, she wasn't sure why. She said,

'Take him on, then,' and Oliver asked idly, as if he didn't already know,

'Do you teach art, then?'

'Yes, but I don't think there's a lot I can teach you,' said Maggie, regretfully. 'Why don't you work in oils? This style of thing rather lends itself, don't you think?'

'I never have. And wouldn't it be a bit difficult, when we're living in someone else's caravan?'

'I don't see why. Would you like to?'

Since Oliver had momentarily looked like someone who had been shown the Promised Land and then been refused a visa, Chel thought that she could have saved herself the question, but Oliver simply answered,

'Yes.'

'Then you should,' said Maggie. She shuffled the sketches together and put them back in the folder. 'I've got some paints I haven't time to use these days, you can borrow them. I'll give you a few lessons, if you like, and then if you like the medium, you can buy your own stuff.'

Visa duly issued and stamped.

'Would you really?'

'I said so, didn't I?' Maggie pushed the folder aside and folded her hands round the glass of fresh orange juice that Chel had set in front of her. 'Now tell us, we're dying to know. How come you seem to have become New Age Travellers?'

Mr. Rupert Gittings of Hedge & Hollow, Estate Agents, had arranged to meet Oliver and Chel out at Moor House, that had once been Vellanzoe Cottages, at eleven o'clock the following morning. Judy's mother had loaned her car for the expedition.

'You don't want to be taking that great thing down that lane,' she said, firmly, which was perfectly true. Chel found herself increasingly reluctant to drive it anywhere, let alone down the lanes, although she had driven all the way to Cornwall without really thinking about it. Need, rather than herself, had been in the driving seat then, she thought. Did that mean that her subconscious had decided that the need was now past? Interesting question!

Interesting, too, to find how easily Oliver could by this time manage getting in and out of a normal car, one not equipped with a special seat for the disabled. Either he had begun to make a remarkably swift recovery, or the pressures from his family back in Embridge had held him back more than they had realised. Either alternative held out hope of a better future than they had dared to believe in.

As they drove along the lane towards Vellanzoe, Oliver looked about him with interest - a quite different interest from their last visit, Chel realised. A *this could be our place* kind of interest whose significance she wasn't slow to recognise. Oliver had had enough of gypsying in a caravan, and since she felt the same, she could relate to that. Only, was it a symptom of a deeper change, or simply present circumstances? And if Moor House proved to be yet another dead end, what then?

Questions impossible to answer.

When they arrived and pulled onto the new gravelled parking place beyond the wall, there was nobody there, no car parked and the house looked shut and secretive, empty.

'So what do you think?' asked Chel, to break a silence that seemed suddenly oppressive. Oliver shrugged.

'It's changed a lot.'

'Yes.'

'There's some slates loose on the roof. That needs fixing before we sign anything.'

Chel hadn't noticed. The slates, she noticed with an odd little twist deep in her stomach, were slipping from the area where the plane had crashed through the original roof. To cover her disquiet, she said,

'They said in the shop that the people who bought it wanted it for a holiday let. I wonder why they didn't use it?' The speculation, meant to lighten her unease, only deepened it. But the house looked blandly innocent under the April sun.

'People's circumstances change,' said Oliver, adding, for once without bitterness, 'Ours have, after all.' He pulled back his sleeve to look at his watch. 'So - where's this Mr. Gittings who's supposed to be meeting us?'

'Do you want to have a look round the outside while we wait?'

'Could do.'

'OK. I'll get the chair out.'

'You won't,' said Oliver, fiercely. Their eyes met. They had had a tussle of wills over bringing the hated object in the first place, and Chel had thought she had won. Now, she saw that she hadn't.

'It didn't just come for the ride, you know,' she said.

Oliver felt a gut reaction that was pure pantomime, and only with an effort restrained himself from saying, *oh yes, it did!* Chel, reading the words in his expression, was horrified to hear herself saying,

'Why do you *always* have to be so obstructive?'

She didn't expect to get an answer, least of all one so devastatingly honest.

'Because I am sick to death of pity,' said Oliver, precisely, and they stared at each other in mutual shock. Chel swallowed.

'Nobody pities you,' she said, without conviction.

'Don't patronise me, Cheryl! You know they do - *you* do. So do I, if it comes to that.'

He never called her *Cheryl.*

'Self-pity is despicable!' retorted Chel.

'There you go again! *Stop it,* I've had enough!'

There was a silence, while they both stared out through the windscreen, speechless. Then Chel said, tightly,

'We've got to stop doing this.'

Oliver tilted his head back against the headrest and closed his eyes.

'OK. I'm sorry.' He didn't sound it, but it was something.

Pause.

'Shall I get the chair out then?' asked Chel, in a small voice that she despised in herself but couldn't help. 'Just to go around the garden while we're waiting?'

Pause.

Chel wanted to fill the silence by pointing out that although there were no doubt chairs in the house, standing around in the garden while they waited for an indeterminate length of time would be far worse for Oliver's injured back than walking about, at which he was getting quite adept now, but he knew that perfectly well - better than she did, probably. She tried hard to blank all traces of sympathy out of her face and waited. After a moment, Oliver said, roughly and unreasonably,

'Well, get on with it, then.'

The manoeuvre was accomplished in silence. In silence too they passed through the gate and under the arch onto the lawn. Oliver tilted his head to look up at the façade of the house, narrowing his eyes thoughtfully.

'If it was only done as a speculation, there's been an awful lot of money spent on it,' he commented. Chel, relieved that his fury seemed to have evaporated as suddenly as it had come, launched into a too-effusive explanation, heard herself, and winced.

'They think at the shop that maybe he intended to live in it - and the man who bought it certainly did - only -' She broke off.

'Only?' prompted Oliver, into a pause.

'People's circumstances change,' repeated Chel, unconvincingly, feeling that she was required to say something, even if it was further obscuring the truth. She couldn't get out of her head that story about the builders who walked out. Had the builder really been bothered by ghost stories, she wondered. Or had he, as Sally Tregillis had it, simply run out of money? No use in speculating, she didn't know whom he had been, and if she did, she could hardly go and ask him. Of one thing she was certain, on the sweet spring air there was no lingering breath of tragedy, not today.

'You're right, the conservatory's good,' observed Oliver, in a speculative tone that made Chel prick up her ears.

'Full of light,' she offered.

'Be hot as hell on a summer's day.'

'You can open the doors.'

'Would it do, do you think?'

'Depends what indoors is like. Depends what they want for it. Depends if it's even to rent.'

'I like to hear you being so positive.'

They both laughed, at ease again. It was into this moment of unity that Mr. Gittings strode, clutching a clipboard. Absorbed in the house, they hadn't even heard his car.

It wasn't an auspicious meeting. He hadn't expected the wheelchair. Chel read the surprise in his face when he saw it and watched as he visibly dismissed Oliver from his calculations and turned to her instead.

'Mrs. Nankervis?' He held out his hand. 'Gittings, from Hedge & Hollow. I understand you have approached us on the possibility of renting this property?' He sounded as if he had already written them off as potential clients, and Chel felt her hackles rise.

It would have been easier if Oliver had said something, but he didn't. Chel took the proffered hand awkwardly. It was barely a handshake, he dropped her fingers as soon as they touched, and swung the keys of the house round his finger on their ring.

'I suppose we may as well have a look, since you're here. I should say at once, however, that it isn't a suitable house for a disabled person, and I doubt it Mr. Williams would agree to the installation of rails or a stairlift, since he is trying to sell the property. I understand you are not in a position to buy.' It was a statement, not a question. As such, Chel and Oliver felt it required no answer, even if in both of them a disinclination to confide their private affairs to Mr. Gittings hadn't arisen like choking fog. In any case, he didn't wait for any comment, simply turned on his heel and strode back through the arch towards the porch. Chel, not daring to meet Oliver's eyes, followed with the wheelchair. Oliver's crutches, on which he could get around very well these days, were in the car. Neither of them felt like drawing further attention to his disablement by asking Mr. Gittings to wait while they were fetched.

Mr. Gittings didn't quite ask them to be careful of the paintwork going through the door, but he made a tutting noise under his breath which they both heard as he opened a door to the left of the little tiled lobby just inside - new since their first visit, part of the added porch.

'This is the downstairs shower room, put in so that children can shower when they come back from the beach, and not tread sand through the house.' Was the reference to children deliberate, to point the unsuitability of the house for themselves? Chel, not a person given to such negative responses, found that she hated the estate agent. But there was no time to analyse the feeling, the door to the shower was slammed shut before they barely had time to glimpse the room behind it. Mr. Gittings swept on through into the main part of the house.

Both Chel and Oliver still carried in their heads the recollection of the house as it had been when they first explored it. The contrast with what it now was stopped them in their tracks.

'Oh goodness!' said Chel, before she could stop herself.

The rubble of their last visit, the broken bath, the gaping roof weren't even a memory. It was as if they had stepped into a completely different place.

The ground floor had been gutted. The lobby opened directly into a dining area with a table and four chairs, and a sideboard against the wall. Beyond that, a breakfast bar divided kitchen from dining area; there were cupboards and worktops, built-in cooker, a fridge-freezer and a washing machine. The only interior wall that remained on the ground floor divided the kitchen from the living area beyond, against it, a flight of polished wood, open-tread stairs led upwards; the remainder of the divide had become a wide arch, supporting the upper floor. Both Chel and Oliver saw instantly that he would be unable to manage the stairs, but it wouldn't matter, the spacious downstairs would have everything he would need, inclusive of personal space in the conservatory.

Mr. Gittings gestured perfunctorily towards the kitchen.

'As you can see, it is all fitted out for holiday occupation,' he said, labouring the point a second time with impatience that he didn't bother to conceal. 'Through this way is the living room and the conservatory.' He led the way, briskly.

The living room occupied the rest of the ground floor. When the shutters were folded back, sunlight poured in through the windows and the french doors to the conservatory, filling the space with warmth and brightness. The furnishings were simple, a sofa and two armchairs, coffee table, a television, all ranged around a wood-burning stove in the old hearth, a bookcase with some well-thumbed paperback novels on its shelves, and against the back wall, a cheap sofa-bed. A second arch had been created beyond the french doors, once more to replace the old dividing wall, adding character to the big, uncluttered room, and beyond this was a curtain rail and a long, heavy curtain that could be used as a room divider at will. It was obvious that the intention was that the far end of the room could be used to make an extra bedroom for a big family on holiday, even if Mr. Gittings hadn't made it his business to point it out, adding,

'I believe I should be open with you, Mrs. Nankervis, and inform you that we have felt it our duty to point out to Mr. Williams that we do not feel it would be in his best interests to let this house on a long-term basis. We felt bound to point out that he would retain more control over the property, since he wishes ultimately to sell it, if he let it as it was originally intended to use it, as a holiday cottage. The income, of course, would be much higher, and such an arrangement would leave him in a stronger position should a purchaser be found.'

'That was very thoughtful of you,' said Oliver, in a tone of voice Chel hadn't heard from him for weeks now. 'Couldn't he work it out for himself?'

Mr. Gittings focussed his gaze on a point just over Oliver's head, and addressed Chel as if Oliver hadn't spoken.

'There are also, of course, other considerations to be borne in mind. Mr. Williams was not aware of your husband's disability, since you hadn't seen fit to inform us of it.'

'Should we have?' asked Chel, blankly. Were there rules and regulations about letting houses to people on crutches? Health and Safety, perhaps? Surely not... but Mr. Gittings was speaking again. He looked, she thought, like a camel. A particularly supercilious camel, belching in someone's face. Hers, for instance. And Oliver's.

'This house, as you can see, is hardly suitable for an invalid, and of course, there's the possibility of damage from the wheelchair. Mr. Williams would need to take this into consideration, I don't know that he would be prepared to take the risk, or even that we could advise him to do so. The house is in new condition.'

This was true, but then, if gossip didn't lie, it had never been lived in since its conversion. Chel opened her mouth to point this out, but Oliver got in first.

'Why don't you just tell us outright that you would much prefer to take the commission on summer lets for him?' he asked, and Mr. Gittings made his tutting sound again.

'Could I see upstairs?' asked Chel, hastily, and then was angry she had asked, because it seemed to set Oliver aside. For a moment, she thought Mr. Gittings was going to tell her it would be a waste of time, she almost saw the words, like a cartoon think-bubble, rising from his head. But instead, he looked from her to Oliver, just as if, she said later, he suspected them of being a pair of con-artists after the spoons.

'Will Mr. Nankervis be all right down here on his own?'

'No, I shall go roaring round in my wheelchair, wrecking the furniture!' said Oliver. 'Why don't you ask me? I'm not deaf and dumb!'

'I think...' said Mr. Gittings, flushing a little, and headed for the stairs without saying anything more. Chel followed him, pausing halfway up them to look down at Oliver. He met her eyes defiantly, and she turned away and followed Mr. Gittings onto the landing.

There were two double bedrooms, a single, and a bathroom upstairs, the doubles plainly and sparsely furnished as downstairs had been, one with twin beds, one with a double. Holiday cottage furniture, that didn't quite match and had been bought on the cheap, but adequate for its purpose. The small bedroom contained a single divan bed and a wooden chair, nothing else.

'It's a completely unsuitable house for someone like your husband, as you can see' said Mr. Gittings, and added, with a false sympathy that grated like rough sandpaper, 'It must be very difficult for you.'

'No, not really...' But Chel was hardly listening. They were in the twin bedded room overlooking the garden; here, in the roof above their heads was where the little plane had crashed through and its pilot had been trapped and called fruitlessly, uselessly, for help as his life slowly drained away with his blood... but there was nothing here now. Just the stuffy feeling of a house that had been left shut up too long, characterless, a blank page waiting to be written upon. But of course, the building had been old long before the plane crashed. It must have seen a lot of people come and go, tragedies as well as happy times. Nothing remained of any of them now. She believed she would know if it was otherwise, among many other hard lessons, the horrible bungalow had surely taught her that.

Back downstairs again, Oliver had relapsed into a nail-biting silence, and Chel felt a painful pang of pity for him. He had no more idea of how to handle Mr. Gittings than Mr. Gittings had of what to say to him, and even had they met on equal terms she couldn't imagine that they would have seen eye to eye. She felt guiltily that the present impossible situation was her fault, it was she who had insisted on using the wheelchair for the garden. Mr. Gittings had tilted his head so that he could look at them down his nose - not purposely, she hoped.

'Shall I tell Mr. Williams, then, that you find the property unsuitable on closer inspection?' he asked. Chel looked to Oliver for a cue, but he unhelpfully avoided her eyes.

'But we don't know that we do,' she objected. Mr. Gittings looked at her with his supercilious camel expression.

'If your husband can't manage the stairs, that seems rather to settle the question.'

Chel had already mentally shifted the sofa-bed into the little bedroom, moved Oliver's own adjustable bed, at present in the bungalow in Embridge, into the vacant space and placed the single divan beside it. She did not say so because she had no chance.

'Tell Mr. Williams,' said Oliver, 'that we're still interested.'

But he wouldn't, both Chel and Oliver knew that. If Mr. Williams heard anything at all, it would be that they were quite unsuitable tenants. Mr. Gittings said,

'I shall be in contact with him later today and putting him in the picture.'

End of visit. It was as clear as a drawn line. End, too, of any chance they had of living here, thought Chel. They had no way of tracing Mr. Williams for themselves and Mr. Gittings had his own agenda, made no secret of it. She allowed herself and Oliver to be herded back to the front door.

Chel and Oliver drove back to Church Farm without speaking to each other, but when they were back in the caravan, Oliver said,

'That's that, then.'

He looked stormy and resentful, and more tired and drawn than he had looked for a long time, as if the morning had drained him of all energy, and Chel busied herself with the kettle to avoid looking at him.

'We'll see,' she said. She had fallen in love with Moor House, its easy open plan and its sunlit aspect, and her disappointment, probably unreasonably, had found its focus in Oliver's attitude there. Years of practising on his family had made him too skilled at giving offence in the fewest possible words. Even had Mr. Gittings not made it too obvious that he considered him negligible because of the wheelchair, Oliver's attitude had certainly hardened his. There would be no attempt at cooperation here, the house would go for a summer let, Mr. Gittings would make sure of it. Oliver's next words showed that he realised it, too.

'Not just no help, a positive hindrance,' he said bitterly, and on the words, Chel's resentment vanished. It must have been horrible for Oliver to have to sit and be patronised by a camel. She turned to face him, leaning her back against the worktop, an empty mug in each hand.

'Don't start that,' she said. 'After all that time you spent under the sea, I would have thought you'd have learned that it was stupid to bite sharks, but if you didn't, you didn't, and I doubt if it made any real difference. He'd already made up his mind before he even got there.'

'You think so? I think it was me who tipped the scales. The *cripple*.'

'He didn't say that.' He hadn't needed to. She made her voice light. 'It isn't the end of the world, anyway. There'll be other houses. Probably much nicer, too.'

Oliver didn't comment directly. Instead, he said,

'You won't set your heart on it, will you? Our only chance of getting it is to buy it, you can be sure of that.'

'The bungalow might sell tomorrow,' said Chel.

'Watch out of the window, you may see a flying pig! Who in their senses would want that place?' The bitterness in his voice was frightening. Chel, who had originally chosen the bungalow - or more accurately, allowed herself to be talked into choosing it by Susan, said, trying to laugh,

'Thanks for nothing, Oliver! Don't you think you might be a tiny bit prejudiced?'

Oliver dismissed this with the contempt it probably deserved.

'Even if it did sell, it wouldn't realise enough to buy that place.'

'Oh, come on Oliver. It's only a country cottage, not even particularly pretty! The bungalow is a town property, and in a sought-after position too!'

'You sound like Mr. Gittings,' said Oliver.

'It's true.'

'You've overlooked something. It mostly belongs to my father and the Building Society.'

'Your father meant it as a gift,' said Chel, hesitantly, because this was old ground.

'We can manage without charity, thank you.'

How? Chel asked herself, but silently. The kettle boiled and she began to make the tea. 'We don't know that Mr. Williams will want to be bothered with holiday lets,' she said, trying to look on the bright side.

'It won't make any difference. Gittings will be on the phone as soon as he gets back to his office, telling him not to put his faith in Mr. Nankervis because Mr. Nankervis is a cripple, and he'll be right.'

There was no answer to that which would convince Oliver, so Chel made none, but into her mind, unbidden, slipped once more the echo of Judy's almost throw-away comment - *this house has a way of sorting things out for itself.*

Well, it had sorted her and Oliver out, that was certain.

'Maybe it just doesn't want anyone to live there, ever again,' she said, before she had thought. Oliver, understandably, stared at her as if she was mad.

'What on earth are you talking about?'

'Nothing. Just something Judy said. It doesn't matter.'

Oliver must have known more or less what she meant, though, for he laughed and said,

'Hard luck for Mr. Williams, if so.'

V

In spite of what she had said, Chel had never really thought Judy intended her comment to be taken seriously, so that it gave her a shock when she went into the village shop a few days later and found the whole place in a ferment with excited gossip. The shop seemed to be full of people, although in fact there were only half a dozen or so, crowded round the till area where a customer, bright-eyed with the sensation she was causing, was telling a tale.

'...gave her such a turn, she had palpitations for half an hour afterwards,' she was saying, as Chel came in. 'After all the tales folks tell, there was this voice calling, *help, help!* and she took and run halfway to the farm before she realised as there'd been a car there, and the front door ajar. But she weren't going to go back on her own, not her, and she went to the farm and got Will to go down there with her, tho' what help she thought the poor old bugger would be, only the Lord knows The voice was still calling, ever so weak now she says, and when they went inside, there was this poor man lying on the floor at the foot of the stairs with his leg broke. Taking an inventory, or something, he said he was, and somebody pushed him on the stairs, but that's the shock talking, he just slipped and fell of course, and laid there all day, calling. The bone was sticking right through his leg, Will said, and broke in two places, ever such a mess. They took him off to Truro to have it put right, and they say he'll be there weeks yet.' She ended on a note almost of triumph, and her hearers shook their heads in sympathy.

'It's always been a queer place, that,' said one of them. 'They won't make much of a holiday let out o' that, if you ask me, whatever they may think.'

'Is that what they're planning?' asked someone else, and the original speaker said,

'So Jenny said the fellow told her while they was waiting for the ambulance. Gittings, his name was, he's from Hedge & Hollow, over to Penzance. His wife runs an agency for summer lets.'

A packet of frozen peas slipped from Chel's fingers and dropped through to the bottom of the freezer. It might have been because they were cold. She swallowed, and reached for them.

'Remember what the tiler said about that place?' said the second speaker, with relish. 'They slates kept sliding off where that hole used to be, he said, and nothing he could do would stop 'em, although the rafters and that was all new.'

'Come on, Ted!' cried Sally Tregillis, laughing. 'We all know that was just storm damage and shoddy work! Using it as an excuse, that's what he was doing.'

'Ah well, maybe.' Ted shook his head as if he didn't really think that at all. 'You can't deny they stopped work on it in the end.'

'That wasn't the reason,' said Sally, beginning to ring up the till for the next customer. 'Them's just stories, and you know it. He ran out of money.' She looked up and saw Chel standing there. 'Morning, Mrs. Nankervis, did you hear what happened yesterday out at that Moor House you was asking about?'

'Most of it,' said Chel. She was sorry for Mr. Gittings, at least, she hoped she was, but she couldn't help hoping too that he would find himself sitting in a wheelchair for a bit and have people pitying him and talking over his head as if he simply wasn't there. Just for long enough to know how it felt, she told herself.

'Wanting to buy that place, weren't you?' asked Sally.

'We hoped the owner might rent it to us on a long let,' said Chel.

'Going for a holiday place, that is,' said the ghoulish Ted. 'A shame too, when young folks down here need homes.' The group was launched on another perennial grumble, and Chel put the peas in her basket and went on with her shopping.

Nothing had offered to push her down the stairs. They were perfectly safe, ordinary stairs.

Nonetheless, she suddenly found herself wondering, if she and Oliver paid a builder to put the slates back on the roof, would they stay there?

Disquietingly, she half-suspected that they might - but of course that would only prove the truth of what Sally had said - and if Mr. Gittings had persuaded the unknown Mr. Williams to use Moor House for a summer let, the matter would never be put to the test. For a regrettable moment, out of her own surprisingly bitter disappointment, she was glad that the agent had fallen, whatever the reason - slipped, undoubtedly, to think anything else was absurd, and serve him right after his snide remark about Oliver and those same stairs.

An uneasiness remained.

The following week, in response to a pressing invitation, they borrowed Millie's car once more and drove to Maggie and Jack's cottage on the moors behind Zennor for dinner, on a cool, spring evening when the sky overhead was the colour of a duck egg and as clear, and there was still enough nip in the air to make the fire that

69

Maggie had kindled against their arrival a welcome sight. The children were all in bed and more or less asleep, and Jack was an easy host, pouring drinks while Maggie cooked. There was good vegetarian food, all organic as Maggie assured everyone, and home-made blackberry wine winking crimson in the firelight, pleasant conversation... the eggshell sky had darkened in the windows and Maggie drew the curtains across when she rose to make coffee - dandelion coffee, of course - at the end of the meal, heavily because her time was almost on her, but moving with a clumsy grace, the perfect earth mother.

'I'll clear up when you've gone,' said Jack, forestalling Chel as she went to gather the empty pudding plates. 'Come and sit round the fire, it's still cold by this time of night, although the evenings are drawing out. How're you making out, back in that motor home of yours?' For the first visitors had turned them out of the static van back into their own.

'Oh, it's warm enough,' said Chel, holding her hands to the blaze - not that she was cold, but for the sheer pleasure of feeling the heat on her palms. 'Cramped, though. We shall have to think of something soon.' She tried to keep the trouble from her voice. Jack said, watching her,

'I drove past that house at Vellanzoe the other day, I could hardly believe it was the same place - it always beats me how someone can look at a disaster like that and see something that can be made of it. I suppose I've no imagination.'

'Well, my petal, we all know that,' said Maggie, patting his arm as she passed on the way to the kitchen. 'Of the earth, earthy, you are.'

'Good thing someone is, in this house,' said Jack. 'Did you get to see inside it before it all went pear-shaped on you?'

'Yes...,'said Chel, hesitantly.

'Unfortunately, it isn't an option,' said Oliver. 'It's going to become a summer let, so no good to us.'

'We mightn't have liked it out there anyway,' said Chel, dismissively. Jack laughed.

'Depends how credulous you are,' he suggested. 'Did you see any ghosts on your visit of inspection?'

'No, of course not!' said Chel, and realised immediately that she had spoken too vehemently, her mind full of climbing stairs. The others were looking at her, and Jack was grinning.

'Come on Cheryl, you said that almost as if it wasn't true!'

Did he fall, or was he pushed? And if he was pushed, why?

'Well, I didn't,' said Chel, getting up hurriedly to clear a space on a small table for Maggie, who had come in with a tray of mugs. 'There you are, Maggie - there aren't such things as ghosts, anyway, not in the way you mean.'

'If there were, that would probably be as good a place for them as any,' said Oliver idly, and Chel looked at him in surprise, and Jack in despair.

'Come on Oliver, not you too! We men should hang together on this one!' cried Jack, and Chel said,

'You don't believe in ghosts.'

'I never said that,' said Oliver. 'I've never seen any - but then, I don't think I'm the type that does. That doesn't mean there aren't any, necessarily. I'm damn sure, for one thing, that I've felt them.'

Maggie took her seat on a fireside stool. She looked interested.

'Have you really? Where was that?'

'Oh... out at Vellanzoe I suppose, once. Not this time.'

'You never said,' cried Chel, swiftly, and he looked at her.

'Neither did you, but I knew even so there was something wrong,' he pointed out. 'If you weren't letting on, why should I? Anyway, it was only a feeling, I didn't hear anything. But what about that bungalow of yours?'

'Please stop calling it mine,' begged Chel. 'I hated it. I'd never have let Susan talk me into it if I'd known - ' She broke off.

'Known what?' asked Maggie.

Chel didn't want to be drawn into a discussion of the bungalow and its unhappy history.

'Oh... the people who lived there before us were old, and they had troubles...' she said.

'Did they die there?' asked Maggie, interested. Chel stirred her dandelion coffee with great care, looking down at the brown swirl of it with feigned fascination. The alternative had been herbal tea.

'I believe he did, yes. Not her.'

'Ah...' said Maggie.

The way she said it set Chel on the defensive.

'When you come to think about it, at least with older houses, there can't be many places where people haven't died.'

'It can make a difference how,' said Maggie.

'Come off it, Mag!' protested Jack.

'But it can,' Maggie persisted. 'If people are very unhappy - if there's been a suicide, for instance, or something like that - then it isn't a ghost exactly, but they can leave bad vibes behind them...' Her voice tailed off. Oliver had gone very still, and Chel went on stirring her coffee. Maggie said, with sudden certainty, 'There was - wasn't there, Cheryl?'

71

'I believe one of the neighbours did say something.' said Chel, uncomfortably.

'If you and Oliver both felt it, it must have been a pretty strong vibe,' said Maggie. 'But that's not like ghosts - that's just a feeling left behind - I have an idea that ghosts are perhaps a bit more than that - well, some ghosts, anyhow.'

Chel thought yet again about Mr. Gittings falling down the stairs, and the persistently slipping tiles of Vellanzoe, and rejected them firmly. She must be losing her marbles to think... what she occasionally found herself thinking.

'I can accept that there might be something happen in a place that caused such a strong surge of emotion at the time that it got... well, sort of left behind on a kind of permanent replay, I suppose,' she said. 'I believe that - if you think about most ghost stories, it's easy to believe, but more than that? It opens up too wide a field. How *can* you believe it?'

'It would mean that we live on somewhere,' said Oliver, quietly. 'And are accountable, maybe. I'm not sure I like that idea. I'd sooner come to an end and be done with it.'

'People who come very near to death come back with some strange stories,' said Maggie, and Chel wondered if she realised how near Oliver himself had been. She looked at him out of the corners of her eyes to see his reaction, but he simply looked mildly interested.

'Such as?' asked Jack. He sounded sceptical. Maggie hesitated.

'Oh...' she said, slowly. 'A place where there are people... spirits, I suppose... waiting to guide them on. People they knew, who've died already...' She hesitated again. 'Some people, apparently, particularly if they die suddenly, don't immediately understand that they're dead - that's when you get ghostly manifestations - they can't, or won't, accept it.'

'Says who?' asked Jack, derisively. The other three ignored him.

'So ghosts - that sort of ghost - might not even leave a permanent feeling behind them?' said Chel. So, no feeling at Vellanzoe... she had stopped thinking of it as Moor House, but hadn't realised it.

'I suppose not.' Maggie's corroboration couldn't possibly be deliberate, she knew nothing about falls downstairs. 'Or at least, only when they decide to appear.' *Ouch!* 'I suppose that's what there might have been at Vellanzoe, and now that the house is all different, he's realised what happened and moved on.'

And it was just as possible that it had been a genuine fall.

'I do hope so, for his sake,' said Chel, meaning it. Maggie looked pensive.

'I'm no expert, of course, although I've read a fair bit, but I think it would be very comforting to feel that we didn't just fizzle out when we died - it would be nice to know that if we make a mess of things here, we can have another go somewhere else.'

'Or perhaps, if someone makes a mess of things for us,' suggested Oliver, not as lightly as he might have done.

'Much better get it right first time,' said Jack, briskly. 'Maggie, my love, you talk a lot of bullshit!' He got to his feet and began lighting a second lamp. 'That's better, anyone would think it was Hallowe'en! Enough of ghosts - shall we bore you with our Australian photos instead? I got a beaut of the dunny spider.'

But it hadn't escaped Chel's eye, as maybe it hadn't escaped Jack's either, that Oliver was looking tired, a sure sign that it was time they left.

'Next time,' she said. 'We should be going now - we're not used to living it up like this.' She added, with wonder in her voice, 'I hadn't thought about it, but it's the first time we've been on the tiles for a year.'

'Really?' Maggie looked flattered. 'I'm so glad it was to us, then.' She got to her feet. 'Before you go, I've got something for Oliver.' She reached behind a chair and brought out a flat wooden box. 'Oil paints, as promised. There's a pad of oil paper here, too. I'll slip over when I've got a minute and show you a few things.'

The door opened, and the child, India, sidled in, in a short white nightshirt and dragging a teddy bear behind her by one leg, like an illustration from *Winnie the Pooh*.

'Maggie, I can't go to sleep,' she whined.

Her grizzly arrival effectively brought a swift end to the evening, with no prolonged goodbyes. Chel and Oliver left, promising to repeat the occasion some other time, some other place.

'We'll have a house-warming,' promised Chel.

'When we have a house to warm, that is,' added Oliver.

Maggie and Jack stood on their doorstep, waving, the child on Jack's shoulders and the golden lamplight spilling through the doorway around them.

'Either make it quick, or hang on a month,' called Maggie. 'I have a previous engagement!'

Goodnight, goodnight...

They tumbled into bed without talking very much, but when they lay together in the quiet dark, Oliver suddenly said,

'Do you believe that - what Maggie was saying?'

Chel had been drifting into sleep, it took her a moment to focus.
'About what, particularly?' She yawned, hoping he would take the hint. He didn't.
'About life after death. Do you think there is anything?'
'I don't know, do I? Shut up, Oliver, it's too late at night for this.'
Oliver was silent for so long that she wondered if he had gone to sleep after all, but after a while he said,
'If there is something, it puts us under some sort of obligation. It makes a difference. Life becomes, not something that's just there, but a gift. All I've done with mine so far is please myself, and never mind if it hurts anyone else. I've deliberately got into stupid trouble, done dangerous things for my own satisfaction, regardless of how it worried other people - even you, and I love you. I think - ' He paused briefly. 'This is going to sound terrible. I think you're the only person I've ever really loved.'
Chel found nothing useful to say to this, merely wishing that he would give over and let her sleep, but after a short pause, he went on.
'I've never let anyone come close to me, except you, and even you I've succeeded in alienating from your own family. I must be a perfect monument to misendeavour! I deserve to burn for eternity, and that's what it often feels as if I'm doing.'
There was no sensible answer to that, either - no answer at all that Chel could think of.
'You're just tired, and it's making you depressed again,' she said, trying to offer comfort where there was none and hoping that he would stop, but again, he didn't.
'Is that so?' He gave a short, smothered laugh. 'Well, perhaps I am, and can you wonder at it? It's more than a year now, and I'm hardly more mobile than when I left hospital. Surely, by this time...' He paused, and the darkness pressed around them, velvet black. It seemed to have an almost tangible quality, like an extra blanket. There was no moon tonight, Chel thought confusedly, no light outside, and in Oliver's mind, even yet, darkness. He couldn't still be hoping for miracles, he couldn't -
'You know what really gets to me?' he asked, and answered himself, harping a familiar tune. 'It was *people* who did this to me - people who didn't even know me, not for any reason but that I was in their way and they felt like it. They didn't have to, there were half a dozen of them, I was hardly a threat, was I? *They just felt like it*, as if I was a football or an old tin can to be kicked down the street... can you imagine how *dirty* that makes me feel? It's like looking into the abyss...'
'It shouldn't make you feel like that,' protested Chel. 'You were

doing a brave thing - '

'Being bloody stupid, you mean. It was *sick*, and I feel as if the sickness is smeared all over me, for ever.'

'Oliver, stop this. Go to sleep,' commanded Chel, but she thought he didn't even hear her, hardly pausing, but baring his inner thoughts in a way that she had never heard from him before, never imagined that she would..

'I often wonder why I survived,' he said, but more, Chel decided, following a line of thought of his own, seeking for some answer, perhaps, than directly to her. 'I lie awake sometimes, knowing that everything that made me *me* has gone for ever. All the things I did, all the things I knew... they're no use to me any more. No use to anybody. So what am I doing here? I must have been as good as dead that night, but I lived. So why, *why?* Just for this? Just to sit around aching, a burden to you and to myself? It isn't fair, we had so much... I meant to give you so much...'

'Oliver - ' began Chel, and stopped. A wave of pity, of deep compassion, swept over her and left her speechless. She sought for something to say that wouldn't sound trite and failed to find it. She said, 'Everything has its price - perhaps this is ours.'

'It's never worth it,' said Oliver flatly.

Chel had thought - hoped - that all this was behind them. She reached out and laid her hand on him, feeling his flesh warm under her hand, alive... but not, now, with the joyous zest for life that she had first loved in him. She had no idea what to say.

'Oliver, don't - please don't. It's only tearing yourself up for nothing, and it'll pass, things do. You'll get better, we'll make new plans. It'll be all right, I know it will, you'll be of use again, only you mustn't give in.' She wasn't certain which of them she was trying to convince, if it was Oliver, the attempt failed.

'I can't give in,' he reminded her, grimly. 'This is the road that has no turning - no diversions, no lay-bys, no escape lane...' But there was an escape lane, and the knowledge that he had tried to take it was in both their minds. He stirred, uncomfortable with the memory, and Chel heard him catch his breath as if even that slight movement was too much. Oliver said, quietly, 'I dream, you know. Almost every night, I dream - not quite a nightmare, but somehow worse, because everything is always distorted by those damned drugs, I suppose. I'm climbing - not a mountain exactly, a tall, endless cliff. It leans over on top of me and there are very few handholds or footholds, all round there's just pale blue, blazing sky with no clouds in it, if there were clouds it somehow wouldn't be so bad. There's nothing below me, just this cliff going down, and so there's nothing to do but keep on climbing. There's no end, nothing to climb for, but I have to go on and on for ever... and then sometimes, very, very occasionally, I fall off, down and down into deep water, and I dream instead that nothing ever happened and I'm diving again on the *Hesperides* or sailing among the icebergs in the Southern Ocean... and that's the worst of all.'

Chel buried her face in his shoulder, unreasonably guilty.

'You never told me.'

'I don't quite know why I'm telling you now - except that I love you... and I can't go on like this, I *can't* - so - '

She heard it then, the warning note, loud and clear as a bell.

'I love you,' she said, helplessly, repeating a well-learned lesson. 'I'd do anything to help you, if I could, but I can only do my best... it isn't good enough, is it?'

'You do all right,' said Oliver. He said no more after that, but Chel wasn't sure that he slept, she thought not. They lay side by side in silence, and the long night went on.

Chel slept in the end, and waking early, lay for a while watching the sunshine dappling through the curtains, wondering what this new day would bring. Sometimes, Oliver's fits of depression evaporated overnight, sometimes they hung on for days. She hoped this was one of the overnight times, and wondered if Jack's home-made blackberry wine had been in any way responsible. People put funny things in wine, she had read somewhere. Although, come to think, probably not super-organic vegetarians such as Jack and Maggie. She thought of the dandelion coffee, and shuddered. Perhaps there was some depressant substance in dandelions?

Beside her, Oliver slept, a deep frown between his eyebrows as if even in sleep his mood was dark. Repressing a sigh of frustration, she quietly slid out of bed and made herself a cup of real coffee, sitting in the despised wheelchair to drink it. She stirred it thoughtfully, thinking about him and trying to feel her way towards deeper knowledge of him and failing. Whatever lay concealed behind his sleeping face, it belonged to a different Oliver, one that she didn't yet know - one that he didn't, she suspected, know himself, but whose acquaintance he desperately needed to make. She sipped her coffee and wondered.

Almost as if he felt her thoughts, Oliver stirred and opened his eyes. He looked at her for a moment, drowsy with sleep, and then he said,

'Chel?'

'Hullo,' said Chel, neutrally. 'Want some coffee?'

'Mmm, sounds good. What's the time?'

'Just after seven.' She made the coffee without speaking, hardly daring to after last night, but she saw with relief that the frown had disappeared, so perhaps he had just been dreaming again. She carried the mug over to him and he took it with a muttered thank-you. After a few minutes, while they drank in silence, Oliver said,

'I was sounding off again, wasn't I, last night? Why you don't just tell me to shut up, I shall never know, before I drown us both in a sea of self-pity. I don't deserve you... or all your understanding, your loyalty. What can I ever give you in return?'

'I don't deserve that you should talk about my loyalty,' countered Chel. 'Anyway, you've already given. Full measure, for two wonderful years. It's my turn.'

'And for how long? I shall hold you back for evermore.'

Chel paused, thinking this one out. When she spoke, it was hesitantly.

'Just answer me one thing. If you hadn't been married to me, how would you have spent those two years?'

'All right,' said Oliver, after a moment. 'But Chel, you dear, fool girl, two years is only two years.'

'If things had fallen out differently, how long would you have reckoned our marriage to last?' asked Chel. He looked surprised.

'What do you mean?'

'Two years, three years... ten years... life?' Then, when he was silent, she said. 'It was all right for you, when I was holding you back. So what's different?'

'You're rationalising, and you know it.'

'You're talking nonsense, and you know it.'

They smiled at each other then, a sudden contentment between them that they hadn't felt for a long while. Chel yawned, placing her mug on the tiny worktop, and stretched luxuriously.

'It's a lovely day. Any plans for it?'

Oliver's eyes went immediately to Maggie's wooden box, sitting in the corner behind the passenger seat.

'I thought I might play with Maggie's paints. Unless you have other ideas?'

Freedom from constant attendance on an invalid was one of the precious blessings of their new but erratic lifestyle. Chel said,

'I might take Millie's bike and go down to Lamorna. Unless you feel like coming too, you could paint there just as well. Better, maybe.'

Oliver knew that the things he wanted to paint were all inside his head, however beautiful he knew Lamorna Cove to be.

'No. You don't want to haul this great thing down that narrow lane. I shall be fine here.' He hesitated. 'You could ask Judy to go with you.'

'I couldn't keep up. She rides a *big* bike, I've seen it, I can just imagine me pedalling frantically along behind! Anyway, we haven't seen Judy for a while, she's probably busy.' Not since Maggie and Jack reappeared, she suddenly realised. Was there a connection there?

'We must sort out this transport problem,' said Oliver, but not as if he meant to do anything about it himself.

'The accommodation problem, too,' said Chel.

'We can go back in one of the vans soon.'

'It's not good enough, though, is it? Only until the middle of June.'

'Long enough for all kinds of things to happen,' said Oliver, with that scary irresponsibility that Chel was slowly coming to realise had always been an integral part of his personality. She sighed, but on this beautiful morning, without pathos.

'Old lap of the gods thing?'

'Exactly,' said Oliver.

VI

April drifted towards May, and in the days before her baby was born, Maggie came up to the caravan site and gave Oliver advice about oil painting, bringing with her books which, Chel suspected, he actually found more helpful. She didn't think that Maggie, who taught pupils of secondary school age, had a lot to teach Oliver who must once have been one, for the more he painted, the more she found herself wondering just what she had started.

She had no idea of the artistic merit, or otherwise, of the work he produced, for Maggie made no comments to her, possibly considering her a philistine on whom such comments would be wasted, but she couldn't fail to be aware of two things, one, that the more he worked the more deeply absorbed he was becoming, and the other that he was totally obsessed with the sea. He had never drawn another cat, but sheet after sheet of paper, both oil and watercolour, had been covered with waves and rocks and flying spray, with empty storm-swept beaches, soaring cliffs, ships of all shapes and kinds, all wild and exciting and unrestful, full of the stimulation and risk and adventure that had once been the breath of life to him. Working it out of his system, Chel suspected, and also suspected that they were good, although she knew that her opinion was totally uninformed, and therefore probably valueless.

Then, after ten days, Maggie failed to appear and Jack came instead, grinning all over his face, to say that they had another little boy, and she would be back just as soon as she could. Chel thought that Oliver was slightly relieved. She knew that she was.

Vellanzoe might have slipped through their fingers, but it showed no disposition to move out of the headlines. The evening after Jack and Maggie's son was born, Judy and Keith reappeared, strolling up the field in the warm spring evening, Sheba at their heels.

'Earth-mother having been safely delivered, we thought it was safe to come back,' said Judy. 'Ma said she was practically living here.'

Chel thought this was a fair comment, she had even been feeling rather excluded and had begun to take long walks when Maggie appeared, which she knew to be childish and of which she was slightly ashamed. After all, she liked Maggie, who had never done her any harm and who was trying to help Oliver in a way in which she herself couldn't.

It made her squirm a little inside to wonder if this was the reasoning behind her long walks and mild but growing irritation. Judy, however, was cheerfully forthright.

'Don't misunderstand me, but that woman really gets on my tits,' she said, grinning. She had, Chel remembered, said something like it once before. She returned the grin, immediately feeling better.

'Don't let her drive you away,' she said.

'She hasn't. Here we are. We wondered if you'd fancy a drink at the Cornish Arms?'

The Cornish Arms was the pub in the village. Walking distance, but not for Oliver. Chel opened her mouth to make some excuse, but Oliver said, unexpectedly.

'Good idea, make this chair earn its keep. We can leave it outside, and with a bit of luck, someone will pinch it.'

'Hang on to it, I would,' said Keith. 'You'll be the envy of all, the chairs in that pub make standing up the preferred option.' And amazingly, Oliver laughed. Was this a side-effect of finding something that he could still do, and do superlatively well? Chel wondered, but knew she wouldn't ask. She locked up the van and they all went down the field together, Keith pushing the wheelchair and Judy and Chel strolling along ahead.

The pub was fairly full, and they entered to a hail of greetings. The village had found out about Oliver, and he and Chel had ceased to be outsiders. Not only Oliver's local roots, but to a certain extent his fame too, and their interest in Moor House, were now in the public domain, and people rushed to keep them informed, while Keith ordered up a round at the bar.

As soon as they had settled at a table by the window, Sally Tregillis was standing beside them.

'Cheryl!' She was Cheryl now, not Mrs. Nankervis. 'Cheryl, have you heard what happened out at Vellanzoe?'

'About the git, Gittings?' asked Chel.

'No, since that.' Sally dismissed Mr. Gittings' mishap on the stairs, some weeks ago now and old history, with a wave of her hand. 'The people who were in there last week left early and asked for their money back! They said the place was haunted, and nobody should ask them to stay there. What do you think of that?'

Chel was startled. Not, probably, for the reasons that she should have been, but because she thought that if there was a ghost there she should have known, and she had been aware of nothing... nothing at all. Not this time.

'They must have heard the stories,' she said.

80

'No, they hadn't. They told the agents that the children said there was a man in their room, and the place was terribly cold at nights, too. And the woman said she saw funny lights drifting across the landing, and heard someone whispering. Spooky!'

There had been strange lights at the bungalow. But that had been passing cars... hadn't it? Chel felt a thrill run up her spine.

Cars must drive past Moor House, too.

If there was a ghost, why was it not appearing to her any more?

Jim had joined Sally.

'Say what you like, someone must have told them about that plane crash, and they just used it as an excuse. They didn't want to stay. Overspent on their holiday, probably.'

It sounded convincing.

'The people there over Easter didn't like it either, they went home early,' said Sally, throwing out a challenge. Jim laughed.

'They didn't say nothing about any ghost though, did they?' he asked, as if that finished the argument. Sally exchanged a glance with Chel, which Chel tried, and failed, to avoid.

'That place has always been one for tales,' said Sally. 'I expect you're some glad you're not living there, aren't you?'

'I liked it, actually,' said Chel, but with caution. 'If there is a ghost there, I didn't feel it.' Not the last time, anyway, she added guiltily, to herself.

'It might have been different at night,' said Sally. Unanswerably. It was mostly the nights at the bungalow.

Jim looked at his wife with affection.

'Few weeks back, you were saying there wasn't any ghost,' he reminded her. 'Just talk, I think it was you said, and an excuse for skimping on the work. So what's changed your tune?'

'Those poor little mites,' sighed Sally, sentimentally. 'Scared out of their wits they must have been, poor lambs.'

'Didn't sound like it to me, from what their mum was saying,' said Jim.

They moved away as Keith came over with the drinks.

'What an odd thing...' said Chel. She paused, and went on thoughtfully, '*If* there's something there, why would it appear to everyone else, and cut me dead?' She tried to speak lightly, make a joke of it. Oliver grinned at her.

'Chasing everyone else out, you think, to get us in?' he asked. 'Grow up Chel!'

Chel looked uneasy. It was too near what she herself had tried to avoid thinking.

81

'You go in for seeing ghosts then, do you, Cheryl?' asked Keith, with a grin that was alive with his own scepticism, and Judy said,

'Call her Chel. Oliver does, and so do I.'

Had she changed the subject deliberately? Chel didn't know but was grateful anyway. Keith, successfully distracted, eyed the pool table at the back of the room, and looked at Oliver.

'Reckon you can play pool sitting in that chair?' he asked.

'Reckon I can bloody well try,' said Oliver.

Judy and Chel declined the treat, and the men borrowed all the 50p pieces they could scrounge and went off together. Chel watched them go and then dropped her eyes to her glass.

'Keith is good for Oliver,' she remarked.

'Making him behave normally, you mean? Time he did, if you ask me.'

'I have tried,' said Chel, defensively.

'Hey, don't raise your hackles at me! I only meant, you're too close to the problem.'

'Sorry.'

'You need other people,' said Judy. 'Even Mother Earth - I've no doubt she does her bit, in her own hippie way.'

'It just seems,' said Chel, still staring down into her drink, 'that right at the moment, other people can give him more help than I can.'

'Then perhaps,' said Judy, ever practical, 'that means that you can let up on yourself a bit. Have fun.'

'Fun?' queried Chel, as if the word was new to her.

'You poor thing,' said Judy, with mock sympathy. 'On your bike, in the immortal words of Mr. Tebbitt. Why not? Or better still, on mine.'

'It's your mother's bike,' said Chel, captiously.

Judy looked at her thoughtfully.

'Have another drink,' she suggested, getting to her feet and reaching for Chel's glass. 'Then perhaps you'll tell me what's really on your mind.'

And perhaps not. Chel watched her weaving her way through the crowd, stopping now and then to exchange a few words with friends. Behind her, round the pool table, a crowd, mostly men, had gathered and a cheerful uproar had broken out in which Keith's voice seemed uppermost, offering some kind of challenge. A long-lost but nonetheless familiar normality swept over her, which made it as unexpected to herself as to Judy when she asked, as a fresh drink was set before her,

'Who was he?'

'Who was who?' asked Judy, slipping back into her seat.

'The pilot - the one who crashed into the cottages. Does anyone know, or is it just folklore now?'

'It's real enough - it wasn't that long ago.'

'That isn't quite what I meant.'

'No.' Judy paused for a moment, considering. Because of the involvement of her Uncle William, the details tended to be clearly remembered in her family, but even so they weren't dwelt upon, and she needed to put her thoughts in order. 'His name was Matthew Sutton,' she said. 'He was one of the St. Ives artists' group, he learned to fly before the war and flew all through it, so he should have known what he was doing. Bit of a lad too, from all accounts. He liked young girls.'

Chel wrinkled her nose. She was short of sympathy for a middle-aged pervert.

'No great loss, then?'

'I don't know about that. He was a pretty good artist - famous, too. I wouldn't mind finding one of his pictures in my attic, I can tell you. When he was killed, he left a nice little nest-egg to some dewy-eyed Lolita, a college student or something, and there was a great to-do over it, big scandal, you can't imagine it now, can you? Lousy way to go, though, stuck in the roof, and the fog all around.' She shivered.

'Was it because of the fog that it happened?'

'God knows. Nobody else does, that's for certain. I don't think they ever found the actual cause. Just one of those things.'

'He must have been quite experienced if he flew through the war.' It was half a question, but of course, Judy had no answer for it.

'You'd think so, wouldn't you?'

'So what became of her - Lolita?'

'I've no idea. History doesn't relate.'

Chel said nothing. The sad little tale made pictures in her head, but they were nothing to do with the house as it was now, or as she had first seen it. She looked upwards in her mind's eye and saw the sturdy chimney pots and roofs of the original cottages, but dreadfully distorted by the shape of the little smashed plane, swimming through the swirling mist like the ghost that Matthew Sutton had, perhaps, become. She shivered, although the pub was warm.

'It made a lot of fuss in its day,' Judy said. 'Not just locally - he had pictures in half the important collections in the country, and did commissions at prices that would make you blink, in those days anyway, and of course, when he was killed the papers made a lot of it. It's just a story now though. Something to frighten the tourists.' She made a face. 'Ghost stories - they ring the bell every time.'

'I thought you believed in them,' said Chel, a challenge in her voice. Judy didn't meet her eyes.

'Not ghost *stories,* not things that go bump in the night. And nor do you, if you're sensible.'

If Chel thought that there was a bit of lateral thinking going on here, she decided that in the pub was not the place to say so. She said, instead,

'I wish we could find somewhere to settle.'

'You can have a van again next week, Dad said.'

'But only for a while. I want to get rid of that great camper and be able to get around easily - not just me on the bike, both of us. It seemed like a good idea at the time, but now, if we want to get down to the sea it's like a military operation - grinding down these tiny lanes now there's so much more traffic about, and I'm terrified I'll meet a tractor towing some fearsome machinery that won't reverse... it's not good enough. I feel permanently stretched, like elastic.'

'There must be *somewhere,*' objected Judy.

'We've looked - or I've looked, on the bike - at one or two places, but there's always something... steps, or neighbours right on top of you, or no proper access... it's not as easy as you might think. It's not just the summer, I have to think about the winter too... and if it's somewhere temporary only, we might as well stay as we are.'

'You might have to re-think your requirements then. There's other places, in the town.'

'Oliver won't live in a town.'

'Oliver is a man. That's to say, he's a selfish bastard.'

'True, but that isn't the whole story.'

'Nothing ever is.'

Chel said, slowly,

'As a matter of fact, I don't think that Oliver's too bothered. Not about a house, anyway, he'd settle for an accessible bathroom. I don't think...' She hesitated, but she liked Judy and she had to say it to someone - and it certainly wasn't going to be Maggie. 'This is going to sound stupid when you consider the circumstances, but I don't actually think Oliver wants to settle anywhere.'

To her surprise, Judy understood - better than she did herself, in a way.

'Why should that surprise you?' she asked.

'He was so dreadfully injured.'

'I think,' said Judy, thoughtfully, 'that he's frightened of the word *settle* - except, I suppose, as it applies to butterflies. Keith thinks so, too.'

84

Put into words like that, Chel knew that it was something she had been afraid of for some time.

'There's nothing I can do about it,' she said.

'No. And you must have known before you got yourself into it.'

True.

'So if you look at it like that, does it matter if you flit from van to van?'

'Except for transport. Oliver can't ride a bike.'

Judy emptied her glass.

'For God's sake, Chel! Buy a car then. And it's your round.'

As Chel waited at the bar, she wondered what was the matter with her that she couldn't see the obvious any more. *Buy a car.* There was nothing stopping them. They couldn't afford a house, no, but a good second-hand car wasn't beyond them. She knew, from borrowing Millie's car, that it didn't need to be specially adapted any more, Oliver could cope with anything reasonable. It was the motor home that was blocking her view, telling her that they already had a car, when logically, they hadn't. What they had was a... not a house. A home? A mobile bedroom? And if she pursued that thought to its logical conclusion, since the word had come into her mind, if they had a car, their own van would be enough. Oliver preferred being outside anyway, and the summer was coming. They didn't need to keep moving from van to van on the campsite. They could just park their own and live, not in it, but out of it... leave it sitting there and get out and about... free.

'God, I am stupid!' she said, not realising that she was speaking aloud, and the man standing beside her turned and grinned at her.

'Any particular reason, my bird?'

Chel knew she had made a fool of herself, and grinned back.

'I need to buy a car,' she said.

'Now that *is* stupid! What sort of a car?'

'Wheel at each corner, and an extra one to steer with? Engine would be good.' It was her turn to be served, she placed her order and then found that he was still beside her, still grinning. She had thought he would be gone.

'How much d'you want to pay?' he was asking. Chel, who had no idea, was surprised.

'What's it to you?'

'Only, I've the garage down the road. You come and see me, happen I can do something for you. That your hubby wiping the floor with 'em all back there?'

Chel took a swift glance over her shoulder. Oliver, who was finding the wheelchair at about the right level for sighting along the cue, was about to make a shot. Keith was waving both clenched fists in the air and crowing. Two locals leaned on their cues with resigned expressions.

'Could be.'

'Right on!' He nodded, and moved away. Chel went back to Judy, who was laughing.

'The hour produceth the man,' she remarked, as Chel sat down. 'Did he try and sell you a car?'

'Should I buy one from him?' asked Chel, but Judy's reply was drowned out by a huge cheer from the pool table.

So, one way and another, it had been a good evening. Chel, lying in bed later on, reflected on its events and found herself quietly optimistic. Something of a novelty. Finding that he could beat half the local pool team had pleased Oliver disproportionately - although, maybe not, on second thoughts. For him, these days, it must have felt like conquering Everest. And she probably would go along to the garage and ask about a car, once she had spoken to Oliver and they had worked out what they could spend. He might, of course, reject the idea out of hand but she didn't think so. The thought of being able to go where they wanted, when they wanted, was wonderful, and would represent a significant step forward. Chel snuggled down into her pillow and closed her eyes. A good evening. A better day. Maybe things were on the move at last.

Her eyes snapped open again onto darkness. On the move, to where? Not to Vellanzoe.

The ghost... Matthew Sutton. He didn't appear to her.

Jim Tregillis could be right, of course, and he didn't really appear to anyone. Some people were very suggestible.

On the other hand... she was one of those *some people*, or had been in the past. So, was the ghost at Vellanzoe simply stepping aside for them, clearing their way out of sympathy for a fellow artist, on their side?

No. Ghosts weren't on anybody's side but their own, that was why they were ghosts. Or so she had always understood. And Oliver and Matthew Sutton were hardly in the same class, if half what Judy had told her was true.

So, no ghost. It was a comforting thought. Stories, hysteria, feelings maybe, she had experienced all of them, but no ghost. Having thought this out to her own satisfaction, Chel closed her eyes again. Something would turn up. Something always did, look at tonight. Think of a car, hey presto, a car salesman appears! On that happy thought, she slept.

The possession of a car and the growing warmth of the year made all the difference. It no longer seemed necessary to rent a static van when their own had all the necessary facilities like shower room and cooker, and they had the whole great outdoors in which to sit and not feel cramped up. Jeff helped Chel empty the holding tank when it was necessary, and apart from the lack of a house, life looked good. Oliver and Chel enjoyed the greater freedom of rational transport, no longer tied by need to the van they picnicked on cliffs high above the sea, relaxed beside golden beaches, allowed life to develop into one long holiday, Chel sometimes thought. Except that Oliver painted as if his soul fed on it, and even Chel could see that his pictures were changing.

Maggie had returned, walking up the field from time to time with her new baby held in a sling against her breast, sometimes with the toddler in a pushchair, although thank goodness she never brought the grizzly India. Most of her attention was focussed on Oliver, which although understandable, Chel found annoying, it left her to entertain small Giles and to keep an eye on the baby - unasked, which made it worse. Expected. She liked Maggie, at least, she supposed she did, but at close quarters she was beginning to see all too clearly why she irritated Judy so much. Maggie still excluded her, that was the trouble, reducing her to the rank of unpaid baby-sitter in return for her own advice to Oliver. An increasing feeling that it wasn't quite fair began to steal over Chel, and a growing resentment that she tried her best to squash.

One afternoon, as she prepared to leave, Maggie surprised Chel by inviting her to walk down the field with her.

'It's such a lovely day...' she said vaguely, by way of explanation. Chel, in whom shame worked to make her agree to an invitation she didn't welcome, agreed.

'I can walk on and get some more milk at the shop,' she said. 'Just let me get my purse.'

As they walked down the field together, Maggie said nothing and Chel didn't feel it necessary to start a conversation herself, this was Maggie's idea after all. But when they reached the entrance gate, Maggie said,

'Let's sit on the wall for a minute - we need to talk.'

Chel, quite unreasonably, felt a defensive prickle up her spine.

'What about?' she asked, and feared it was rudely. Maggie smiled at her.

'There's no need to be like that,' she said kindly. 'About Oliver, of course.'

Worse and worse. Bad enough being shut out of something that was obviously so important to him, without Maggie lecturing her about him.

Chel sat down on the low wall that flanked the gateway with a bad grace, and Maggie settled beside her.

'You must have noticed,' she said, without preamble. 'He's not been taught much beyond GCSE standard, but he's got tremendous natural style - A-level possibly, I suppose, but that still leaves him in the beginner class. What are you going to do?'

This sudden challenge caused Chel's jaw to drop in amazement.

'Me? What can I do? Anyway, does it matter... if it's only a hobby?'

Maggie gave her a pitying look.

'Well, he could be the Grandma Moses of Trelewan, I suppose, but I think it would be a waste. He should go to college as a mature student. You should make that possible.'

Chel stared at her.

'Maggie, what are you trying to tell me? Would you mind giving it to me straight.'

Maggie sighed, as if in the presence of extreme stupidity.

'I'm trying to tell you that Oliver has all the hallmarks of incredible talent - as if you didn't know.'

There was a silence, while Chel got her breath back, and wondered if Maggie knew what she was talking about. After a moment, Maggie said,

'I can help him a little, but only so far. I'm not bad, but I only teach school kids and paint local views for the undiscriminating. I've never seen, let alone taught, anything like this. Now he knows about the mixing of colours and the basic techniques - and he hardly needed showing, really - he's way beyond me. I think he was probably born there. I can't tell him anything now that he won't get as easily from books, and it won't be nearly enough.'

Chel was surprised at Maggie's honesty, since it would separate her from daily contact with Oliver, but perhaps over painting she couldn't deceive herself. In that moment, Chel liked her better, but liking didn't help. Solve one problem, and the solution made another, like the endless cliffside of Oliver's nightmare, climb, climb, climb, and never reach safety at the top. Chel knew quite well that Oliver wouldn't go back to college, even if he was acceptable as a student - and that, too was debatable.

'I don't see that we can do anything, except take it a day at a time. *I* certainly can't.'

'He could make a good living for you both,' said Maggie. 'Have you thought of that?'

Perhaps oddly, Chel had not. She had thought of painting simply as an expression of Oliver's natural gift, as salvage for his self-esteem, on a par with beating the village lads at pool. As a form of release, not as a means of earning a living. She now saw that she had been wrong not to see that the two must go together. The fact that he could no longer provide for her without what he chose to refer to as charity, in whatever guise, was yet another of the things that caused Oliver deep distress, and she knew it all too well. How could she not, when it kept rearing up through the calm surface of their healing but directionless life like the snout of an infuriated shark, and any share he might yet receive from the salvaging of the treasure ship *Hesperides* would do little, or nothing, to make things better. The present, far more than the past, needed to yield its treasures. Even so, she felt herself on the defensive once more, protecting Oliver from unrealistic expectations.

'There's no money in art,' she denied. 'Everyone knows that.'

'Do they, indeed?' said Maggie, smiling at her pityingly. 'Believe me, there is in what I suspect will turn out to be Oliver's sort of art, Cheryl dear. Tell me, does his mother starve in a garret?'

Chel felt unreasonably patronised.

'No,' she said, sullenly.

'So think about it,' Maggie advised. She hesitated, and then said, 'Don't you feel bitter about it, ever? You sound so calm always - I'd be tearing the world apart if it had happened to Jack.'

'Calm!' exclaimed Chel, sweepingly angry suddenly at Maggie's words, which sounded to her both critical and self-indulgent, and realised immediately that she had spoken too forcefully. 'No, I'm not calm. Yes, I am bitter. I lie awake at nights sometimes, burning up with sheer hate, wishing I could batter those brutes in return - but what good does it do? That sort of thinking will only bring us down. We have to make the best of things as they are now, don't you see?'

Maggie paused, re-aligning her approach, conscious of reluctant admiration. She said, quietly,

'Oliver should be the pupil, and ultimately, I suppose the master, of a master.'

Chel was furious, without quite recognising why.

'So what? He'll have to settle for second-best, then, won't he? He'll never know, if you don't go telling him!'

'Don't bet on it. He isn't stupid, and I've told you already, he's a born painter.'

'Look Maggie,' said Chel, getting herself in hand. 'I know you mean well - but you don't help when you say things like that. There are a lot of things that Oliver can't have, and if that's one of them, at least this time he can blame himself, he's the one who's always turned away from it after all. We've enough troubles without you adding to them, please.'

Maggie got to her feet, cradling her baby against her in a protective gesture..

'You don't know what you're saying,' she said, and then, as if she had realised she had spoken out of turn, 'but perhaps only another artist could really understand. Come on then - if you want to go to the shop, we'd better go, or it'll be closed.'

There were no further stories of ghosts out at Moor House, but it wasn't a success as a holiday let. There was a lot of grumbling, Sally Tregillis told Chel when she went to the shop for her stores. People staying there came into the village to shop, and grumbled about faulty wiring, a leaking roof, draughts, and things that were missing from the inventory. Someone got hit with a falling slate one stormy day, and someone else had an accident to their car and had to return home before the end of their holiday - although this last surely couldn't be attributed to the house. Chel didn't repeat these stories to Oliver, and in fact she now had something else, of more immediate concern, on her mind. Long before Hedge & Hollow wrote to Oliver, in the middle of June, she had lost patience entirely with Maggie.

'She's always under my feet,' she told Judy, indignantly. 'Every bloody day, it's beginning to seem, she appears on the scene on some excuse or other! It doesn't even seem to matter where we are - the other day she appeared when we were down at Sennen trying to get away from her. What's she after, anyway, she says herself she can't teach him any more.'

Judy gave her a sideways look.

'If you don't know that, darling Chel, who am I to tell you?'

Chel rubbed her nose thoughtfully.

'Well, I do know, of course - but why should she fancy my husband when she's got a much better one of her own? And a home and children - doesn't she ever spend any time with them?'

'She brings the children with her, I thought - those that aren't at school,' said Judy.

This was another festering thorn in Chel's emotional flesh. She looked rebellious.

'And leaves me to mind them while she talks to Oliver. About art, art, art - and deliberately shuts me out. And he's beginning to do it, too. I feel like a child-minder!'

'Oh Chel,' said Judy, in exasperated sympathy. 'Why let her, if it winds you up?'

'How can I stop her?' asked Chel.

'You should have worked out the answer to that one before you married the dish of the day,' Judy told her.

'I never needed to before,' said Chel, and it was true. 'Oliver's never seen girls coming - too involved in his own affairs - but Maggie's different. She *is* his own affairs.'

It was too true for her to explain. Maggie was different because of what she brought with her. Knowledge, books, a common interest, and it was also true that Oliver encouraged her. Physically frustrated, his mind went out after knowledge like hounds after a fox. He picked Maggie's brains, read her books, and seemed happy to talk with her by the hour, while Chel pushed Giles on the swings in the centre of the field, and walked the baby in its pushchair up and down the grass. She had caught herself out in possessiveness once or twice before, but never like this. Resentment - of both Oliver and Maggie - grew in her mind, the more unreasonably since she knew quite well that Oliver couldn't be unfaithful to her at present if he wanted to - and probably the most unreasonable part of all was that she didn't believe for a moment that he did want to. After her own brief and abortive affair the previous year, it was ironic that it should be she who felt jealous and shut out. A taste of her own medicine, she told herself wryly, and one she could have done without.

It was because Maggie made no secret of her... well, infatuation, was the kindest word Chel could find, and because she could give Oliver something which Chel, for all her own love, couldn't, that she was so infuriating. The sight of Maggie sitting there unable to take her eyes off him, talking, talking, and excluding Chel was the most maddening thing in the world.

And Chel didn't want to look after Maggie's baby. Only last year, she had lost her own, and walking this one round the field, cuddling it when it cried, with the warm, milky baby smell in her nostrils was even worse than watching Maggie making up to Oliver.

Judy had little or no time for Maggie at the best of times, although she knew nothing of the lost baby.

'Tell her to bugger off if she's getting up your nose,' she said, crudely, but that, too, was easier said than done, because it was true that Maggie offered Oliver something that he couldn't, situated as they were, get from anyone else.

'If only it was that simple,' said Chel.

'All right then,' said Judy. 'Next time she comes, just say you're going to Penzance with me, and leave her to mind her own children. You make it too easy for her - that Giles of hers is a real ball of fire, she'll have to take her eyes off Oliver then.'

Chel looked wistful.

'I'd love to, but he has so little, it wouldn't be fair.'

'Look,' said Judy, firmly, 'you're going to have to stop putting Oliver's interests quite so far ahead of your own. All right, he had a rotten break - but men are selfish enough without you actively encouraging them! And martyrs, let me tell you, are very uncomfortable people to live with. If you take up martyrdom as a pastime, you'll drive him into her arms - and at present, if you ask me, it's a very one-sided affair.'

'If I thought it was *any* sort of affair, I'd kill her,' said Chel, and Judy grinned.

'That sounds better.'

'I don't see what she hopes to get out of it, anyway,' added Chel, bringing the conversation round in a circle, and this time, Judy laughed.

'Chel *dear*! She's still on maternity leave, a bored housewife with half a dozen little children, and a husband who spends all his spare time surfing and diving. And he's gorgeous, and romantic - and disabled, so that she can fantasise about him to her heart's content, and the most jealous husband in the world isn't going to have a glimmer of suspicion. He's a gift to her - and you're gift-wrapping him!'

'Oh, bother her!' said Chel, not sure if she was angriest at Maggie or at herself. 'I always promised myself I'd never be a possessive wife, and now look at me!'

'Possessiveness is a relative thing,' Judy suggested. 'There must come a point when the lack of it could get a bit confused with not caring at all. I don't think Oliver needs to feel you don't care at all, do you?'

'But it's just because I do that I'm putting up with Maggie,' said Chel, indignantly.

'You've got a problem then,' Judy told her unhelpfully. 'Well, sort it out your own way - but if I was you, I'd get right in there and stake a claim. Why don't you tell him how you feel?'

But that was a road too full of pitfalls. Oliver's dread of being possessed, particularly now that he had lost most of his precious independence, and his need for Maggie's help could easily combine to produce the row to end all rows. Chel couldn't face it, not over another woman, it would be so undignified.

'It'll all be fine when we have somewhere proper to live,' she said, hopefully, but Judy only asked sceptically,

'Why?'

Chel was not so naïve, either, as to believe implicitly in what she had said, but she was so torn between Judy's view of things and her own that she stuck to it almost in desperation. Judy thought that she was being stupid, and really ought to tell Maggie to push off and take her children with her, and perhaps she was right from Chel's viewpoint - but from Oliver's? Chel hadn't forgotten the hard-learned lesson that love wasn't enough. She could give him that, no question, and had no serious doubts that it was returned. And in fact, it had been enough at first, but now this painting business was taking her out of her depth again. The mere fact of being disabled had thrown Oliver back onto resources that he hadn't known that he had, it was no part of either love or understanding to hinder their full development.

But Maggie, deep in her new part of guide and mentor was, in Chel's growing opinion, coming very close to over-egging the pudding. Feeling superfluous to their activities as was becoming usual, she returned from a walk around the field and a trip to the swings with the children and found Maggie sitting on the grass going through one of the books she had brought, talking knowledgeably about colour balance and texture, and Oliver, who didn't appear to be listening, experimenting happily all over a new daler board that she had brought him. His absorption in what he was doing was absolute, and he was no more aware of Chel than he was of Maggie's comments. For some reason that she couldn't satisfactorily explain this single-mindedness, that excluded both herself and Maggie, gave Chel a jolt.

But Maggie didn't like exclusion, particularly where her own pet subject was concerned, perhaps she felt that it relegated her, too, to the ranks. She looked up as Chel approached with the children, defending her position with a rueful smile.

'I think you've lost your husband for the next hour or so,' she said. 'I'm sorry, it's my fault.'

'Oh?' asked Chel, who had long accepted that the initial fault, if fault it was, was her own for starting this in the first place. Maggie ignored the challenge implicit in her tone and laughed instead.

'Artistic people are like that - when I'm painting, I forget everything - children, mealtimes, the lot. It's lucky that Jack is patient and understanding.'

Chel had a distinct feeling that Maggie had drawn a deliberate line, herself and Oliver on one side of it, creative, single-minded, different, and on the other Chel and Jack, ordinary, and therefore both less interesting and exploitable. The red tinge from her hair crept, without her meaning it, into her voice.

'How lucky for you - and the children,' she said, but sarcasm was wasted on Maggie, who laughed again.

'Oh, Jack understands. You'll learn.'

Some things, Chel had no intention of learning. The tilt of her chin should have warned Maggie that she was venturing into enemy territory.

'Well, since Jack isn't here, perhaps you should know that your baby needs changing, and Giles wants his tea.'

Maggie's eyes flew to Oliver, a short distance away, and so immersed in his painting that the rumble of warfare had passed right over his head - apparently.

'I ought to stick around, Oliver might want me,' she said. 'There's a clean nappy in that bag over there, Cheryl, would you be a dear and see to it? Giles will be all right with a biscuit for now.'

Chel drew a breath to answer her - and let it go again. Giles's eyes, round and altogether too intelligent, were going from his mother to herself as they spoke, she couldn't make him, or his baby brother, a bone of contention in front of him. Feeling that she had been emotionally blackmailed, she swallowed what she had been about to say, picked up the indicated bag and dropped it into the pram, and taking Giles by the hand, stalked off to the washroom. There was no way she was changing nappies in the close confines of their van.

'Why you angry, Cherry?' asked Giles, but Chel only replied,

'I'm not angry,' and folded her lips together in a way that would have warned a far less bright child than Giles.

She attended to the baby and fed Giles with biscuits, but this time she didn't remove them from the vicinity of their mother, in spite of Maggie's hints that she should do so, and eventually Maggie took them away, raising her eyes to heaven as she went. Oliver gave her an absent-minded goodbye, but when she had gone, he laid down his brush and looked at Chel, speculatively.

'You shouldn't have let her get away with that,' he said.

'With what?' asked Chel, belligerently, gathering up the remains of the biscuits and a cup that had held milk. Oliver didn't answer her directly.

'You don't have to be a nanny to Maggie's kids if it upsets you. I'm just sorry they can't be your own.'

'It isn't that - ' said Chel, before she could stop herself, and broke off abruptly. The devil and the deep blue sea, here they were again.

'Ah,' said Oliver. He began to clean his brushes carefully, but Chel thought there was a glimmer of amusement in his eyes, to which she felt he wasn't entitled. After a while, he said,

'She's a very stupid woman in many ways. I wouldn't let her rile me, if I was you.'

'She's an artist,' said Chel, suddenly not caring if she did sound jealous, but Oliver only smiled at her.

'Of a sort. Not so much of an artist as she would like us to think she is. Come on Chel, what do you think goes on between us while you walk round and round the field with those tiresome brats of hers? Mad, passionate love?'

'No,' said Chel, woodenly.

Oliver held out his hand to her.

'Come here, and stop being ridiculous,' he told her, and when she had come, slipped his arm round her waist and looked up at her.

'Where mad, passionate love is concerned, you're the only one,' he told her. 'It'll be all right on the night, I promise. Just bear with me a while longer.'

He was no longer laughing. Chel touched his cheek, hesitantly, Maggie forgotten, unimportant. She felt the moment tremble on a delicate, unseen balance.

'Oliver - '

'Anyway,' said Oliver, briskly abandoning pathos, 'I'm not fit to cope with Other Women, I've trouble enough with the one I already have. Come on, slave to Art with a capital A, and clear up this mess for me. I'm tired.'

Oliver might appreciate Chel's point of view, and he might think Maggie stupid, but he was also, as advertised, fearsomely single-minded. He didn't discourage her from visiting, except in so far as he suggested that Chel might get fed up with minding her children. Maggie was hurt over this.

'You should have told me, Cheryl,' she said, reproachfully. 'You didn't have to bother Oliver - poor darling, he's got enough to manage. I wouldn't have minded.'

'I didn't bother Oliver,' said Chel, flattening her indignantly. 'Didn't it occur to you that squalling babies and toddlers around him are the last thing he wants, or needs? I'm only surprised he didn't say so before.'

'Oh!' said Maggie, staring at her, and then rallied to say, 'But you never told me that, either.'

Chel shrugged her shoulders. Oliver had absolved her from the sin of possessiveness, and she could afford to be generous.

'We're both very grateful, you know, for the way you're giving up your time for him,' she said. 'But he isn't nearly fit yet, and it really would be better if you found a babysitter - you don't mind me saying?'

Or perhaps that hadn't been so generous after all. Maggie turned a slow scarlet and turned away from her.

'Oh,' she said.

Chel, who had meant her to feel an outsider in return for being made to feel one herself, wondered if she felt sorry, and decided that she didn't. She remembered that she quite liked Maggie, and that to fall out with her would be to deny Oliver not only her help, but the friendship and company of Jack. A few *Keep off the Grass* signs wouldn't hurt her.

The discovery that another woman could still fancy her husband in spite of his disabilities made Chel look at him with new eyes. The relief of finding that love could slowly grow again between them, and the peaceful isolation of the last few months, had made her begin to take him for granted. She found to her surprise that while she had been swanning along with her eyes shut, he had grown spectacularly attractive. The outdoor life they were leading now and the late spring sunshine had kissed his skin with familiar gold, and the introduction of painting into his life had rekindled a flame that had lain dormant for too long. Even in the wheelchair, he retained grace, in the gestures of his hands, the turn of his head, however much he had lost elsewhere. It wasn't complete recovery yet, but an assurance that might herald it, not a return to complete health and strength, but the departure of that haunted fragility that had been so disturbing. He was less prone to slide into depression, was beginning at last to fight back at pain. They had, she realised with surprise, passed some milestone, and if Maggie had contributed to that - as she had - she should perhaps be thanked, not blamed.

'What's the matter?' asked Oliver, catching her eye. 'Have I got paint on my nose?' He rubbed it as he spoke, leaving paint where there had been none before, and grinned at her. 'You're making me self-conscious.'

Chel shook her head, laughing.

'I think I was just falling in love with you all over again,' she said.

'Had you fallen out?' asked Oliver, with a confidence that already knew the answer.

Chel could never make up her mind whether it was the effect of spiritual release that worked its silent alchemy, or more prosaically, whether he, like herself, was reawakened by the discovery that in spite of everything, he could still be attractive. The old days had gone for good, but she had married a man who was both generous and imaginative, and gradually the physical expression of tenderness and love began to creep back into their lives, and if it had to fall a long way short of the heady passions of other days, it was still a great step forward and a new bond between them.

The summer and the expression of love grew together out of the black winter that had gone, and with them grew Oliver's talent. Let loose with paint and brushes, he lost track of time, erected a deliberate barrier against physical pain, and worked with the dedication of a high priest. Chel hadn't expected this result to her experimental therapy, and watched from the sidelines with increasing fascination and, recalling what Maggie had told her, the faintest stirring of apprehension.

She had never imagined anyone working as Oliver did. He seemed to have a clear mental picture of what he wished to put onto paper or canvas, and no scruples as to how he did it. He would use brushes - both ends - palette knife, even his fingers, to achieve the effect that he wanted, and some of the results were startling. Once he had got the feel of oil paint as a medium, and it took him remarkably little time, all his early pencil sketches became transmuted into angry representations of wild seas and spray-darkened rocks, scudding clouds, little ships half-buried in mountainous waves. He painted daylight, moonlight, darkness, but above all, he painted anger, as if all his own pent-up frustrations found unspoken outlet in a series of wild, rather uncomfortable pictures, all the more convincing since they were drawn from his own experience. Now, as never before, when he could no longer be on or in the sea, Chel began to understand the particular relationship he had with it. She had never before had such a clear picture of what he had seen, what he had done, or what he had endured. It gave a startling and illuminating new slant to familiar knowledge.

While he painted, she made a few half-hearted attempts to find a house, but it was hopeless now the summer was gathering momentum. There was nowhere she liked available to rent permanently when the visitors would pay so much more, and back in Embridge, the bungalow had still not attracted a buyer. She sometimes suspected that Oliver was relieved about it, and under the summer sun it was easy to be philosophical.

Dear Mr. Nankervis,

Following our discussions earlier in the year, our client, Mr. George Williams, has asked us to enquire if you would still be interested in renting his property, Moor House. It appears that it is too far away from beaches and amenities to be successful as a holiday let, and he would be prepared to reconsider his earlier decision in the event that you should still be unsuited.

Should you be interested in this proposal, Mr. Williams would be prepared to let the house to you for an initial six-month period, payable in one non-returnable instalment, and renewable thereafter at three-

monthly intervals, for a guaranteed minimum of up to one year.

It has been explained to Mr. Williams that you have special problems, and he wishes us to say on his behalf that he has no objection to minor additions on the ground floor to accommodate you, provided that you give an undertaking that these would be removed and the decoration made good at the end of your tenancy.

It should, naturally, be born in mind that the property is to remain on the market, and that no guarantee of tenancy after the period specified can be given, although further periods of three months, if appropriate, might be considered thereafter.

Perhaps you would be good enough to let me know either way, so that we may make other arrangements if necessary on our client's behalf. The property has been unlet from the first week of July, and we are anxious to arrange matters very soon.

With best wishes,
Yours sincerely,
R. Gittings
For Hedge & Hollow

VII

Up until the day they moved, Chel had succeeded in rationalising the experiences at the hated bungalow, together with all that acceptance of them implied, half-fearing, half-disbelieving in the possibility of clairvoyance, and had even brought the reluctant Judy round to the idea of the move..

Moor House, or whatever spirit inhabited it, very soon turned her thinking upside-down.

She had visited it twice since they entered into a contract with Mr. Williams, once to remind herself of its possibilities, once to oversee the fixing of grab rails in the downstairs shower, the only modification necessary to the easy open-plan layout of the ground floor. On both occasions its innocent, sunny simplicity disarmed suspicion and left her certain that it was now clean and empty, the stories about it just that, stories.

The day they moved in, the weather changed from warm sunshine to a day of clouded blue, a little too bright, with a brisk wind bending the wild flowers that grew in the walls and in the long grass. There was a watery look about the brightness that meant it wasn't going to last, and Chel was relieved to be able to drive out to the house, unlock the door, and take possession. An old colleague of Oliver's, who had worked with him for Bill Rowlands, the salvage diver who had masterminded the search for the *Hesperides,* was due around mid-day with a vanload of their smaller possessions that had been left stored in the bungalow and one or two essential items of furniture. In the meantime, she had the camper van to unload of their clothes and bedding and the few personal items they had brought with them. Once that was done, and the van from Embridge had been and gone, she would take the camper to the garage in Trelewan, where her acquaintance from the Cornish Arms had already found a buyer for it, walk back to the camp site, pick up the car and that would be that. Their nomadic existence would be over. She wasn't sure if she was glad or sorry.

In order to retrieve their things from the bungalow, it had been necessary to contact her sister-in-law, Oliver's stepsister Susan, who had the key. It had not been accomplished without an argument.

'If they know where we are, they'll be down on us like a ton of bricks,' Oliver had objected, his mouth set mutinously.

'Oh, get real Oliver! We've got to do it sometime, the only thing that amazes me is that they haven't had private detectives out after us before this!'

'Maybe they have,' said Oliver, a gleam in his eye. 'They haven't found us though, have they? Now here's you, selling us to the enemy.'

'Wouldn't you like your bed back? That nice grandfather chair from the sitting room? All our books and clothes and pictures and china? Decent pots and pans?'

'Pots and pans,' said Oliver, 'are not an object with me.'

'Well, they are with me! I'm sick of managing with two saucepans and an electric kettle, and the stuff in that house isn't much better!'

'The shops are full of them. Buy some more.'

Chel looked at him, and he looked back at her. Dominating her with his will, that was stronger than hers. *You're going to have to stop putting Oliver's interests quite so far ahead of your own...* She took a deep breath. *Here goes, then.*

'I want my home back,' she said. '*Our* home. I want to stop living in limbo. I want to be able to tell my parents where we are, and maybe have them visit. I want my sister to bring her family and spend time with us, I want to see Tracy's kids and have them play on the beach and in the garden. I want to be able to write to my brothers and have them write back - and I want to see Richie and Louise's new baby before he's into long trousers! I can't help it if you come from the world's most dysfunctional family, I don't. And come to that, I'd like to see your sister Debbie, get to know her a bit better. And so should you! Thanks to you and your attitude, we're practically strangers!''

She paused. That was pushing the boat out with a vengeance, and she held her breath. Oliver shrugged his shoulders and picked up a brush, dipped it in a squirl of paint on his palette.

'OK. On your own head be it.'

As simple as that. Or was it?

Talking to Susan, which naturally fell to her lot, was less easy. She had long been forced to acquit Susan of deliberate malice, but she was, Chel thought, a very spiky woman, with her values in all the wrong places, and let's face it, the mother from hell! It was the Dreaded Dot, she knew, who was root, trunk, branch and leaf of the main problem, but it had to be faced. She went into the van, where Oliver wouldn't hear her, and dialled the fateful number.

'Susan! How are you?'

'Oh, it's you,' said Susan. She didn't sound pleased. Chel decided to cut the social niceties and go straight to the point.

'Susan, Terry Gage needs to get into the bungalow to collect some of our things, can you let him have the key?'

'The house agent has one,' Susan pointed out, unhelpfully.

'True, but Terry's at work when they're open. He needs to pick it up one evening.'

'Doesn't he have a lunch hour?'

Terry, as Oliver had been, was a diver. He spent his days and quite often his nights too, on, or even under, a boat. Susan knew this as well as Chel did, she was being deliberately obstructive. On the whole, she reluctantly thought that she sympathised. Susan, like Oliver's father and her own family, had wished them no actual harm. They must have found it hard to understand why they had been so conclusively shut out - although Debbie, she thought, might have made a guess. Debbie, half-sister to both Oliver and Susan, and younger daughter of the Dreaded Dot, was different... as so, too, was Jerry, her father, in a way... groping after a new idea, Chel nearly missed Susan's next remark.

'Are we going to be allowed to know where you are if you're planning to settle down?' she was asking. 'I presume you are, if you want your things.' There was hurt in her voice, making Chel feel guilty. She had meant to come clean with Susan anyway, it was more than time. She said,

'Of course we are. Have you got a pen handy?'

She dictated the address - Moor House, Trelewan, Penzance, Cornwall, and added the previously withheld number of the mobile - and presumably Susan wrote it down. After a moment, Susan said, grudgingly,

'You'd better tell Terry he can call for the key tomorrow evening, we're out tonight. And tell him to be sure to bring it back.' She rang off then, abruptly, and Chel sighed. She had almost been friends with Susan at one point; more than anyone, she realised in retrospect, Susan had supported her through the worst time, albeit in her own bossy way. Now they were enemies again. She sat for a few minutes with the mobile in her hands, half expecting it to ring, but it didn't. Either Susan hadn't passed on the information, or her mother was out. Chel switched off the phone, just to be on the safe side, and sat down to write a letter, passing on the same information to her own parents. When you wrote things down, you couldn't be interrupted, lose the thread, and lose your temper after. People had to accept what you wrote in the spirit in which you wrote it. She didn't, however, mention motor homes or caravan sites. Some things were better glossed over.

Now, on the day in which they were moving into their new home, she had still not heard from anyone, and wasn't sure if this was a good thing or a bad.

It wasn't an easy morning. Oliver stood around getting angry because he couldn't help her as she carried armsful of clothes and bedding in from the van, underfoot and infuriating. Partly, she thought, it was the idea of meeting Terry again under these circumstances, but it seemed unfair to take it out on her. In the end, she flung wide the french doors leading from the conservatory to the garden and ordered him outside.

'I don't care what you do! Paint a picture, or walk up and down, or just plain sulk, just get from in my way!'

It was easier after that, but she was conscious of him, sitting in one of the upright rattan conservatory armchairs and glowering at her as she went to and fro. His paints and brushes and boards were all unloaded, but he didn't touch them. Like a ten year old, she thought furiously. A spoilt little boy who wasn't allowed to play with the big boys.

Terry arrived shortly after eleven, and he had a friend with him.

'Hope you don't mind. Your sister-in-law suggested it, some of this stuff's heavy.'

The bed, particularly. Chel had been wondering how they were going to manage that between the two of them, and thanked Susan in her head. Officious as ever - but undeniably right, that was Susan to a T. Jack and Keith had changed the divan from upstairs round with the sofa-bed the previous night, making things as easy as possible for them. She helped unload the smaller stuff, boxes and crates and bags of clothes, and piled them in the dining area. Terry, she saw, had found Oliver and gone through to speak to him. She switched on the kettle to make coffee, and while she waited for it to boil, reviewed the heap on the floor. It was strange to see it all here, and there was a lot more, she was sure, than she recalled packing and labelling with her mother's help when they closed down the bungalow - for that journey east to her home which had turned into a flight west, but best not think about that. Possibly, though, her memory was playing tricks on her. She lifted a cardboard box to put it on the table and look inside. It was heavy, but she could just about manage it, or at least, she thought so until the bottom fell out. A cascade of books fell out onto the floor and scattered in all directions.

'Bugger!' said Chel. She placed the remains on a chair and began to gather up the scattered books, and as she did so, realised why there was so much stuff. This wasn't just the things she had asked for, these were all Oliver's diving and sailing books: Susan had cleared out the loft.

How just like Susan, she thought angrily - and unfairly, for Susan could quite naturally have supposed that she wanted *all* the boxes, she hadn't been specific. But how typical of Susan it was to chase them into sanctuary with all the things they were trying to leave behind. She almost suspected her of doing it on purpose, but surely Susan wasn't capable of such calculated cruelty.

Her mother was. Her lips tightened at the thought. She imagined she could hear her now, sugar-sweet - *And don't forget the things in the loft, Susan dear. Those are Oliver's, I expect Cheryl will want to keep them, you know how sentimental she is.* It was so real that for a moment she almost saw the woman smiling as she said it. She placed the pile of books she held on the table and looked at the other crates and boxes. If the books were here, then Oliver's wet suit and air cylinders were in one of those crates. She would have to get Terry to get it all upstairs, out of the way, which she hadn't meant to do. Damn! It would have to go in one of the bedrooms for now. She went into the kitchen to make the coffee.

She walked through into the conservatory with the tray, and a smile on her face.

'Terry, I'm awfully sorry, some of that stuff is going to have to go upstairs after all, I'd forgotten how much there was. Would you mind?'

'No problem.' Terry took his mug and smiled back at her. 'We'll do that for you, and then we must be off. I don't want to be too late back, got to dive tomorrow.'

Although it was good to see him again, Chel found that she was glad about this. The two halves of their lives, so neatly divided, nevertheless seemed to her to be grating together. Oliver had come out of his sulks, but he didn't look relaxed. Terry's friend, a stranger to him, was trying not to be embarrassed by his disability, and it was making him, like Mr. Gittings of evil memory, slightly patronising. For the first time she wondered, dismally, if there had been some excuse for the dreadful Mr. G. But if Oliver had simply broken a leg he would still have been on crutches, and nobody would have patronised him then.

The friend - she never did remember his name - now got to his feet.

'Show me what you want moved,' he said, helpfully. 'I'll do it while I drink my coffee - it's too hot - ' Glad to get away and find something useful to do, Chel thought. Oliver had a cynical look, she refused to meet his eye. She left him with Terry and went back into the main house.

The friend made light work of the unmarked boxes that needed to go upstairs, fortunately Chel had written things like *China, Books, Linen* on the downstairs ones, it made the job simple.

'That the lot?' he asked. Chel made a quick check.

'Yes - thank you.'

He held out a folded sheet of paper.

'I found this on the floor, I think it must have fallen out of that dodgy box you dropped. You'd better have it, it might be important.'

Chel took it, unfolding it mechanically without looking at it.

'Thanks.'

Terry came in from the conservatory carrying the tray of empty mugs, ready to go.

'Good to see you both again. Keep in touch. I told Oliver, Bill will be writing to him, there's another report on the ship out.' He touched her shoulder, lightly. 'Love the pictures. Keep him at it, it might turn out a nice little earner down here. Tourists like pictures.'

The next person who said that was going to get a mouthful back, Chel decided. Neither she nor Oliver had the smallest idea how to market paintings seriously, and Maggie's experience was confined to hanging them in cafés with a price ticket stuck on the corner, she couldn't see Oliver's paintings in that setting, somehow. She waved Terry and his friend off and went slowly back inside. Through the glass doors, she could see Oliver beginning to sort through his painting gear at last, piling it insecurely on the conservatory table. She wondered whether to leave him to it, unhandy though he was being, or to go and give him a hand and risk offending him again. Then, realising that she still had the paper in her hands, she put off the moment of decision by looking to see if it was important, or one for the bin. Her breath stopped.

It was a letter, dated the end of March in the previous year.

Dear Mr. Nankervis,

I hope that you won't find this letter an impertinence from a complete stranger, but I and some friends of mine have a proposition to put to you, in which we hope that you might be interested.

Basically, it is this. We should like to put an entry into the next Round-the-World Race, which as you know is scheduled for the end of next year. This, as you know is an expensive business, as well as requiring a great deal of knowledge and experience, and although we have an offer of sponsorship (which as you will know is essential for this kind of enterprise) they are insisting that the skipper of our entry is someone who has that experience. Someone, in fact, like yourself.

We are therefore wondering if we can interest you in joining our team and leading us to victory! You would, of course, be allowed to select your own crew members to a large degree (although my friends and I hope that we might be included!), and your name behind us would undoubtedly enable us to raise further sponsorship and launch an even better challenge!

I realise that this is over a year ahead, but I don't need to tell you that it is none too early to start thinking about it. We have no boat as yet, although we have a couple in our sights, and some input from you on this subject would also be both appreciated and useful.

If you might be interested, perhaps you would write to me and we can arrange a meeting with the sponsors to discuss the full details. I can assure you that this is a genuine proposition, and that we all hope very much that you will join us.

It was signed *James Filedale-Brown*. Chel had never heard of him.

She folded the paper slowly and slipped it into the back pocket of her jeans. Poor Oliver. Poor, poor Oliver - that letter must have arrived only days before the Meridew Street incident. He had never mentioned it to her, she didn't even know if he had replied to James Filedale-Brown, or what he had wanted to do, but the recollection of it must have been at the back of his mind all the time he had been in hospital, slowly coming to terms with the fact that all that part of his life was over - and for good. She didn't even think, *he would have left me and the baby then, for months and months, however long it takes.* She was only tearingly sorry that he hadn't been able to go.

She went slowly back into the dining area, feeling as if she was walking on eggshells - which was ridiculous. However he had felt at the time or afterwards, Oliver must long ago have put it behind him, and she must do the same.

She made herself open the box marked *Linen*, pulling out sheets, duvet covers, pillowcases. She would make the beds, and then she would get some lunch, and then she would finish unpacking. Life had to go on, and in a way, it was extraordinarily heartening the way it did so even when it was apparently falling apart.

After lunch, Oliver lay down thankfully on his own bed at last, and fell instantly asleep, leaving the conservatory in chaos. Chel, going back to her own unpacking, found herself feeling slightly resentful, he could at least have stayed awake and talked to her, even had he been able to contribute nothing else. It wasn't how she had imagined today, back in a home of their own choice at last, although she supposed she could be glad that he could crash out like that, only a few weeks ago he couldn't have done it.

She remembered that upstairs there were a few additional problems waiting for her to sort through, courtesy of Susan. The sooner they were dealt with, the sooner she could put them safely out of her mind again, and while Oliver was asleep seemed like a good time. He wouldn't ask questions about what he didn't know. She went upstairs.

Up in the back double, Terry's friend had piled the crates and boxes haphazardly under the window, and dumped a load of loose items onto the bed. Not only, she found to her dismay, Oliver's wet suit and

105

compressed air tanks, which she had expected, but the watercolour painting of *Lawley's Girl*, in which he had sailed so triumphantly round the world, and which had been Susan's wedding present to them, which she had - almost - forgotten about, it had never hung in the bungalow. How could Susan have been so thoughtless? She couldn't have known that Oliver wouldn't see it, she might have used her common sense to interpret her instructions! This was the rock on which their new life could founder, if founder it was going to, they couldn't look back for ever with regret, they simply couldn't, or they would never be whole again - and nobody should try to make them. In this respect, she knew, Oliver was doing better than herself, and it made her ashamed. She ought at least to do as well as he.

She really ought to do something about Oliver's diving gear too, for he would never use it again. She reached out and fingered it gently, and wondered if the day would ever come when she would look back without pain because something else had replaced ships and the sea in his life, indulging what she promised herself must be the last, the very last, orgy of nostalgia that she was ever going to permit herself. *They that go down to the sea in ships, that do business in great waters, these see the works of the lord...* oh Oliver, oh my dear, what is going to become of you?

Quite suddenly, it was cold in spite of the summer sunshine, alternating today with heavy showers but still seasonably warm. The sunshine poured through the window and bathed the muddle on the bed with light, but Chel shivered and hugged herself against a sudden chill. Perhaps she should go downstairs again, she was upset by the sight of all these things, and it probably wasn't the best moment for burying memories. She could push most of it out of sight into the wardrobe and deal with it when she felt less emotional, that was the thing to do. She picked up Oliver's wet suit briskly, but the feel of it brought back a great wave of recollection. She sat down on the bed, cradling it in her arms, and felt her throat tighten painfully. She was cold and miserable, and felt dreadfully cut off and alone... nobody she knew for miles now, and Oliver asleep... perhaps this hadn't been such a good idea after all. She wanted to cry, but the tears wouldn't fall. She wished they would, because the need for them hurt so much.

She didn't consciously close her eyes, but she must have done for there in front of them were the flickers and flashes that follow on clenching the eyelids tight against bright sunlight. They ran across her vision like blips on a radar screen, spun and whirled into a ball, spun again above the foot of the bed like a catherine wheel, throwing off bright sparks to glitter and fade against the white wall. Bewildered, she blinked hard to clear her sight, but found the ball unaccountably still there, spinning, breaking up a little in the centre now as if it was spinning itself into an open-ended cone, flickering and dispersing into nothing. There was almost something there, colours fragmented like the scattered pieces of a jig-saw puzzle, green and gold and flesh-tints - but the last spark died and there was only the wall, blank and uninformative, and a shaken feeling that was almost, but not quite, fear.

The sun was warm on her cheek, on her hands. She found that she was clutching Oliver's wet suit to her almost as if she was protecting it - or expecting it to protect her, maybe. Her heart was banging as if it was trying to get out through her ribs.

Wake up! You nodded off staring at the sun, that's all. She laid down the wet suit and got to her feet, annoyed and surprised to find her knees wobbling, but pleased to discover that she no longer wanted to cry. In fact, she felt quite different, as if the strange ball of light, dreamed or actual, had held wisdom. We can't put it behind us, she found herself thinking, it isn't behind us, it's part of us, and we've got to live with it and make it a natural part of our lives, not run away from it. Susan was wrong, when she told me to hide it all away in the loft that day, but she's right this time. If I do that, and worry all the time about what will remind Oliver, I'll rob him of thirty years. I can't do that, not when so much else has gone too. At the bungalow, he must have felt as if I had rejected everything he ever stood for, totally. It's never been his courage that's been at fault, but mine is.

She tiptoed downstairs again with *Lawley's Girl* and propped it up on the mantelpiece. Later, when Oliver was awake again, she would fetch a chair and hang it on the empty hook above the fireplace, and it would be there where they could see it as they sat in the evening, or lay in bed in the morning, and it would make them both remember. Memories were for always, they didn't spoil like photographs but neither could they be torn up and thrown away. She had been wrong about not looking back - but one should never look back with regret on what wasn't in the least regrettable, and that had to be true, because if you did that you would never go forward.

She spent the remainder of the afternoon digging into boxes that hadn't been touched for months, rebuilding, had she but realised it, not the bungalow they had so hated but the flat where they had once been so happy, as if the happiness had been packed away with the material things, and as she did it she began to feel more and more lighthearted, safer, like herself again. She began to enjoy herself, tiptoeing up and downstairs with forgotten treasures like a little girl at Christmas. On her last trip she came down with her furry Pink Panther, that Oliver had once won for her at a fair, in her arms, and found that he was awake again, lying pensively looking at the picture propped on the mantelpiece.

'Hi there,' she said, and he turned his head to smile at her.

'I see the *Girl* has come out of hiding.' He didn't say what he thought about it, and allowed his eye to roam around the room with interest. 'You have been a busy little bee, haven't you? Aren't you tired?'

'Not in the least,' said Chel, who hadn't felt so energetic for a year. 'Do you like it?' She sat down on the bed, tossing the Panther onto her own.

Oliver lifted himself into a sitting position, with audible thanks for modern technology. He noted without comment that things such as coffee tables and standard lamps and odd stools had been banished to allow the maximum amount of clear floor for him to stumble around on, a consideration he hadn't been given in the bungalow and would have died rather than asked for, and the reappearance of all his technical books as well as the watercolour painting of his round-the-world companion. The world seemed to be turning the right way up, he reflected, and concentrated for an annoying moment in swinging his legs over the side of the bed and putting his feet in contact with the floor. When he was sitting beside Chel, he slipped his arm round her.

'It all looks great.' He spoke with such obvious satisfaction that Chel gave him a startled look.

'Good. I'm going to make a cup of tea now, do you want one?'

Oliver said that he did, and she went off to make it while he got himself from the bed to his familiar upright armchair, going into the kitchen without mentioning her peculiar experience upstairs. Oliver might laugh at her, she thought - which she probably deserved, but for some reason she didn't want to be laughed at. She told herself that it had been because she was tired and under stress, plus the shock of seeing all those things again - and of course, it probably was. And it had been nothing like the horrible atmosphere of the bungalow. Whatever it was, if anything at all, had gone, and left the air clean behind it.

And what was she trying to imagine that it had been, anyway? It was one thing to believe that people could leave an atmosphere behind them, if they had been sad or happy enough - at least, she supposed it was. Quite another to think....

Chel stopped thinking abruptly. She had a house to run, and a temporarily invalid husband to care for, this was no time to start imagining ghosts. There were no ghosts.

Matthew Sutton, whoever or whatever he had been, was not only dead, but gone.

Gone!

For a few days, it rained persistently, and Chel and Oliver were left in peace to settle into this new phase of their lives. It also blew hard, but no amount of heavy gusts shifted even one of the slates that Jack had nailed back onto the roof for them, and Chel found that a vague uneasiness left by her experience upstairs was beginning to show a tendency to creep back if she left her mind unoccupied too much, together with phrases such as *out of the frying-pan, into the fire.* Fortunately, there was plenty to do, things to unpack and put away, meals to cook, trips to the village for shopping - it was like playing houses, and to start with Chel enjoyed it wholeheartedly, in spite of the rain. Oliver painted, grumbled about the light when the clouds came over extra black, and made the conservatory, and to a degree the rest of the house too, reek of turpentine and linseed oil. It all began to be as much a way of life as gypsying it at Church Farm had been, only more comfortable and a whole lot more practical.

This went on for four or five days, and then the rain and wind let up a little and Judy walked over from the village, with an excited Sheba dancing at her heels.

'You never walked all the way!' exclaimed Chel, for by road it was a two or three miles.

'There's a footpath from the farm,' explained Judy, raising her voice above Sheba's excited barking. 'It comes out about a hundred yards up the road, it's not a bad walk if you're not in a hurry. Be quiet, dog!'

Sheba had caught sight of Oliver, painting in the conservatory, and wanted to say hullo, she was practically strangling herself on the lead. Judy gave her a sharp tap on the nose that had no noticeable effect, and apparently immune to the noise, looked around her. The big room had effectively become a bed-sitting room, the effect was unusual, but there was enough space for it not to be cluttered thanks to the open plan.

'That's better,' she said, with approval. 'It looks much less like a miserable summer let.' She raised her voice. 'Hullo, Oliver!'

Oliver looked up from his painting and waved his brush at her with an absent-minded smile, and Chel suggested that her friend might like to sit down.

Sheba had run out of bark. She made a brief, frustrated attempt to climb onto the sofa and settled down, bright-eyed and alert, at Judy's feet. A sudden peace descended on the room.

'Coffee? Tea?' suggested Chel, and Judy agreed with alacrity.

109

'I thought you'd never ask, coffee'd be great! Sheba's OK, she's
been drinking puddles, but I'm parched after slogging all this way. I'll
help you make it, but can I just have a quick wash and brush up first?
I'm not exactly clean.'
'Help yourself.' Chel, turned to the kitchen. 'Go upstairs, will you?
I took the towels out of the cloakroom to put in the wash this morning
and I haven't got around to putting them back.'
'No problem.' Judy disappeared up the stairs, and Sheba began
barking again. Chel took her through into the kitchen area with her and
gave her a biscuit to shut her up, and was peacefully making the coffee
when there was a sudden loud shriek, the slam of a door, and running
footsteps on the landing, and a moment later Judy came hurtling down.
She was as white as a sheet, and obviously greatly shaken, and Chel,
and Oliver who had just wandered through from the conservatory,
stared at her in astonishment. Chel went to her, alarmed.
'What's the matter? Here, come and sit down - have your coffee.'
Judy sat down in an armchair and accepted the mug. The liquid in it
rocked and jumped like a disturbed sea because of the shaking of her
hands, and she sipped it without speaking. Oliver said, after a pause,
'What's the matter? Spider in the bath?'
Judy shook her head, still speechless.
'Tell us,' Chel invited. Judy looked at Oliver, and then at her.
'I don't know if I should...' she said.
'I think you had better,' said Oliver, but kindly. Judy took a quick
gulp, choked because it was hot, and drew a breath.
'There was a man in your bathroom,' she said.
'What?' said Oliver, startled, and Chel said, more practically,
'What kind of a man?' and Judy looked at her in surprise.
'Have you seen him too, then?'
Chel edged away from this question by asking,
'Tell us about him.'
'Well,' said Judy, and hesitated. She was calming down a little, Chel
saw with relief, the necessity for thinking about what she had seen
steadying her. She gave a shaky little laugh. 'It'll sound really stupid.
You won't believe me.'
'You'd be surprised,' said Oliver. 'We believe anything, us.' And
this time, Judy told them.
'I was just washing my hands, and I saw him - thought I saw him - in
the mirror,' she said simply. 'He was just an ordinary man - wearing a
sort of heathery green sweater and a white shirt under it... middle-aged,
I suppose. Fairish, floppy sort of hair... he looked quite normal. I mean,
not blurred, or transparent or anything, not - not *ghostly*.' She bit her

lip, shot a look at Oliver from the corners of her eyes, and took another sip of coffee. 'I thought he was the window cleaner - honestly. I was a bit embarrassed - and then I realised that the window was shut, and the door locked - and I ran - '

'Was he actually there?' asked Oliver, with slightly scandalised interest. 'I mean, was he just in the mirror, or was he really there behind you?'

'I didn't look,' confessed Judy. 'I just wanted to be out of there.'

Chel got to her feet.

'I'm going to look,' she said.

'No - don't - ' said Judy, and Oliver said,

'Leave it, Chel.'

'Don't be silly,' said Chel, more bravely than she felt. 'If there really is a man up there we need to know about it - and if there isn't, then whatever it is isn't going to hurt me.'

'Chel!' said Oliver, and when she continued on her way to the stairs, swore violently and reached for his crutches. Judy stopped him.

'I'll go,' she said, quickly. 'It's all right, truly - it was just the surprise. I'm fine now.' Oliver subsided with indignant reluctance and fury.

Chel and Judy went up the stairs together. Chel had no more enthusiasm for ghosts than Judy appeared to have, and still wasn't convinced about them, but obviously this thing had to be investigated. For one thing, apart from anything else, she had always believed that ghosts made no reflection in mirrors, cast no shadows, and if there was a real intruder, they needed to know how he got in. She opened the bathroom door with extreme caution and faltering courage, half expecting a fist in the face.

There was nothing there.

Judy crowded into the small room behind her, and they looked carefully around. The window was still firmly closed, the mirror reflected only their own startled faces.

'I must have been imagining things,' said Judy, with relief.

They peered into the three bedrooms and even into the airing cupboard, but there was nothing to be seen. The upstairs rooms of the little house were quiet, sunlit and deserted. They went back down to Oliver and found him at the foot of the stairs, still furious - more at himself than at them by this time.

'There's nothing up there,' said Chel, taking him by the arm. 'For goodness' sake, stop raging about! I can stand anything, short of a house haunted by you!'

They sat down again, and Judy said,

'I'm so sorry, I didn't mean to make a fuss and upset you both.'

Chel didn't say that she hadn't, because Oliver was still so obviously upset that it would have been futile. Instead, she said,

'Have you ever seen things before?' in as normal a voice as it was possible to say something so unusual. Judy looked at her doubtfully, and she went on. 'We just moved out of a house that was very queer indeed, and although we never saw anything' - (True? Not true?) - 'when we first saw this place, years ago, when it was still a ruin, we both thought it was a bit strange, as you know. So we won't laugh - I promise you.'

'Most people would,' said Judy. 'It sounds silly for a doctor's wife, we're supposed to be practical people, although I can never understand why - and Keith would have fifty fits and start prescribing Prozac - but yes, I do see things sometimes. I told you, didn't I? She sounded defensive.

'About knowing things - not actually seeing them.' Chel tried to keep accusation out of her voice, it would be unfair. After a moment, Judy shrugged her shoulders.

'Oh well... if you really want to know, I suppose... when I was little, before we came to Church Farm, we lived on a farm miles out in the country. It was quite old, about two hundred years. There was someone there who used to sing... when you were alone, or quiet, you could hear this high, clear humming somewhere in the house. And at night, sometimes, I'd wake up and there would be someone in the room - a woman. She felt kind, and she wore a long grey gown and a sort of bonnet. I was never afraid of her that I remember, I've thought since I grew up that perhaps she was an old nanny, just pleased to see a child there. It was a particularly happy house - and then once, on a school trip abroad, I went into a friend's room, and she was talking to someone I had never seen before. I asked her later who it had been, and she said she hadn't been talking to anyone, what had the person been like, and I described her - and she said, that's my friend Sheila from home, I was thinking about her - and she gave me a funny look, but it wasn't for ages that she told me Sheila had been killed by a hit-and-run a month before.'

'Ugh!' said Oliver, expressively. Judy looked at him.

'Perhaps I was imagining things then, too. But I've heard it said that a lot of children see things like that, but they grow out of it and forget. Only... I don't seem to have grown out of it.'

'The dog didn't make a fuss,' said Chel, slowly. 'Animals are supposed to know.'

'The dog was downstairs,' said Oliver. 'Come to that, she *was*.'

112

'I wish I hadn't mentioned it,' said Judy, although how else she could have accounted for such full-scale panic was a question.

Chel gave a slightly nervous laugh.

'There's no horrid atmosphere in this house.'

Judy was calming down, she spoke more sensibly.

'There wasn't in the house where I grew up, either. I wouldn't worry about it if I was you, if you have got a ghost, it's obviously a friendly one.'

'You screamed,' Oliver reminded her.

'Wouldn't you, if you thought you were alone in the loo, and some strange female peered over your shoulder?' said Judy, and Oliver laughed, and said that he would certainly be rather disconcerted.

Judy, beginning to be slightly embarrassed by what had all the appearance by this time of a major social *gaffe*, changed the subject by asking how the pictures were going, and why didn't Oliver try to sell some of them?

'How do you sell pictures?' asked Chel, still wanting to know.

'You hang them on a wall somewhere and put a price tag on them,' Judy told her. Much what Maggie did, in fact. 'Or, if you're a well-known artist, some gallery sells them for you and people ask you to do commissions. It seems a pity to waste them all.'

That was certainly true, Chel thought. The smallest bedroom upstairs, the one with the displaced sofa-bed, was beginning to look like an artist's studio with all the paintings stacked around it, and the number was undoubtedly going to grow. Oliver had painted over one or two of his earlier attempts at oils, but Chel had rescued most of them.

'Or at least,' went on Judy, 'you could frame some of them and hang them on the walls here, they are a bit bare, and you've only got two pictures of your own - is that the boat that you went round the world in, Oliver? Is it one of yours?'

'Yes - and no, thank you very much,' said Oliver, giving it a swift look. He had always been slightly scornful about it, Chel remembered, which she was by this time beginning to understand. 'The grey blob at the wheel is presumably a speaking likeness of me.'

'Keith says that cats and trimarans are nautical abominations,' said Judy, getting up for a closer look.

'She got me round,' said Oliver.

'She got you into the record books, too,' Chel reminded him, and Oliver said,

'Only until someone else does it quicker,' very offhandedly.

'It's a terrific likeness!' said Judy, peering at the blob, and laughed nervously before changing the subject again, feeling, as Chel did, thin ice crackling beneath her feet.

Shortly afterwards, Judy gathered up her dog and left, hoping to dodge the next rain squall, and Chel collected the mugs and took them into the kitchen to wash, not because she was particularly bothered about unwashed mugs lying around but because small, fussy jobs like this were what filled her time just now. Oliver had gone back to the conservatory and his current painting without comment when Judy had gone, but Chel wasn't deceived into thinking he had dismissed the morning's alarm. Was he, like herself, thinking with distaste of the bungalow, and wondering if they had made another mistake?

Except, it was true that this was different. The bungalow had had a horrible feeling about it from day one, this was a happy house.

But once, it hadn't been so...

... green and gold, and flesh-tints...

....*a fair-haired man in a heathery green sweater...*

The recollection of the day they moved in swept over Chel in a sudden wave, tingling to her fingertips, incredible and rather sobering. Suppose that hadn't been imagination? Judy, it had to be assumed, had really seen a man, although what man had yet to be established.

What had this Matthew Sutton looked like?

If it could be proved - if she could prove beyond all doubt that Judy had seen a man who was supposedly thirty years dead, it would be like opening a door on sunshine. Her dead baby son, Oliver's life sentence of disablement, she might even be able to forgive them if she could believe that they weren't all there was going to be.

Forgiveness is for angels... I suppose that when more time has passed we shall get used to it, learn to live with it, but will we ever stop thinking if only it had never happened, and hating those yobs for what they did to us?

It was an unanswerable question. Chel hung the mugs on their hooks and went back into the living area, but Oliver was engrossed in his picture and didn't even look up. She picked up a newspaper and sat down with the intention of glancing through it until it was time to get the lunch, but it failed to get her attention. Hardly surprising, she thought, laying it down with a sigh. It wasn't every day that somebody thought they saw a ghost in your house. She thought about Judy's visit, feeling herself tip-toeing round the idea of it. Judy had a tendency to sweep through life like a small, dark hurricane, whisking up thoughts and ideas and scattering them broadcast as she passed on her way, but in among the fallen leaves was the odd chestnut. On impulse, Chel got to her feet again and went upstairs to the room where she had stored Oliver's pictures.

114

She had propped them round the walls like the stock-in-trade of a secondhand shop, and she knelt on the floor and began sorting through them, leaning them up so that she could see them properly. About ten oils, in all, by this time, and a portfolio of watercolours. You could tell which were his earlier works, she decided, but he had done some impressive stuff recently. Not restful, exactly, but full of impact. She herself and Judy and Maggie were quite right, and it ought to be possible to sell them, but she had no more idea of how to set about it than she had had at the beginning. And it probably wasn't as easy as it sounded, particularly here in Cornwall where there were so many artists, some of them famous, and very good indeed.

She was holding in her hands a picture of a night-time sea, swirling over a shelf of rock and eerily lit in fitful moonlight that sent uncertain shadows and sudden splashes of light among the clefts and irregularities of the rock face and the spilling surf. Out on the dark sea were the lights of a small coaster, battling her way through a brisk chop, a dim outline under scudding clouds, momentarily lit on their edges with fugitive touches of silver light. In the far distance, the red light of a lighthouse flashed its warning. One of Oliver's quieter efforts, and one of his most recent... funny how often light crept into his pictures as if it was something solid and tangible... he painted light like the Almighty... she was suddenly conscious of the oddest prickle up the back of her neck, linked with the thought that had spun so idly through her free-wheeling mind... just like a catherine wheel spinning in her imagination against a blank wall... the sensation died abruptly, and left her with the strangest idea.

Was Oliver really brilliant? Maggie, as she knew by now, was given to extravagant comments that she didn't necessarily mean to be taken literally, but just suppose, for that once, she had spoken the absolute truth?

She *had* spoken the absolute truth. It came to Chel with certainty, as if it was in the air around her, tangible. It was something that had happened to her in the past, and proved right too often to ignore, but this time at least it was something pleasant - part of the link that ran between herself and him. She had no idea how it worked, or where it came from.

Chel got to her feet hastily, as always made uncomfortable by the exercise of whatever power it was that she had, and realising as she did so that, for once, she hadn't tried to rationalise it, whatever that might signify. She left the room, closing the door firmly behind her, and went downstairs with the lighthouse picture tucked under her arm. Oliver looked up as she came into his view, and called through the open french doors,

'What are you planning to do with that?' as if he was actually interested.

Chel held it out at the length of her arms to give it another look.

'I thought I might get it framed and hang it somewhere,' she said. She had been vaguely planning to hang it in one of the spare rooms to make it look more homely should they ever have guests, but it was really too good for that. Her eye went meditatively to a Constable print which she had hung above the sideboard. It was a nice print, nicely framed, and whatever Susan had said about it (and she had) Chel liked it, but it would look equally well in a spare bedroom. Better.

'Which one have you got?' Oliver was asking, and she turned it around to show him.

'It doesn't make me feel as seasick as some of your others,' she said, and he laughed. Chel leaned the picture against the empty wood-burning stove and stood back for a better look. 'Do you mind?'

'Why should I? Logically, I can only be flattered.' There was amusement in his voice, and affection, and something else that she couldn't quite identify. She looked at him quickly, but he had gone back to his picture, touching in detail with unusual deliberation for a painter who was normally swift and sure in his approach. Perhaps she had imagined it, whatever it had been. She hoped so, for it had seemed to have a sharp edge.

'What did you make of Judy's experience in the bathroom?' asked Oliver, carefully painting.

'Odd,' suggested Chel, cautiously. There didn't seem to be a better word to describe it.

'Do you think she really saw something?' He laid down his brush and began to squeeze paint onto his palette - green paint. Sea, sea, always sea. He had a fixation about it. Chel shivered, without knowing why.

'If it was that pilot, if that's what you're thinking, surely by this time he would have realised he was dead.' She hadn't meant to sound quite so challenging. Oliver didn't look up.

'Some ghosts hang around for centuries, if ghost stories are to be believed.' He sounded sarcastic.

'But those aren't quite the same,' said Chel. 'They've lived in the places they haunt, they have associations...' She wasn't quite sure of her ground, and her words tailed off into nothing. Oliver was mixing his green into a sort of turgid greeny-brown, which on the palette looked horrible, and on the picture would blend in so beautifully that the next time she saw a real sea, Chel would find herself trying to pick it out.

'Perhaps he doesn't want to realise,' he said. He was something of an expert, he reflected wryly, in not wanting to realise things. He could sympathise.

'But why should he want to spend thirty years in our roof space?' asked Chel.

'Perhaps he hasn't. Maggie never said anything to suggest that such spirits can't move around. Perhaps they can.'

'When we first came here, I thought I heard voices,' said Chel, rather too defensively. 'I suppose it was just the wind, really - and I haven't heard anything since we moved in, even with all the wind we've had lately. Have you?' She threw out the question like a gage of battle, but Oliver ignored it.

'But what have you seen?' he asked, and Chel said firmly that she had seen nothing, and if they were going to have any lunch, it was time she did something about it. Domestic chores to the rescue again, so they had some use.

This question of their ghost was a difficult one, she thought, washing lettuce at the sink. She was conscious of a vigorous opposition to becoming convinced, still less involved.

For Matthew Sutton had been a famous painter, and Oliver, untrained as he might be, was a natural artist... and his resistance had been, perhaps still was, low enough to allow the spirit in the bungalow to manipulate his actions. She didn't put it more clearly to herself than that, but she was aware at the back of her mind of a great but unspecific thankfulness that Oliver would probably never go upstairs.

VIII

Three days later, Chel left Oliver resting after lunch, and drove into Penzance for a quick visit. She walked into the heart of the town with Oliver's picture under her arm, turning into a narrow side-street up which she had noticed a little shop called the Cosgrove Gallery which sold pictures, and which also displayed a sign announcing that it carried out framing. As she walked up the street between the tall buildings, that seemed to shut out both light and air on this warm day, she was turning over the bathroom incident, and other things, in her mind, and no single breath of prescience touched her, which she was afterwards to consider odd, and an on the whole comforting reflection on her own powers, which very firmly put her in her place as an ordinary mortal like the rest.

The little shop was empty when she pushed open the door, and at first nobody responded to the *ting* of the bell. She stood for a few minutes looking about her with interest. The gallery sold nothing but pictures, all originals, and extremely diverse in both subject and execution. There was a huge nude study in the window, propped on an easel, and around the walls everything from factual still life to incomprehensible post-modernism and naïve art. The prices were as diverse as the subjects. She had heard of none of the artists, but that didn't surprise her. Some of them looked to her decidedly amateur, but of that she knew she was no judge.

'Good morning. How may I help you?'

Chel jumped, and turned round hurriedly. A man had appeared behind the tiny counter, smiling at her. He was neither young nor old, like a little gnome in the gloomy back of the shop.

'I'm sorry, I didn't mean to startle you. A picture for framing, is it?'

'Please.' Chel laid Oliver's painting down on the counter, and he picked it up, turning it towards the light and looking at it through narrowed eyes.

'What sort of a frame had you in mind?'

Chel had always thought of pictures as coming ready-framed, and the task of choosing a frame kept her happily occupied for some time. Eventually she settled on a simple gilded moulding with a deep red inset line, that picked out the red light from the lighthouse in the picture.

'That one.'

118

'A very good choice,' he said, approvingly, writing it into a book, together with her name and address, and then he picked up the picture, carrying it over to the window where he could see it properly. 'A nice piece of work. Your own?'

'My husband's,' said Chel.

'Really?' He continued to look at it, turning it this way and that. 'Yes, a very nice piece of work. I deal in pictures, you know.' He looked at her. 'If your husband had any others that he wanted to sell, we might do business - twenty per-cent, and I do the framing at a discount. What do you think?' His voice was casual, almost uninterested.

'I don't know without asking him,' said Chel. 'You don't buy pictures yourself?'

'No, I only sell on commission. Take it or leave it, the offer's there.'

'I'll tell him,' said Chel.

She arranged to pick up the picture in a week and said goodbye. He held the door for her as she went out, bowing a little old-fashioned bow, but when she had gone he went back to the counter and picked up the picture again and studied it with knit brows, humming to himself, before finally carrying it through into the back of the shop. There, he thought for a moment, and then reached for the telephone that stood on his cluttered desk.

He dialled a number that he didn't have to look up.

Chel, meanwhile, drove home full of a bubbling excitement.

'Hey, guess what!' she greeted Oliver, practically dancing into the house.

Oliver had spent the afternoon in an uneasy doze that had left him feeling heavy and unsatisfied, half-dreams haunted by things that he hesitated to tell his wife since he considered that she had enough on her plate to worry over already. He was therefore not in the best mood to be swamped with optimism.

'What?' he asked, rubbing his eyes with his knuckles, trying to catch up with her obvious enthusiasm and finding it hard.

'The man in the framing shop - he said he'd sell some of your pictures if you wanted. He has a little gallery there, I think he sells pictures for his customers. He takes a percentage and gives you a discount on the framing.'

Oliver, more dazed than if he had slept properly, struggled to get his thoughts in order and treat this news with the respect that Chel apparently felt it deserved. It wasn't one of his best efforts.

'That sounds a well-organised way of earning a living. Catch your customers coming and going - I like it!'

'Wake up!' cried Chel, indignantly. 'You're supposed to be all pleased and excited!'

'Oh, I am, I am.' He yawned, breaking into a laugh when he saw the expression on her face. 'Sorry, sweetheart, you might let me wake up before you spring things on me.' He reached for her hand and held it, knowing that he had disappointed her and unsure of how to undo it. He lifted the hand he held so that he could see it, touching the gold circle of her wedding ring with his fingers. Rather painty fingers these days, particularly round the edges of the fingernails, more than ever those of an artist rather than an adventurer, and at the moment, rather tense. He loved her, and these days, he suspected he was entering another downward spiral of always hurting her. 'Chel, I do love you. Believe it.'

'Oh, I do...' said Chel, failing to meet his eyes.

There was something wrong there, and she couldn't help being a little disappointed. Her news about the Cosgrove Gallery seemed to have fallen rather flat.

She had more success with it later in the day, when Jack and Maggie dropped round after supper. Like Judy, they were on a visit of inspection, and they brought with them a bottle of their blackberry wine and a card with a silly joke on it, which Chel placed on the mantelpiece among several others - Keith and Judy, her own parents at last, her sister Tracy and her family, her two brothers, Debbie... but not Susan, or Oliver's parents. Placing Maggie and Jack's card reminded her of this and made her feel sad.

'A house-warming bottle!' cried Jack as they came in, waving it about. 'Come on, Cheryl, where's that corkscrew?' He kissed her, and stepped aside for Maggie to push past him, clutching a large flowering plant which she dumped, with the card, into Chel's hands without ceremony.

'And a house-warming present, I grew it from a cutting,' she said. 'Doesn't it all look nice, with all your own things around? Not a bit like a holiday let! Have you settled in all right? We can't stop long, we've left Jack's mother baby-sitting and they all run rings round her .' She swept on past, heading for the conservatory and Oliver, and Jack followed, saying,

'Just long enough to help with the bottle - come on Cheryl, where's those glasses? Trot 'em out, chop chop!' and leaving Chel to open the card, have her moment of depression, and find the corkscrew.

She put the plant on the dining table and went into the kitchen to hunt out glasses, where after a moment, Maggie found her working at the cork.

'Oliver looks tired,' she announced. 'Should he be working this late, do you think? It can't be a good idea, surely?' and it was to stop her fussing over Oliver as if his own wife couldn't look after him that Chel told her about the gallery.

'George Cosgrove?' said Maggie. 'I know him - he frames pictures for one or two of my friends sometimes. He belongs to the Society of Artists - he paints himself, did you know?'

'I never met him before today,' said Chel, resisting a facetious answer involving woad. Judy would have laughed or said it first, Maggie, never. 'Do you think he can really sell some pictures for Oliver, or is that just bullshit?'

'He sells a fair number,' said Maggie. 'It's a matter of supply and demand though, isn't it? If people want to be blown and hurricaned at off their walls, then they'll buy Oliver's pictures, you can't make forecasts about it. Personally, I find them a bit over-stimulating, good though they are. I like more restful pictures.' Her own walls were covered with her own landscapes and animal paintings, which Chel found rather childish in style, like nursery-rhyme illustrations, but she could see what Maggie meant. Oliver did rather hit his canvases like a tempest. But you had to hand it to her - she could be objective, it was one of the things that Chel couldn't help liking in her, her unflinching artistic integrity. Now, Chel gave a sigh.

'I suppose it's a start,' she said, and Maggie agreed that everyone had to start somewhere, with a little of the enthusiasm that Oliver had so signally failed to raise.

Back in the living area, Oliver had come out of the conservatory and sat down in his chair, and he and Jack were discussing diving. As Maggie and Chel came through with the wine, Oliver said,

'Chel, have we still got my diving gear? I know it sounds stupid of me, but I have no idea.'

'I think it's upstairs,' said Chel, knowing perfectly well that it was but not wishing it to seem an issue with her. 'Why?'

'Jack can get rid of it for me, secondhand - there's no point in keeping it after all.' That sounded blessedly matter-of-fact, but it gave Chel a jolt just the same. She was wondering how to reply when Jack said,

'I know someone who wants to start diving, he'd be glad to take it off your hands.'

'I see,' said Chel. 'All right. I'll get it down for you before you go.'

They would be better off with it out of the house, it only served as a permanent reminder of what was lost - not to Oliver, of course, who couldn't see it, but to her. Silly to feel as if she had just volunteered to cut off Oliver's right hand, even so.

The other three had resumed the diving discussion that the arrival of the wine had interrupted. Jack was doing most of the talking, but Oliver was listening quite placidly, and he was perfectly capable of changing the subject. There was nothing that Chel could usefully contribute, and after a while she put down her glass and slipped quietly away up the stairs.

It was all there, piled together on the bed where she had left it: the air tanks, emptied by Bill before he returned them, with their valves and harness, the breathing regulators, pressure and depth gauges, weight belts, all the expensive paraphernalia of Oliver's old life and work. She pulled a cardboard box out from beneath the bed and emptied the few books and papers it still contained onto the floor and began to repack it. She supposed that Oliver had meant his wet suit too, it had been handed back to her rinsed free from salt, and she had put it away carefully - why, heaven knew, but she had. She laid it in the box and began to pack the valves and gauges, and was suddenly furious to find that after all this time and all her trying there were still tears running down her face. She dashed them away angrily with the back of her hand. If Oliver saw that she had been crying, he would be upset, and if he had any reservations of his own about this, they would all come to the surface. They had had enough emotional upsets to last them a lifetime already, this wasn't even new ground.

She sat on the floor with Oliver's mask, that he had no further use for, in her hands, and sank her teeth into her lower lip. She wouldn't cry, she would not! It was her own silly fault, she should have got rid of this lot when she got rid of Oliver's old sports car and been done with it all at once. She stared ahead through an angry mist, blinking hard to try to clear it, feeling the tears trickling hot down her cheeks. It was a good thing it was all going, if she was going to be like this every time she saw it.

There were no whirling lights, no catherine wheels. He was simply there, sitting on the end of the cluttered bed watching her, exactly as Judy had described him. A thin, fair-skinned man with floppy light brown hair, ten or fifteen years or so older than Oliver, which yes, made him middle-aged, nice-looking without being particularly handsome. He wore grey trousers, a dull green sweater with the collar of a white shirt showing at the neck, she even noticed that he had brown lace-up shoes and grey socks. She sat on the floor and looked at him and he looked back at her. There was something comforting about him, she thought, but before she had properly formulated the idea, he wasn't there. It was as simple as that. He didn't fade, or disintegrate or dissolve, he just... wasn't there. She told herself that she had imagined him. She hoped that she had.

But, just as on that previous occasion, she found that she had been left with insight. Oliver, she suddenly saw, was tough, pragmatic, unsentimental. He would bury his own emotions in order to survive. It was she herself who cared about things until they hurt. There was no point in trying to project her own feelings onto him, he simply didn't have them. She whispered,

'Thank you,' and immediately felt foolish.

She heard footsteps on the stairs, and Jack's voice calling,

'Cheryl, where are you? Can I help?'

'I'm in here.' She hurriedly picked up a weight belt and put it into the box as Jack came in through the door. 'Nearly done. You can carry it downstairs. I'll bring the tanks.'

'Great. Sorry we can't stay longer, but my mother gets into a tiz. It's good to see you both settling in so well.' He swept the box into his arms and stood smiling at her over the top of it. 'It'll be all right, Cheryl, you'll see.'

He might be right, Chel thought as she followed him downstairs, but she couldn't yet see why he should think so. It seemed to her that they were still drifting, in spite of apparently positive action. She thought of the Cosgrove Gallery and was vaguely comforted. That would be positive, surely.

Oliver refused to show any real interest in choosing a couple of pictures to try to sell, once he had painted them he appeared to want to forget them, so positive it was not after all. Chel chose at random an oil and a watercolour that she rather liked herself and took them into the town with her when she went to collect the lighthouse picture. This, although it was handsome in its new frame, Oliver looked at casually and then ignored. She hung it in place of the Constable print and tried not to feel too disappointed.

It could have been the weather, of course. From being merely warm, it was becoming hot, humid and thundery, and even in the garden Oliver was finding it stifling and unbearable. He had never minded heat in the past, he had absorbed it like a salamander even in the burning sunshine of the Mediterranean, but this year, because his options for getting cool were limited, he became languid and irritable, lost his appetite, and had little energy even for painting. It was made no better by the knowledge that, not so far away, the cool sea surged around the rocks and onto the beaches, and other people were swimming and diving and surfing and sailing, making full use of the opportunities afforded by the blazing summer days. He seemed to want to do nothing but lie in the shade through the heat of the day, lost in private thoughts that didn't seem to please him very much, with a sullen look on his face.

Chel felt sorry for him, of course, but her sympathy was definitely qualified. She was feeling the heat as well as him, and she felt that she could hardly rub salt into an open wound by rushing off to the beach and going swimming when he, for the moment, could not - or would not, but it came to the same thing. A thundery headache of her own, and a heat-induced lassitude gave rise to an unidentified conviction that all this was somehow his fault, feeding a familiar resentment that had led them into serious trouble back in Embridge and that she had believed left behind there. Thrown too much together, a major row was, as then, perilously close. She told herself that he was as selfish as an invalid as he had been as an adventurer, and a whole lot less fun!

There was nobody there to shake them both out of it. Judy and Keith were on holiday in Spain, Maggie up-country on a visit to her parents with the children, Jack away on a course. The spare room, when she went up there in search of she knew not what, was deserted. There was only Oliver, surly and preoccupied, moody, falling a long way short of the standards set by the heroes of romance, wanting nothing from her but to be left alone, deeply depressed by pain, heat and circumstances, and almost impossible to live with.

It was inevitable that there should come a breaking point. There was a day when the enervating, breathless heat had built up to a peak, when huge anvils of cloud clustered on the low horizon, and the blue sky overhead had a brazen look to it. It was so close, both inside and out, that it felt difficult to breathe. Oliver, weary with the heat and with depression, had taken himself and his paints into the garden, but was doing nothing with them. He had sat out there for most of the morning, limp and motionless and virtually speechless, while Chel pulled weeds with a vicious fury and sweated until her hair stuck to her hot forehead and her temper sizzled. Not that the garden really needed weeding, she told herself morosely, but murdering something, even a weed, made her feel better.

Or did it?

In the house, the eternal housework was no doubt lurking in wait for her, but she was growing to hate housework. Never very domesticated, it was beginning to spell prison bars for her. She sat back on her heels, wiping her hand across her hot face and leaving a muddy smear. There was going to be a storm, she could feel it, thunderstorms always gave her this caged-tigerish feeling in the stomach, made her want to bite people and be angry. Unfortunate, then, that she was confined to this house and garden with the one person whom she mustn't bite under any circumstances. Poor Oliver, disabled and insecure, who mustn't be upset.

She shot him a look across the lawn, sorry and annoyed in a curious mixture. He didn't look nearly so well as he had done, there was a dragged look about him, a listlessness, that she hadn't seen since they left Embridge. As dreary and bored as she, perhaps, but at least he had his painting to amuse him if he would only pull himself together. A spurt of irritation caught her like a thunderflash, and she heard herself saying,

'Why don't you get on with something, instead of just lying there?' and Oliver came right back at her as if he had only been waiting for the excuse.

'How can anyone concentrate on anything, with you fussing around them wasting time?'

It was the kind of snappish retaliation that, up until now, had sent both of them running for cover, backing away with conciliatory excuses, but the caged tiger was looking for an excuse to fight. Chel felt it flexing its claws.

'You look ill,' she told him, not at all sympathetically.

'Well, I'm not! And if I was, is that a reason for you to hang round me?'

Muscles rippling beneath striped skin, the purring snarl of frustration. A twitching tail beginning to lash itself into a rhythm of rage. Not an Embridge tiger this time, destructive and wounding, but a thunder tiger, tensing itself for the spring with claws half-sheathed.

'You've hardly spoken to me for days,' said Chel, in the tone adopted by neglected wives the world over.

'What did you want me to say?'

'Anything - anything you like!' said Chel, wildly. 'You sit there, day after day, painting, painting, or staring into space, in your own world somewhere, and it's getting on my nerves!'

'Obviously,' said Oliver.

'What do you mean - obviously?' she flashed back.

'Just that - obviously.' Sticky discomfort, a thumping headache and a strong sense of injustice sent Oliver leaping to meet the tiger. 'Nobody asked you to make a martyr of yourself - if what I choose to do displeases you, go out somewhere. Nobody's stopping you!'

'How can I?'

'Quite easily, you often did. Just open the door and go!'

Dangerous ground. Chel skated over it, breathless with fright.

125

'Where's the point?' she demanded, knowing that she was winding herself up but somehow unable to help it. 'Even if I do go out, you're not the smallest bit interested in anything I might have done. There's no fun in coming back and not even being able to tell you about it!'

'So what do you do, that's so earth-shaking?'

He had, Chel realised, used a typical male ploy of turning the whole thing round so that it was herself, not he, who was on the defensive. She turned it back with vigour.

'I do things for you, to try to help you, and you haven't even the grace to *pretend* to be interested!' She drew a breath. 'You're not interested in a thing I do, in or out of the house, and since it's all quite as much for you as for - '

'Is that meant to imply that I don't do anything?'

'No, of course it isn't.'

'Then what did you mean? All right - so I don't do anything. I bloody well can't do anything, and you know it! Do you think I enjoy being stuck here all the time, watching everybody else running around and having fun - '

' - oh, if you're going to start in with the self-pity - '

'Self-pity!'shouted Oliver, releasing his hold on caution and even on common sense. 'Never mind about *self*-pity, a bit from you now and again wouldn't come amiss!'

'If I pitied you, you'd hate it! You hate it from anyone.'

'You're not just anyone, you're my wife.'

'Oh, the slave, nobody!'

'*Now* who's wallowing in self-pity?'

Chel had long since given up on the weeding. Now, she stood in the middle of the lawn in a red-haired rage, screaming at him, exulting in the dangerous freedom of self-expression.

'All you think about - *care* about - is painting, painting, painting! You'll talk to Maggie about painting by the hour, but you never talk to me - '

'At least it leaves you free - '

'I'm never free!' cried Chel, on a wail. 'I'm degenerating into some second-class citizen who's good enough to sweep the house and dig the garden, but too ignorant and uncouth to be taken into your confidence!'

'Now, look here - '

'No, *you* look here!' The pent-up, scarcely recognised grievances of weeks suddenly boiled to the surface. 'Ever since you first picked up a brush, you've shut me out - ever since you've been painting you've gone further and further away and shut me out! Even if I try to help you can't be bothered with me, you snub me and treat me like a moron, and the only person you'll talk to about what interests you is Maggie - Maggie - always Maggie!'

'So who bloody started it in the first place?' roared Oliver, thoroughly incensed after the manner of someone with a sneaking suspicion that they are somehow in the wrong after all.

'I bloody did!' Chel roared back. 'I bloody did, and I wish I never had! I've always taken second place in your life, ever since we met - first it was diving and sailing, now it's painting! You don't take me into your confidence about anything, even going off all round the world on some stupid race, or where you decide we're going to live, even things like that I'm not important! I feel like a chattel! You don't need people, Oliver Nankervis, not even a wife you don't need - you never did! You haven't time for them! The trouble with people is they have feelings - ships and water and paint are inanimate, they don't get hurt, or cry - they don't want to look after you, or worry about you, they leave you alone, and *alone* is the only thing you've ever wanted to be! I don't know why you ever married me - '

'Shut up!' said Oliver, between his teeth. 'Just shut up for a minute, and listen! What the hell's the matter with you?'

'I'm bored, that's all!' shouted Chel, revelling in the noise she was making. 'Life's boring - you're boring - everything's boring!'

'Shut up!' he shouted back at her. 'How can anyone get a word in with you ranting away all the time?'

'I'm not ranting!' ranted Chel.

Oliver knew such a strong impulse to jump up and shake her until her teeth rattled that imagination had taken him halfway there even while reality kept him sitting in his chair. He positively snarled at her.

'Stop being so bloody silly!'

'I'm not being silly.' She caught her breath on an unexpected sob, struggled to calm her voice and speak reasonably, shaken at the fury she could see in his face not realising that at least half of it was directed against himself. She spoke more quietly. 'Yes. I'm bored. And lonely, and I feel that I'm wasting my life. I'm not blaming you, it happened to both of us. All I want is for you to understand. You take all my sympathy, and I'm not denying that you deserve it, but you spare none of your own for me in return.' Her voice broke into a howl, suddenly she could take no more. The one thing she wasn't going to do was to stand and weep and plead in front of him while he was looking at her like that. 'Oh, it's useless! The only person who matters to you, is you!' She broke off and ran blindly for the house and sanctuary. Upstairs, where he couldn't follow, she would be safe -

'Cheryl!' Oliver shouted. She didn't stop. The tiger had slunk back

127

into his cage, ashamed, and all she wanted to do was to hide.

She went straight up the stairs and in through the first open door like a rabbit into its burrow, slamming it behind her with a shattering crash, and collapsed onto the bathmat in a heap. She was shaking, she found - shaking, and all of a sudden, rather frightened. The spectre of their life in Embridge gibbered in the corners, behind it, the memory of the unresolved quarrel, the first they had ever had, on the day of his accident - for want of a better word - grinned and mocked, reminding her of the long hours of useless weeping that she had almost forgotten in the horrors that had followed. He had run out that time, intent on his own affairs, glad to get away. The second time they had fought like that, she had been the one to run out, and what she - and he - had done then would forever be on her conscience. And now, a third time.

She lay there for some time, her head hidden in her folded arms, crouched on the floor beside the bath, sobbing and miserably sorry for herself. Boredom, loneliness, frustration, fear of the future, jealousy, unspecified disappointment, all drenched the bathmat for some time, and then quite suddenly, like the last bit of water gurgling down the plug, they were gone. She realised instead that her head was aching, and she had almost cried herself sick.

This was stupid - childish. She reached up a shaking hand and pulled the towel from the rail, mopping her hot, wet face with it, gulping back heavy sobs, and then sat up with her back pressed against the bath and thought about what had taken place, still convulsively shuddering with suppressed sobs and sniffing unromantically.

She had quarrelled with Oliver - again. She, and he, had set about it with thoroughness. They had gone at it hammer and tongs, covering a wide range of issues, including housework, painting, and you-only-talk-to-Maggie, and one or two others that she hadn't realised until now were issues at all, and not one of them had even Oliver tried more than half-heartedly to link with his disablement. They could have quarrelled about the same things in almost exactly the same words if he had been as fit and strong as he had been the day she married him.

An ordinary quarrel.

Anger had finally drained away, leaving her limp and spent. Chel got to her feet, went over to the basin, and splashed cold water over her sore eyes and reddened face. As she dried it, she peered over the towel at her reflection in the mirror, without admiration. She looked terrible, and she felt worse. Men, on the whole, weathered rows better than women did, but she had never encountered Oliver in the aftermath of one, for one reason and another, and she had no idea what to expect. She ought to go down to him. This had been one row that he couldn't run out on.

While she wept and raged, the light in the windows had gone dark, the blue sky swallowed in black clouds, text-book anvils full of menace. It was raining, she saw, great thundery drops, not hard yet, but threatening worse to come. She stood on the landing for a moment or two, listening, but there was no sound downstairs to tell her if Oliver had come indoors or was still in the garden in the rain. The house was completely quiet. Uncannily quiet. It had about it that waiting stillness that precedes a really good storm, and beyond the open landing windows, the heavy, swollen raindrops plopped onto dusty leaves unstirred by a single breath of wind. Temper and crying hadn't improved her headache, which was starting to verge on migraine.

The house felt empty apart from herself, but in the half hour or so since she had run upstairs, there was nothing that Oliver could have done, nowhere he could have gone. No racing out into the streets and away this time, the garden gate was about his current limit. And she kept all his medication in the bathroom cupboard. She had never thought about why she did it, but just for a second she felt physically sick.

She realised that she was purposely putting off the moment when she must go down and face him. Deliberately harrowing her own feelings in order to cool her remaining resentment, and it was a mistake. Resentment would either go on its own or remain, just as it did for anybody else. They had listened for too long to people telling them how badly hurt Oliver was, and it had frightened them both into highly artificial behaviour. The day they quarrelled, she had once told herself, they could count themselves on the road to a real recovery. Well, here was the day, and here the moment of truth, and if once she let what Oliver had been through serve as an excuse for anything he did, she might as well give up.

She went quietly down the stairs and stood for a moment at the bottom, waiting for some reaction, but Oliver hadn't heard her come. He had come in from the wet, she was relieved to see, and laid down on his bed, half-propped so that he could see through the open window. He was staring out, totally abstracted, biting at his fingernails. Because this turned his head away from her, she couldn't see his face, just the line of his jaw and the curve of his cheek.

'Oliver?' she said.

He turned his head and looked at her, strained and speechless, very much on the defensive, hopelessly at a disadvantage because his fear of losing her finally had so many barbs to it, and his natural male dominance was being humiliated yet again. He made no further move, waiting for her to give the lead.

She didn't know what would be the right thing to do, or what might tumble the whole house of cards. She walked across the room without saying anything and sat on the bed beside him, putting her arms round him, and for a while they stayed like that. Then she said, quite naturally,

'I'm sorry.'

The jumbled confusion to which their lives had been reduced shivered and began to fall back into place at last. Oliver reached up and gripped her arm tightly, without speaking.

'We were quarrelling,' said Chel.

'I know.'

'It doesn't matter. I still think you're the best thing since sliced bread.'

'If it comes to that, I'm sorry too. I know I'm a bastard, but it's this stupid helplessness... it diminishes me, Chel. I hate being dependent, not just for me, for both of us. It's cruel.'

From anger and resentment, Chel suddenly found herself swept with love. The contrast made her speechless, allowing Oliver space in which to continue.

'I feel as if I'm in a permanent dead end,' he said. 'I can't turn round and get out, and for all your help and your generosity, it isn't even a bearable dead end. Being made to realise you're in it too, simply makes it bloody.'

The sound of the rain roaring onto the glass roof of the conservatory, was the only thing to break a long pause. Then Oliver said,

'I'm not me any more. I can't seem to get to grips with the person I'm having to be instead.'

The purpose of storms, of any kind, was to clear the air. Chel ventured a remark, inexplicably heavy-hearted.

'It's this house, isn't it? Things have gone wrong since we came here, just like they did for those other people.'

'You've been listening to too many ghost stories,' said Oliver. His fingers were digging into her upper arm so hard that later on she found a group of pitch-black bruises there, thumb and four fingers. 'It's nothing to do with the house this time, I like it here - so far as it goes. It's me. I feel as if I've fallen off the edge of the world - my world, my God, was it flat all the time? I'm in limbo, I don't belong - you and Judy and Keith and Jack, you all talk and laugh together about things that don't - can't - concern me any more, so that when Maggie comes and talks about things that I can still have, and do... well...' He let the sentence trail into silence, and Chel said nothing.

The rain was getting harder, Chel thought that she saw a flash of lightning, and in the distance a faint growl of thunder sounded. The air already felt cooler.

'If I tell you something,' said Oliver, slowly, 'will it make you feel better, or worse?'

'It depends what it is,' said Chel, cautiously.

'Might-have-been...'

'Don't you think things like that are best forgotten?'

'I did think so, yes - but - ' He broke off, and started again. 'How did you find out about the Round-the-World Race? I never told you. I would have liked to, but there never seemed to be a good moment, and then...'

'I found the letter, the day we moved in. It fell out of a book. From James Brown, or whatever his name was.'

'I wasn't planning to leave you, you know,' said Oliver. 'I know what everyone said about me - but I wouldn't do that. Not unless you chose.'

'*I* chose?' said Chel, stupidly. 'You mean, you wouldn't have gone, if I'd said you shouldn't?' She didn't believe him.

'I mean,' said Oliver, deliberately, 'they said, if you remember, that I could choose my own crew. Do you think you would have liked it? Ocean racing is bloody hard work, mind you.'

She stared at him, all the ground cut from under her feet, her mouth open.

'Me?' she said.

'It doesn't take that long - months, at most. And I should have liked to show you the Southern Ocean... it must be the most beautiful place on earth,' said Oliver, not looking at her. 'The baby - Jeremy - he would have been nearly eighteen months old by the time we sailed. I thought maybe your mother, or Susan... they could have brought him to the stops...' He broke off, and then said, in a strangled voice, 'They must be qualifying now.'

Chel sat perfectly still. All this time - ever since she had known him - she had believed what she had been repeatedly told. *He'll leave you, he'll go off on some adventure, he'll never stay at home...* and instead... *I should have liked to show you the Southern Ocean.* She knew that it would have been totally impractical, but his loss was her loss too, and she sat still with the thunder grumbling round the house and plumbed the full depth of it.

The rain spattered on the windows through a long, long silence, while she wondered what she could possibly say. Set against the banality of their present existence it was brutal. Pointless now to wonder whether she would or even could have gone or not, it was enough that he had wanted her.

The silence went on too long. Chel got off the bed and went to close the french doors in the conservatory, for a wind was getting up and blowing the rain through onto the tiles. She pulled them shut, and the roar of water on glass, thus enclosed, nearly drowned her words as she walked back through.

'At least you have your painting,' she said.

She knew that it was both clumsy and inadequate, but she wasn't prepared for his reaction. His laughter was immediate and derisive, and she had the impression that the derision was for himself.

'Painting is a hobby.'

Chel walked slowly towards him.

'If Mr. Cosgrove Gallery can sell them for you - ' Oliver's face stopped her speaking.

'Dear Chel,' said Oliver, but quite kindly, 'I know what's been in your mind, but believe me, it's just a dream. All right, he might sell the odd picture for me - four, five a year perhaps, in a good season and if I was lucky. At maybe a couple of hundred pounds a go on a good day, say, and with him taking twenty per-cent, and deduct from that the cost of materials and framing - oh, at a discount, of course - and what are you left with? It isn't worth the bother - the pictures aren't worth it.'

It dawned on Chel slowly, but with conviction, that this was all the cause of their present problem, and that for all his improved health, Oliver's wings were still clipped. The free-as-air adventurer with whom she had fallen in love and married had lost the knack of dreaming dreams and making them come true. Grounded. Worrying about what he was doing to her, worrying about the future, trying to be what he was not in order that she might have security. And yet, in their original flat high above the harbour they had lived on a lot less than they had now, and never been happier - perhaps never would be happier. Now - well, now he had ceased to believe in himself, needlessly, weighted down by a sense of responsibility and his loss of freedom.

'But your pictures are good, they'll fetch a lot more than that,' she said, remembering the prices she had seen in the gallery. 'Anyway, maybe you'll be a runaway success and be famous all over again, and make a fortune, you don't know.' She was taken with her own idea and tried to sound encouraging, but Oliver simply looked at her as if she was speaking a foreign language.

'I don't think having more money, or not having it, is the solution to anything,' he said. 'Luckily, for in case you hadn't already realised, I've blown that as well as everything else. You didn't exactly pick out one of life's success stories when you married me.'

Flash, crash, rumble... When the noise had died away, Chel said, 'Don't be so silly. You must know you're good, anyone can see it.'

'Oh, the boy is quite talented, in an untutored sort of way,' said Oliver, but without enthusiasm. 'Probably, I should have done what everyone tried to tell me at school - but I didn't listen to people much in those days, and hell, how could I tell this was in store for me?'

'What did they try to tell you?' asked Chel, curiously.

'To try for a place at art college.'

'So, why didn't you? After all, you went on to university, so you didn't have a face set against higher education, or anything.'

'Oh...' He gave the matter some thought, and finally answered, 'I didn't want to teach, or go into commercial art.'

And you didn't want to owe anything to poor Helen, thought Chel, but it was old history and she didn't say anything. What was done, was done. She said, instead,

'So you chose Political Science instead, and where did you think that would take you? It's a Mickey Mouse subject if there ever was one!' And that was why; she had answered herself. Oliver's answer was only a little different.

'A scary subject, actually - and that's me all over. Still is, come to that. A mobile - more or less mobile - disaster area.'

Another huge crash of thunder, almost simultaneous with its attendant lightning, interrupted them, and Chel flinched, she had never liked thunderstorms. Almost, she lost the thread of the discussion, grasping it with an effort to say,

'Even so, I don't see that that means that you've blown everything. You've still got the talent - you're not exactly over the hill, for heaven's sake, you've all the time in the world to catch up and learn.'

'From whom?' asked Oliver, in a tone of voice that startled her.

'From Maggie... from books.'

'If Maggie could help me, she wouldn't be teaching school kids.' He said it quite naturally, without any conceit, stating a simple fact as if he were quite unaware of the implications, and Chel was startled all over again. She could have laughed at him and told him not to be so pleased with himself, but she didn't. His utter detachment and the recollection of Helen's enormous talent alike prevented her.

'Ah...' she said, and could think of nothing to follow it. Oliver went on, sounding disturbingly more like his old self than he had done for a long while now.

'I don't know if it's a fault in me, or a virtue, you tell me. But if I do something, I want to do it best. I'm a professional at heart, I can never be an amateur. Not when it matters. I can't change that, not even if I wanted to. And I don't.'

'Perhaps something will turn up...' said Chel, helplessly, out of her depth, and Oliver, rather to her relief, gave her a perfectly ordinary grin, and said,

'I bet nobody ever said that to Leonardo.'

'I bet his wife said it all the time,' said Chel, before another crash of thunder silenced her. This time, it was so close and so loud that she fled the last few feet across the room and scrambled onto the bed beside him, burying her face in his shoulder. 'I hate storms!'

'I well remember,' said Oliver, who had asked her to marry him on the heels of a thunderstorm, when her behaviour had been very similar.

Chel stayed there in his sheltering arms, her ear against his heart hearing the steady thump of the life that had failed to die in him, indefinably happier than she had been for weeks, in spite of the roaring storm, for he had spoken to her at last about what was closest to his heart, dismissing Maggie in one annihilating sentence.

And then, something very strange happened.

She had the oddest sensation, as if time had slipped, and she was looking back on today from some moment in the future, laughing about it from the solid base of a security that neither of them had ever dreamed of, or even wished for. *Sir Oliver and Lady Nankervis* - the names whisked into her mind and were gone again, together with a clear picture of Oliver, curiously in monochrome, several years older and more good-looking than ever, with a bloom of fulfilment and success on him... and the first step along the path that led to that was so close that before they went to bed tonight, they would have taken it -

'Chel!' said Oliver, and gave her a shake. The shock, although it was a gentle one, made her gasp, she had been so far away.

'What?' She raised her head, looking straight into his eyes, so close to her own.

'You weren't breathing - you weren't moving - '

'Catatonic,' said Chel, snuggling closer. 'Isn't this nice and wicked, in the middle of the afternoon?' She had scared him, she suddenly realised, so no moment this to tell him she thought she had seen into the future, and anyway, how silly it would sound! But the effort to be normal was immense.

Was that how fairground soothsayers worked, she found herself wondering, and if so, had the one they had once consulted in fun seen what would happen to Oliver? If she had, she hadn't told him. What an awful responsibility, if that kind of thing became a habit.

It felt odd to think that, and yet at the same time not to believe wholly in what she had seen. A sceptic, and she could easily make herself be one, could say with truth that she had imagined it because it was what she wanted. Except that she had never wanted anything so way-out as to be *Lady Nankervis*. The sceptical Chel would then say, *not consciously*, of course.

It must be down to the storm. Electrical disturbances, or something.

Except that there was something about this house, and she wasn't alone in finding it so.

'If your mind is set on being wicked...' said Oliver, and the rest of the thunderstorm passed almost unnoticed.

It poured with rain and roared with thunder for most of the afternoon, the noisy culmination of the sultry, unbearable week, but by four o'clock the skies were clearing, leaving the air cool and fresh. In the same way, the afternoon's quarrel had lightened the atmosphere indoors. More fully aware of how each other were feeling, Chel and Oliver were also more at ease with each other than they had been for a long time, almost as if their mutual confessions had carried with them the relief of absolution. Indeed, a question had been answered that had tormented Chel on and off since she had known him, and in way that she had never for a moment expected. The knowledge that he considered her so much a partner that he would, literally, have taken her to the ends of the earth with him - if she had wanted to go - was a gift beyond price that vindicated her own belief in him that others, who thought they knew him better, had constantly tried to undermine.

She wondered, as she started to prepare their evening meal, if her spur-of-the-moment vision would ever be reality, and the idea began to take root in her mind, not as something that would definitely happen, not graven-in-stone certain, but as a possibility. Everyone needed a dream, and Oliver more than most right now. She tried to see again if this was something that might come true, but if she had truly caught a glimpse of the future, she found that she couldn't yet do so at will. Perhaps, she thought, with an involuntary giggle, she should get a crystal ball to help her, and then, immediately, disturbingly, that *if* it was true, she shouldn't have long to wait to find out. *Before they went to bed tonight.* It had been, in her thoughts, absolutely clear.

'Just look at you!' she said, going back with a colander of peapods to where Oliver still lay luxuriously on his by now rather rumpled bed. 'Never mind round the world, you look as if round the room would be an achievement - like a rather decadent sultan!'

'Really? Well, I'm willing to give decadence another go, if you are.'

'Certainly not, what can you be thinking of?' said Chel. 'There's our dinner to get - you can shell the peas, if you're just planning to loll about for the rest of the evening.'

'Nothing very decadent about shelling peas,' said Oliver, regretfully. 'All right, then. If you insist. I just hope I don't get them in the bed.'

'Like the princess,' said Chel. 'You could get off it, of course.'

Oliver had found that the quarrel and its pleasant aftermath had depleted his energy, and he couldn't be bothered. He smiled at her, lazily, but made no attempt to move. She was about to settle down to help him with the peas when the doorbell rang.

Since apart from their close friends, who were away, as yet they had few visitors, Chel went to open it haunted by her constant, irrational fear that she would find Oliver's parents on the doorstep, a treat that they had so far been spared, but which could only be a matter of time. Not this time, however.

The man on the doorstep was a total stranger. Mid to late sixties, slim and dapper with greying dark hair, gold rimmed glasses, and a frighteningly elegant city suit. Behind him in the road Chel could see a large, expensive car, that looked as if it had probably been speckless before it encountered the post-downpour Cornish lanes. She thought he must have stopped to ask the way. But -

'Mrs. Nankervis?' he asked.

'Yes,' said Chel, but warily. Double-glazing? Insurance? Praise the Lord, and thus save your soul?

'Good afternoon.' He held out his hand. 'Gifford Thomas. I wonder if your husband would be in, and able to see me, dear girl?'

Chel took the proffered hand, not knowing what else to do with it, and had her own warmly shaken, while she wondered what this unmistakeable old queen could possibly want with Oliver.

'If he should not be back from work yet, perhaps I might wait?' Giff smiled at her, a smile that she thought had something in common with the one reputed to be on the face of the tiger. 'I've come down from London, just for one night, and I would particularly like to speak with him - oh, I'm so sorry!' He took a card from his breast pocket and placed it in her hands. 'My card.'

Gifford Thomas. The Ladbourne Gallery, and an address that Chel thought, vaguely sounded like the West End, but she wasn't too familiar with London. She looked at the card a little helplessly.

'You'd better come in,' she said.

Oliver had lost the peas somewhere, probably they would find them under the duvet, but he had not had time to do anything about the state of the bed, or to get himself off it and over to his chair. Chel thought that the way they had spent the late afternoon must be obvious to anyone. The air of rampant, but interrupted, sex was to a degree at least misleading, and she felt a giggle, long unfamiliar, rising under her ribs. Gifford Thomas, she was interested to see, didn't bat an eyelid.

'My husband,' said Chel, waving a hand. 'This is Mr. Thomas, Oliver, he wants to see you.' She gave him the card, and he looked at it blankly.

'You won't know me,' said Giff, and again extended his hand, exuding grace and charm in about equal quantities. Oliver, embarrassed at being caught at a disadvantage, took it awkwardly.

'Excuse me, won't you,' he said. 'A bit of back trouble... I'll just get up.' He had dropped the crutches on the floor and couldn't reach them. He gave Chel a murderous look that she didn't deserve.

'No please - I shouldn't dream of disturbing you, dear boy.' Giff seated himself gracefully on the foot of Chel's bed, in a move that somehow disarmed any awkwardness. Chel didn't quite like to ask for the vanished peas so that she could finish shelling them, and offered Mr. Thomas a chair, which he declined.

'No no, thank you. I shall be wonderful right here, my dear girl.' He turned immediately back to Oliver. 'A slipped disc is it, dear boy? That can be very painful, I know, but at least it means I found you.' He crossed one elegant leg over the other, very much at ease. 'You must be wondering why I'm here.'

'Why are you?'Oliver asked. Chel began to retreat towards the kitchen, but Gifford Thomas stopped her.

'Please stay, Mrs. Nankervis, you may find this interesting too.'

Chel sat down on the sofa. A good thing the times of meals in this household weren't immutable like the tides, she thought ruefully. Gifford Thomas smiled at them both, impartially.

'I had your name and your address from George Cosgrove at the little gallery in Penzance,' he told them. 'I should explain, first, that I have a gallery in London - fine arts and paintings, exhibitions, you know.' He dismissed it with a deprecating wave. 'We have earned ourselves something of a reputation for discovering new talent over the years - not simply innovation, or daring, the thumbs-up at the establishment, you understand, I'm speaking of the real McCoy, there's not so much of that as you might think. Perhaps once in a decade, we discover someone whose work will outlast time.' He named a couple that even Chel had heard of, and went on. 'My old friend George Cosgrove scouts for me. There are a great many artists in Cornwall, as no doubt you know, good, resoundingly bad and sadly indifferent. Some of them take their pictures to George to be framed, many more will exhibit in his gallery. If he comes across something that he thinks will interest me, he gives me a call, and if it seems worth my while I come down to see for myself. Many wasted journeys, but always the chance that one day he will have found that one in a decade for me.'

Something jumped inside Chel, sending her pulses galloping crazily, and she gave Oliver a quick look. His face betrayed nothing but polite interest. Mr. Thomas was watching him too, like a cat at a mousehole - no, a lion at a waterhole. His smile deepened - the smile, Chel decided, of a hard bargainer on the trail of a juicy deal. He said,

'I came down from London today, Mr. Nankervis, to see some of your work. I cannot, of course, base my judgement on two paintings. I was hoping you could show me some more.'

'I haven't done that many,' said Oliver, and Giff said, very gently, that he realised that.

'They're upstairs,' said Oliver. 'My wife will show you.'

'Perhaps Mrs. Nankervis will allow me to help her to bring them down?'

'I can manage,' said Chel, getting to her feet. 'They aren't any of them framed. Do you want them all?' She looked at Oliver, and he shrugged his shoulders.

'Might as well.'

Chel went upstairs and stacked as many pictures as she thought she could carry safely in one go onto the portfolio of his watercolours. Downstairs, she could hear Mr. Thomas talking and Oliver answering, although the words were indistinguishable, but when she got down again with her pile it appeared that they had been discussing nothing more interesting than the afternoon's storm.

'Ah...' said Giff, rising to meet her and take the tumbling stack from her. 'Now, let's see...'

The pictures were ranged around the furniture, and Giff sat for some while, turning the watercolours over on his knee, gazing at the oils, meditating deep within himself. Finally, he said,

'This is everything?'

'Except for a couple over there, in the conservatory, that aren't finished,' said Oliver, and Chel went to fetch them. One of them, she saw, was the mixture as before, but the second one was in a completely different mood. A quiet bay, full of mist, with the tide creeping up underneath and spilling around mud and shingle. Giff looked at that one for some while, and Chel suddenly said,

'There's all those drawings you did.'

Giff didn't wait for anything Oliver might say.

'Find them for me, will you, dear girl?' he asked, absently. Chel found them pushed into a drawer. The room was beginning to look like a rather untidy shop by this time, and she had to sit on the foot of Oliver's bed to watch Giff go through them. Finally, he shuffled the drawings together and put them back into their folder.

'Of course, you've been nicely taught by somebody,' he said. 'George Cosgrove could undoubtedly sell your work as it is, and make a name for you locally. You have both style and sensitivity.'

'But no technique,' said Oliver.

'Oh, I wouldn't say that, dear boy.' Giff narrowed his eyes and looked again at the half-finished misty bay. 'Let's say, your work lacks as yet that certain something that would lift it above the good average. You should, I think, work under an expert. Of course, I realise that you have commitments, but I have to tell you, Mr. Nankervis, if you did as I could advise you, maybe a year, two years from now, I would guarantee an exhibition that, if it didn't precisely set the art world ablaze, would certainly kindle a small, warm fire. I think that it would be an acceptable gamble.'

'So, what would you advise?' asked Oliver. He sounded calm and objective, but there was a shiver of excitement about him that Chel hadn't seen for months.

'There's no way that you can consider this a hobby,' said Giff, thoughtfully, almost as if he was talking exclusively to himself. 'To be at the top of any art or profession requires a total dedication. I know nothing about your circumstances, of course. Do you have children, Mrs. Nankervis?'

Chel was startled at this apparent *non sequitur.*

'No,' she said, shortly. He gave her a strange look, as if he had read more into that brief syllable than she had intended.

'That, of course, makes it easier. There are grants available, and I imagine that you could be eligible. I have an old friend who has a studio in St. Ives, a well-known painter of considerable standing, who will occasionally take pupils of promise, and I would suggest that I send you to her with a letter of introduction. She would, I think, agree to let you work in her studio.' He looked from Chel to Oliver. 'I realise this is something that can't be decided all in a moment. I can't promise that you will turn out to be the one in a decade. If you gave up your normal employment and took my advice, and in the end I was wrong, you could stand to lose a great deal.'

Oliver said, slowly,

'That isn't a problem. My employment has already given *me* up.'

Giff rose to his feet, graceful and urbane, placing the folder of drawings carefully on the foot of the bed.

'You must discuss it with your wife, of course. I shall be staying in

Penzance overnight - if I leave a telephone number, perhaps you could give me a ring in the morning? After that, of course, I shall be back in London, but you can take all the time you need. I can always write or telephone to Anona Fingall, it will make little difference in the end.' He turned to Chel, holding out his hand again, smiling. 'I hope we shall meet again, dear Mrs. Nankervis.' And to Oliver, 'Think very carefully. I should like to arrange that exhibition.' He paused, and coughed delicately. 'Excuse me, dear boy, but are you sure we haven't met before? I wasn't going to mention it, but there is definitely something...?' He allowed his words to tail off into a question mark, and Oliver said, firmly,

'No, I'm sure we haven't.'

Giff allowed his eyes to rest, thoughtfully, on the picture of *Lawley's Girl* above the mantelpiece. He said, half-apologetically,

'Then I think, perhaps, I may once have known your mother, you have a look of her, I believe. I didn't, of course, know your full name when I came here, but surely, you're the Oliver Nankervis who sailed around the world - Helen Macken's son?'

'So?' asked Oliver, stiffening, but Giff had more tact - and cunning, be it said - to trespass where warning signs were so clearly displayed. It was an unexpectedly interesting situation, he thought, it would be fascinating to see how it developed. He shook Oliver's hand with composure.

'So, I'm doubly glad to have made your acquaintance, my dear fellow. That explains a great deal. I shall look forward to hearing from you.'

He left, kissing Chel's hand at the door, and Chel went back into the house and looked at the shambles his visit had left behind.

'Do you think he knew - about me?' asked Oliver, directly. Chel sat down on the arm of the sofa, clearing up could wait.

'I think he must have, don't you? He must have known as soon as he realised who you were.'

'He didn't say anything.'

'Perhaps he feels it doesn't matter.'

'Anona Fingall may feel that it matters.'

Chel privately thought that, whatever Anona Fingall did or didn't feel, the whole scheme had serious flaws in it. Driving to St. Ives and back, presumably on a daily basis, sounded so simple, but it this case it was far from it. Apart from the fact that it would tie up her time as well as Oliver's, which Gifford Thomas wouldn't have appreciated, they were not discussing the harmless and gentle pursuit of a hobby here, but a serious programme of work. Art was a job like any other, if you wanted to succeed, or so she supposed. Oliver, at present, wouldn't cope with that, and Anona Fingall, whoever she was, would quite possibly not want the responsibility anyway.

'Have you ever heard of her?' she asked, to cover an awkward pause. Oliver frowned.

'Vaguely, but as you know yourself, I'm a bit of a philistine about art. Still life, I think, or portraits. I don't really know.'

'And do you think that the flowery Mr. Thomas meant what he said?'

'I didn't get the feeling that Mr. Thomas was in the habit of saying things he doesn't mean. Did you?'

'No,' said Chel. She met his eyes consideringly. 'What are you going to do - dear boy?'

'What do you think? It concerns you as well.'

Chel thought. On the face of it, Mr. Thomas had suggested the impossible, but his visit had come right on cue. She could hardly say that to Oliver. She hedged.

'What do you want?' she asked him.

'I'm afraid...' said Oliver, and went on more firmly. 'I'm afraid to want anything, in case I can't have it.'

'You want to work under Anona Fingall?'

'More than anything in the world.'

Go with the flow. She either believed she had been in touch with some truth, or she thought it was all baloney. One or the other, she couldn't have it both ways. She got to her feet.

'Then,' she said, 'we must leave it up to her. She'll know how many beans make five the minute she sets eyes on you, if Mr. Thomas doesn't tell her first. She can only say no. And even if she does, you're getting better all the time now. If you wait a bit - '

'I'm sick of waiting,' said Oliver, more quietly than he felt. 'I want here and now. I want to be able to do something - to do this - that will make my spirit whole again. I never wanted anything half as much, and if I can't have it because of that bloody stupid mugging - ' He broke off, biting his lip, and she felt an already half-sensed desperation leaping into full flood. 'Chel, I'm sorry. I must have it.'

And if he couldn't, what then? Chel asked herself, as she carried the pictures back up the stairs. A year from now, and what promised to be a violent and abortive explosion might have been a sunburst. Now... the premature release of unsuspected brilliance would have to be served at any cost, she knew it. The true fire, and with it, the true temperament. *I must have it* - she had thought that she had known how he felt, and she hadn't had the smallest idea. If he could have this one impossible thing, he might even count the rest well lost. If it had to wait, it would serve a different end. A good end - not today's end.

And yet, she had seen....

'She mustn't say no,' said Chel, into the silence of the empty little room, knowing that even if Anona Fingall said yes, that was only the beginning of the problem.

Back downstairs again, Oliver was ruining his nails and had forgotten what he had done with the peas on the spur of the moment. Chel found them eventually under her pillow, and shelled them herself.

IX

It was Chel, not Oliver, who in the end went to see Anona Fingall. Gifford Thomas, still without comment on what he must surely know to be Oliver's physical condition, had set up the meeting before he returned to London, and advised on what pictures would be best to take, and the arrangement had been that Chel would drive Oliver to St. Ives at the appointed time. As it turned out, Oliver awoke that morning with a crippling migraine that nothing would shift, quite probably, Chel thought, because of tension over the importance to him of the coming meeting, and it was quite obvious that he wasn't going anywhere.

They had the address of Anona Fingall's studio, but no telephone number, and she didn't appear, under that name at least, in the directory. An attempt to contact the Ladbourne Gallery proved abortive, there seemed to be nobody there, the phone rang and rang, on and on seemingly forever. Chel, still lacking a crystal ball, had no way of knowing that Gifford Thomas sat beside the phone watching their mobile number showing on his call recorder, making a policy decision not to answer. Giff had been fascinated to find what house he was visiting, and who it was that lived there, and he thought that even if he hadn't already meant to steer the unidentified artist Nankervis in Nonie Fingall's direction, he wouldn't have been able to resist the temptation. He never had been able to resist temptation when it came to meddling with the lives of other people, as the late Matt Sutton could have testified.

Simply to cut the appointment would be unforgivably rude, and might well ruin whatever faint promise the situation seemed to hold. Unable to see what else there was to do, Chel left Oliver to his misery and drove to St. Ives on her own.

When she arrived there, she was glad that she had, however frustrating it was for Oliver. It was the summer holidays now, the little town was seething with crowds of tourists and she had to park the car on the edge of the town and walk. On business she might be, but she had no idea if there was parking space at Anona Fingall's studio, and had no wish to find herself trying to back and turn in the narrow streets. She hefted the pictures under her arm and set off through the wandering crowds of visitors, following a roughly sketched map that Giff had drawn for them.

Anona Fingall, as she discovered eventually, had her studio up a cobbled back street, very steep and narrow, that ran into a small courtyard and out at the other side, getting narrower all the time. Three sides of the courtyard were taken up with the walls of other buildings, the fourth was the studio. It was situated over a gallery, obviously made out of a converted shed or store, for the shop-front had been put in behind the original big sliding doors, which could still be rolled across and padlocked at night. The gallery was given over to a selection of very beautiful, high quality local crafts and paintings, which Chel longed to browse around, and that, at least, was certainly on the phone - had she known it was there. The studio was above, approached by a flight of steep stone steps. She knew that it had to be the right place, for a carved wooden plaque beside the door announced STUDIO *Anona Fingall*, so that there was no possibility of mistake. It was generally an attractive place, in good repair, the granite blocks of its construction clean and well-pointed, the upper storey rendered and whitened. There were bright salmon pink geraniums in tubs spilling down the granite steps.

'Oh shit!' said Chel, inelegantly, looking at them. There just had to be steps, didn't there! Their presence effectively aborted the mission before it had fairly got under way. She went up them anyway, bitterly disappointed, and knocked on the open top of the stable door. The big room beyond was full of light, canvases everywhere, and a big easel with a half-finished still-life of apples and pears on it. The familiar smell of turps and linseed hit her nostrils, and she wrinkled her nose. She could hear someone moving about inside, and after a moment, the person came to the door.

Chel had vaguely imagined Anona Fingall to be young and 'arty', something like Maggie, maybe, but more up-market, but she wasn't a bit like that. She was a tall woman of at least fifty, slender to the point of being thin, with short, curly, white hair still streaked dark at the back, brown eyes, and a lively, intelligent face. She wore jeans and a polo shirt, both liberally smeared with paint. She looked at Chel with an enquiring lift of her eyebrows, still strikingly dark.

'Hullo there.' She looked at the pictures under Chel's arm. 'The gallery's downstairs.'

'I wasn't looking for the gallery,' said Chel. 'Mr. Thomas made an appointment. Well, it was for my husband really, but he couldn't make it.'

'Ah.' Nonie Fingall unlatched the bottom of the door and opened it. 'You'd better come in - please come in,' she added, realising that she had sounded ungracious. She had been irritated with Giff to start with, trying to land her with an unwanted pupil, and now he hadn't even

144

bothered to turn up in person. Sod's law!

Chel, sensing her lack of welcome, wondered just how honest she ought to be, but then, fudging the issue wouldn't alter anything. If there was nothing else to be gained from this meeting there would be an informed opinion, and there might possibly be advice to lighten her own ignorance and help her to help Oliver.

The light, airy studio had an old sofa and two armchairs arranged around an empty fireplace. Nonie waved Chel to a seat. Because she knew she had been ungracious, she now heard herself over-compensating.

'Do sit down. I used to live here, you know, so at least there's a comfortable chair. I'm sorry your husband couldn't make it, Giff seemed to think he was worth getting excited about. Are these the pictures?' She held out her hands for them, and Chel gave them to her, before perching nervously in the indicated chair. Why should it feel like being at the dentist? Nonie ranged the pictures against the wall and stood back, looking at them consideringly. There was the lighthouse, looking quite different since it had been framed, two other oils, and a folder of watercolours and pencil sketches. She studied the oils for some time, took the sketches and looked through them again more closely, and then sat for a while on the arm of a chair, just thinking. Giff had not identified this unknown artist to her, leaving her to come to an objective decision on her own as to whether she bothered to see him or not, but he had, of course, assumed that once they met, she would realise who he was. As things had turned out, she still had no idea. Nankervis was a Cornish name, an unfortunate coincidence that brought back bad memories, but there were many of them about, particularly here in the west. Nor was she impressed by the fact that he hadn't come in person.

'Of course,' she said, at last, 'I should have to meet your husband before I came to any decision. It isn't possible to work with everyone. I like his style.' She looked at Chel thoughtfully. 'Giff looks a bit of a poser, I know, but he's a clever man. He isn't often wrong about painters, he has a built-in sensor for potential success, that's why he's successful himself. Your husband could do worse than go along with him, if not with me, with someone else. How does he feel about it? He must have considered it seriously, or you wouldn't be here.' Not seriously enough, or he would be here himself. Whatever she thought of the pictures, there were a lot of talented people who lacked that essential spark that drove them forward. She couldn't be bothered with them.

Chel thought that she had gauged Oliver's feelings on the subject fairly accurately. They had discussed it enough in the past two days, and one thing stood out like a beacon.

'He hasn't thought as far ahead as Mr. Thomas and his gallery,' she said. 'He hasn't thought any further than working with you - with any first class painter. He has a tremendous thirst for knowledge, I suppose. He knows what he doesn't know is necessary to do the work that he feels he should be able to do. It's the thing itself, not the money it might make, that drives him.'

'Did he say that?' asked Nonie, interested.

'Not in so many words, no.'

But he still wasn't here himself. Nonie returned her gaze to the oil paintings against the wall. They included the half-finished misty bay with its creeping tide and perfect stillness. It reminded her of that last morning on the beach with Matt, and she felt the twist of an old pain deep inside. She said,

'I should like to say straight out that he can come and work here any time he wants, but I'm not going to. For one thing, you haven't explained why he hasn't come himself. In spite of what you say, that doesn't look as if it matters that much to him.'

So Gifford Thomas had kept anything he might have known or guessed not only from them, but from Anona Fingall too. A devious man then, working for his own ends - and not often wrong, apparently. Chel said,

'He got involved in a... an incident. A sort of fight. It left him disabled.'

'How badly disabled?'

'Too badly to get up your steps, at the moment,' said Chel.

'Is that why he isn't here?'

'We didn't know about the steps. He gets good days and bad days. This was a bad one, but there aren't so many now.'

Nonie still had her eyes fixed on the mist-filled bay. There was mist in her head, too, like a safety curtain, shutting something out that she half-knew and didn't want to confront. She said, with regret,

'This is where I work. Does Giff know?' She answered herself. 'Of course he must. He's met you both.' She paused. 'He should have told me.' The unspoken comment that if he hadn't done so, he must have had his reasons, remained hanging in the air.

'I suppose that's it, then,' said Chel.

Nonie said, slowly,

'I don't teach as such, you know. I take pupils, as Giff must have told you, but they aren't beginners. They're people like your husband who already have some skill and more talent, but lack experience, and they come here and do their own work and I advise them if they want. No more than that - too much teaching is death on originality. But if it's worth it, if they're good enough, if I feel that I can really help them... then I let them come and go as they please. Your husband couldn't do that?'

'I don't see how,' said Chel.

'Then it was very unlike Giff to suggest it. Are you sure that he knew?'

'He might not have realised how bad....'

'Will he mind - your husband? Will he be disappointed?'

'He realises there might be problems, if that's what you're asking. But yes - he will be. He's set his heart on it, but if it can't be done - and it obviously can't - then it can't.' Her voice was stony with the knowledge of Oliver's disappointment to come. Perhaps this coolly pragmatic Anona Fingall heard it, too.

'He can still go on working,' she said. 'One day, perhaps, he could go to college as a mature student and study properly. Or perhaps he already has - I really know very little about him. What did he do - before this accident? It presumably wasn't painting.'

'He was a delivery skipper - or a diver, whatever turned up. He sailed round the world single-handed.'

'Oh, my God!' said Nonie, unable to stop herself.

Giff wouldn't - would he? She answered herself, yes Giff would. Giff would know that she would walk a hundred miles barefoot before getting involved in the lives of Helen, Jerry and Dot a second time. Giff was a conniving bastard! She looked at Chel. Nonie was good at faces, naturally enough in a portrait painter. This one, blunt, freckled and determined, had charm and character and would be good to paint, but it was, at the moment, thought Nonie, who was something of an expert on the subject, the face of someone who had been through hell and thought they had come out on the other side, only to find that the light at the end of the tunnel was the proverbial oncoming train. Oh bugger you, Gifford, but not in any way that you might enjoy!

She turned her head to look again at the pictures, with new eyes. With a stomach-wrenching shock, she realised why they were so beautiful. Not necessarily skilled, she had seen that at once, but beautiful. Strong, bold colours laid on canvas by a man who had been there, done that, and come home wearing the T-shirt. Even his sketches had the same bright strength, and his watercolours were hardly like watercolours at all. She shuffled them absently through her hands, her thoughts in chaos.

'He should try gouache,' she said, turning the sheets of paper over, but really what he needed to learn was control - control over the richness of his own experience, pouring onto paper and canvas like an avalanche in full cry. Avalanches were strong meat for most people.

'*Oliver* Nankervis,' she said, already knowing the answer. Chel said nothing, it was too obvious. Nonie dropped the sketches onto the seat of the chair on whose arm she sat, and got to her feet where she stood irresolutely. 'I think I'll make some coffee. Would you like a cup?'

'Thank you,' said Chel. Nonie crossed the room to where the worktop and sink still remained from her past occupation and concentrated on filling the kettle while she tried to think what she should do now, leaving Chel on her own, where she sat for a while feeling miserable on Oliver's behalf, her eyes roving, but only half-seeing, round the studio. It was a big room, with bare rafters, perhaps it was converted out of an old herring loft, with big skylights let into its roof, bare floorboards, a painter's trolley scattered with tubes of paint and bits of rag, a couple of easels with canvases resting on them, Oliver would envy Anona Fingall its possession. There were more canvases stacked around the walls as well as hanging on them, some facing inwards, some outwards. Oliver seemed to have had the artist pretty well to rights, portraits, flower studies, still life. Modern in execution, vibrating with colour and highly distinctive in style. Confident pictures.

She had lived here, she had said, so the doors at the far end must be to living quarters. Maybe she herself and Oliver could live in a place like this one day, Oliver would like that, and it was comfortable enough. This end of the room, where she sat, had a worn, but still bright rug on the floor and was comfortable with its sofa and chairs grouped around the fireplace, and the windows either side that looked down over tumbling steps of slate roof to the harbour, glimpsed between the chimney-pots in flashes of water, granite pier, and fishing boats. The seething holiday crowds were out of sight behind the houses, but in the gutter of the house immediately below on the cobbled hill, a seagull had built its nest. It was empty now, but Anona Fingall, if she was interested in such things, must have had a ringside seat in spring.

A sturdy low table to take mugs of coffee and magazines, a bookcase with the books all higgledy-piggledy on its shelves and a big picture hanging on the wall above it completed the furnishings. A high-quality print of an oil painting, she saw, not one of Anona Fingall's unless her style had dramatically changed. An idealised landscape, seen from above through a golden haze but still brilliant with spilling light; hedges, rivers, woodland in dark wedges, a water mill, a tiny pony cart in a winding lane, all painted, it would appear, from a lark's-eye view. It was made all the odder by a Christmas-present framework of things in the foreground that sent the perspective spinning and tumbling, among them a pile of books, musical instruments, and bizarrely,what looked uncommonly like an old twin-tub washing machine from the sixties, with a stethoscope coiled like a snake on its shining top. The general effect was of a joyous surrealism that by its dazzling inconsequence gave a strange lift to the spirits, the original must be stunning. Apart from that, there was only one other picture at this end of the room, a portrait over the fireplace. Chel, all unsuspecting, tilted her head to look at it almost idly, and the world rocked.

A face she knew, friendly but unsmiling, concentrating, lost in what he was doing. Light brown hair, grey eyes, quite unmistakeable. She felt the jag right through her, like several thousand volts of electricity.

Matthew Sutton's face. If there had been any doubt, which there wasn't, it would have been resolved by the wooden plaque screwed to the wall below it, the twin of the one outside, only this one read STUDIO *Matthew Sutton*. His studio. His sunlit, golden landscape then. Not lark's-eye view - pilot's-eye view. And here, in this room with her...

Matthew Sutton's girlfriend, his lover, Judy had said. Anona Fingall who, thirty years ago would have been - what? Twenty? Twenty-five? Not more, but certainly not less either. So rumour lied about them... what else was lies?

'He was a friend of mine, a long time ago,' said Nonie, behind her. 'This was his studio. He painted that picture on the wall - well, it's only a print, but the original hung there once. It got too valuable, when I moved into the cottage it had to go into a gallery. He called it *Tomorrow* then, but of course, it's yesterday now... it was only a few years after he painted it that he was killed in a flying accident. *C'est la vie.*' She tried to speak lightly, realising that she had maybe put too much into words.

'I'm sorry,' said Chel, and the blood drummed in her ears.

'It was a very long time ago. More than thirty years.'

Matthew Sutton, looking down at her from his gilded frame... she heard the clink as Anona Fingall put down the tray she was carrying.

'A stupid accident,' she was saying. 'He came all through the war, flying bombers over Germany, only to fly into the roof of a house in the mist. Do you take milk?' When Chel didn't answer, she found herself constrained to go on, although her throat was closing against the words, almost as if they were determined to speak themselves. 'He died there, before they could get him down.'

Chel's hands felt damp and her heart was thumping in a rhythm with the drumbeat inside her head. She turned to face Nonie, standing beside her with the milk bottle in her hand and her eyes looking blankly back over the years. When Chel faced her, she gave herself a shake.

'Listen to me! That's old history, you don't want to hear about that!'

'I know the house,' said Chel, and would have added that she lived in it, which of course, Nonie didn't know because of the changed name.

'Then you'll have heard the stories,' said Nonie, wryly, before she could speak. 'The locals said that he haunted the place, calling and calling... I imagined it was to me. Once, I went back to listen - to try to tell him that it was all right. We'd had a bit of a disagreement, you see... it made it doubly hard.'

Chel understood that very well.

'He wasn't there,' said Nonie, bitter with an old disappointment. 'Of course, I understood in the end that it was only tales. People don't stay after they're dead - not people you know - just tales, and the wind.' She was amazed at herself. All these years, she had said nothing to anybody, and now to this complete stranger she had said the unsayable. But Cheryl Nankervis had been down that road too... only for her, there had been a way back.

'He was there,' said Chel.

As he was here. She could feel his presence almost as a solid entity, close beside her. Matthew Sutton, using her as a medium through which he could reach the girl he had loved, and who grieved for him... *Anona*. The name came into her mind, quite definite and unmistakeable. *Anona, I love you. Anona, don't grieve, I love you still.*

It dawned on Nonie quite suddenly what Chel had said. She stared at her, mouth stupidly open.

There was a scent in the room, very strong, heavy and flowery. *Roses are for remembrance...* the drumbeat was deafening. Nonie had gone pale.

'Is he here?' she said, in a very odd voice indeed, and that was the last thing that Chel remembered as a huge cold wave swept right through her, tingling to the ends of her fingers and toes and blanking out consciousness, as if some chilly otherworld entity had walked right into her body and taken it for his own.

The next thing of which she was aware was a firm hand in the back of her neck, pushing her head down as she sat in a chair, and the sound of somebody crying, and she slowly realised that Anona Fingall was responsible for both. She struggled to sit up, pushing away the hand, and there Anona Fingall was, tears on her cheeks, kneeling beside her chair.

'I'm so sorry,' said Chel, confused. 'I never did that before.'

Nonie sniffed, and brushed at her tears inelegantly with the back of her hand. She looked different - softer and happier, younger even. Chel felt as if she had been away for a hundred years, like Sleeping Beauty, and wondered how long it had actually been. And what had happened while she had been gone? They looked at each other in mutual embarrassment. Chel started to get to her feet.

'I had better go - '

Nonie pushed her back. She felt as Chel did, but she couldn't send her away like this.

'No you don't. Drink your coffee first, you can't go straight out after that. No - wait a moment.' She got to her feet, went to the kitchen cupboard, and returned with a bottle of brandy, which she poured liberally into both the mugs. The small action helped a little. Chel, who truth to tell felt abominably shaky, sat and watched her without speaking. 'Here.' A mug was thrust into her hands. It was still hot, so she hadn't been... absent?... for very long. She sipped gratefully. After a while, Nonie said, reluctantly,

'Do you do that sort of thing very often?'

Chel shook her head, speechlessly.

'You aren't a medium, or anything like that?'

She hadn't thought so. Chel found her voice.

'Didn't Gifford Thomas tell you where we live?'

'Trelewan, he said. Somewhere called Moor House. Isn't that right?' Nonie already knew what the answer was going to be, and she was right.

'They changed the name,' said Chel. 'It used to be Vellanzoe Cottages.' The coffee was warming her, and the brandy having its due effect. She felt better - not right, not yet, but better.

'It's derelict,' objected Nonie, as others had done before her.

'Not any more.'

Matthew Sutton, if he had been here, was gone. The room was empty of everything but their two selves and its furnishings. But Chel knew that she had seen his face before she had seen his portrait, and they were the same.

She had been wrong, she realised, to wonder if he perhaps wanted to influence Oliver. It was she herself, she was the link. She felt overwhelmingly relieved. Now he had what he had wanted, perhaps Matthew Sutton would be able to leave Vellanzoe too. Now that he had been able to say his goodbye, perhaps he would admit that he was dead. The house would be theirs, and theirs alone.

Whatever had taken place, it wasn't going to be discussed. Anona Fingall was asking her if she was fit to drive home, and she said that she was. She couldn't wait to get away, and her reluctant hostess, she thought, was anxious to see her gone.

She was half-way home before her mind began working again. The first thing she realised was that she had left all Oliver's paintings behind in Anona Fingall's studio, the second, that nothing on earth would make her go back for them after what had just taken place there. Too, too embarrassing, she felt herself going red even thinking about it! And then she thought, wait a minute here. There are too many pieces in this puzzle. And Oliver is one of them.

After that, she didn't know what to think.

Nonie Fingall didn't know what to think, either. If she believed in what she thought had taken place this afternoon, then something very wonderful had happened, and her godson's wife, with her interesting face and her strange eyes had brought a gift beyond price.

But did she believe? Had it really happened? Was such a thing even possible?

'Matt?' she whispered softly, but there was no reply, no feeling of him remaining in the room. Just his dear, familiar face looking down from the wall as always. She buried her face in her hands. Unbelievable, unbelievable... but she had smelled the scent of the roses he brought her, felt the thorns on her hands and the comfort of his arms around her, his kiss on her mouth, and her heart had known it was truly him.

When she raised her head, drawing her fingers down her tear-wet cheeks, the first thing she saw was the picture of a quiet and misty beach.

Unfinished.

X

It was some days before Nonie felt able to reach a decision, and it hadn't been easy. More than thirty years ago, she had a lost a lover and seen his reputation savaged. She had later, in a different way, lost a much-loved friend, witnessing what she believed, in her darker moments, to have been a deliberate ploy to bring that about. And she had been denied contact with her godson, a dear little boy whom she had loved very much. Most of this was - possibly, she had to be fair about this - directly attributable to one person, and the very last thing she desired now was to return to the orbit of Dorothy Shipham/Worthington/Nankervis. Oliver Nankervis, that little boy grown up, was a stranger to her: she had realised, talking to his wife, that he could have no idea she had ever been his godmother. The stairs up to her studio, that he wouldn't be able to climb, made a perfect excuse to send back the abandoned pictures with a polite note of regret, and maybe a recommendation to some other artist.

If only she could trust Giff to behave.

And if only that girl with the beautiful eyes hadn't seemed to bring Matt into this very room.

In the end, she didn't make a conscious decision at all. The pictures had to be returned, it would be absurd to send them by courier. Four days after Chel's visit, she put them into the back of her car after lunch and drove to Trelewan. She made no appointment, although Giff had given her their mobile number. If they weren't there, she would simply leave the pictures in a safe place and put a note through the door. It was like tossing a coin into the air. She reasoned no more clearly than that.

Even so, it took an effort of will to drive along that lane and park outside the house where Matt had died. There was a car in the parking space alongside, she noticed as she pulled up outside, so they were probably in. Was she glad, or sorry? She still didn't know.

The gate moved smoothly under her hand, she walked up the short path to the front door with the pictures under her arm and knocked, and while she waited, she looked about her, wondering. It had certainly changed, and thank God for that. If she hadn't known what had happened here, she would have thought it a pleasant house.

Nobody came to the door. After a moment, she knocked again, waited again. Still no response, so they must be out after all. With a certain relief she turned towards the gate leading to the lawn. She

153

would find somewhere to put these pictures and make a run for it, the coin fallen tails up, the decision made for her, no more heart-searchings, end of story. She pushed the arched gate open and stepped through.

The first thing that met her startled eyes was Oliver, sprawled fast asleep in a garden chair, full in the sun on the little patio.

'Oh *sugar*!' said Nonie, under her breath, and paused to collect her thoughts. The first of these, absurdly, was *how he's grown*, which in more than twenty-five years was only to be expected. She had seen him on television, when he had sailed into Falmouth after his circumnavigation, and what a disquieting surprise that had been, but that was significantly different from seeing him in the flesh, and in the last few years he had aged. The sleeping face was that of a man who had known illness and suffering and frustration, who even yet knew pain. For the rest, he was too thin, brown from the sun, casual in jeans, faded blue T-shirt, bare feet. Helen's beloved son, her godson, Dot's stepson. An unknown quantity, and her cool shadow falling across his sun-warmed feet had woken him.

In the first moment of waking, seeing her against the light, Oliver thought that he knew her. The silhouette standing over him was of somebody known, bringing with it a strangely familiar feeling of pleasurable anticipation. He blinked, and as his sight cleared he saw that the woman standing there was a stranger. They looked at each other with mutual caution.

'I'm sorry, I didn't mean to wake you,' said Nonie, and immediately found that the direct - over-direct, some thought at the time - little boy hadn't, essentially, changed a jot.

'What did you mean to do, then?' he asked, with interest.

'I was going to put these somewhere safe and leave a note - there didn't seem to be anybody in - ' She was over-explaining, there was no need for all of that. She stopped, and said what she should have said in the first place. 'I'm Anona Fingall. I've brought your pictures back.'

A silence followed this introduction, during which Oliver had time to remember the black awfulness of the last few days, his passport to a possible future snatched away by his hated disablement, the door slammed in his face. He had tried to keep a brave face in front of Chel, but inside, the disappointment had eaten like acid at his tentative hopes and ambitions, burning them to nothing before he had fully admitted them even to himself.

'I see,' he said. Nonie looked at his shuttered face, and the words spoke themselves.

'We need to talk,' she heard herself saying. She placed the pictures on the garden table and pulled out one of its upright chairs. The scrape of metal against stone sounded unreasonably loud. She sat down, uninvited, and Oliver said,

'We do? About what, exactly. I thought any discussion between us had ended before it had even begun.'

'Because of my steps? Is that why you didn't come yourself?'

'I didn't know about them,' said Oliver. 'How could I? I had a migraine. It's one of the side-effects of being kicked in the head.' The bitterness in his voice shocked her. She stepped back from it, hastily.

'After your wife had left, I found that I couldn't put you out of my mind,' she said.

'Really? Trying for you.'

'Don't be like that,' said Nonie, gently. 'You paint well, you must know that. What did you hope for from me?'

Oliver closed his eyes, and tried to control a probably unreasonable resentment.

'Guidance?' he said.

'To what end?'

Oliver spoke precisely, savagely,

'To make a living and support my wife.'

'Well, that told me,' said Nonie. Oliver opened his eyes again and looked at her, stormily. She said, 'Angry young men are old news these days. Put your hackles down, for God's sake, we're going nowhere together if you insist on being so confrontational. Forget your financial problems for the moment, and give me a proper answer.'

'I'm not quite sure what the question was.'

Nonie said,

'I'm a mainstream painter. I don't do anger and I don't do sensational installations - if you want half a sheep preserved in formaldehyde, or a pile of old bricks or an unmade bed, then I'm not your answer, to me that may be clever, but it isn't truly art, just artful. But if you want to paint pictures, then maybe we can come to some sort of understanding.'

'Half a sheep?' asked Oliver, amazed out of his attitude problem.

'Where have you been?' asked Nonie.

'Playing ostriches,' said Oliver, again with that bitter undertone.

'Apparently.'

'All right,' said Oliver, with sudden rage. 'Since you ask, I'll tell you. I want to be the best bloody marine artist in the world. Will that do?'

Nonie let out a long sigh. It was like coming home.

'Perfectly,' she said.

Chel had been to the village. She had gone via Judy's footpath, with no particular end in view but space and peace and an outlet for her nervous, frustrated energy. Living with Oliver over the last few days had been difficult, not because he had ranted and raged and been impossible, but for the very opposite. He had been quiet, considerate, and frighteningly good, but he hadn't painted a thing. That could be because his half-finished picture was in St. Ives, she told herself, but knew that having half-finished one picture had never, in the past, been a barrier to starting another. Because it would have infuriated him, she had had to hide how sorry she was for him and try to behave normally: it had been a severe strain.

She would have to go and fetch those pictures, she knew that. Anona Fingall had had long enough to send them over if she had been going to do so, and perhaps when he had them back, Oliver would be different. Or perhaps not. The only thing was, that after what had happened there, she really didn't want to face Anona Fingall again. Their meeting had shaken her more than she would admit, even to herself, and she had told Oliver nothing, for where was the point? She was beginning to feel like an onion, being peeled back skin by skin, and by this time she was half-scared of what she might find at the core of herself. The only mercy was that the incident seemed to have exorcised Moor House once and for all - and even to think that way was crazy in itself.

Bloody Oliver! she told herself, angrily. Always having to win, always having to be top of the heap, and if he wasn't, then he wouldn't play at all! Couldn't he just settle for an occasionally lucrative hobby?

And answered herself, no, he couldn't. Oliver was a maverick, yes, but he needed to achieve. For some reason, he needed to achieve to the point of obsession, and looking back, he always had. Only, when he was fit and well, it hadn't made so much impact.

Helen, and Jerry Nankervis, and the Dreaded Dot had really loused him up between them!

Furious, without quite identifying why, Chel slashed at the bushes that overhung the path with an angry hand. Bugger them all!

She bought one or two things at the village shop, since she was there, and exchanged a few pleasantries with Sally and Jim before returning to the footpath and making her way home. Or trying to make her way home.

She had reached the village without any trouble because the church tower served as an unmissable landmark, but on the way back there was no such helpful sign. She missed the footpath somehow and found herself, not climbing the stile into the lane above Moor House, but on the far side of the field behind.

'Shit!' said Chel, who was both tired and hot. It was annoying to be so close, but the field of standing maize between herself and home formed an impassable obstacle to a crow's flight return. She had two choices, retrace her steps and see if she could find the footpath, or walk round the edge of the field and try to find her way through onto the road. Neither choice looked good.

'Oh well,' said Chel, to a passing blackbird. 'I suppose the field might turn out quickest, even if not easiest.'

The blackbird hadn't stayed to listen, he was off on his own affairs. Sighing, because her small bag of shopping, which had felt quite light at the start of her walk, now felt as if it held half a field of turnips, Chel began to make her way along the hedge, her eyes fixed on the distant goal of home.

Brambles caught at her jeans and snagged her light cotton top, and here between the well-grown maize and the overgrown hedge it was stiflingly hot, full of tiny biting flies and airless. Like a jungle, thought Chel, irritably dashing at the flies, and moreover she had a growing, horrid suspicion that she was on a fool's errand, and there was no second gate. If she couldn't climb over the garden wall, which she rather suspected might be the case, she was going to have to do a complete circuit of the field and find her way back the way she had come - unless, maybe, she could squeeze through or under the hedge onto the road, she thought, a little wildly, but it was full of brambles and hawthorns, and remarkably solid. William Nankervis was obviously a man who took his hedges seriously, although close relations seemed to be another matter, for they had not yet made his acquaintance. Thinking this, and other increasingly disagreeable thoughts, Chel fought her way on down the side of the hedge, stumbling in ruts, slapping flies and catching her feet in brambles, and eventually she reached the garden wall in a flaming temper.

There wasn't a snowball's chance in hell of climbing over here, she saw at a glance. It would take a skilled mountaineer to scale that wall, which was not, at this point, the ubiquitous and prickly Cornish hedge but a high breeze-block construction that enclosed the new parking space. Moreover, as if that wasn't enough, ahead of her lay a thick tangle of nettles and brambles that reached right out into the field. An outcrop of rock, possibly, or maybe the septic tank, that must be out here somewhere. Whichever, it was seriously in the way. Chel switched the bag to her other hand, rubbed the sweat off her forehead with her wrist, swore, and began to struggle past, wishing very much that she had gone back to search for the footpath after all.

She was about halfway round the obstacle when she realised that it was neither rock nor septic tank. In among the brambles she caught a glimpse of twisted metal, and casually curious, pushed them aside to see better, expecting to find an abandoned farm implement or even an old car. She did not.

In among the tangled briars and brambles, rotting away among the nettles and red campion and coltsfoot, was the bent and buckled skeleton of a little plane.

Chel stood perfectly still. The thorns prickled her hand, but she didn't feel them. She was aware only of the thumping of her heart and a trickle of sweat running down between her shoulder blades, cold against her hot skin.

She stood there for quite a long time.

Above her head, a lark tumbled in the warm air, singing his bubbling song, but all Chel knew was the silence... silence, and the cold touch of mist on her skin. After a long time, she released the spray of bramble that she was holding and stepped back, allowing it to spring back into place. She rubbed her fingers where the thorns had dug into them.

Nobody had told them that was there, not Judy, nor the Tregillises, nor anyone in the village. Perhaps they had all forgotten it, it was so very long ago. It would probably be better to forget it herself, it was so sad, so lost, in its tangle of briars. Already, it was fragile with decay, looking as if she could crush it with her hands. One day soon it would rot away altogether and Will could clear the brambles and move the last of the pathetic debris, and it would all be over. A story to tell the tourists, until that was forgotten too.

She could hear voices, on the other side of the wall that bounded the garden, a murmur that was Oliver, and a woman's voice, talking quietly, bringing her sharply down to earth. Bloody Maggie, come to poke her nose in again! They hadn't seen so much of her since they had moved out of the village, and although Chel quite liked her, she wasn't in the mood for her now. She remembered that she was on her way home, and that she was hot, cross and tired, and could do with a cold shower and an iced drink, and maybe a trip to the beach for a swim. But she would take one last look before she left. She reached out her hand and pulled the screen of leaves away for a second time.

There was no plane. There was only an old, fallen tree, half-smothered in undergrowth and rotting quietly into oblivion, returning to the earth in a pile of crumbling bark and splinters.

But once, it had lain there, however briefly, she knew that without knowing *how* she knew. Not forgotten and disintegrating as she had seen it, but newly broken and wrecked, lifted down by some crane and laid there to await transport onwards. Splattered with Matthew Sutton's blood, hacked and cut where they had removed his body from the tangle. They had put it there, she thought unexpectedly, to keep it away from the sightseers, the gawpers. They had died together, Matthew Sutton and his little plane, and been hidden privately away while they were parted from that final embrace, and what she had seen was a memory that had aged with the passing years.

Holding the briars away with her already scratched and bleeding hands, Chel worked all this out in her head and was quite unable to stand back and laugh at herself.

'Oh God...' she said, on a long breath. 'What am I...? I must be losing my marbles.' Her hands fell to her sides, she had long since dropped her shopping to the ground. For a long time she went on standing there, biting her lip, lost in a different world, until a burst of laughter from beyond the Cornish hedge that stood between herself and her home brought her back to here and now. With a dismissive shrug that had no real heart in it, she stooped down for the mundane plastic bag full of bread and sausages and apples.

And there it was, right beside her foot.

At first, she thought it was a strange-shaped stone, kicked out of the soil as she struggled round the thicket, but then her brain registered its strange regularity, and she bent and picked it up, brushing loose earth away with her fingers. It seemed to be some kind of cylindrical metal object, a little box perhaps, but it was too encrusted to be sure, With vague recollections of archaeological finds in ploughland, she hesitated a moment, then dropped it in with the shopping for proper examination later. Roman remains, or something of the kind, would be a lot easier to accept than what she had imagined she saw, and at least the object was real. She could hold it in her hands, touch it, feel its shape. It's obvious reality was very comforting.

And now it was time to find her way home. Thinking about how to do so put welcome distance between herself and the... the what? The figment of her imagination? The ghost of a lost plane? With an effort that was near to physical, Chel pushed such speculations right out of her mind.

Beyond the thicket of brambles, the back walls of their outhouses backed up against the hedge. If she could get through to the base of the stone wall at that point, Chel estimated, she might be able to climb up and then over the roof of one or the other and jump down on the other side, and so it proved. Tossing her shopping up ahead of her, she was able to use both hands and the hedge itself to aid a scramble up the wall, and from there it was comparatively easy to crawl onto the slates.

She lay there on her stomach, and looked with amazement at the scene below, where Nonie and Oliver were so absorbed in their conversation together that they hadn't even heard her puffing and panting as she climbed.

'Hi!' she called, and they both turned to look at her.

'What in the world,' said Nonie, 'are you doing up there?'

'Looking for a way down.' Chel rose cautiously to her knees and crawled to the edge. The renovation, she was pleased to see, had been thorough, and she wasn't heavy. She dropped the shopping to the ground - luckily nothing was breakable - and gripping the edge of the roof firmly, she swung herself over, dropped to the length of her arms, and ended up, breathless but safe, on the grass.

'My word!' said Nonie. 'You must be fit!'

'Hi, you look a mess,' said Oliver, less admiringly, and grinned at her.

'Thanks.' Chel dusted her hands together and picked up her shopping. 'I love you, too!' She smiled at Nonie. 'Two older brothers and an older sister,' she explained. 'I had to be extra-fit if I wanted to keep up. You remember these things. I'm sorry, I should have come for those pictures. I was going to.' Their bantering reality was wonderful, she basked in it like sunshine.

'I'm glad you didn't.' Nonie gestured to Oliver. 'I wouldn't have met him, if you had. We've come to an arrangement. If he can't come to me, then I'll have to come to him. If that's all right with you?'

Chel stared. Nonie said, hurriedly,

'Oh, not every day, don't be alarmed. Once or twice a week, or when he needs me. Is that OK?'

'It's extraordinarily good of you,' said Chel, finding her voice. She looked at Oliver. He, in turn, looked as if all his Christmases had come at once. 'How can we thank you?'

'Don't,' said Nonie, with a smile.

Chel went indoors to clean up and fetch cold drinks. Tipping her shopping out onto the worktop, the strange round object slid out with the packet of sausages. She picked it up, but her mind was too full of what she had just heard to bother with it now. She wrapped it in a piece of kitchen roll and dropped it into a drawer to look at later, where she promptly forgot all about it.

Nonie arrived back at the studio in a very different frame of mind from that in which she had left it. From being deeply reluctant to put herself in the path of involvement, she was now supremely glad that she had done so.

'He's the business, Matt,' she told the portrait above her fireplace. Over the years she had continued in an early habit of talking to him when things were particularly important. She had never stopped missing him; although her life had been full, successful, and generally a happy one, his absence had been like a perpetual thorn sticking into her heart, often fading into the background but always there. Except for that one time, when Chel had been here, he had never come to her, even in the emotional days immediately after his death, but she liked to imagine that he was in some sense still near to her and be comforted.

Dropping her car keys onto the draining board, she switched on the kettle, and while it boiled walked to the window, looking down over the tumbling roofs as she had so often done in the past, with a new, springing optimism. Helen's son - all Helen's talent, possibly more. It didn't matter that he had no idea of their connection, if Helen and Jerry wished to repudiate that heart-warming compliment, that was their affair. They couldn't shut her out of his life. To do them justice, she didn't think that it was either of them that had tried. A residual bitterness that she hadn't even realised remained began to sweeten. Her godson, the nearest thing to a child of her own that she would ever have now, and he needed her. It hadn't all been a waste of emotion, fate - and Giff - had thrown them together again.

Giff. That was another thing. Matt had always laughed about Giff, saying that he had the Midas touch, every artist he touched turned to gold. Her godson, she obscurely felt, could do with being turned to gold. He had come late to serious painting, and reluctantly, that much she had already concluded simply from talking to him. He had always dabbled in odd moments, he had told her, sometimes settled a debt by painting a picture, often in tavernas and lodging houses in the Mediterranean when he had been waiting around for a flight home or a berth on a boat after making a delivery, but he had never considered it as a career. With disarming honesty, he had confessed that he had always thought of it as lightweight. A small, but saleable talent, no more. Handy in an emergency. He had laughed at himself, cynically. You never knew what you might be driven to do. Beneath the cynicism, unspoken, was the realisation that the small, saleable talent was more important to him than he had wished to believe, and not just because of its potential income value. He had shut it away, kept it hidden, for whatever private, unrecognised reason, and now the door to the secret place was cruelly jemmied open and all the treasures spilling out.

And not just treasures, if she wasn't mistaken. It was a real Pandora's Box.

The kettle boiled. Nonie made herself a coffee and carried it to the settee, sitting cross-legged in the corner in her old, habitual way. She took a sip.

'I can't work those two out,' she confessed, to Matt's portrait. 'They seem to have cut themselves adrift somehow. It's like one of his pictures, some of them are frighteningly wild, Matt, you should see them. There's a wind blowing them, and I get the feeling that there's rocks on every side. That girl is so tense you could play her like a cello. And Oliver... he's swept overboard, and I'm not sure there's a lifebelt handy. Unless it's her... and that's hard on her, if it's true.' She tilted her head to look up into the painted eyes. 'Matt, do you see me as a lifeboat? The good ship Anona, sailing to the rescue? I wish I did. Their lives have been cut in two by this disaster.' She frowned, trying to express in words something that she half-suspected. 'I get the idea that the knot that joined them together has ended up on the wrong side of the cut, and perhaps that's why they're drifting. And that the pictures are pushing them further apart, that there's nothing for them to share any more but problems. Am I being fanciful here? You'd tell me if I was, wouldn't you?'

The painted lips were silent.

'I hardly know them, of course,' Nonie admitted. When she considered the experience she had shared with Chel, and that she had first met Oliver when he was only days old, the statement sounded ludicrous. That they could use some help was apparent, that they warded it off with both hands, ran from it, feared it, was equally obvious. Only over-riding need had allowed her within the palisade. Any attempt to coerce them in any way would very soon see her outside again, and the pair of them in dissolution. Why should thinking that immediately make her think of Dot? 'She was a destructive woman,' she said, musingly. The *non sequitur* wouldn't bother Matt, if he happened to be listening. She made a wry face, half-humorous, half-despairing. 'All that teacher training, it's going to come in useful after all. You may well laugh, but we won't get this one to go to art college, that's for sure, and I'm not sure it would be right if he did. He's too... grown up, I suppose. And someone's been helping him recently, and whoever they are, they're not bad at the job. He's taken more interest, over the years, than he's going to let on.'

She had finished her tea, she twirled the mug round her finger by its handle and frowned, thoughtfully. It was going to be interesting, that much was certain. And Giff...

'Gifford Thomas, manipulating lives again!' she said, getting to her feet. 'Let's hope he knows what he's doing. He missed the boat with Helen, after all.' Although that hadn't been Giff's fault. It was Helen who had chosen to go to another gallery. Cutting all associations, storming out with her hurt and her resentment. Did she ever see Jerry, Nonie wondered, did Dot allow it? But mothers must be more difficult to vanquish than godmothers.

And if she was to talk of manipulating lives, Dot was the acknowledged queen of the art.

Yes, it was certainly going to be interesting.

Nonie, who deliberately included Chel where Maggie had excluded, very soon found a way in which she could make a useful contribution to Oliver's interests. It happened, in the end, quite naturally.

'You don't want to keep paying good money to George Cosgrove,' Nonie said. 'Why don't you do your own framing?'

'Kind of awkward, at the moment,' suggested Oliver. 'I need my hands for myself. Is it a sit-down job, do you think?'

Nonie frowned.

'Well, I suppose it wouldn't be impossible. But actually, I was thinking of Chel.' Like Judy and Keith, she had very soon adopted Oliver's name for his wife. They both looked at Chel now, sitting doubtfully with a glass of iced juice in her hands. Oliver's glance, at first amused, became speculative.

'Would you be up for it?' he asked.

'I've never done any woodwork,' said Chel. 'At least, not since first year at the comp., and that was more playing with bits of wood and glue.'

Nonie grinned.

'Did they make the boys do domestic science? Yes, I thought they might have. Much more useful for them, of course.' She pulled her face straight. 'I learned at college. It's hardly rocket science, I could show you easily.'

'I don't mind having a go,' said Chel, cautiously.

'You don't have to,' said Oliver. 'You should have your own life. You've lived mine for long enough.' He was still acutely conscious of the fact that he was a brake on her, where he had once promised her adventure and excitement.

'I'd like to,' said Chel, surprised to find that it was true. Now that freedom was slowly coming back into her life, she was finding it less important. 'I could make canvases too - couldn't I, Nonie?' *Miss Fingall,* like *Cheryl,* hadn't lasted the first morning.

'Sure thing. It won't take up her whole life,' Nonie assured Oliver. 'She'll have plenty of time left to do what she wants.'

Whatever that was, thought Chel, but did not say. Time of her own unweighted by a sense of responsibility was still a novelty, she needed to rediscover herself and her own choices.

A little to her surprise, Chel found making canvases and frames comparatively easy, and the fact that Oliver was now painting increasingly accomplished pictures on canvases that she had made drew them together in a common aim and began to re-forge secure links between them. Life began to fall into a pleasant, easy pattern, forward-looking at last, and with no more ghosts to disturb it.

Maggie, when she returned from her visit up-country, was piqued to find that she had been superseded. She had begun to look on Oliver as if she had some sort of exclusive rights to his talent and she didn't like finding herself reduced to the ranks *in absentia*. Oliver had perhaps been a little brusque with her - he had treated her, Chel recalled with a private grin, rather like a book that he had finished reading, but he hadn't meant to be unkind. Perhaps, for Maggie, that made it worse, but it was Nonie who was valuable now to Oliver. Maggie was simply Chel's friend. It was unfortunate that she had made it so clear to Chel that she was Oliver's friend.

It might have been unconsciously that she had tried to rock the boat, but Chel was never quite certain with Maggie.

'Don't you ever feel that you want to be yourself for a change?' she asked. She was trendily concerned with her own identity, but Chel was beginning to find that she didn't mind one way or the other. She wondered occasionally, when she had been listening to Maggie for a while, if there was something the matter with her, but the truth was that for now she rather enjoyed being the practical face of Oliver's brilliance. In any case, she seemed to have her own uneasy ways of achieving identity if ever she summoned the courage to use them. She had no need to feel herself second violin to Oliver's lead, surely, when she carried this difference within herself.

'I am being myself,' she said.

'You're so lucky,' said Maggie, with a soulful sigh. 'I wish that I was naturally domesticated.'

It was the last phrase that Chel would have used to describe herself. No really domesticated woman, she suspected, could live in peace with an artist and survive as an entity on her own.

'Who's naturally domesticated?' she answered lightly. Maggie had ceased to annoy her since Oliver had ceased to need her, she even felt a little sorry for her.

Maggie evaded a direct answer, by saying,

'I'd find being tied to the house all the time so frustrating. I think I'd go mad.'

Chel laughed.

'I'm not tied to the house, not these days. Anyway, I think I might keep goats.'

'Goats?' asked Maggie, blankly.

'On that rough bit of garden at the end,' said Chel, kindly, as if to a child.

'We had goats before we went to Australia,' said Maggie, rather at a loss.

'I know. And Will's wife has offered me some bantams, what do you think?'

Will had eventually appeared, a bent, elderly figure, with freshly dug potatoes and a bundle of runner beans, grunting a dour greeting. Chel, however, had felt him to be friendly. He hadn't stayed, being not much of a one for chattering, as he had kindly informed her. The vegetables had been delicious.

Maggie must have suspected that she was being got at. She said deeply,

'I do admire you, I really do. You're so brave.'

Chel, who considered that most of the bravery was on Oliver's side, was surprised at this comment, which came out with such spontaneous conviction that she had to believe it was really meant. It disconcerted her.

'What?' she said, laughing, but Maggie only shook her head at her.

'It took courage to stick by him when this happened,' she said. 'Lots of women could never have made the sacrifice - they wouldn't have done it.'

Chel knew that she nearly hadn't done it herself, and was unreasonably annoyed.

'It must be my total lack of imagination,' she informed Maggie, tartly, annoyed on Oliver's behalf quite as much as on her own, and no longer certain if Maggie was trying to put her down or not. She could never make up her mind if Maggie was stupid, as Oliver had once said, or simply inclined to over-dramatisation. Judy, she knew, couldn't stand her, but she herself often suspected that Maggie had found marriage a disappointment, nice as Jack was, and far more than Chel herself, needed drama and excitement to get through her days.

Maggie, however, took the wind right out of her eye.

'It can sometimes be a bit of a curse to be too imaginative,' she agreed, and left Chel giggling and thinking how much Judy would enjoy the joke.

XI

Debbie came first, Oliver's young half-sister. She came in September, unannounced and unexpected, bringing with her a not, by this time, unwelcome breath of that other life that they had abandoned for sanctuary. Her visit was timely, the coming autumn was making Oliver restless and he needed distraction. Chel thought she knew why. The Round-the-World Race was on television, in the newspapers, almost ready to start now, and if that wasn't enough, the turning year was heralding change. The leaves rustled dryly on the surrounding trees, browning a little at the edges, ready to fall, the mornings were misty and cool. It was time for something new.

'Whatever brings you here?' asked Oliver, surprised but not displeased, of all his family, Debbie was the only one for whom he had much time. Chel, who had seldom seen the two of them together, watched their meeting with interest. Debbie laughed.

'Curiosity? I was down this way anyway, so I thought I'd drop in - see what you were up to.' She paused, her eyes taking in the picture on the small easel resting on the conservatory table. It was of one huge wave beneath a cloudy sky, a single shaft of sunlight struck through the rearing wall of water, turning it clear, glassy green rippled with white foam. Across it, two birds flew, dark shapes against the lovely colour, above them hung the broken white of the curling, curving crest. It was simple, moving, beautiful. Quietening at last from the raging storms and full of light. 'I never expected this,' said Debbie.

'Got to do something to pass the time,' said Oliver. Debbie looked at him thoughtfully, Chel thought that she was sufficiently like him not to be deceived; although Dot's daughter rather than Helen's, each probably had enough of their father in them to understand the other. She had always thought that she would like Debbie, if she ever had the chance to get to know her, but Debbie, like Oliver, steered clear of the family whirlpool. On three occasions, they had met, every one a family crisis. Her wedding to Oliver, Chel remembered, the mob attack in the alley accompanied by the tragic, premature birth of their son, Oliver's dramatic suicide attempt that had followed her own departure to return, abortively, to an old love. Disasters, all of them. She had been like a storm petrel, flying in on the wings of the hurricane.

But not this time. This time she sat, calmly discussing Oliver's painting, perched on the arm of one of the conservatory chairs, and if there was a storm brewing, Chel thought, this time it was for Debbie herself.

'I'll make a drink, shall I?' she asked - asked herself, she thought, for brother and sister hardly noticed. With a smile, for it was good to see Oliver being civilised to one of his own, she went into the kitchen to see to it. After a short while Debbie wandered in to join her.

'Nice house,' she said, lounging against the worktop. 'Bit of a surprise though - I would have thought you'd be nearer the water.'

Chel laughed.

'Yeah, right... you should see the prices.'

'Dad would have helped,' said Debbie, and made a face. 'All right - don't say it. I understand really.'

Chel paused, a milk bottle in her hand, staring unfocussedly out through the window at the field beyond.

'It'll change, the bungalow will sell one day, and if Oliver's pictures are a success...'

'Has he done many?'

'A fair few, by this time. I'll show you later - they're all upstairs in one of the spare rooms.'

'Will he mind?'

'I should hope not.' Chel grinned, and poured the milk into the three mugs. 'If he objects to people looking at them, he's not going to get far with an exhibition, is he?'

'Is that what he's doing - stuff for an exhibition?'

'Yes. Some time next year, probably, the gallery's all lined up and waiting.'

'St. Ives or somewhere, I suppose. Nice work.'

'London,' said Chel, with satisfaction. 'West End.' And watched Debbie's face, which registered amazement and pleasure in about equal measure.

'Wow!' she said. 'Good going! How did he swing that?'

'Coincidence. Luck.' Fate.

'It's doing him good,' said Debbie. 'I haven't seen him so... well, un-tense, I suppose... oh, not for years. Not for long before... what happened. You know our family.'

'Dysfunctional, isn't that the word?' She had used it to Oliver, she remembered. He hadn't denied it, and neither did Debbie, now.

'The very one.' She looked down at her feet, pushing her fingers through her shaggy, blonde hair in a tired gesture. 'Oh well, I don't think the show's got much longer to run, actually.'

Chel looked at her in surprise.

'Debbie? What do you mean?'

'Oh... it was all wrong from the start, wasn't it? You learn things as you get older, see them differently. And Dad, I think, blames Mum for what you two did... running off like that. You frightened them, and when people are frightened the truth comes out... it really put the cat among the pigeons.'

'I'm sorry.' This, she hadn't expected. She looked at Debbie, uncomfortably. 'It was as much Oliver's fault, you know - that they never got on. I know that. Oliver, too.'

'Oliver was a child,' said Debbie. 'It's nice of you to try, though.' She looked up, and she was smiling. 'It isn't the end of the world, you know. If people are unhappy, they shouldn't stay together. It's just a waste of life. I'm the world's expert - I don't suppose they told you I broke up from my bloke? He turned out a bit of a mistake, after all that fuss.' She screwed her face into a grimace. 'You should have heard them all - but - where was I? Oh yes - they're my parents, but that doesn't mean that I don't see them clearly. I've done that for a long time.'

Had she? Chel wondered. Dot was her mother. Did any child see their mother that clearly? Useless to ask, and Debbie had in any case long ducked out of family life and gone to live her own. As she was, no doubt, doing now. Something stirred in Chel's mind, and was as quickly suppressed. No! Go away! Debbie pushed herself away from the worktop and stood up properly.

'Let me take that tray for you - you can bring the biscuits.' She paused, tray in hands, looking at her sister-in-law with her brother's eyes, blue-grey, disconcertingly dark in her fair face. 'I just wanted to let you know, that's all. So you were warned.'

'They'll be here soon?' said Chel, reading her expression correctly.

'They will. Dad has done his best, but he can't keep her away for much longer. She'll fuss and make trouble, all with the best intentions, and it's me that should apologise, not you.'

'Oh well,' said Chel. 'Thanks for the warning.' Forewarned was forearmed - but she had known, in any case, that the inevitable visit of Dot and Jerry would be a bummer. She had, however, less faith than Deb in the purity of Dot's intentions.

Oliver had cleaned up his brushes and set his painting aside, a clear indication of his pleasure in Deb's unexpected visit. She looked at him assessingly.

'You look better,' she said. 'In fact, you look better than you've looked for a while now.' She put the tray down. 'How's it going?'

'All right.' He was getting about more easily now, but still having trouble lifting his feet properly. He was walking, Chel realised, from the hip rather than the knee, she was beginning to wonder if it would be permanent. But getting stronger all the time, it wouldn't be long now before the crutches were a thing of the past. It was much in the mind as in the body, she thought. Debbie took the answer at face value and didn't pursue it. Oliver didn't pursue it either.

'You never answered my question,' he said. 'What brought you to Cornwall? Not sisterly devotion, you can't kid me!'

'Well, no.' Debbie looked at him with the glimmer of a smile. 'Not that I'm not devoted to you, of course, brother dear. No, would you believe business?'

Debbie worked in a drawing office in London. Oliver looked sceptical.

'Pull the other one, it's got bells on.'

'Not *that* business,' said Debbie. 'I'm going for a career change. I'm fed up with London. I'm fed up with graphics, too.'

Oliver looked interested.

'Really? What about whatsisname - Robin? I thought you were joined at the hip.'

Debbie, who had caused a major family disruption by electing to move in with her boy friend at a very bad moment, had the grace to look abashed. She had been hurt by whatever had happened, Chel thought, she was being too casual now. But there were to be no confidences.

'It turned out to be a bad move,' she said, and shrugged. 'Time to move on.'

'To what, then? I wouldn't have thought there'd be anything for you this far down.'

Debbie leaned forward.

'Remember Tim? Used to be a boyfriend of mine. Tim Howells - come on, you must remember.'

'Thin, fair, spectacles. Sailed a Flying Fifteen. Bit of a geek,' recalled Oliver, smartly. Debbie looked as if she wished he hadn't remembered quite so clearly. Her laugh was only half amused.

'He wasn't that bad. You didn't really know him, and if you had, you wouldn't have had much in common.'

'Don't tell me you're getting back with him. Please.'

'No. He's married, anyway. She doesn't sail but she's OK. Anyway, her aunt died this year and left her a house on the Helford. A big house, with water frontage and outbuildings, it's got its own jetty and boathouse, the aunt ran it as a guesthouse. Tim and Lesley thought they'd turn it into a sailing school and run holidays for people who want to learn to sail. They asked me if I'd join them.'

Again that quiver of knowledge. Chel closed her eyes, once more fought it back. She didn't want to know things about people's private lives, didn't want to see into their future. There was the crackle of a fire in her ears. Her eyes flew open.

'As an instructor, or as a chambermaid?' Oliver was asking, with a lift of his brows.

'Oh, as an instructor - catch me being a chambermaid! I've time before they open to get all the bits of paper, Tim's got them already, he works with the Sea Scouts.'

'He would,' commented Oliver, and Debbie gave him a fierce look.

'Don't be so unfair!' she said. 'We hope to kick off in the spring. Lesley will run the guesthouse side, Tim and I will do the teaching - we may need someone else on that side, if it takes off, we're going to see. Anyway, to get back to your question, we came down to have a look at it, see if it would work, and it looks as if it could.'

'It sounds as if it could be fun,' said Chel. 'Does... Lesley, is it? - does she know anything about catering?'

'No, but it can't be that difficult. Just feeding people and making beds,' said Debbie, blithely. Chel, who had been in professional catering all her working life, looked sceptical, but made no comment. Debbie was off again, talking to Oliver about sailing dinghies, good secondhand Wayfarers, whatever they were, ideal for the job, but she could see that his interest was merely peripheral, he wouldn't get involved.

'Was Tim so awful?' she asked him, when Debbie had taken herself off to rejoin her friends in Helston, and Oliver laughed.

'Probably not. A bit colourless, rather earnest, you know? He wouldn't have done for Deb, it was a mercy she took herself to London before it got too serious.'

'But nice enough?'

'Oh yes - probably very *nice,*' said Oliver, and a faint whiff of charring seemed to hang in the air. Once more, Chel shut her eyes, trying to shut it out. When she opened them again, Oliver was looking at her more closely than she liked.

'Anything the matter?'

'No,' said Chel. She got to her feet and walked to the open patio doors. 'There's a change coming in the weather. Autumny. Someone's got a bonfire, I can smell it on the wind.'

The wind smelled of mown hay and a faint whiff of cow. She gave herself a mental shake.

'Come back here,' said Oliver. He reached out his hands as she came, taking hers. 'Come on, Chel, what's the problem? That's two or three times this afternoon that you've looked as if you've been stung by a wasp. Tell me about it.'

Chel tried to draw her hands away, but couldn't. Oliver's hands were strong, she gave up the struggle.

'It's just...' And then it came spilling out. 'Suppose you knew - or thought you knew - something that was going to happen to someone in the future, just caught a glimpse of it... what should you do, do you think?'

Oliver looked at her seriously.

'This is that clairvoyance thing, isn't it? Do you still get it, then?'

'Occasionally,' said Chel, avoiding his eye.

'Since we got here, isn't it? I've thought, once or twice, there was something. Is there?'

'It's gone now,' evaded Chel. Oliver dropped her hands.

'This afternoon, then. About Deb?' Chel nodded. 'Good or bad?'

'I don't know. I didn't reach for it. I just know it was there, something's going to happen for her.'

Oliver noted her choice of words.

'Something's going to happen for all of us, one way or the other. Was that all, just a feeling?'

'Yes,' said Chel, because it was true, she hadn't reached. She had chosen not to. Her fear, unspoken, was that one day she would have no choice.

Oliver said, selecting his words with care because he could see she was troubled,

'The fortune-teller at that fair up at Tregothen, the one you made me see... she knew what was going to happen to me, I'm bloody sure. She didn't tell me, and it wouldn't have made any difference if she had, it would still have happened... because you don't think of things like that when life's just going on around you.'

'She told you to be careful,' accused Chel.

'And I wasn't. I forgot... no, that's not quite right. I couldn't *not* have done what I did. I couldn't have walked on while someone was screaming for help. So... what's it worth, this fortune telling?'

'You mean, I might know, I might tell Debbie, but it wouldn't, in the end, alter a thing?'

'Something like that, I suppose, yes. But you don't know, you say.'

'I think I could know, but it seems intrusive.'

'Then forget about it, is my advice,' said Oliver, gently. After a pause, he asked, 'Does this often happen to you?'

More often than I like.

'No,' said Chel.

171

*

Debbie's visit had been an unexpected pleasure. Less amusing in every way was the visit of Jerry and Dot. Fortunately, Jerry, whose motives after Debbie's visit Chel, at least, was beginning to wonder about, had insisted that they stay in a big seafront hotel in Penzance, which meant that they only visited Moor House, they weren't staying there. Even so, it was bad enough.

Their visit was, in any case, timed at a bad moment. The start of the Round-the-World Race was on every News channel, on the sports page of every paper, unavoidable unless you shut your eyes and ears and blanked it out. Chel thought that Oliver had done that. He had gone very quiet, working hard and laughing seldom, and, she thought privately, deliberately tiring himself in order not to have to think. She made no attempt to stop him, thinking that physical tiredness was better than brooding and bitterness, although that last, too, must be there. It was hard for Chel too, even though she was getting more understanding now about Oliver's moodiness - she hoped that she was. But the last thing that either of them needed at that exact moment was a visit from the Dreaded Dot.

'You naughty things!' cried Dot, surging through the door the minute it was opened to her. 'We couldn't rest until we had been to see you both and made quite certain that you were really all right! You can't go by what Deborah says, she's young and sees what she wants to see.' She gave a playful smile. 'I told Jerry, we must come now, tonight, or I shouldn't sleep a wink! We've been so worried about you, you naughty children!' She made a dive to kiss Chel's cheek, but Chel countered it by stepping past her to greet Jerry. She liked Oliver's father and felt sorry for him in a way. Oliver couldn't have been an easy son, and his wife was awful, poor man! She had never understood how he could have swapped beautiful, talented, warm Helen for unimaginative, plain and stout do-gooding Dorothy, although maybe she hadn't been plain and stout at the time. A self-inflicted wound, obviously, but probably no less painful for that, she cynically thought. She had forgotten how implacable Dot was. Like an advancing army, she gave no quarter, but unlike the army, smiled all the time. She swept onwards now, looking for Oliver, giving Chel's cheek a forgiving pinch in passing that made her flinch.

Jerry brushed her cheek with his lips, an undemanding gesture of genuine affection.

'You're looking very well,' he told her, and asked, as his wife had not done. 'How is Oliver?'

'He's fine.' Chel took his arm to lead him into the living area.

'Come and say hullo, see for yourself.' No help for it, but Oliver would hate it.

It had become their pleasant habit, when the light faded and the evenings drew in, to sit together and read, watch television, listen to music, talk together, discovering all kinds of shared or opposing interests and tastes that they had never had time to explore before, the other side of the coin that fate had tossed to them. Often, friends dropped in - Judy and Keith, Jack and Maggie, others whom they were beginning to meet through visits to the pub or the beach. Even a fellow artist, known simply as "Charlie" had wandered into their orbit, apparently by osmosis, and become a regular drinking companion. Oliver's pool skills were much in demand at the pub, and Jack had introduced him to the surfers of Sennen. None of these people appeared to pity him, taking him easily at face value, and their life had taken huge strides towards normality over the summer months. Nonie, too, staying on after one of her teaching visits, or inviting them to her cottage, had become friend as well as mentor. In front of any of these, Oliver was perfectly happy to be found lazily propped up on his bed, resting his back which still bothered him a bit after a day spent painting, relaxed and at ease, unembarrassed by what everybody knew and took for granted. Not so, in front of his stepmother.

She knew better than to make any attempt to kiss him, but there were other ways of getting at him, although she may, of course, Chel told herself firmly, have meant it kindly.

'Oh Oliver, dear!' she cried, throwing her hands up. 'Deborah said you were so much better, I *knew* she wasn't telling the truth! All this living on your own with nobody to help you - no wonder you both look so tired! Cheryl here with great shadows under her eyes, and you looking so poorly! How could you both be so silly!'

Oliver looked as if he would like to bite her. He pushed himself completely upright and swung his legs off the bed, reaching for his crutches. Dorothy reached out.

'Oh no - no. You lie there and be comfortable. You look so frail still.' She tutted anxiously. 'I'm not at all sure that all this rushing off to Cornwall was the best thing for you, but there, you young ones always have to know your own business best.' Oliver, taking no notice, got to his feet.

'I'm not in the least frail, thank you,' he said icily. 'And who else is qualified to know our business?'

His stepmother patted his arm and told him, soothingly, not to get excited.

'So bad for you,' she cooed. 'Now come and sit down.' But he shook off her supporting hand, and she looked around her at the room instead. 'What a strange little house you've found for yourselves!' Tinkling little laugh. 'I don't like open-plan myself, but so practical with your special needs, of course.' She smiled widely. 'We won't say anything about all that wasted space upstairs, shall we? But perhaps it would have been more sensible to have a bungalow, right in that nice little village we came through, don't you think?'

'It's their affair, Dot,' suggested Jerry, placatingly. He took the chair Chel offered him and sat down, looking, she thought, as if he wished he was somewhere else. 'Oliver. Good to see you.' He looked apologetic. 'We worried about you, you know.'

'I'm sorry about that,' said Oliver, stiffly and insincerely. 'We did keep telling you, we're OK.'

'Oh, you were good about keeping in touch, but we did wonder where you were.'

Neither Chel nor Oliver followed this lead. Best not to mention campsites and caravans, Dot would go ballistic, Chel thought wearily, even though Oliver had obviously survived and, in spite of what Dot chose to say, thriven. She squirmed inside with helpless fury as Dot began to walk around inspecting everything with the indulgent smile of one prepared to see good in anything, even if there was none. She tutted over the french doors open, through the conservatory, to the evening air, telling Chel that she must shut them at once.

'It gets chilly on these autumn evenings, after the warm days. You don't want poor Oliver to catch a chill, dear. Not after all that trouble he had with his lungs last year.'

Oliver had been on a respirator after the attack, but that, at least, he had long put behind him.

'I've never had a chill in my life!' he said, indignantly, but Dot shook her finger at him and told him he must take care of himself and not be naughty.

And then, she found the lighthouse, standing sentinel over its angry sea, hanging over the sideboard in the dining area. She gave another little laugh.

'What a very dark and gloomy picture!' she exclaimed, adding artlessly, 'It's an original, isn't it? Cheryl darling, you shouldn't waste your precious money on silly luxuries, should you dear? Food and warmth and the rent, those are surely your first priorities.' She smiled kindly. 'You two never did know how to be sensible with your money, did you?'

Jerry, maybe feeling that most of this comment was unnecessary - although why he should have singled out just this one was a mystery to

Chel - said, with interest,

'A good original can be an investment. Who's the artist, or is it part of the fixtures and fittings?' He got up - he had looked unsettled in his chair anyway, and crossed the room to have a look for himself. 'I don't know as much as I would like about art, admittedly, but I must say, I rather like it. It has atmosphere.'

'Thanks,' said Oliver sardonically, and Chel said, unaccountably nervous,

'Oliver painted it.'

Jerry looked startled, even taken aback, but Dot stepped smoothly into the opening, indulgent smile firmly in place.

'Really? How splendid!' There was a sour little tang behind her enthusiasm. 'There now - we all said he should take up some little hobby! Has he done any more, Cheryl dear? Perhaps I could take some home with me and sell them among our friends. It would give him a little income, help you out a bit. Make him feel of some use, you know, it will all help.'

It occurred to Chel that Oliver's stepmother, for some reason, resented his painting and was belittling it on purpose. Her offer just *might* be as self-importantly genuine as it was crushingly insensitive, although Chel doubted it somehow, but her own generosity in offering her patronage was definitely giving her satisfaction over and above the obvious. Totally self-deceiving, or deliberate? Smug, anyway. More than a little sadistic, if she could deliberately poison a dream for someone she had brought up from a child.

She must be imagining it, surely, Chel thought, for why should Dot resent Oliver's pictures? - but at the same moment, saw Oliver's expression, which was compounded about equally of outraged fury and indignation, and hastily and unwisely hastened into the breach.

'I don't think - ' she began, just as Jerry said quickly,

'If Oliver wants - '

Their simultaneous rush to Oliver's defence defeated its own object. They each stopped speaking to allow the other to finish, and into the resulting silence, Oliver said dangerously,

'I should try to be a little less preoccupied with our affairs, if I was you.'

His stepmother didn't appear to see the red light. She leaned over and patted his cheek. Chel reflected that she was lucky not to lose her fingers, Oliver looked wild. She would as soon have patted something stripy in a jungle herself.

'Now Oliver dear, we mustn't be so touchy, must we? Poor Cheryl has a lot of responsibility and worry, and you must learn to be good and let us help you where we can.'

'You can help best by minding your own business!'

Chel hurtled in without taking a breath, and heard her own voice babbling jerkily,

'It's kind of you to offer, but really it isn't necessary. Oliver has all the help he needs from Anona Fingall - you've probably heard of her - she - ' She broke off. Jerry's face would have stopped her, even if Dot hadn't turned a dangerous puce and started spluttering.

'*Nonie Fingall?*' exclaimed Jerry, and Dot, getting her breath back, cried,

'That woman! I thought she was gone from our lives, and good riddance!'

Their joint reaction was so totally out of the blue that both Chel and Oliver simply stared at them, startled. After a moment, Chel said, absurdly,

'You know her?'

Jerry answered as if he was choosing his words with care.

'She was at college with Helen. They were friends.'

'Huh!' exclaimed Dot, betrayed into speaking like ordinary people for the first time that Chel had ever heard. 'With friends like her, who needs enemies!'

'Shut up, Dot!' said Jerry, with a sharpness that was as innovative as Dot's idiomatic comment. Some deep undercurrent was being disturbed, in both of them, not just in Dot.

'So what did she do?' asked Oliver, in a flat voice, beneath which lay a whirlpool of conflicting instincts and emotions, not hidden well enough. Dot seized on the question.

'Someone that your mother cared about died because of her,' she said, and the triumph in her voice was unmistakeable, Oliver was playing into her hands. But she had herself under control again. 'She wasn't a very nice girl, Anona Fingall. Running after that dreadful artist, at least twice her age, and playing God with people's lives the way she did. Arrogant. I don't suppose she's changed much.' She spoke dismissively. Destroying Nonie, and feeling her way towards bringing Oliver down with her. She hates him, Chel thought, startled. She really hates him, or is it Helen that she hates? I've wondered before, but this proves it, it's always been a running battle between them. And she'll win, if Nonie hurt Helen, for all he thinks he doesn't like her, he won't accept help from anyone who did that. It'll be finished, unless Giff can find someone else. She can't know that.

Into this jumble of thoughts and impressions, Jerry spoke quietly.

'You know that isn't true, Dorothy.'

176

'So what about it is untrue?' asked Dot. Their eyes locked. This was an old dispute, Chel thought, one that had lain too long unresolved. She didn't understand, but she felt the deep currents whirling, breaking up, destructive.

'The slant you're putting on it,' said Jerry. 'If Nonie was at fault, then so was I. And it's easy to be wise after the event, as I seem to remember pointing out at the time.'

'You *were* at fault,' Dot told him. 'That's why Helen left you.' There was a note of triumph in her voice. 'If Anona Fingall is worming her way back in, then Oliver should know the truth.'

Jerry said, with devastating honesty,

'Nonie was never *out* by my wish, and therefore your choice of words seems inappropriate.'

Dot's reply sounded strangely as if she was on the defensive.

'If she chose to live her own life, was it my fault?'

'Well, was it?' asked Jerry.

'You never received a single word from her.'

What a strangely ambivalent way of putting it, Chel thought. Jerry must have thought so too. He gave Dot an odd look.

'No, I didn't, did I?'

'Under the circumstances, don't you think that a clear statement of intent?'

'Somebody's intent, yes.' Jerry scowled, and looked momentarily so like Oliver in a mood that Chel's heart turned over.

Jerry and Dot seemed to realise together that they were committing the cardinal sin of rowing in front of the children. They fell silent, and into the space Oliver asked,

'What *truth* should I know?'

Dot opened her mouth, and Jerry said hurriedly,

'This isn't the moment, and it was all a long time ago. Come along Dorothy, I think we should leave. Before something is said that we shall all regret.'

Oliver began to speak, but Chel caught his eye and shook her head.

'Not now,' she mouthed, and then, aloud, trying to defuse the atmosphere, 'Would you like a drink before you leave? Coffee or something? We haven't been very hospitable.' *Please don't say yes!* It was like taking a step back in time to those awful sessions at the bungalow, when Dot and Susan had trapped her in the kitchen and given her advice. This time, to her relief, everyone recoiled from the suggestion as if she had suggested a night out with the Borgias.

Jerry gave her a crooked smile.

'Nice try, Cheryl, but I think we'd better go out and come in again, don't you?'

Dot gave a wide smile, but although when she spoke it was pure Dot, some of her self-satisfaction seemed to have evaporated. If it hadn't been silly, Chel would have said the woman was nervous about something.

'Now Cheryl dear, you mustn't worry that anything Oliver has said has upset me, I quite understand. I hope I know my duty as a Christian better than to take the words of a sick man in any spirit other than that of true charity.'

'Bloody hell!' shouted Oliver, and his father took Dot hastily by the arm and pushed her towards the door.

'Come along, Dorothy, we're all tired. Tomorrow.' He pushed her out ahead of him into the lobby and turned to Chel and Oliver. 'Tomorrow,' he repeated. 'I'll come over, if I may. There's something we must discuss, Oliver. You too, Cheryl.'

'Don't bring her,' said Chel, unintentionally rude, but she didn't soften it. Jerry met her eyes.

'No,' he said.

They were gone. After the door had closed behind them, Chel waited until she heard the car start before she said,

'Well!'

Oliver said, sombrely,

'What was all that about, do you think?'

'Storm in a teacup?'

'Sounded more like skeletons rattling in the family cupboard to me.'

Chel hesitated.

'Didn't anyone ever tell you - how your parents' marriage broke up?'

'Obviously not the truth.' Oliver looked stormy. 'Nonie never said she knew Helen. Why not, do you think?' A rhetorical question, Chel hoped, as she had no idea. She shook her head.

'Search me. But all that just now, it was a private quarrel, nothing to do with you.' Most of it, anyway. 'Deb said she thought they were on the final straight, didn't she? I think she could be right.'

'But *killing* someone?'

'She didn't say that.' Dot had said a lot of things tonight, without appearing to say them, Chel thought, it was a classic Dot trick. She pondered for a moment. 'Perhaps it was an accident of some sort. She's got it in for Nonie, you could tell that. You should sympathise really, she's got it in for you, too. And I don't think she was one of Matthew Sutton's admirers, either, you could hear it in her voice. *That dreadful artist.* It spoke volumes.'

178

'I thought things were coming straight at last,' said Oliver, with angry despair.

'Maybe they are. Maybe they have. You shouldn't judge without a hearing. You shouldn't judge a rabid rat on what your stepmother has to say.'

'True.' But he looked unsettled. Chel cursed Dot in her mind. Call herself a Christian, she might, but she had deliberately made trouble here tonight. Only, for once, it might rebound on her own head, and she had no idea where that thought came from, unless from Jerry's final, downright, *no*.

'Put it out of your mind for now,' she advised. 'Tomorrow - maybe - someone will tell us, we can't do anything tonight. It's not even worth discussing it.' She paused, looking at his troubled face. 'And don't worry over it. Whatever it is, it can't hurt us, it's too long ago, surely.'

'She never said she knew Helen,' said Oliver, for the second time, and Chel had to admit that that was certainly strange.

'She may not even know that you're Helen's son.'

'Come on Chel, let's get real here. She *must* know.'

Chel said,

'People in Embridge know, you grew up there after all. Why should Nonie?' and knew that she was offering false comfort. Of course Nonie knew. Dot notwithstanding, it was odd that she had never said.

'Gifford Thomas knew Helen, he said so,' said Oliver. 'He must have told Nonie, even if she *didn't* already know. Anybody would.'

'Then perhaps she didn't think it relevant,' said Chel.

'For which she must have had her reasons,' said Oliver, and fell silent, wondering uneasily what those reasons could possibly be, and what effect they might have on his recent discovery of the other side of himself, and on his new and over-riding ambition.

XII

Breakfast in the hotel dining-room, with its panoramic views of Mounts Bay, was a silent affair. Dot, although not in general sensitive, knew that she had stepped over some invisible line last night and that she must be more careful. She had never had reason to doubt her possession of Jerry, from the day that she had won him from Helen, but suddenly, she was afraid, in some hidden place inside her head, that she just might lose him, even after all this time. The years had changed Dot, as they change everyone, no longer the single-minded young woman determined to have the man she thought she loved, she had over time become, in one way at least, a more honest woman, openly proud of her standing in the town in which she had been born. Status was important to her, the fact that she had stepped all over Helen to get where she was had never troubled her. That she might have also stepped all over Jerry was a new, and disturbing idea. She had no illusions any more that he had ever loved her, but she had thought that she had been a good wife and had made him content. It was unnerving, now, to have the phrase *for the sake of the children* reverberating through her mind like a mantra, and to find herself wondering if contentment and a beautiful home had ever been enough. For Helen, it was true, in spite of Dot's efforts, had never quite gone out of his life, although neither had she definitively come back into it. The son that they shared had held them together, however tenuously, and what Jerry thought about this had never been discussed.

And now here was Anona Fingall, whom she had never liked, turning up in the life of that wild and delinquent, trouble-making son of Helen's - she never really thought of him as Jerry's - and, as she had always managed to do, creating waves and making people confront issues that were, in Dot's view, better left in abeyance. It was too bad! Thinking about Anona would bring everything back. Instinct told Dot that this was a bad time for retrospection, all the trouble and fuss over Oliver and his tacky little wife had already started shaking at the family foundations in a way that shook her complacency too, when she made herself think about it.

So she ate her breakfast quietly, attending to her husband's wants as a good wife should and holding her peace. She was rewarded, at the end of the meal, by Jerry throwing his napkin onto the table and getting abruptly to his feet.

'I'm going out,' he said.

'I'll just go and powder my nose,' said Dot, who still used such phrases where other people had long abandoned them.

'I'm going out, I said - not *we're* going out. You go and enjoy yourself round the shops.' He spoke as if what she did hardly mattered, dismissively. Dot was indignant.

'The shops are in the centre of the town. How do I get there, may I ask?'

'You walk,' suggested Jerry, not unkindly. 'It isn't far.' Dot wasn't in the habit of walking.

'You could drop me off.'

'I'm not going through the town,' said Jerry. Dot sniffed.

'Going to see *Oliver*,' she said. "How you will explain everything, I should be interested to hear.'

'Well, you aren't going to, so save your interest,' said Jerry, more shortly than he had meant.

'Well, if you want to be like that!'

Jerry did. He was surprised to find how much, as if all the bitter regret and resentment of years had suddenly crystallised when Dot - he couldn't avoid knowing - had done her best to rob Oliver of Nonie Fingall, and Nonie Fingall, for the second time, of Oliver. He didn't know if it had been on purpose, or simply Dot just being Dot, he only knew that, in that instant, he had actively hated her.

'I'll see you later,' he said, and was gone. Dot sat where she was, looking out at the road along the seafront, but Jerry's car never went past. She concluded, with an uneasy jolt, that since he wasn't going into the town, when he came out of the hotel car park, he had turned, not right for Trelewan, which would have taken him past the window, but left - for St. Ives. A horrible feeling that time was running out came over her, but where it was all running to, she didn't know. And it was so unfair. She had been a dutiful wife, she had put up with his dreadful son and given him a lovely daughter. She couldn't bear the humiliation of being deserted, divorced, everyone knowing that Jerry had got tired of her. It couldn't happen to her, not after all these years. She hadn't done anything.

Jerry, meanwhile, was on his way over the moor, headed for St. Ives, as she had thought. He had only visited Nonie's studio once, when he had called for Helen, who had been staying with her, before Matt's funeral, but he remembered more or less where it was. He didn't know if it was still hers, but someone there would know where she had gone. Those fishermen who had kept their gear underneath, maybe, or whoever had the studio now. He hadn't thought further than that, there

181

was no point. He had to speak to her, to do that he had to find her. The studio was the starting point.

And the finishing point, he soon discovered. It looked rather different now, with the gallery underneath instead of the boat store, and everything smartened up. Anona Fingall, of course, was well-known in her own right these days, she wouldn't be short of the price of a geranium. He viewed the improvements with approval. Successful himself, Jerry felt at home with success.

Success in some things anyway. Material things. He had not, he thought gloomily, made much of a success of either of his marriages, and Nonie, sensible woman, hadn't even tried it so far as he knew.

The top of the stable door was open, and Jerry, after a brief hesitation, took his courage in both hands and mounted the steps. To see Nonie again, he knew, would bring back memories that he had deliberately buried, both sweet and bitter. She had been so much of a part of his meeting with Helen, his life with her, of the time when they were all young together and thought that happiness was for ever. As it hadn't been, not for him, and not for Helen, and certainly not for Nonie. With each step upwards, as if he walked back into the past, he saw clearly that for each one of them Dot had been a catalyst. Oh, she had not been responsible for Matt's death. But for the destruction of his reputation and for the additional trouble and grief that had caused to Nonie, yes, she probably had been. By the time he had reached the top step, his mind was clear.

She would not do the same to Oliver.

Nonie had people with her, an American couple, walking round and examining the pictures that glowed against the white walls. The man spoke knowledgeably, his wife admired. They looked set for the morning. Nonie turned as the lower door clicked open, and for a moment stood there, startled into immobility. Jerry, who had been prepared for their meeting, found his voice first.

'Hullo, Nonie,' he said.

'Jerry!' He hadn't changed greatly, she would have known him anywhere. Broader, a bit grizzled at the temples, but he had kept his hair and developed what could only be described as a presence. Like him, she recognised success when she saw it and wasn't surprised. Jerry had always been going to succeed materially. It had made him, she had often thought, complacent. It had no doubt come as a shock to find that material things weren't everything. As to whether she was pleased to see him in her studio after all these years, Nonie decided that the jury was out.

The Americans looked at him with interest, but they were here for pictures and soon lost it. Nonie gestured towards them.

'I'll be with you soon. Sit down.'

The Americans obviously felt that their intention to spend several thousand pounds here entitled them to take their time over their decision, and Jerry wouldn't argue with that. The interval while they talked and discussed colour, texture, subject, form, whether their first choice would complement their interior design, gave him time to put his thoughts in order. Even so, when they finally departed, promising to return when they had agreed on a picture, they left Jerry feeling that they had been hurried. The first thing he did, therefore, was to apologise to Nonie.

'I'm sorry. I seem to have chosen a bad moment.'

Nonie went to the door, removed the sign that declared her studio to be open, and closed both sections.

'Coffee? Or is the sun over the yardarm?'

'Don't tempt me! Let's stick to coffee.'

Filling the kettle and finding mugs gave Nonie, too, time to think. Or more precisely, to wonder what to think. While the kettle was boiling, she came to perch on the arm of the sofa.

'So? What brings you here after all this time?' She sounded cold, which Jerry thought he might deserve.

'Several things.' He hesitated. 'First and foremost, I wanted to thank you for what you're doing for Oliver.'

Nonie shrugged.

'It's my pleasure. And anyway, it's Gifford Thomas you should be thanking, not me.'

Another memory.

'I haven't seen Gifford in years,' said Jerry. 'Helen exhibits with other people since... well, these days. Mainly in America right now.'

Nonie said, carefully,

'You see Helen, then?'

'Not if she sees me first.' Jerry made a wry face. 'We tried to remain friends for Oliver's sake. But mainly, I think, on my side.'

'Hmm.' The kettle boiled, and Nonie got to her feet again. 'So what did you expect? Or think you deserved, come to that?'

'She behaved quite unreasonably. You know that.'

'Do I?' Pouring water into the *cafetière*, Nonie felt the stirring of an old anger. 'Well, maybe she behaved *impulsively*. But unreasonably? I suppose that depends on what you think constitutes a reason.'

'Look,' said Jerry. 'I didn't come here to rake over dead coals with you. I came to tell you something.'

Nonie set milk to heat on the ring. She knew that she was making a production of the coffee, but it kept her hands occupied and her face turned away from Jerry. It was surprising how much the sight of him sitting so coolly there, after all these years, upset her.

'So?' she said.

'You haven't told Oliver that you know Helen. You haven't told him that you're his godmother.'

'Neither had you,' said Nonie. Jerry flushed a little.

'Yes... well... you took yourself off, didn't you? Never wrote, never even sent a birthday card. What would have been achieved if we had reminded him?'

'Hold on a cotton-picking minute!' said Nonie, swinging round indignantly. 'I was told in no uncertain terms to keep away!'

Jerry looked uncomfortable at the memory.

'Yes... well... I never meant you to take it quite so literally.'

'Oh, really? So what became of all the cards and presents I *did* send?'

'What? We never saw any.' They looked at each other. Nonie sneered at him.

'Less of the *we* might be more appropriate, then. And what about that wonderful picture I gave him for his christening?'

'It's in the bank,' said Jerry, obviously not knowing what she was talking about.

The milk boiled over. Nonie turned to deal with it.

'It is, that's true. My bank, actually. It's been there twenty years.'

Jerry had got to his feet.

'Nonie, believe me, I had no idea. I was going to give it to him when he had a home of his own... but he never did, and when he and Cheryl moved into that bungalow, I had other things on my mind. I swear I never knew!'

'You know now,' said Nonie, busy mopping. She sounded angrier than she felt, at least with Jerry, because it was one way of fighting back the tears that prickled behind her eyes. That gesture, more than any, had hurt, she had never admitted how much. Matt's beautiful picture, rejected, together with the love that had prompted the gift... She said, rubbing it in, 'She sent it back with a letter, saying that it was unfit to hang in a Christian household, or some such crap.'

'She had no right!' exclaimed Jerry.

'Oh, rights never bothered her much,' commented Nonie.

They were getting away from the point, Jerry realised. Probably they would have to come back to it, because he must take it up with Dot, and to do that he must be sure of his ground, but now wasn't the moment. A surge of anger took him unexpectedly. She had no right to do that, the picture wasn't hers, and moreover it was very valuable. Probably, knowing Dot, she hadn't even given that a thought. She only ever saw one thing at a time.

Nonie handed him a mug of coffee and led the way back to the chairs grouped round the fireplace. When they were seated, she said,

'Are you here to tell me I *should* tell Oliver?'

'No,' said Jerry. 'I'm here to tell you that, as of last night, Oliver knows, at least that you were at college with Helen.'

'Ah.' Nonie set her mug down on the table. 'Don't tell me. Dot told him.'

'She did more than that, I'm afraid. She allowed him to think that you were in some way responsible for his mother walking out, and have therefore hidden the connection from him.'

'Yes, that sounds like Dot.' Nonie clasped her hands to stop them shaking. 'She always did have a very individual way of telling the truth.'

'It *is* true, in one way, that's the point.'

Nonie considered this. Dot had obviously not changed much. She said,

'She's a mischief-maker, Jerry, always has been.'

'The trouble is, you never know how much is deliberate,' said Jerry, for whom this was no longer news. His conscience twinged momentarily.

'*You* never did, true.'

'I still don't, although I accept your estimate.'

Nonie recalled, belatedly, that there were some aspects of Dot on which she, too, had reached no definite conclusions. She said, half in despair,

'I never understood why you felt you needed to marry the woman.'

Jerry, too, was beginning to suffer from *déja vu*. He remembered that he had frequently found Nonie's point of view uncomfortable.

'Well, you always had a down on her, didn't you?'

Nonie gave him a sardonic smile.

'Oh, so you're happy as the day is long, are you? Darby and Joan personified?'

It was tempting to lie, but Jerry resisted it.

'If you really want to know the truth, she's become a very difficult woman, and once Deb is off our hands I think that will be the end of it.'

'Deb?' Nonie was astonished. 'Your daughter? She must be in her twenties, surely!'

'Twenty-four. That's still very young.'

'She's a remarkable anachronism, if she's still *very young* in this postmodern era! Does she live at home?'

'No. She hasn't done that for years now. She works in London. Lived with her boyfriend up until recently, but that's over now she tells us.' He sounded resigned.

'I rest my case,' said Nonie.

'Oh, I know what you're saying, and you're right, of course. It's just...' He paused. Why was he trying to justify himself to Nonie, of all people? She always had inhabited a different planet.

'Just what?'

Jerry said,

'It's just that I would like to get things right for just one of my children. Dot says a saint couldn't have handled Oliver right, but that can't really be true... and Susan, poor little brat, is trapped in what I suspect is a not altogether happy marriage with two children that she hardly sees being looked after by an *au pair*, and in self-defence has become a lady who lunches. An empty life.'

Nonie remembered a solemn little girl in a pushchair: round brown eyes and tumbled curls.

'Henry was a dear,' she said.

'There's a lot of good in Susan.'

'Ho!' said Nonie. 'Do I hear faint praise, damning the poor girl?'

'She admires her mother, of course, is under her influence.'

Nonie noticed that he didn't use the word *loves*. She let it pass.

'I heard that Oliver was a problem teenager through my mother, but he turned up trumps in the end, surely?'

'I think that to say *problem* is to put it mildly. He was a menacing tangle of galloping resentments.'

'He and Helen were very close. Poor little boy, he must have been devastated.'

'He never cried for her,' said Jerry. Their eyes locked.

'Really?' Nonie's heart ached for the happy child she remembered. 'And does he see her now? How do they get on?' She sounded satirical. Jerry flushed.

'She had access, of course,' he said, with dignity. 'When she had calmed down.'

'And?'

'In the end, Oliver refused to go with her. Now - well, he sees her occasionally. If he's made to, but he spent so much time abroad...' He looked uncomfortable.

Getting away, thought Nonie, poor Oliver. Getting away from everything, but unable totally to repress the gift he had from equally poor Helen, running, running, and always taking something of her with him. She looked at Jerry with an emotion verging on dislike.

'You must be proud,' she said, ambiguously.

'Since you mention it, no.'

'You're lucky that he's come out of it as well-balanced as he is. You should be thanking your lucky stars that he had the strength of character to find a way to handle it. Even if you didn't approve of the way he chose.'

'He did his best to make what was already difficult, impossible,' said Jerry.

'Don't blame him. It was your choice, nobody forced you.'

Jerry said nothing, and Nonie, slamming the point home, said,

'And was it worth it? Did Dot go on worshipping you, make you feel good about yourself?'

He shook his head, but it was a moment before he said,

'No. I'm not sure she ever did, when you come down to it.'

'Well, go to the top of the class! She had a crush on you, she resented Helen because she took you away, and she did everything she could to break up your marriage, and then, when she had you, she didn't want you any more. Anyone with half a brain could have predicted it.'

'She married Henry,' said Jerry, defensively.

'Why are men so *stupid*?' Nonie asked the empty air. 'She told me why once, and in as much as I believe anything Dot says, I believed her. But it was all part of her obsession with *you* when it came down to it, and you were wrong to have ever encouraged her. It was marital suicide!'

'I didn't encourage her!' cried Jerry, indignantly.

'Oh? How often did you tell her to bugger off and leave you alone, then?'

'Now look here - '

'No, *you* look here! You may think that you were making a stand, being kind to a friend and a client, sorry for her even, but what you were actually doing, and were too dumb to see, was letting her destroy Helen. You *loved* Helen, for God's sake! Why did you do it?'

'She admired Helen. It was Helen - '

Nonie took a deep breath.

'You poor, deluded creature, and after all this time! Can't you be honest with yourself, just the once? She hated Helen's guts, she was jealous of her, she wanted what Helen had. Is that clear enough for you?'

There was a pause, while they glared angrily at each other.

'Well, she never got it,' said Jerry, stiffly. Nonie's eyes narrowed speculatively.

'Is that so? Then I hope you were pleased with yourself for what you did!'

'You've grown into a very hard woman, Anona Fingall,' said Jerry, and rather to his surprise, Nonie laughed.

'End of conversation. OK. Aren't you going to ask me about Oliver's pictures?'

'What's there to ask? It's kind of you to take the trouble. I've thanked you already, he needed something to take his mind off things.'

'Jerry Nankervis, there are times when I think you were standing behind the door when eyes were being handed out! Have you *seen* them?'

Jerry looked uncomfortable, there was a spark in Nonie's eye that made him so. He fidgeted.

'There was one hanging in the house. I don't know much about it, but it looked quite competent.' He had said the wrong thing. He knew it. Nonie gave a snort.

'*Quite competent!* Honestly, Jerry! No wonder Helen despaired of your understanding.'

'Better than that?'

'I should say so!'

'So?' asked Jerry, after a pause. 'How much better?'

Nonie got to her feet and gathered up the untouched coffee mugs.

'This is cold. And now, the sun really *is* over the yardarm. D'you fancy a glass of wine? I'm afraid there's no beer in the fridge these days.'

'How much better?' persisted Jerry. Nonie paused, the mugs in her hands.

'Does it matter to you? Or has Dot made you write him off as a has-been? Jerry, if you blush any deeper, you'll have a stroke!'

He couldn't repeat to Nonie some of the things that Dot had said. They constituted, he realised, several of the nails in Dot's coffin, the casket that held what had become their travesty of a marriage. He fell back on what had been said last night, unsure what was expected of him.

'It's good for him to have a hobby. I suppose he might sell some of them, that would help.'

'Philistine,' said Nonie. She poured the cold coffee into the sink and opened the baby fridge beside it. 'I suppose, if you only saw the one, I shall have to forgive you though. Oliver, Jerry dear, is going to be first class. Think of Helen, and all her talent and success.' She paused, a bottle in her hands, and watched him thinking. 'He's every inch her son. You get the idea?'

'But he never even went to art college! He was given the chance - '

'Oh, shut up,' said Nonie, wearily. 'College isn't everything. He was born with it. Helen knew. Only you insisted on sending him to that silly playgroup because Dot said so.'

'Nonie, stop rubbing it in, will you?'

'Smarts, does it?' She poured white wine into two glasses, and handed one of them to him. 'Drink up, it'll do you good. And before you whinge about driving, it's low alcohol, and one glass won't hurt you.'

'I wasn't going to whinge.'

'Good, that's one mercy. I thought Dot might have made you sign the pledge, with all her Christian values and rubbish.'

Jerry made a feeble attempt to carry the war into the enemy's camp. He might have known he would be routed.

'You think Christian values are rubbish?'

'Not genuinely held ones, no, although I don't see why the Church thinks it has the monopoly. But Dot's, definitely. Look at her track record.'

Jerry abandoned the unequal contest. It was true, Nonie had become hard, perhaps it was because she had never married, he thought, and then realised that he was being anti-feminist and patronising.

'You're blushing again,' said Nonie, critically.

'You mean that, about Oliver?' asked Jerry, before she could ask him why. He could feel the sand shifting under his feet, and knew better than Nonie how unstable it was. He wasn't about to pour his heart out to a woman who, he felt, had always held him in very slight contempt.

'I don't fantasise about things that matter,' said Nonie. 'Unlike some.' She raised her glass. 'Here's to him. Here's to his amazing talent, and here's to his inevitable success.'

Their glasses clinked together.

'I can drink to that,' said Jerry.

Chel had spent most of the previous night wondering if she had been reading too much into the events of the evening. She had long since decided, on good evidence, that Oliver's stepmother was a self-righteous, mischief-making, interfering pain in the arse who manipulated people to get her own way - but this time, she had had nothing obvious to gain, and yet her attempt to demolish Nonie Fingall in Oliver's estimation had been quite blatant and not wholly explained by her dislike of him. Chel thought it boded no good but couldn't work it out, and she was therefore not best pleased when a taxi deposited Dot on the doorstep.

'We were all tired, last night,' she said, bustling in before Chel could stop her - although how that could have been achieved, she had no idea. 'Jerry was cross with me, I know, so I thought I would come and make my peace.'

'Where is he?' asked Chel, peering over her shoulder but seeing only the departing taxi. Her heart sank.

'Oh, he's gone to St. Ives to look up Anona - they are old friends, you know. To see what can be done to help Oliver, I expect.' Honey-sweet, much-to-be-dreaded Dot, dripping poison over everything, full of helpful advice and false sympathy. Chel almost shuddered.

'Oliver doesn't need help,' she said.

Dot had surged past her into the living area, where she couldn't help seeing Oliver, sketching in the conservatory. He reached out deliberately when he caught sight of her and pushed the doors closed, but they didn't quite catch. Ignoring her, he went on sketching with his head turned away. She tutted forgivingly as she sat on the sofa, pulling Chel down beside her.

'Of course he does! You must be more practical, Cheryl dear. You must know that there are all sorts of schemes for people like poor Oliver nowadays. You should ask at your local job centre, they'll run rehabilitation classes for people who are unemployable through injury. They would teach him to do something useful, something within his ability. It would give him back a little pride, that's so important for them.' She gave Chel's hand a cosy pat, and Chel cringed, aware that Oliver could hear every word.

'Would you like some coffee?' she asked, trying to change the subject, but Dot couldn't leave it alone.

'You know I wouldn't dream of interfering, don't you dear? But you poor children, you've been through such a terrible time, it's up to us as true Christian parents not to stand aside and let you struggle on alone. Anona Fingall trained as a teacher, she won't work for nothing, I know, and you must let Jerry help with the fees, you don't want to be beholden to her.' Pat, pat.

The subject of fees had never been mentioned, at least in Chel's hearing, but now that Dot had brought it up, she found herself thinking that they had been taking advantage, which was just so typical of Dot. Unless Oliver had come to some arrangement, it would now have to be discussed the next time they saw Nonie, which among so many other questions that needed to be asked and answered after last night, would probably be the end of her visits. Why had everything suddenly become so complicated?

Easy answer. One word. Dot.

No, correction. If Jerry was discussing fees now and there was no existing arrangement, maybe they would never see her again, which would solve one problem, even if it presented them with another.

Bugger!

'Coffee,' said Chel, for the second time, and got determinedly to her feet. To her annoyance, Dot followed her into the kitchen.

'I would prefer tea, dear. And could I just powder my nose, do you think?'

'Of course.' The downstairs shower-room was full of boots and coats, and since it had been raining on and off for the past few days, quite possibly mud trodden in from the garden. 'The bathroom is upstairs. First door on the left.' At least that was clean, she had taken out her anger on it yesterday, when Jerry and Dot had left. Dot, thankfully, vanished upstairs, giving her a respite. Clattering mugs, she didn't hear Oliver come out of the conservatory until he spoke just behind her.

'What the hell does she want?'

'To apologise, she said,' said Chel. She turned and leaned against the worktop. 'Go back into the conservatory. I'll deal with her.'

'Where's my father? He ought to keep her on a lead.'

'Gone off on his own affairs.' She wouldn't tell him where. 'Go on - go, before she catches you.'

A desire to do just that warred in Oliver with a vague but chivalrous feeling that it would be unfair. He scowled.

'I can't leave you to face her venom on your own.'

Chel thought that it might be easier if he did. She was about to say so when a door opened and closed upstairs, and Dot came tripping back down. Chel thought that it hadn't been the bathroom. Taking the opportunity to nose around, no doubt. She felt unreasonably annoyed, after all, there was nothing to hide up there.

'Oliver!' cried Dot. 'Now you didn't have to stop your drawing to entertain me, you know. Cheryl and I are getting on like a house on fire!'

I wish the house *was* on fire, thought Chel, she might go then. She poured water onto the teabag in Dot's mug, and Dot smiled widely.

'No teapot, Cheryl dear? And I *would* prefer a cup, if you have one.' A comment about the superiority of loose tea hung unspoken in the air.

Their wedding-present cups and saucers, seldom ever used, were still in a box in one of the spare bedrooms, and they had long since mislaid the teapot, it was quite possibly still in Embridge. Chel only just repressed a sigh.

'I'm sorry,' she said, without adding excuses. She picked up the tray and carried it through to the coffee table. This time, she avoided sitting beside Dot by waiting out of reach until she was seated and then taking the armchair. Oliver, she saw with regret, feeling robbed of his options had taken the grandfather chair and was preparing to be as difficult and unco-operative as possible in the hopes that his stepmother would take the hint and go. This time, her sigh was unintentionally audible.

'Poor little Cheryl,' said Dot, sympathetically, which at least made a change from *poor Oliver*, although probably not for long. 'It must be so hard for you, dear. You should find a little hobby of your own while poor Oliver is busy with his painting.' There, Chel knew it couldn't last. 'It would do you good.'

Chel thought of the beautiful paintings stockpiling in the room upstairs. Dot had looked at them, of course. Prying old witch! She said,

'It's more than a hobby,' and immediately wished she had kept silent, as Oliver had for once had the sense to do. She should have known better than to expose Oliver's ambitions to Dot.

'He's obviously been working hard,' said Dot, indulgently. 'All those paintings, my goodness! But you mustn't let him get depressed, dear, all those boats and things, looking back all the time - I'm not at all sure that it's the best thing for him, you know.'

'Looking back?' queried Oliver, in a tone of voice that should have warned her.

'Oh, darling!' she cried. 'All that rough sea! You really would do better to put all that behind you, don't you think? There's such pretty countryside, and so many interesting things round here, why don't you draw some of them for a change and get out in the fresh air? It really would be healthier, and I'm sure *they* would sell like hot cakes!'

Oliver's rush of indignant fury was its own undoing, he took such a sudden breath before launching out at her that he choked on a mouthful of hot coffee. Dot took the mug from him like a nursemaid and put it back on the table.

'Now, don't fly off the handle, dear, you always were a moody boy. I'm only speaking for your good. I did bring you up from a child, after all, I know you - perhaps better than you know yourself.'

'And are you proud of the job you made of me?' asked Oliver, getting his breath back, but she pretended not to hear the question and looked flustered. Chel rushed into the breach, with unfortunate results.

'Tell us the family news,' she said, it was the first thing that came into her head. 'We know about Debbie, of course, how is Susan?'

Dot bridled, it was becoming a lost art but she could do it.

'Deborah, of course, is behaving in a very headstrong way.' Chel thought for a moment that she was about to blame Oliver for it, but she didn't. The opening she had been given was too tempting. 'Susan is trying for another baby. Now that Annabel and Sebastian are at school, she misses having something in the nursery.' She smiled indulgently.

'Oh, great,' said Chel. Susan was a tiresome woman, but she wasn't sufficiently interested in her to bear malice at this distance, and wished her luck. Dot gave her a sly look.

'And what about you, Cheryl dear? It's over a year since your miscarriage, and you shouldn't leave these things too long. It's time you had another try at starting that family.'

Chel almost gasped. This was too much, surely, even for Dot? She did *know*, didn't she? Or didn't she?

'Oh, I don't think so,' she said, avoiding Oliver's eye, but Dot wasn't to be stopped. She had, Chel realised angrily, used - possibly even invented - Susan's unlikely wish for another baby as a deliberate stepping-stone to a new and more dangerous vantage point for needling Oliver. Dot shook a finger at her, playfully.

'Now, you mustn't let Oliver be selfish. It's more than time you had another little baby to replace the one you lost. Men don't understand how women feel about these things, and of course, with Oliver being so ill at the time, perhaps he doesn't realise all that you went through. I can see I shall have to have a little talk with him!'

'No, please - said Chel.' She was aware of Oliver, very still and watchful, but couldn't bear to look at him. The injuries he had suffered in the attack, Chel knew all too well, made it unlikely that he would ever father another child, but even if Dot didn't know that, as *maybe* she didn't, she had no right to interfere in what was, after all, a very private thing. Her involuntary plea fell with the impact of a shout, but Dot, for whatever reason, chose to ignore it.

'Now Cheryl, you mustn't be self-sacrificing and silly.' Again, the admonitory finger wagged. 'Of course, I know it may not be as easy as all that for you both.' She broke off, with a trilling little laugh. 'But I know of a very good private clinic that can work miracles, I assure you, and of course we shall be happy to foot the bill, you know that. After all, we know you *were* both fertile, and I had a word with Dr. Smithers, and he assures me - '

Oliver cut in before she could finish, his own voice throbbing with such anger that it stopped her in her tracks.

'How dare you!' he said.

She turned to him, smiling and placatory, all innocence, and Chel felt a coldness in the pit of her stomach. Faced with a dilemma which both Nonie and Jerry would have found familiar, she found herself reluctant to condemn and unable to exonerate. She felt sick.

'Now, Oliver dear - '

'Don't you *Oliver dear* me! How dare you discuss our private affairs with other people? How dare you think that you can buy the right to interfere in our lives - is there one area of our privacy that you haven't violated in the short time since you came here? Just keep out of it, if you please!'

'Now Oliver dear,' she repeated soothingly. She sounded as if he was still in the nursery, which was more or less how she had behaved to him all morning. She leaned forward and began gathering up the empty mugs, busily putting them onto the tray. Chel might as well not have been there. 'It's high time you pulled yourself together, Oliver,' she said, and in the pause that followed it would have been possible to hear a pin drop. 'I know that at the time nobody told you exactly what happened, when you were so badly hurt, but poor Cheryl was very ill too and it's time you understood that. You can't be self-centred all your life you know, and it's time you started considering this poor child as a woman - as a wife. Women need children - '

'I don't want them!' cried Chel. 'It's our business, not yours, please keep out of it - '

'Don't be silly, please, Cheryl. Women have a natural instinct towards maternity,' said Dot, as if she was laying down the ten commandments. She turned again to Oliver. 'Poor little Cheryl nearly broke her heart when her little baby died.'

'Mine, too,' Oliver reminded her, in a voice like cracked ice. 'Chel's right, it isn't your business.'

'It is our business. You're our responsibility, you're our son. Your wife should be allowed to have children - '

'Will you shut up?'

'Now Oliver dear, don't go making a scene. Just listen to me, for I'm going to give you some very good advice if you want your marriage to last. Remember, I'm your - '

'If you say you're my mother, I won't answer for the consequences,' said Oliver, dangerously.

Incredibly, she smiled at him.

'At least admit that I've been a better mother to you than your own ever was.'

There was a moment of stillness, before Oliver said, quite quietly,

'That isn't true.'

'She abandoned you!' cried Dot.

'She did nothing of the kind,' retorted Oliver. 'She was pushed out - by you. I don't know why I never saw it that way before, but you've always interfered in my life when I look back, so why not hers too? Long before you bust up her marriage - no, don't bother to deny it! Helen had got something you wanted, hadn't she, and you took the very first opportunity that offered to take her for everything she had!' He paused, and in the stunned silence that succeeded his accusation, said, 'Even me. But mother to me, you were not. You made perfectly certain that I grew up motherless.'

'That's a terrible thing to say!'

'It was a terrible thing to do.' Oliver narrowed his eyes. 'You're a cuckoo. You never wanted her child, you never cared a damn! You just didn't want her to have me, to have anything.'

'I reared you like my own!'

'Then heaven help Debbie and Suse.'

'Cheryl!' cried Dot, although why she thought Chel would be on her side, Chel had no idea. In any case, there was no stopping either of them now. 'Are you going to let your husband sit there and say such things? After all the things you *know* I've done for him!'

'You've done nothing for me!'

'I brought you up!'

'I wouldn't boast about it, if I was you.'

'I did my best - you were such a difficult, unloveable child - '

'I was an *unloved* child, I agree.'

'She neglected you!'

'She loved me, at least. As much as she was allowed.' A chip at himself, too? Chel wondered. This was developing into the kind of slanging match in which all kinds of things best left buried, rose stinking to the surface, and without Jerry there Chel had no idea how to stop it. She found that she was trembling.

'Please - ' she heard herself saying, uselessly. Neither of them took any notice.

'You never loved her in return!' cried Dot. 'You had no love in you, even as a young child you were cold and wild and uncontrollable, totally self-centred! Look how you're treating Cheryl now - she knows - and Jerry - you only married her to spite us all, but you could at least consider her feelings!'

'Oh yes, I did love Helen!' shouted Oliver. 'She and I used to understand each other, I thought, until you - *you* told me different! I was six years old, my God, what would you have done if some troublemaker had come waltzing in telling you, oh so kindly, that your mother had more important things to do than look after you?'

The row had escalated into a whirlwind, until they were shouting at each other at the tops of their voices. None of the three of them had heard the knocking on the front door, none of them had heard it open.

'Did you say that, Dorothy?' asked Jerry, unexpectedly.

The quietness of his voice brought the combatants down from their soaring high quicker than a bucket of cold water on a pair of fighting dogs. Oliver looked shocked, Dot suddenly lost and deflated. She said, uncertainly,

'I don't know. I might have. I meant it for the best. She was a totally unsuitable woman to have charge of a child.' Her voice gained confidence on the last words. She sounded more like herself, with the support of Jerry behind her - if support it was. Chel said, her voice pulsing with rage, taking up the fight where the other two had dropped it,

'Oliver is exactly the same, but he's quite suitable, apparently!'

'Helen is an artist. She thought it gave her some great privilege denied to the rest of mankind!' retorted Dot, spitefully.

'Oliver is an artist, too,' said Chel.

His stepmother's eyes flickered over him with scorn and dislike, and the will and ability to hurt and humiliate.

'Oliver is a cripple,' she said.

When Chel had been unpacking all the treasures from the flat, she had placed at either end of the mantelpiece a pair of antique fishing floats, one a dark, glowing red, one a vibrant and beautiful blue, that had been brought up from a wreck at the bottom of the sea. The mantelpiece was close to Oliver, in a movement swifter than Chel had realised he could make, he had the blue one in his hand, weighing it like a bowler before a wicket, more furiously, blindly angry than she had ever expected to see him.

'Get out!' he said, and he didn't sound like Oliver at all. 'Get out, and stay out!'

Chel was across the room and had caught the movement of his hand before it had barely started, in the same instant as Jerry caught Dot's arm and pulled her sprawling from the sofa to the comparative safety of the floor.

'Don't!' cried Chel. 'Don't, Oliver - ' Fighting his arm down was like pitting her strength against steel, getting about on crutches had developed the muscles of his shoulders and arms to a pitch that she hadn't expected. He gave in quite suddenly, and the ball dropped onto the floor, hitting the edge of the stone hearth and exploding as it went. The sherds lay on the mat, holding in their broken curves the deep, shining blue of the Mediterranean. Nobody spoke.

Dot regained her breath first. Her voice shook as she spoke.

'Jerry - did you see that, Jerry? Your son might have killed me!'

Jerry watched her scrambling inelegantly to her feet, making no attempt to help. His face was rigid with anger.

'You ever do that again, Dorothy- to any one of my children, and that's *it!*' He added, more quietly, 'And don't think I don't mean it.'

'He was trying to kill me!' she repeated, on a rising note. 'He's out of his mind, he should be under restraint - '

Chel's teeth were chattering so that she had difficulty saying anything.

'Go - p-please go.'

Jerry took Dot firmly by the arm and swung her away before she could speak, giving her a push towards the door that was far from sympathetic and made her stagger. He looked at Chel and Oliver with such pain in his face that Chel felt tears sting behind her eyes.

'I'm sorry. She was meant to be shopping. Will you two be all right?'

'Yes...' said Chel, on a whisper.

They went. Dot said spitefully, over her shoulder,

'You had better take care, miss, or you'll be sending for the men in white coats - '

The door slammed, cutting her off.

Chel let out a long breath.

'Whatever did you do to make her hate you so?'

'I'm just beginning to understand,' said Oliver, but didn't explain. His face frightened her. He reached for the hated crutches and got, rather unsteadily to his feet. 'I'm going outside. Please leave me alone.'

It was an order, but Chel, shaken by that moment of uncontrollable jungle fury wouldn't have stood in his way in any case. She picked up the tray of mugs and went the opposite way, to the kitchen. Returning after a few minutes with the dustpan, she saw him on the lawn, pacing up and down with his shuffling step, the jungle animal forever caged and churning with rage and frustration, and could have wept. She knelt to collect the broken sherds, and their brightness was misted with her unshed tears. For a moment, wrenched with pain for him, she just stayed there, still, the biggest of the sherds in her hand and the dustpan ignored beside her.

The misty, beautiful blue cleared before her eyes and became the wine-dark sea, the land-locked Mediterranean, lapping the shores of a headland. Not a big headland, but not so small either. Rising to a hill towards the mainland, climbing olive groves ringed its shingly beaches, black cypress trees pointed to the blue, blue sky. A village of little

197

white houses tumbled to the shore under its protection, encircling a harbour where caiques and yachts lay at anchor or ranged along the quay, tavernas and shops crowded on the quayside. And a path leading steeply through the village, to a balconied villa set above the water, white among the cypresses. A dream... a time that was gone... the whisper of water along a curving hull and the creak of a sail in the wind....

'It's so bloody *unfair*! cried Chel, aloud, and was immediately sitting by the hearth with a curved sherd of blue glass in her hand, and horribly familiar tears running down her face.

Everything in pieces, not just the beautiful glass ball. She swept the broken fragments together, tipped them into a cardboard box and took them out to the dustbin. It had begun to rain quite hard now, as if the weather was in sympathy with the mood in the house, and she was glad, when she came back inside, to see Oliver heading indoors. She watched for a moment as he struggled with the step up onto the terrace, was it her imagination or was he finding it easier? Imagination of course, nothing good was going to come out of today. She turned away from him and went upstairs. He didn't want to talk to her, nor she to him. Now was the time for thinking and for being alone.

Later, she came downstairs and walked quietly into the living area, wondering what she would find, but Oliver was once more drawing in the conservatory. He looked up as he became aware of her moving beyond the french doors, not an unfriendly look but not smiling either. She pushed the door open and went in to join him, they had to meet sometime.

'Hi,' she said. Oliver gave her a nod, as if he didn't yet quite trust himself to speak, and returned to his drawing. But he wasn't drawing the sea, she saw over his shoulder, he had taken his stepmother's unkind advice and exercised his talents on a stone circle. He felt her eyes on it, and said,

'Since she's so into the beauties of the countryside, she can take this one home to the Women's Institute.' He tore it from the top of the block and held it at arm's length, studying it critically through narrowed eyes. 'That should shut her up, don't you think?'

Chel whisked it out of his fingers and stared at it in utter consternation. He had used his gift for caricature in a way that had turned a simple landscape into a gross distortion that sent a chill down her spine. The stones stood black under a stormy sky, in an attitude of waiting that made them look hideously alive. Ink-black shadows held lurking, half-seen, half-imagined horrors, nasty little watching eyes peered from tangled bushes, evil pulsed off the paper. It was quite the most horrible picture that she had ever seen, a distilled essence of torment, misery, and the blackest deeps of despair. It scared her.

'Oliver - '

'Oh, don't worry,' he said, with a sudden, unexpected grin. 'It's not really me - just the side-effects of some of those drugs I used to have to take, junkie that I was, but she isn't to know that. And although you look far too sane ever to have experimented with hallucinatory drugs, she knows that I did, and at least it should stop her boasting about the way she brought me up.' The spark of amusement died, his hovering depression surged back like a breaking wave. 'Oh God - now I've made you unhappy.'

'You shouldn't antagonise her,' said Chel, obscurely troubled.

'Why not? She does it to me.'

Chel wanted to say, but she's much better at it, and didn't. She could feel Oliver's antagonism like a third person in the room, and that sort of thing was maybe OK for the totally fit and healthy, she supposed, but not for the chronically sick. Annoyed with herself, for she had thought of Oliver as injured, tiresome, desperately unfortunate, all sorts of different things at different times, but never before as chronically sick, which he was not, she said,

'At least let me get rid of this horrible picture,' and to her relief, he agreed. He had discovered that he didn't much care for the idea of hitting at his tormentor at his wife's expense.

'All right. Bin it, then.'

Chel took it into the kitchen, tore it up and put the pieces on a plate. She found a box of matches in a drawer and struck one with fingers that shook a little. The tiny flame from the match licked round the shreds of paper, caught, burned up. She pushed them all together round the funeral pyre until the last one had been reduced to black ashes, and tipped the ash out of the window into Will's field beyond, brushing the last of the fine dust away with her fingers, rinsing both them and the plate thoroughly under the tap when she had done. She couldn't bear the thought of even the ashes in the house. There had been an implication behind that stone circle that had made her cold all over, although she couldn't identify it. There were things there that she didn't know, didn't want to know, and was certain were best forgotten. It was better as ashes, scattered on the brown earth.

But in her mind, against her will, as she put the plate away, were memories of betrayal, heartbreak and suicide, and the twisted metal bones of a broken aeroplane.

It wasn't going to be as easy as Jerry tried to make out, thanks to

Dot, Nonie thought as she drove over the moor the following morning, headed for Trelewan. The only thing that Jerry had probably done right was to leave it to her to explain, and she wasn't even sure about that, and it had taken her the best part of twenty-four hours to summon up the courage to try..

Her worst fear, as she drove through Trelewan, and a prescient one, was that Dot had somehow been before her. True, Jerry had driven off with the car and left her at the hotel, but she was quite capable of not taking the hint. From what Jerry had said, she had thrown a cat among the pigeons, it would be just like Dot to send a pack of hounds in after it. She parked beside Moor House with unaccustomed trepidation.

It was too grey and cold these days for even Oliver to paint outside, but knowing that he would have the french doors wide open regardless, Nonie went round the house through the garden, she had no wish to run the risk of having the front door closed in her face, and wasn't at all sure of her reception. It irked her to feel so uncertain, emotion should never stand in the way of the work, but she could see Oliver's likely point of view. There was no reason why she shouldn't have mentioned that she knew Helen unless that reason was a bad one. A child could work that out. She wondered what the relationships between them all really were, it was unlikely that Jerry had been totally honest, even with himself.

Oliver was painting in the conservatory, he looked up as Nonie appeared on the patio, but for once there was no warmth in his eyes.

'Oh, it's you,' he said. 'You took your time.' It wasn't a good start. Nonie paused in the doorway.

'Will you listen to me? Or are you going to cut off your nose to spite your face?'

'Oh, I would never do that. You know I need you.' His voice was as cool as his eyes.

'Then may I come in?' She had never felt she had to ask before.

'I can't stop you.'

'Oliver - ' She stepped over the threshold. 'Can we talk sensibly?'

'Is there anything sensible to say? Apart from the fact that I am sick to my soul of people keeping things from me and lying to me, that is, and that I didn't expect it of you.'

'I would have mentioned that I knew Helen, but you obviously didn't remember me, or know my name, and it was all a long time ago now.'

'*Remember* you?' Oliver laid down his brush. He recalled that she had been fleetingly familiar when he first saw her. He frowned.

'I've known you since before you were born. I was godmother at your christening.' In one sense, he had been at Matt's funeral.

'So Helen was your friend, but still you hurt her.' A statement, not a question.

Peachey hurt her, Nonie thought. He set it up deliberately, and he would be laughing himself sick if he could see how well it's worked out. Peachey loved Helen and Dot loved Jerry, and neither of them knew the real meaning of the word, so between them, they had ruined several lives and a reputation.

'May I tell you about it? Then you can tell me what you would have done in my place - and in your father's.'

'If my father was running true to form, he swept whatever it is under the carpet,' said Oliver, with bitterness. 'And you? *Playing God*, my stepmother called it. So am I to hear the truth at last?'

Nonie could feel his sarcasm creeping into her own voice, and disliked herself for it.

'Will you have the full version, or the abridged?'

'Just give it straight, and leave out the flowery bits.'

Flowery bits? Had there been any? Nonie took a deep breath and took the first dangerous, unsteady step down memory lane, knowing that someone - not her, but someone - owed it to Oliver and wishing that it hadn't fallen to her to pay. She wondered where Chel was, and the thought that she was keeping out of the way brought no comfort.

'Helen and I met at college. We made a threesome, me, Helen, and Helen's boyfriend, Dan Peachey.' She caught Oliver's eye. 'No, that's not a flowery bit. It's the whole point, just wait and see.'

'Sorry,' Oliver had the grace to say.

'We were all young, having a good time. To Helen and me, nothing was very serious. To Peachey... I ought to explain Peachey.' She hesitated, for how to do that? At the time, she had taken him at face value, and her hindsight was coloured by Matt's opinions, forcefully expressed.

She settled for, 'Peachey was unstable,' and in retrospect, found it an understatement. 'Matt thought - ' She broke off, swept with unexpected pain. *You want to watch it, Anona Fingall. You're beginning to say* Matt thinks *at the beginning of every sentence.* Past tense now. She took a breath, conscious that Oliver was looking at her curiously. She began again. 'Matt thought he had a drug problem. That wasn't as common in the sixties as it is now, whatever you hear, but it certainly happened, even in places like Embridge. Helen told me later that it was true. Perhaps that was why... he did what he did.'

'Matt?' prompted Oliver, for all he knew at this point, of course, was that an artist called Matthew Sutton had crashed into the roof here and died, and there was no obvious link.

'Matt Sutton. He was a lecturer at the college,' said Nonie. Her mouth curved into a tender, reminiscent smile. 'A very bad one, actually. It's where we met.' She paused momentarily, choked by emotion. Oliver looked at her with no discernible sympathy.

'Go on,' he said.

'Helen lived with her grandparents, her father - but you'll know all that,' Nonie interrupted herself, remembering what he had said about flowery bits.

'No,' said Oliver. 'Why did she live with her grandparents?'

Nonie stared at him.

'Don't you know *anything at all*?'

'Why?' reiterated Oliver. Nonie said, blankly,

'Her mother, their daughter was dead, and her father married again. He lived in Edinburgh, but the art school in Embridge was particularly hot on ceramics, which was always her particular thing, so she lived with her grandparents. There wasn't anything sinister about it. She was welcome in her father's home, and in fact she often stayed there in the holidays. OK?'

'Yes. Go on.'

Nonie was settling into her story now. No need to go into details about Matt, ultimately that could only make bad, worse. She said,

'Jerry's parents had been friends of her mother's, when she was alive. Her grandparents thought it would be nice to get them together - Jerry and Helen - and they arranged it.' She gave an involuntary laugh, remembering that meeting. 'She'd spent months ducking and diving, trying to avoid meeting him, and he had told everyone that he had already got a girlfriend, putting up a smokescreen, and then they met, and bang! They both looked extremely foolish.'

'Can you come to the point?' asked Oliver, stony-faced, and Nonie remembered how that fairy-tale meeting had ended. She said,

'Peachey resented it. He loved her, in so far as he could love anyone, I don't think she realised it. She was simply too wrapped up in Jerry. At first...' She hesitated. At first, Peachey had thought it was Matt, but that was her story and probably irrelevant here.

'At first?' prompted Oliver.

'It doesn't matter. Flowery bit.' She gave him a wry smile. 'Anyway, he crashed out of college - in fact, we all did, for one reason and another. Helen was the only one who finished her course, and that was in Edinburgh... but you don't want to hear about all that. What matters is what Peachey did... and me... and Jerry.' She fell silent, and this time Oliver said nothing. After a while, she found the words.

'It was her wedding day. I was chief bridesmaid. She was upstairs with her father, and the phone went, just as the first wedding car drew up to the door... I answered it.' Her throat closed, remembering what followed, and she swallowed. 'It was Peachey. He said... he said, if she didn't go to him at once, he was going to kill himself, and I thought... I thought...' She broke off. She had imagined, over the years, that she had managed to put it behind her, but she hadn't. There were tears in her eyes. Oliver waited, watchful now. She thought that he knew what was coming, but he didn't help her. She said, simply. 'I was wrong. He meant it. He hanged himself while she was driving to the church to marry Jerry. She never knew - oh, she knew he had committed suicide, but she didn't know why, or exactly when. Jerry and his parents, and her grandparents... and me... we all kept it from her. We were wrong, but it looked as if we were right at the time. It was so cruel.' And that was ambiguous, if you like!

There was a long pause. Nonie, who was still standing at the door, looked out over the drizzle-swept lawn and tried to bite back tears that she hadn't expected, and after all this time, deeply resented. After a while, Oliver spoke.

'And when she found out, she blamed you both? Is that it?'

It wasn't, not all of it, but it would do for now.

'Yes,' said Nonie. Oliver said,

'Did she love him, then?'

The question was unexpected, and one that Nonie had, in fact, never considered. She looked at him in surprise.

'No - no, not in that way. She never did, it was a boy and girl thing for her, although obviously not for him.'

'Then it seems to me a gross over-reaction to break up her marriage over it, not to mention your friendship - or am I missing something here?'

'So you think we were right to keep it from her?' asked Nonie, too quickly.

'Don't ask me for absolution,' said Oliver. 'I wasn't there, was I? If you were in the wrong, this Peachey character was more so... I would say. But two wrongs never made a right. On the other hand, what good would it have done for her to know? Look, I can play devil's advocate all day, if you want me to, but it isn't going to alter anything.' He broke off, and said, in an irritated way, 'Oh, do sit down! You're making me uncomfortable, standing there as if you thought you were on trial!'

Nonie thought, if she had been, she had been acquitted, although exactly what of she wasn't certain. She sat, and was about to relax when Oliver said,

'And one day, when you feel like it, you can tell me the rest - which I take it, since you left it out, is nothing to do with you?' He made it into a question.

'I don't think it's for me - ' began Nonie, but, he interrupted.

'Not at all, it's your godmotherly duty.' He smiled, crookedly. 'Just answer me one question. This girlfriend my father claimed to have. The Dreaded Dot?'

It had been Helen's name for her, and it was strange to hear it on her son's lips. She said,

'Who else?' and made an expressive face.

'So, was it true?'

Nonie thought back, searching for an honest answer.

'About as true as that Peachey was Helen's boyfriend, I suppose. One-sided, or at best, unequal. As with him, maybe it became an obsession. Obsessions are dangerous things. Obsessions of any kind, Oliver. You should remember that yourself. They can rebound on your own head and clobber you flat.' She spoke robustly, anxious to close the subject.

Oliver felt as if she had turned the tables on him, disconcerted. He backed away from the further questions he had been going to ask, feeling rather as Judy must have felt when she thought she saw a man in the bathroom. The thought, unprompted, made him want to laugh.

'Chel's down in the outhouse,' he said. 'Give her a yell - if she can hear you above the sawing. I'll put the kettle on for some coffee, unless you'd sooner have tea?'

Saved by the bell, Nonie thought, as she went out onto the damp patio to do as she was told. Things were not quite the same as they had been, but Oliver had taken it all more calmly than she had expected, and for that, two reasons were obvious. One, she was wise enough to understand, was self-interest. The other had something to do with overkill, he couldn't handle any more, or didn't want to. The subject might be reopened one day, she must be prepared for that. But as for her godmotherly duty, where did that lie?

XIII

.Matthew Sutton returned to Vellanzoe on a misty November night, when summer's leaves lay rotting in the ditches and the air smelt crisp, and smoky with a dozen sweet-scented bonfires. Desperate and unfulfilled, tied by a need that couldn't be served, unable to tear himself free and move on. Coming back, always, to the place where he died, urgent to communicate yet unable to get through. Haunting...

'Oliver is obviously going to be one of the great seascape painters,' said Judy, who knew nothing about it really, but rather liked her new cousin. She was curled up before a sparking log fire lit behind the open doors of the woodburner, and looking admiringly at the latest picture, which was propped up against the back of the sofa. Exhibition work by this time, Nonie said, worlds away from his early pictures that now collected dust upstairs. Still water, dark, steep cliffs, curling mist, a sensation of dawn and birds flying... treasures from a storehouse of memory, leaping to life to be shared.

'You would know, of course,' said Oliver, and Judy laughed.

'I expect I'm about on a par with the rest of us general public. *I don't know much about Art, but I know what I like,* you know?'

'It's the critics he needs to beware of, not morons like you,' said Chel. 'Gifford Thomas says that they may well slay him just because he is who he is, accuse him of cashing in on his past reputation. Or it could work just the other way. He'll have to be brilliant before any of them forget it, and if it turns out that he is, and they do, other artists who've gone through college and then had to struggle for years and paint on sackcloth and social security in garden sheds for peanuts, are going to resent him terribly. He can't actually win.'

'*On* sackcloth or *in* sackcloth?' asked Oliver, and Judy said,

'It serves him right for being such an exhibitionist.' She got reluctantly to her feet. 'What's the time? I must go, Keith will be thinking I've eloped with the postman. Oh Sheba!'

Sheba had sneaked up beside Oliver, where he lay, or lounged, said Chel, in mock disgust, propped up on the bed as he did most evenings. Sheba considered it a splendid habit. He never pushed her off, and for all her exuberance she behaved towards him with an instinctive gentleness that was quite irresistible. Oliver at least made no attempt to resist it.

'Just look at them!' said Judy, disgusted. 'He spoils that dog rotten!'

Sheba flattened her ears and moved her tail gently, defying Judy to remove her. She had long ago worked out that for some reason beyond dogs, being close to Oliver spelt protection from forcible coercion.

'Come on, rotten dog,' said Judy, and reached for her collar.

Sheba flattened her ears still further, and a very low, warning rumble came from her throat. Judy withdrew her hand with a half-scandalised giggle.

'My goodness, she is getting partial! Come here, stupid dog!' She patted her knee invitingly, but the only response was another rumbling growl. The hairs along the dog's back began to rise up, making a rough crest on the smooth golden fur. Oliver laughed and fondled her ears affectionately.

'Go on, fool, you can't stay here all night.' He gave her rump a shove, but she bunched into a ball against him and stuck, grumbling. An attempt by Judy to haul her off bodily only resulted in a volley of sharp barks and a plea from Oliver to stop.

'I'll get up,' he said hastily. 'I can't be used as a battlefield in my state of health.' But when he left her to Judy's mercy, Sheba dived off the bed with a whine and took refuge under it. Not an easy thing to do, she had to flatten herself like a kipper to squeeze in.

Nothing would persuade her out, and quite suddenly, in the middle of the tussle, Chel felt her own hair rise on her arms and on the back of her neck, and a prickling sensation that ran the whole way down her spine. She abruptly stopped laughing at Judy, beginning to lose her temper on her hands and knees beside the bed. There was nothing that she could put her finger on, nothing to see, and the fire was warm on her legs as she sat beside it, but the oddest conviction that Sheba was aware of something that they were not took hold of her. Not in this room, maybe, but definitely in this house, and trying, as on another occasion, to use Judy as a channel. Sheba hadn't minded Oliver's touch... but Judy had been an open door to the spirit world since childhood, more instantly receptive than herself and less resistant. Like an aircraft homing in on a radio beacon, would Matthew Sutton go for the strongest signal?

Matthew Sutton? Again? Matthew Sutton had got what he wanted and gone.

Or got part of the way to what he wanted, and come back for the pay-off. Beside her on the sofa, Oliver's picture, the best that he had yet done, sat as a mute witness to the incredible. Chel knew it to her soul.

Matthew Sutton needed an artist of his own stature.

He had used her to bring Nonie to Oliver, not, as she had thought, simply himself to Nonie. That had only been the first step.

Every instinct to protect leapt immediately into action. She had no idea what Matthew Sutton could be looking for, but every story that she had ever heard of possession came into her mind and stiffened her resolution. He wasn't getting anywhere near Oliver.

Her heart began a slow, sickening thudding under her ribs and the palms of her hands had gone damp. Nobody could pitch their wits against the supernatural and win, surely.

Bell, book and candle. It sounded outrageous, even in her head. If it hadn't been so serious she would have laughed.

Judy sat back on her heels, hot and cross and dishevelled.

'She won't come out,' she said indignantly. 'She tried to bite me.'

Chel got to her feet. If she was going to defy Matt Sutton, perhaps first of all she should make quite certain that he was really there. He had been absent for months, after all.

If he had even been there in the first place.

Bugger!

'Leave her to get over it for a bit,' she suggested. 'I'm just going to take this picture upstairs - come with me, and I'll show you some of the others. Oliver won't mind.'

Judy got to her feet, dusting her hands. Chel wasn't too fanatical about cleaning under beds. She followed Chel up the stairs, asking, 'When is the great day to be, anyway?'

'Probably next October, November maybe, and even that's a miracle - getting a gallery, and in the West End too, so soon.' said Chel. They were on the landing now, if Matt Sutton was anywhere, it would be somewhere up here, he had been seen in the spare double and in the bathroom, but never anywhere downstairs, he seemed only able to go into areas where he had been in life, or in this case, as he died. Of all the rooms, the small spare room that she used as a picture store, and since the weather got colder, as a workroom, was the one where he might feel most at home. She had taken up the carpet and rolled it away and put a small, sturdy table under the window to take her tools. She pushed the door open. 'Gifford Thomas wanted it even earlier, which is a great compliment apparently, but Nonie told him not to be so greedy - told Gifford. She says Gifford is very knowledgeable, but too fond of making a fast buck and it would be much better from Oliver's point of view to wait - ' She stood aside to let Judy go past her into the room and stepped in after her.

'Goodness!' said Judy, 'It's like Siberia in here. Oughtn't you to have some heating, with all these pictures? They might turn out to be valuable, after all.'

The storage heater against the wall was set to give out a constant background warmth. Chel leaned dark cliffs and flying birds against the table, and after a pause, Judy said sharply,

'You told me he'd gone!'

'He's back tonight,' said Chel.

She hadn't switched the light on, although Matthew Sutton seemed unconcerned by either daylight or artificial light it had seemed an irrational action for a ghost hunt. They stood there side by side in the light that came through the open door. It lay in a wedge just inside but left the corners of the room in shadows that were not absolutely pitch dark. On Chel's worktable, pushed under the window, the metal tools caught the light and flung it back as a subdued sparkle. There was no sound but their own breathing.

The misty night seemed to have got into the room with them, the sparkle by the window was growing dimmer... which was strange, when the window was closed. It gradually became possible to see that the mist lay in an apparently localised cloud, lit along one edge by the light from the doorway and seeming to breathe with a life of its own. Chel reached out and grabbed Judy's hand just as Judy grabbed for hers, they held tightly to each other, wanting to leave but held where they were by a mixture of natural curiosity and an emotion that wasn't quite fear, but akin to it. They had both of them seen - some might say *imagined* they had seen - Matt Sutton before, but there was something about this manifestation that was indefinably different. It made them glad they were together.

He appeared both gradually and incompletely, as if after such a long interval he found materialising difficult. Just his head and shoulders in the swirling cloud, and an overwhelming sense of need. The soundless, gaping cry for help was in the room with them, a clamorous silence in the still night, and then in the blink of an eye it was all gone. The room was empty of all save their two selves, and gently warm from the heater. Nevertheless, Chel was shivering, and Judy reached out abruptly and switched on the light. The cluttered, familiar room sprang into view.

The urgency of that cry for help was still with them. Judy and Chel looked at each other, each seeing in her friend's face shock, doubt, and a futile desire to pretend that nothing had happened. Judy swallowed.

'What are you going to do?' she asked.

'Do?' asked Chel, uncertainly.

'He'll stay here for ever if you don't do something,' said Judy. 'It wasn't like before....' She didn't finish the thought, and had no need to. Matthew Sutton hadn't worried her when he appeared in the bathroom, any more than he had worried Chel in the bedroom, once they had got over the initial shock, because he had been benevolent. Tonight he had been desperate.

In local folklore he was desperate, too.

Matthew Sutton, whom she was increasingly sure needed, for some reason of his own, to make contact with Oliver... but Oliver was out of his reach, the one as certainly trapped downstairs as the other was upstairs. His only contact was through the medium of another person.

Matthew Sutton, who hadn't been prepared to die... Chel knew it. There must have been some overwhelming motive for him to feel that way, so strongly that in fact he had been unable completely to do so.

'We should help him,' continued Judy, with some of Matt Sutton's own urgency. 'We can't just leave him - not to cry down the years as a lost soul....' She stopped, disconcerted by the picture that her own words had made. 'We just can't,' she ended.

'Perhaps we could make him see that he's dead, somehow, and then he'd go,' said Chel, without conviction. People who were dead shouldn't be hanging around - at least, she supposed they shouldn't. As to where they were meant to be, that was another thing entirely. Also, Matt Sutton, if what she suspected was true, was perfectly well aware that he was dead. His problem, much like Oliver's, was a refusal to accept the inevitable.

But why?

'How do you talk to a ghost?' asked Judy.

'I thought that he got inside my head once - twice, maybe, I don't know if it goes both ways.' Chel hesitated, but Judy made no comment. 'There are ways, though. People hold seances, but I've never been to one. They find a medium who can go into a trance.'

Judy looked sceptical.

'Can you go into a trance? Would you even want to?'

Chel was perfectly sure on that point, without even thinking about it. 'No!'

One of them might have to try.

'We could find an expert,' said Judy, hesitantly, but neither of them liked the idea. They knew too little about the subject, only enough to know that fake mediums existed.

'Or we could ask the advice of a priest,' suggested Chel, willing to delegate responsibility. Judy said,

'I don't want the whole village to know that I see things - I don't want Keith to know. Do you want Oliver to know that you do?'

Oliver, Chel instinctively felt, was different, and probably, anyway, had a pretty good idea already. She felt that he understood - perhaps he more than understood.

'What's the matter?' asked Judy.

Chel wasn't sure what she had been about to realise, and answered with no more than the spirit of her half-formed realisation.

'Nearly forty per-cent of the population can divine water, if only they knew it,' she said, and Judy laughed, relieved to find something to ease the tension.

'I suppose you know what you mean by that,' she said.

Chel said, slowly,

'If it - if he - wants anything, I think he wants it from Oliver.'

Judy looked at her, taking due note of her reluctance, and said doubtfully,

'Perhaps if we knew what it was, Oliver could give it, or do it, and he could move on.' Then, when Chel said nothing, she added, 'He was an artist too.'

'I know,' said Chel.

Oliver was proving amazingly resilient, but not superhumanly so. Fine, when things went right, but prone to depression if they went wrong. Quite often, now, recognisably his old self, or at least a revised version of it. But even had he been completely fit, Chel would have fought to keep him apart from Matthew Sutton; as things were... their experiences at the bungalow in Embridge haunted her, the fear of possession possessed her. She would fight to the last ditch.

'What sort of person was he, I wonder?' said Judy. 'Apart from the obvious, of course - but a lot of older men fancy young girls, it doesn't have to mean all that much.'

Chel looked surprised. Her own thoughts had been quite different, and anyway, she didn't think any more that Matthew Sutton had fancied young girls, apart from one.

'I don't know - is it important?' she said.

'I was just thinking,' said Judy. 'If we knew what he was like, we might have a better idea of what we ought to do. We might even find a clue as to what he wanted. It was only a thought.'

The sudden ring of the telephone downstairs brought the down-to-earth, everyday world back into the tense atmosphere of the little room, and effectively ended the discussion. Chel ran downstairs to answer it, leaving Judy to put out the lights, for Oliver's ability to cope with the mobile depended a lot on where he happened to be when it rang. If it wasn't right beside him, the caller had often given up before he found it.

It was Keith. Spirit possession to *is Judy planning to come home tonight? Her mother's panicking about her car in this mist,* in less than a minute was too much of a contrast, and the effort to accommodate it brought Chel quickly down to earth. Speaking to Keith, who wouldn't believe in a ghost if it shook him by the hand, it was almost impossible to keep the last quarter of an hour clear in her mind - which was on the whole a relief.

Sheba had come out from under the bed as if nothing had happened, and was making up to Oliver with her tail waving and her tongue hanging out like a damp, pink ribbon. Judy grabbed her unceremoniously.

'Come on dog, there's not time for that, we're going to be disowned, if not divorced - ' She was anxious to go, as rattled as Chel, if for slightly different reasons. Her retreat was almost a rout. When she had gone, Oliver raised his eyebrows quizzically at Chel.

'I never realised Keith could so easily put the fear of God into Judy,' he observed.

'Oh,' said Chel, airily, improvising rapidly, 'He's on call, I think, she promised she wouldn't be late. That's why she came in her mother's car...' She was over-explaining. She stopped.

'Oh, really?' said Oliver, disbelievingly, but he couldn't be bothered to pursue the subject.

Chel went through the nightly routine, kettle on, upstairs to the bathroom, reluctantly tonight, nightie, make a hot drink, arrange the logs in the stove so that they would burn slowly and safely through the night, find a book to read herself to sleep - all the usual, taken for granted things that made up the pattern of a normal life.

She lay in bed when the light was finally out, watching the glow from the dying fire in the stove flickering on the ceiling. A real fire in one's bedroom on a chilly night, she now considered, was one of the luxuries of life, but tonight she found it impossible to appreciate. Life in this house wasn't normal.

Matthew Sutton... what did he want? What could he possibly want with Oliver?

Possession...?

The long night crept on.

Chel tossed and turned, dreamed complicated, disturbing, half-waking dreams, and finally fell into a deep sleep just before dawn, from which she awoke on the swing of the pendulum from last night's fears, inclined to laugh at herself. Spirit possession had no substance in broad daylight, and Oliver looked in any case a poor subject for it these days.

He had taken a while to get over that confrontation with the Dreaded Dot, but she thought this morning, as she watched him peacefully mixing colours, that that at least was now behind them, and that in making himself come to terms with its implications he had matured ten years. - caught up with himself, if one cared to look at it that way. Gone for good now were both the selfish, casually charming young adventurer and the self-centred and emotionally unstable invalid who had followed him. Growing out of the shipwreck that the two of them had experienced was a highly gifted man in his early thirties, with confidence in his own talent and a far greater awareness of the rights and needs of other people. If it was Oliver's fate never to be wholly himself, at least his personality was rich enough for either half to stand as sufficient on its own. With a more balanced background and better luck, he would have reached the stars. He might yet.

Oliver looked up, his palette knife poised and with an enquiring tilt to his head.

'You're staring at me,' he told her.

'I was wondering what you would have been like if Helen had brought you up,' said Chel, without quite intending to.

'Good God,' said Oliver. 'Why?'

'I don't know really.' Chel came through the french doors and perched on the arm of one of the rattan chairs, precariously. 'You would have been quite a different person, and I should probably never have met you, let alone married you.'

'Would that be good, or bad?' Oliver squeezed more paint onto his palette and mashed it with the knife, looking at the result critically. 'If I added green, for instance, to this, it would be a different colour - but would it be any the worse for that?'

'Quite disgusting, I should think,' said Chel, looking at it critically. 'I suppose it depends what you want.'

'Well...' said Oliver thoughtfully, picking up a brush. 'I didn't want to be disabled... but that might have happened anyway. With me round her neck, Helen might have been less successful, and whatever she may choose to think, success matters to her... and I wouldn't want to have missed being married to you. Why this sudden burst of philosophy, anyway? Life is just a bowl of cherries, we all know that.'

'It's the turn of the year. I always get philosophical in the autumn.'

'Hmm.' He painted for a minute or two in silence, and suddenly said, out of the blue, 'So what do you think I should do?'

Chel didn't make the mistake of thinking that the remark followed directly on from the previous one, but there was, she thought, a connection. She said cautiously,

'About what, in particular?'

'About Helen,' said Oliver, without looking up from his work. Chel wasn't sure if there was solid ground or cracking ice under her feet. She said,

'Whatever you feel you want to do.'

'I don't know what I want to do. I don't even know what I ought to do - or can do, come to that. Nonie is the first person who's ever given me a straight tale; I'm beginning to realise that I've been fed a load of lies - and I leave you to guess who by. You seem to understand Helen better than I do. Help me.'

'I think it's something that you have to work out for yourself,' Chel told him, grieved at his admission, surprised at the turn the conversation had taken and afraid of saying the wrong thing, all at the same time.

'Do you think I haven't tried? Long before that row with the Black Widow. Ever since you told me how far she was prepared to go for me. That's not just simply saying *I love you*, that's the thing itself. There isn't an answer to it, except the one you can't make unless it's true.'

'You can't make that one?'

'No,' said Oliver. 'No... you can't turn loving someone on and off as if it was a tap. Too much water has gone over the weir for that. Nothing is going to alter the way that I've felt all these years, I felt it and that's that. I can't pretend, and Helen would know if I tried.'

'Then settle for making friends,' suggested Chel. 'I think she would.'

'One of the hardest things in the world is to say *I'm sorry*, and mean it.'

'And can you say that, at least?'

'Oh God, yes.' He made an expressive gesture with the hand that was holding the brush. 'The only thing is, I'm not quite sure if the thing I'm sorry for is something I've done.'

Chel allowed herself to slide from the arm of the chair onto the seat, feeling it rocking unsteadily, probably even symbolically, beneath her. Their rented conservatory furniture was not of the best quality. It gave her a legitimate excuse not to look directly at him.

'Then don't say it. Helen will understand. Just go halfway to meet her, she'll understand that too, and probably prefer it. Apologies are miserable things, in any case.' She hesitated. 'Give her a picture. She'll get the message.'

'What of? An olive branch?'

'Don't be silly.'

Oliver didn't reply to that, and when she looked up again he was absorbed in his painting, oblivious, the switch-over accomplished in an instant as it so often was these days. She leaned back in the chair, knowing that yet another phase of their lives was coming to an end.

The house that had been sanctuary had been invaded, the tide that had begun to turn in the summer was running full flood, the healing time nearly over. After Oliver's family, no doubt her own... after family, old friends. The blending of the old life and the new. She wasn't sure if she was pleased or not.

The brief interregnum didn't last. In the days that followed, the thought of Matt Sutton returned - and not with the scepticism of daylight now, but to torment Chel. Swift glimpses into the future could be laughed off as imagination, which perhaps they were. Matthew Sutton was beginning to scare her. She had thought him well disposed at first, but that had changed. She didn't see him, but his demanding presence was beginning to pervade the upstairs room in which she worked on her framing these colder autumn days, crying out and desperate as he had been when she first sensed him years ago. Far more desperate - so near to what he wanted, but unable to reach out and have it. Blocked - by herself - at every turn. She was very much afraid of what he wanted, convinced that it could only be to live again through the seeing eye and gifted hands of another artist.

Of Oliver.

There wasn't, Chel told herself, with the skin crawling on the back of her neck and on her arms, room for more than one soul in one body. Matthew Sutton could scream for help to eternity if he relied on her for it. The courage and humour that made Oliver himself, the new understanding to which he had been so painfully brought, weren't going to be cast out into limbo for any frustrated artist who ever lived... or died.

Matthew Sutton was dead. Dead, he was going to stay.

Judy still thought that they should try to speak to him, to ask him what he wanted, reason with him if they could. Chel was afraid that if they did so, the channel of communication might remain open. She hadn't forgotten what Judy had said about trances, nor had she forgotten her experience in Nonie's studio, about which she found it uncomfortable to think too closely. She wasn't at all sure that a true medium had any control over the state, and neither was Judy. Every barrier that she could think of was erected against the intrusive spirit in her house, and still he became more and more persistent. She began to hear his voice in every wind that sighed past the windows.

One particularly wild evening, when the wind seemed to be howling even more than usual, Oliver gave her a jolt by remarking that the house was decidedly eerie when the wind blew.

'It sounds almost like voices calling,' he said, and grinned at his own flight of fancy. 'Remember that night we walked around the ruins, Chel? It was like that then, although it wasn't as blowy as this that I remember. I suppose it's because everywhere round here is high, and so flat, the winds can work up a good howl before they reach us.'

Chel had reached no conclusions as to the depth, or otherwise, of Oliver's own sensitivity to spirits, she believed that he wasn't totally immune, that was all. She was so upset by this comment, raising as it did the nightmare thought that perhaps Matt Sutton could reach him from outside without her help, that she allowed it to unbalance her judgement.

Her own and her siblings' private mirth at the eccentricities of an elderly great-aunt who read the tealeaves had conditioned her to laugh at ghosts, while finding that she could apparently see disembodied spirits had frightened her. The one thing working on the other had led her to conceal her peculiar gift from everyone but Judy, who seemed to have it too, and, she supposed, from Nonie who never mentioned their first meeting, but must surely remember it. Not only was she afraid, as Judy was, of being laughed at, a lot of the time she wasn't sure that she shouldn't be laughing at herself. In daylight, with other people around, she could almost believe that Matthew Sutton and everything else too was in her imagination, a dream, a trick or a wish in herself to be somehow special.

Almost...

Upstairs on her own with the wind sighing in the copse beside the road, it was a different thing altogether. Then she could believe in her own powers... and in her own fears.

Her tension was beginning to communicate itself to Oliver. He had asked her several times if she was really happy so far out in the country with winter coming on, and once had commented, not quite in fun, about the reputation the house enjoyed for being haunted. He had begun to watch her, particularly on evenings when they were alone, with a slightly questioning air. It dawned on Chel quite soon after Matt Sutton's reappearance that she was either going to have to tell him the truth so that they could move away, or resolve the problem in some other way.

'Of course,' said Judy, 'you can communicate with spirits without going into a trance. There's always those Ouija board things we used to play around with at school. Remember them?'

Chel shook her head. The large comprehensive to which she had gone had taught her a lot of things, by no means all of them strictly academic, but the use of an Ouija board hadn't been among them.

'It can't be that difficult,' continued Judy. 'Some people say they really work, it might be worth a try.'

Chel had felt unable to state the true extent of her fears to her friend. An Ouija board struck her as frivolous in the context.

'I don't suppose they do,' she said.

'It's worth a try,' repeated Judy. 'I'm not sure I remember exactly what you do with it, but there'll be instructions in the box. You could ask Matthew Sutton what he wants. If we can't get through, you won't be any worse off.'

Instructions in the box. It sounded harmless enough. Chel even smiled at the idea.

'A telephone to the spirit world?' she enquired. Judy looked serious.

'You're really better with someone who's a medium, of course. I suppose either one of us would do.'

Chel wasn't convinced that just seeing ghosts made you a medium, but they either were or they weren't. It was surely only a game, anyway. It couldn't work for real.

'It sounds crazy,' she said.

'We could use it to tell him he's dead, and then he'd maybe go away,' said Judy.

So simple.

'Suppose he turns nasty, and doesn't want to hear?' asked Chel doubtfully, but Judy dismissed this suggestion with a derisive snort.

'Nonie Fingall would never have carried the torch for thirty years for someone unpleasant,' she stated, which was true enough. Chel had found this consideration the only comforting thing about the whole weird business. The thought that women had been mistaken about men before this, she pushed resolutely out of her mind.

'It can't do any harm to try, I suppose,' she conceded.

It took some time to track down a board. In spite of Judy's blithe assertion that it should be easy, it entailed a visit to Plymouth before they located one. Judy, on a day trip for Christmas shopping and the pantomime with the Women's Institute, managed in the end to find one in a strange little alternative lifestyle shop down a side street, and carried her trophy home in glee.

The chance to use it was much easier to find. Keith and Judy had taken to dropping by once a week or so, when Keith wasn't on call in the evening, and the four of them were in the pleasant habit of going up to the Cornish Arms for a drink and a game of pool with Charlie and the boys. Oliver, the hated wheelchair by now relegated to an outhouse, found that his physical restrictions didn't necessarily restrict him from trouncing half the village at the game, although it did require extensive use of the rest, and the discovery had pleased him disproportionately.

216

He was always, Keith observed dispassionately, game for a game. This talent, together with the casual way in which he was coming at last to ignore his disablement, and the fact that he was related to half of them by marriage if not by blood, had made him highly popular among the locals and returned him on equal terms to masculine society. In its way, pool had done as much for him as painting. Judy and Chel, neither of whom had an eye for ball games, usually sat over drinks and crisps and gossiped on these occasions, and since the colder weather set in it wasn't unknown for them to stay at home with the warm stove and let the male bonding go on without them. The night after Judy's trip to Plymouth, they simply stayed at home.

'We must take it upstairs,' said Judy, tipping her purchase from its plastic bag. 'He's never come downstairs. Can we use your workroom table?'

Chel thought that sounded a practical idea, and they carried the brightly coloured cardboard box upstairs, cleared the table, and tipped the contents of the box out onto it.

The box contained a square of polished wood on castors, ringed with the letters of the alphabet inset in a circle, in no particular order, and printed in black on white plastic. A transparent plastic cup, about the size of an eggcup, went with it.

Judy was reading the instructions.

'We sit on either side of it and put a finger each lightly on the cup,' she said. 'Then we ask it questions, and it will slide over the letters, which we write down, and there's our answer. It sounds easy enough.'

Chel was shaken into a nervous giggle.

'You mean, we actually talk to it?'

'Yes. How else can we ask it anything?'

'I shall feel silly,' said Chel, with conviction. 'We shall need a pencil and paper, won't we?'

Judy looked dubiously at the instructions in her hand.

'Perhaps a tape recorder would be better. This recommends a third person to write the letters down. I can't see Keith doing it, can you?'

'There's my cassette player in the kitchen,' said Chel, and went to get it, together with a blank tape and the writing pad on which she made her shopping lists. Judy fetched a second chair from another bedroom, and when Chel came back they sat down, started the tape, and put their fingers on the cup as instructed. Then they sat there for a minute feeling rather foolish. They were both nervous, without admitting it even to each other.

'We'll take turns to call out the letters,' Judy decided. 'What shall we ask it?' She was unable to suppress a self-conscious snigger of laughter.

'Is anybody there?' asked Chel, giggling too.

'Don't be silly!' Judy stifled her own giggles with an effort. 'We must be serious. Think about Matthew Sutton, and ask again.'

The thought of Matthew Sutton was instantly sobering, although tonight his presence could be neither heard nor felt. The little room was quiet and warm, and it all seemed harmless and even amusing. Chel said, more steadily,

'Is anyone there?'

They waited, and in the silence their breathing sounded loud.

'Is anyone there?' repeated Judy, for the third time.

Chel had the oddest sensation that the plastic cup under her finger felt different. It began to move slowly to the left.

'You're pushing it,' accused Judy, giggling again.

Chel denied it.

'I'm not.'

The combined pressures of their two fingers, resisting the movement of the cup, sent it skidding off the edge of the board onto the floor. Judy picked it up and placed it back in the centre of the circle. They began again.

'Don't press so hard this time. Are you there?' asked Judy, and the board, the cup sliding tentatively over the polished surface, replied,

PQRYESR, and fell to describing weak circles in the centre of the ring of letters.

'Who are you?' asked Chel, all desire to giggle suddenly gone. The cup slid weakly from side to side, almost touched D and M, and returned to its feeble circling.

'Ask it something simpler,' suggested Judy. 'Are you Matthew Sutton?'

XSBOBOP

Judy gave another explosive snigger, and hurriedly suppressed it. Her voice was shaking as she asked,

'Do you want something?'

WANTHYES

'Something in this house?' asked Chel.

WANTHWANT

'Ask it who it is again,' whispered Judy, as if the board could overhear her.

'Who are you?' asked Chel, again. The answer came more firmly this time, the cup slipping briskly round the circle of letters as if it was beginning to know its way.

BBBOBOP

Nonie had referred to Matthew Sutton as *Matt* in conversation, but that was no indication as to whether she had, or had not, called him something else in private. Bobop? Bobo? It didn't, somehow, sound like Nonie.

'Is that a pet name?' asked Chel, and the board replied, rather derisively,

HOHOBOBOHO

'Can you tell us what you want?' asked Judy, and provoked a string of random letters, of which very few seemed to make sense.

AGOYQSEEETHPOZXQRFNK (Short pause) PLAF

'Are you sure you're not pushing it?' asked Judy, suspiciously.

'Cross my heart.'

'I don't think I actually like it much.' The quiver, this time, wasn't due to giggles.

'We can stop if you like,' said Chel, who wanted to.

'No. We'll give it another try.' Judy cleared her throat. 'Can we help you?'

The cup made several excited circlings, and spelt out rapidly,

YESYESYESNO

'Can you tell us how?'

SEESEASEAC

The sea was all around them in that room, sweeping across every picture stacked against its walls and on the sofa bed.

'Which of us can help you?' asked Judy, and the board answered her swiftly.

WOULDNTYOULIKESTOKNOWP

'You tell us,' coaxed Chel.

PRZJWK

'*Who*?' asked Judy, with a snort of nervous amusement that made both herself and Chel jump. The jump might have accounted for the fact that the board returned, briefly,

BWPR

'Who?' repeated Chel.

NAN

'Nankervis?' asked Judy, with a quick look at Chel.

NANLIVEHEREBROKEHOUSECINHOLEROOFPRZJWK

Chel took her finger off the cup, hastily.

'I've got cramp in my shoulder,' she announced. 'Give it a rest for a minute. Shall we play it back and see what we've got?'

'All right.'

They transcribed it carefully onto paper from the tape. Some of it appeared to make sense - almost sense, at least.

'*Bobo* could be a name,' said Judy. 'At least, if you discount all the extra letters, it might be. A funny name - ho, ho, ho sort of name.'

'It sounds more like a circus clown than a disembodied spirit,' objected Chel.

'Clowns, presumably, have spirits when they die.'

'Matthew Sutton wasn't a clown. He was a very serious artist.'

'You don't know anything about him,' Judy pointed out, which was true.

'There's a very clear *yes* when you asked him if he was there,' said Chel.

'Or an accidental sequence of letters.' Judy was bothered by all the extra letters.

'It said *Bobo* or *Bobop* three times - and *want* - I think we should ignore the H, don't you?'

'*Ago,*' said Judy, reading down the written page for recognisable words. 'And *see*, or *seethe* without the last E - '

'There's three Es,' said Chel.

'Seethe... see the... go see the...'

'*Poz,*' said Chel, giggling. '*Go see the poz.* What sort of a message is that?'

'There's three *yes*es when we asked if we could help it.'

'And a *no.*'

'Well... they can sometimes get confused,' said Judy, uncertainly. Chel looked sceptical.

'*They*? Spirits, you mean? Judy, that's bullshit and we both know it. All of this is bullshit.'

'It's quite clear about *sea,*' pointed out Judy. 'It says it three or four times, one way and another. And *wouldn't you like to know,* if you forget about S and P.'

'All right, clever, how about *przjwk*?' asked Chel, pronouncing it with difficulty.

'It says that twice.'

'Oh, big deal!'

There was a short pause then, because the last few words suddenly made it apparent that the board was getting more and more lucid with practice. *Nan* was directly associated with the house, either Will or Oliver, and *Nan live here broke house in hole roof* was so nearly sense as to be uncanny.

'Shall we go on?' asked Judy.

Chel hesitated. The board lay innocently on the table with the cup beside it, and the room was still warm. The wind that blew in the copse was just a wind, nothing more.

'All right,' she said.

Their fingers went back on the cup. Judy said,

'Are you still there, Bobo?'

BOBOHEREHEAR

It was easier to follow the words now that they had had some practice, they found.

'Did you make the hole in the roof?'

No reply.

'Tell us who you are,' invited Chel. 'Were you a pilot?'

FLYFLIGHTWARHOLEWANTZPRJWK

'Are you Matthew Sutton?' asked Judy, more directly.

MATHEWSUTTONWHO

'Matthew Sutton made the hole in the roof,' said Judy, and the board replied primly.

NAUGHTY

Judy took her finger off the cup.

'Did Matthew Sutton fly in the war?'

Chel removed her own finger to consider this.

'I believe he did.' Nonie had said something about it at their first meeting that had so nearly been their last. 'But it wasn't in the war he hit the roof - Nonie isn't old enough.'

'Is he? I mean, would he be if he was still here?'

'I should think so. I think she said something about bombers.'

'Let's try again,' said Judy.

As the messages began to make sense, so the sensation that the inanimate plastic cup had a life of its own began to grow. It no longer felt quite like plastic, and to Chel it seemed as if it had begun to beat with a gentle pulse - but that could, of course, have been in her own finger.

'How can we help you, Bobo?' she asked.

PRZJWKGOSEESEASEESAWMARGERYDAW

'Don't be silly,' said Chel. 'We're trying to help you. Tell us what we can do.'

The board answered sweetly,

HELENOFTROYLAUNCHEDSHIPCATAMARANPRZJWK

'What is this *przjwk*?' asked Judy, exasperated, and it came swiftly back with,

DUSBINALLY

Chel's hand flew up as if she had been stung, and the cup shot off the board and rattled into the corner of the room behind a stack of discarded paintings. Judy stared at her in bewilderment.

'What's the matter? What did it say?'

221

Because the letters had been called out so swiftly, Chel wasn't absolutely certain. With fingers that shook, she rewound the tape and played it back, while Judy took down the letters on the pad. When she had done, she looked at what she had written with knitted brows.

'*Dusbinally?*' she queried.

'I think it means *alley*,' said Chel, shaken. 'Those yobs who attacked Oliver left him to die in an alley where they kept dustbins.'

'Ugh!' said Judy, who hadn't known. From knitted, her brows became positively knotted. 'So what about *Helen of Troy?*'

Chel wasn't prepared to go into Helen of Troy.

'I know what it's trying to say,' she said, urgently. 'No, listen, Judy - Oliver's name has six letters. And so has this silly word it keeps repeating - it's got its circuit jammed somehow, it can't spell his name - but it wants Oliver. Look - ' She grabbed the page. 'Every time we ask what we can do to help it, it comes back with that word - '

'But that's only what you've said all along,' objected Judy. 'What's the panic?'

Chel stared at her, round-eyed, and found herself quite unable to say that *dustbin alley* meant only one thing to her. Death. Not Matthew Sutton's - Oliver's. The fear that the conviction brought with it was like a black pall in the room, as if by doing so she could be rid of it, she grabbed hold of the Ouija board and began pushing it haphazardly back into its bright, enticing box. Judy took it from her.

'Here, steady Chel. It won't go in that way, you'll only tear the box.' She turned the board, pushed it inside, and tucked in the flap. 'There. Now, what's the matter?'

'Nothing! Nothing!' said Chel, on a nervous squeak. 'Let's go downstairs, my goodness, look at the time! Keith and Oliver will be thrown out of the pub ages ago, they'll be back any minute.' She ran for the door and out onto the landing, with Judy following more slowly. 'Yes, listen, there's the car now - '

Judy caught her up at the foot of the stairs. The Ouija board, from her point of view, had been rather an anticlimax, and she thought that Chel was being silly. Girls at school, she recalled, had sometimes been the same. For every word that made sense tonight, there had been as many that had been pure gobbledygook. A child's game, *nothing more*.

It hadn't been Keith's car that time, but the next time it was. The time they waited gave Chel enough breathing space to greet them when they came in with smiling composure, and Judy time to hide the Ouija board under her coat.

XIV

That night, Chel found that she couldn't sleep at all. Her mind was alert, her nerves stretched taut by the evening's experiment. She tried reading for a while, hoping that a book might soothe her, but it was impossible to concentrate. Her mind kept slipping back to the room upstairs, and the garbled and silly messages that had held those tiny grains of horrid sense.

She laid the book down on the quilt and looked hopefully at Oliver, but he was far too deeply asleep for a mere look to disturb him. He looked so ordinary, so undamaged, that her heart turned sickly over. He was unbelievably better than she had thought possible this time last year, but presumably almost as well as he was likely to get by now. The pain would go, she now believed, but there was no sign that he was ever going to walk properly, not by most people's standards, or run upstairs, or sail a boat... such a waste, when at this very moment he should have been halfway round the world. Choking tears and familiar anger leapt at her together. One short span was all anyone was allowed, and the mindless brutality of other people could ruin it - unjust, unjust! The insultingly short prison sentences that some of his attackers had received at least offered a second chance. For Oliver, there was no going back at all.

With the same old dreary bitterness in her heart, that she had really thought to be behind her, Chel turned out the bedside light and lay down in the darkness, but her thoughts gave her no rest. They went round and round in circles, as dark as the unlit room.

Oliver's stepmother prided herself on her upright Christianity. She put herself on a pedestal and indulged in good works, and let envy and hate and malice eat her alive, like the little Spartan boy with his fox. Religion hadn't made her a better person, in some ways it had made her a worse one. Religion was a fraud, therefore, and Oliver was right to have nothing to do with it, what you didn't expect, you couldn't be disappointed not to receive.

So, one short span, and then oblivion - and for those who refused oblivion, the nightmare limbo of an earthbound spirit, desperate to live again?

Chel tossed over onto her other side, and lay in the darkness listening to Oliver breathing quietly beside her and her thoughts grew blacker and blacker. The blackness of them seemed to pervade the whole house, growing thicker and more hopeless as the hours ticked slowly by. She hadn't felt this overwhelming unhappiness for months, she felt as if her heart would burst with it and the dawn would never come. *Black... black... black...*

It must have been well into the low, small hours of the morning before Chel gave up the unequal struggle and admitted that she wasn't going to sleep without help. Tossing and turning through the dark night had left her hot, thirsty, and with a pounding headache, and the sensible thing to do would be to have a cool drink and take a couple of paracetamol to calm herself down and fix her head. Then she might sleep at last.

She slipped out of bed and tiptoed across the living area to the kitchen. The ash in the bottom of the stove still held a glow in its heart, but not enough to see by, she groped her way to the foot of the stairs, afraid to put on a light in case it disturbed Oliver. She felt her way upstairs by the bannister rail in semi-darkness, lit only by the light of an uncertain moon, feeling for the treads with her bare feet, shivering a little in the cold, hesitant and oddly reluctant. Perhaps it was just her imagination, or the mental turmoil of the past few hours, but the house didn't feel its friendly self tonight. She would be glad to get back downstairs.

She had her hand on the knob of the bathroom door when she felt it, the cold, cold breath of fear on her neck that froze her where she stood. She spun round, but the landing, fitfully lit by a waning moon, was deserted. She stood still, her own breathing loud in her ears and her heart pumping hard against her ribs. Both breath and heart were jerky and uneven.

Stupid! There was nothing here. Just the tiny landing and four closed doors. If she put on the landing light, she would see that and nothing else. She reached out for it, pressed the switch.

Nothing happened.

Chel stood there in the dark and heard her own heart beating... and over and above it, the steady drip - drip - drip of water... no, of blood. Matthew Sutton's blood, dripping slowly on to the floorboards, as his failing heart pumped his life away. She could smell the warm, metallic scent of it and feel it sticky under her soles. She had never been aware of tragedy in this house since they had lived here, but it was here now. There was no crying voice, no pleas for help... just the piercing awareness of stars shining through the broken roof, the dark shape of the aircraft, the strong smell of aviation fuel and the chinking sounds of hot metal settling... and when she looked down, the pool of blood was stinking around her feet, oozing monstrously between her toes.

Drip - drip - drip - drip - drip.

There was a prickle in the nape of her neck as the hairs rose up in atavistic terror. She could hardly bear the stench in her nostrils, and she could feel the hairs on her arms, too, standing up on end in the age-old, primitive reaction to the feared unknown. Blood, corruption, and all unclean things...

The doors weren't all closed after all. The door of her workroom was slightly ajar. The dark crack against the paler door frame held her attention, held her body stiff against the bathroom door.

And very, very slowly, very quietly, the Thing came seeping through.

It came like smoke at first, and with it came a deadly creeping cold that made the chill of the November night seem, by contrast, like high summer. It flowed out through the crack, thicker and faster, gathering itself up as it came until it crouched, dense and dark, at the top of the stairs. Although it had no discernible face, Chel knew that it looked at her - into her - and it was immediately and unmistakeably the distillation of evil, so that it paralysed her thought and action with the icy depths of genuine Panic fear. The scream that pushed its way up into her throat died there like the unlit light bulb, unreleased, choked in the foul miasma, and every nerve on her skin leapt alive into a screaming network of mindless, extreme terror and pain.

'No - ' she tried to plead, but the word, too, died in her throat. Her hands, stiff-fingered, had released the doorknob. Her head turned away, her eyes, tight shut, refusing to look. Back pressed against the wall, she moved rigidly, uselessly, sideways to escape it... *please let me get away from it, don't let it get me...*

The closed spare room door brought her to a halt. She could go no further. Her hands scrabbled ineffectively for the knob, found it, slipped from it powerless to turn it. But there was no refuge behind the door anyway, she knew that. She heard her fingernails scrabbling against the wood, and wide-eyed at last, turned to face the Thing.

It was moving, slowly, slowly, sliding with fluid ease across the narrow landing. There was nowhere to go, nothing she could do to stop it. The crawling horror would get her and she couldn't stop it... she couldn't stop it... indeed, she had invited it. She and Judy.

By this time, she was spread-eagled against the closed door, pressed against it as if she could push herself through it. Fear swept over her in great, pulsating waves, her mouth opened and she screamed and screamed again, and knew that she was making no sound, a faint, strangled breath, soundless as the summer evening bats, was all that came out. Her mind no longer thought, it was filled with the unheard sound of her own terrible screaming, going on and on into oblivion that was all that would remain.

The appalling smell smothered her, the hunched shape was growing, reaching upwards, until it was a towering black wall between herself and the moonlight. Nothing - nothing but darkness, and a door that gaped on Hell itself, and time that stretched out without meaning into eternity. The presence of bodily death, the stench of rotting flesh, and the chill, damp cold of the grave... and the loss of the soul that would be sucked in by this gross phantasm.

The voice came to her as if from a great distance, and had been speaking for some time before she fully realised it, urgent and insistent.

'Say it, Chel. You must say it. Say it with me - ' And the words of the one prayer that every child brought up in a Christian country must know, repeated steadily. '*Our Father, which art in Heaven* - say it Chel, you must say it!'

At first, her voice wouldn't come, but after a struggle that seemed endless and left her exhausted and sweating, she managed to think the words, then to mouth them, whisper them, at last to speak them.

'*... hallowed be thy name; thy kingdom come... give us this day our daily bread...*' The familiar words were as comforting as the steady voice. The Thing had stopped its advance.

The Lord's Prayer had come to an end.

'Don't stop,' said the urgent voice. 'Pray anything - keep praying - you mustn't stop - '

Fragments of the psalms began to come back to her, that Oliver, who didn't know what he believed in, had recited to her in the far-off days when he was whole and strong and still did such things, simply because he enjoyed the rolling words and the images they called up.

They that go down to the sea in ships, that do business in great waters, these see the works of the Lord and his wonders in the deep. For he commandeth and raiseth the stormy wind which lifteth up the waves thereof... they cry unto the Lord in their trouble, and he bringeth them out of their distresses. He maketh the storm a calm, so that the waters thereof are still.

The waters saw thee, the depths also were troubled. The clouds poured out water, the skies sent out a sound; thine arrows went abroad. The voice of the thunder was in the heaven, the lightnings lightened the world; the earth trembled and shook. Thy way is in the sea, and thy path in the great waters, and thy footsteps are not known.

'Keep it going. You must go on.'

Chel heard her own voice, reedy and trembling, reaching back into childhood, to when everything had been so easy and simple.

'Matthew, Mark, Luke and John, bless the bed that I lie on...'

The Thing had begun to curl in on itself, to shrink, to wisp away into the night. She could see the window, she could move. She slid helplessly down the door to the floor.

Matthew Sutton had never had any connection with those awful deeps of fear and terror... Matthew Sutton had come to save her, and was good and safe and sure... *Four angels to my bed, Four angels round my head, One to watch and one to pray, and two to bear my soul away.*

There were tears running down her face, hot against her cold skin, clean and real. The window was clear now, the square panes of glass outlined against a starlit sky. She could breathe, the sweet cold air of an autumn night, and although she shivered it was with the November frost not the chill of another world.

Defend us from all perils and dangers of this night... the crisp rectangle of window was dissolving in a different mist, wavering and distorting, receding down a long, long tunnel... but she was safe.

She came to slowly, and in confusion, to find herself in nothing but her nightie on the landing, freezing cold, firmly held in somebody's arms and with the light burning brightly overhead. She lay for a few moments trying to remember why she so desperately needed safety, and slowly the recollection came creeping back. She recalled, with a shudder, the horrid hunched shape at the top of the stairs that had oozed and crawled towards her, the vile stink and the mind-bending terror that she had felt... and the clear-sighted courage of a man thirty years dead that had saved her.

'Oh!' cried Chel, and suddenly fully awake, realised two things. The first that the person who held her, and whose courage in the face of evil had undoubtedly saved her from something utterly awful and unspeakable, was no ghost at all, but Oliver.

The second was that it couldn't possibly be Oliver because they were on the upstairs landing.

It was Oliver all right. Even without looking, there was no mistaking his warm solidity for the insubstantialness of Matt Sutton's spirit.

Chel lifted her head.

'Hullo there,' said Oliver.

They were propped, twined together, in the angle that the bannisters made with the floor, herself more or less on top of him where she had collapsed, and he was undoubtedly quite real. Trying to sound light and casual, but white with exhaustion, his dark hair stuck damply to his forehead and his eyes all smudgy and dark. Chel said, more shakily than she liked,

'How did you get here?'

'Just did,' said Oliver airily, but the cost of that struggle up the stairs, lifting the dead weight of his feet from step to step by sheer power of mind over matter was written clearly in his face. He might as well have set out, in all his old strength and fitness, to climb the north face of the Eiger. Chel stared at him, their faces very close because they couldn't bear to let each other go.

'But why? How could you possibly have known...?'

'You called me,' said Oliver, simply.

'I didn't.' She had wanted him, needed him desperately. She didn't recall having called to him. He had been asleep, drugged even, physically incapable of reaching her, of climbing the stairs even had he wished.

He was wide awake now, and he was most certainly here. He put up a hand and pulled her head down against his shoulder, not gently.

'You were screaming your head off,' he said.

She thought that she hadn't been. Desire and intention had been there, no more... and desire had run like a telephone message down the cobweb link that stretched between her own mind and his, and brought him to her when in fact it should have been impossible.

'But Oliver...' she said. The lingering remnants of terror shook in her voice, and she felt his arms tighten round her.

'It's gone now,' he said, tenderly as if to a child scared by nightmare. 'Whatever it was, it's gone. You can tell me in the morning what you and Judy had been up to, never mind now. Try and put it out of your mind.'

'Me and Judy? Up to?' asked Chel, weakly defensive, not wishing to be accused of calling up such a horror.

'You looked guilty as sin, both of you, when we got back. Wherever you got that from, you shouldn't have messed with it at all.' He sounded severe. Also shaken, which was disturbing.

'You saw it?' asked Chel, who had believed it to be a phantasm of her own mind. She could hardly believe it. Oliver didn't reply, and she realised that they were both shivering with cold. 'Come on.' Her voice was stronger now, back on firm ground. 'We're getting cold. Let's go downstairs.'

'In a minute.' He sounded all at once very tired. 'I need time to... I need time.'

To rest, to re-gather strength he meant, but wouldn't say. It seemed so stupid to be exhausted by the effort of climbing up thirteen ordinary stairs, but it had brought him to his knees before the top, and now he was on the floor he wasn't at all sure how to get off it. That, too, he wasn't going to admit.

'Let me go,' said Chel, wriggling free. She was shaken, sick with remembered fright, longing to be safely downstairs again, warm and snug with Oliver's arms round her, where ghosts had never been. She wanted it, at this moment, more than anything in the world. The empty landing, innocent under the light, gave her the creeps, but even so, she understood that if one step up to the terrace was an effort, a whole flight was a marathon. Reluctant as she was to relinquish the sanctuary of his arms, they would both freeze if she didn't do something. The effort to be practical was a help. In the spare bedrooms were warm duvets, blankets, pillows, she fetched them and tucked them round them both, making a warm nest on top of the scrappy landing carpet. Oliver had slid down so that he was lying on the floor, he looked quite comfortable. Chel sat irresolutely beside him.

'You can't go to sleep here,' she said.

'Want a bet?' Oliver closed his eyes. 'Just twenty minutes, maybe half an hour... don't fuss...' And then he would have to stand up somehow and get downstairs again. He pushed the thought out of his mind, irked beyond bearing by his physical restrictions, angry at his own uselessness. He could feel the residue of Chel's fear, her wish to be elsewhere. In a few minutes then... just a few minutes.

He was asleep, Chel thought, before he had even finished speaking, crashing out after physical exertion like a healthy young animal. She found herself wondering if, in fact, he was healthier than anyone gave him credit for these days, it was months since he had had a proper check-up.

'Oliver...?' she said, but he was too deeply asleep to hear. She slid down beside him under the blankets, aware that her heart was beating faster than it should and her breath coming unevenly. A few minutes, she could manage a few minutes. At least they were warm now, if not exactly in four-star comfort, and while the light shone brightly it would be all right. She kept very close to Oliver, even closer than the width of the landing required, her cheek against his shoulder, lying wakeful through minutes that grew into hours, reluctant to disturb him, feeling safer with every tick of time that passed, while the remainder of the night crawled by. It was only when the first streaks of dawn began to brighten the sky that she felt safe to close her eyes and let go, drifting away into deep, healing sleep.

But long before she slept, while her defences were down and her resolution all to pieces, the dream came to Oliver, drifting like a fantasy through the touch of her hand, her breath on his cheek, her body close against his in the dark, spirit-torn night.

She wove herself into his dream at first, the love in her voice as she spoke and the touch of her fingers. Chel, with the sea-green eyes and coppery gold hair, and her healing hands that could drag a man back from the very edge of death... her voice that had called him, pulling him back with the fragile and invisible lifeline that bound them together... and the power that she had that was, all unknowing, making a channel between the living and the dead.

He had no idea how he came to be lying in the grass, but it was there all about him, summer grass, tall and thick and smelling already of drying hay, full of tiny flowers that lay like minute stars against the green and gold stalks, of scarlet blobs of poppies and blue, blue cornflowers. An old-fashioned hayfield, Oliver had never seen one in England. He lay for some time on his stomach with his chin propped on his hands, lying as a child lies, studying the world around him, studying the flowers with delighted appreciation. Such beauty, such detail, for something that as often as not nobody would ever notice, that would grow and flourish, and die under the cutter, wasted. Yet its seeds would grow again in their season to flourish unseen, hidden, perfect and beautiful. Round and round and round with the seasons... round and round and round... round and round...

'Oliver?' asked Chel. She was leaning over him - in reality, in the dream, he couldn't tell - her sea-green eyes shadowed with fears, her red-gold hair shining in the light. He half-saw her, and the shaft of light that threw her shadow on the wall... or on the grass where he lay. But her face was blurring while those strange eyes of hers remained clear and cool, like seawater... somewhere in the distance an aeroplane was droning past in the wintry blue of a different sky, the sound and Chel's face swept together in a mist and just for a split second of time there were trees and the roof of a house - he could see the chimney sticking up through the mist, a warning -

The droning sound was a crop-sprayer. He could see it now, flying over the grass towards him, low, pouring out its poison over the delicate, unseen flowers, killing their transient loveliness, making the tiny seeds barren, great black crosses on its dirty flanks. It was killing the grass too, it was brown and slimy and stinking where the dark, winged shadow passed, like some monstrous bird contaminating the whole world with its filth, until there was nothing left but a desolate brown sea of mud stretching to a wide and empty horizon. By the time it had gone, the crop-sprayer was a nightmare bomber, spewing forth universal death; the War to End Wars, simply because nobody would survive to fight them. The sea of mud was pitted with cracks and deep craters, with oily puddles seeping across the dreary expanse, and on the horizon just one clump of sparse trees, like a cluster of worn-out toothbrushes, to break the bleak, sagging line. There was no more beauty, no more springing life, just death and the smell of decay, broken things starting through the mire, burnt-out tanks and ruined houses, all the detritus of war, and the ache in his back and the stupid weight of his legs... you never thought of the weight of a leg until you had to think about lifting it. There was no Chel waiting to help him this time with her seawater eyes and her courage and love, she had gone with the flowers, barren into nothingness. If he was to get anywhere he would have to get there on his own, crawling with his stupid legs and his feeble spine that could no longer bend into that childish curve, across this dreary and soulless, endless wasteland... crawling to nowhere....

He became aware of the other people only gradually, he who had always boasted that he didn't need them. They were walking across the barren plain in a wavering line in twos and threes, men, women and children, refugees from some terrible devastation. They had no colour and no specific form, they were simply dark silhouettes like shadows against the dull brown land. Some of them walked with hope, some dragged their feet, some stumbled and fell, but they were all impelled to go forward by an overriding necessity to continue, and the stronger ones helped the weakest and carried those that were too tired, too sick or too little make it on their own. They all had to get there, wherever *there* was, and it didn't matter that they were exhausted and starving, up to their knees in treacly black mud, if only they could struggle through. He lay among the blackened stalks where the green and gold grass and the flowers had blown, and knew that he had to join them.

It was a nightmare of effort, an agony that nearly finished him, helpless and damaged as he was, with no crutches, no help, no support for his stupid back, and all the time he heard the voices sighing in a fitful little wind that blew over the wasteland. *You don't need us, you turned us away, you rejected us...* Faces turned towards him... his father's face, Helen's, Susan's, Debbie's, Chel's friendly, close family against whose friendliness he had built a wall. It was too much. He wasn't going to make it, they were going to leave him alone as he had wished and he would be lost. Racked with pain, he lay face downwards in the mud, tasting it in his mouth, feeling it crumbling under his clutching fingers, knowing that he must stay behind for ever... and then he felt someone touching him, lifting him, bringing him to his feet with a supporting arm around him. There were no words spoken, but when he turned his head he saw the man, not so much as a man as an entity.

There were no distinguishing features in that formless face, and yet he knew that he would know this man anywhere, that they had always been destined to come together and their need was mutual, and must be served.

He looked forward then, and now that he could stand, beyond the straggling line of stumbling figures, beyond the sea of black, churned mud with its total lack of hope, he saw their destination. Above the black horizon there rose a springing light, golden shot with rose. It filled the sky, it held out the promise of life like cupped hands offering water in a desert, it was to come... and it wasn't nothingness, it wasn't oblivion -

He awoke too abruptly, not knowing that it was when Chel woke herself and gently withdrew her hand and body from contact, and found himself lying on the landing floor, with her sitting beside him and dawn colouring the sky beyond the window with the gold and rose of the dream.

'Good morning,' said Chel, smiling at him. 'We've spent all night on the floor!' Her relief and pleasure at having survived the awful night coloured her voice, making it ring with amusement.

It took a moment for the flowers and the mud and the springing light to disperse. Oliver looked confused and sleepy, and felt a strange sense of loss, as if a close friend had gone away without a word, and Chel said,

'You were having a very vivid dream - tossing your head about and shouting, and I was just about to wake you when you woke yourself. Was it the same old nightmare?' Her thoughts were with the black Thing of last night, and she was profoundly relieved when Oliver said,

'No, of course not,' although parts of it had been nightmarish enough.

'So?' said Chel.

'So, what?'

'So are we planning to stay up here for ever, or shall we go downstairs?'

From where he was at that moment, staying upstairs for ever looked the easiest option, but Oliver could never resist a challenge.

'Give me your hand,' he ordered, and with her help and that of the bannisters, sat up. Peering through the rails to assess the problem, he decided that going down was going to be better than coming up, once he was on his feet. He had never been on the floor since he was injured. Reaction affecting him in the same way as it had Chel, he began to laugh.

'We're getting hysterical,' said Chel, severely, a few moments later.

'Come on Oliver, pull yourself together! Get on your knees, for God's sake!'

'And pray?' asked Oliver, while adopting this sensible suggestion. From there, with the help once more of Chel and the bannister rail, he got to his feet with surprising ease and leaned there for a minute, thinking. The night's adventure had broken down barriers, and in an unexpected way.

'I reckon I could drive a car, you know,' he said thoughtfully.

'This, from a man who's about to go downstairs the hard way - head first!' retorted Chel. Her heart bumped - with apprehension? With excitement? What had happened last night? Oliver persisted,

'If not right now, pretty soon. It'd probably need to be an automatic, I suppose.'

'Oliver, stop putting it off! Stairs!'

Like standing up, it was unexpectedly easy, as if a wall that had stood for the past eighteen months had come tumbling down, Chel thought, not realising that she was almost echoing Oliver. She could feel the change like a change in the weather; all in a moment, they weren't just making the best of things any more, but going forward. But to where?

It was nearly seven o'clock. Oliver rejected the idea of going to bed, having slept perfectly well on the floor, although Chel would have liked nothing better, and retired into the shower. Using the furniture to get across the room - only one of the hated crutches, she noticed. He looked tired after the broken night, but somehow regenerated. She herself felt as if she had been awake for ever and could sleep for a week.

It was a mental change, she thought, as she sleepily prepared breakfast a little later. A shift in the gears from crawling third to something faster and more ambitious. His painting had been in overdrive for weeks now, everything else stuck in a jam. Now it was all catching up.

It had turned into a black day, cold and rainy, quite out of keeping with Oliver's mood, although Chel's was more subjective. When breakfast was over, she re-lit the fire, which had gone out overnight and curled up in the corner of the sofa with her thoughts, while Oliver pottered in the conservatory, not with any real application for once, but sketching, ignoring two unfinished oils that stood about awaiting attention.

Chel dozed for a little, watching patterns in the flames, imagining faces, wondering if last night was in any way real, or simply fantasy land. But the overwhelming symptoms of terror, the immobility of her petrified limbs, the ice-cold, spreading evil of the Thing were still with her, that was no fantasy. Where, or how had it come? *Had* she and Judy called it with their experiment with the Ouija board? If so, then psychic powers, if she had them, were a two-edged sword that could turn against her at any time. A fairground gypsy and a practising psychic had both, at different times, told her that she would need help. She now began to understand why they had said it. And, not knowing that the answer was already given, she wondered how, if it was so dangerous to reach out to the spirit world, the needs of such spirits - as Matt Sutton, for instance - could be met.

'If I make some coffee,' she thought she heard Oliver say, 'then you can carry it through.'

Chel blinked. She felt as if she was coming back from somewhere a long way away, some unbelievable place where the impossible was possible. The everyday suspension of belief, after what she had been thinking, hit her like a slap in the face. She sat up.

'I'll make it,' she said.

'I'm not paralysed,' said Oliver, but without rancour for once. Indeed, he spoke with a deep satisfaction that surprised her, as if he, too, had made discoveries during the night. He was still only using one of the crutches, she noticed, with an occasional hand on chair back or table as he passed. It went through her mind, quite unexpectedly, that this second screaming woman he had been able to save without offering himself as an alternative victim. Self-image, self-esteem... both those had been damaged. The healing of them was probably as important, or more so, than the healing of bodily injury. The thought was new, slotting him back into a more familiar perspective. Oliver wasn't good victim material, and the role had never fitted him. She got to her feet and followed him to the kitchen, leaning on the worktop to watch him. I wonder, she found herself thinking, how long the ability to get up the stairs has been there, without either of us knowing, just because the over-riding need wasn't? And if it happens that it has been, is it somehow my fault?

Everyone's fault, she answered herself. Don't do that, you can't do this, you'll never do the other again... Oliver was made to believe it, and so it became true. The only person who's told him different is Nonie, and the Dreaded Dot has poisoned that well for him. Last night, the rest of us were proved wrong. I never expected it to be so satisfying to be proved wrong.

'Tell me,' said Oliver, with his back to her.

'Tell you what?' asked Chel.

'Am I a self-centred bastard?'

Chel was about to deny it, but both honesty and what she had just discovered for herself stepped in and stopped her. Don't be patronising. 'You could say that.'

Oliver wasn't given to soul-searching and post mortems. He said, 'Then I'm sorry, because I think you've been the main sufferer.'

'Don't mention it,' said Chel, at a loss. She began drawing on the worktop with her finger, unseen scrolls and lines that meant nothing but kept her eyes from Oliver.

'I've got between you and your family, haven't I? I had no right to do that. How long is it since you saw them?'

Too long.

'We saw Mum and Dad last Christmas.'

'And a right riot of fun that was, if I remember.' He had only just been out of hospital. The festivities had had no joy. 'But your sister and the kids? Your brothers?' He had never met them, Richie and Mike. For the first time, it struck him as awful.

'A couple of Christmases before,' mumbled Chel. 'I suppose. More, for the boys. Trace came when you were in hospital.'

'A long time, then. How often did you see them before you met me?'

'Pretty often. She heard the gurgle of liquid pouring into the *cafetière* and raised her head at last. 'I'll carry that in to the fire. You go ahead.'

'In a minute.' Oliver put the coffee on a tray with the mugs and came over to her, awkwardly but confidently and stood over her. His free hand covered hers, stilling it. 'That's not fair, Chel. You shouldn't have let me get away with it.'

'It's not fair to blame yourself for everything, either. It suited me at the time.'

'But this past year. You've needed them.'

'You didn't.'

'I didn't *want* them, certainly. Needing is quite a different thing, and perhaps I did. Would you like to ask Tracy and Tom and the kids for Christmas? It's a bit short notice, but they might like to come. They must have missed you, too.'

Chel said,

'Have you noticed how tea and coffee have become the solution for all embarrassments? If you can't think of anything else to do - no, I don't mean you, personally - then put the kettle on. Change the subject. Take some caffeine on board and be cosy...' She knew she was what Judy called *waffling*, but she didn't know what to say. She couldn't stop.

'Would you?' asked Oliver.

Chel pulled her hand away.

'Yes. But it isn't that simple.'

'Why not?'

'You have to want them too.' Chel walked past him to the tray, but didn't pick it up. 'Come on. Let's sit down and talk about it.'

'We don't have to talk about it. You've put up with a lot of things you didn't want, it's my turn. And anyway, I do want. That Candy is a real card, we ought to know her better.'

Chel laughed then.

'You might regret it! Remember her being a bridesmaid at our wedding, hogging the limelight on TV? And I didn't even want bridesmaids.'

'And Micky will be quite a lad by now. How old is he?'

'Ten. She's nearly eight.' Talking about them brought them close, she felt a sudden wave of longing for them. Tracy, her sister, was perhaps the closest and dearest of all her family. She sighed, without meaning to.

He didn't comment, but began to move towards the focal point of the woodburner, so that Chel had to follow if she wanted to continue the discussion. She picked up the tray.

'We need to get you a stick,' she said, watching him critically. Changing the subject again.

'Two'd be better,' said Oliver. 'Easier on the furniture.' But he wasn't letting her off the hook that easily. When they were comfortably seated by the fire, he hefted his mug in his hands and said, as if there had never been an interruption, 'It's time you got yourself a life again, Chel. I don't need you now - not in that way. It's time to move on, for both of us. We won't be in this house for ever, living this life. Let's plan for it, you as well as me.'

'October,' said Chel, without thinking.

'What?'

She was confused. October, she realised, was a conviction. It would be some kind of conclusion. The name of the month was accompanied by the number four. If she told Oliver that, he would think she was barking mad, but she said it anyway.

'Something will happen in *four* and it will finish next October.

'Four what?' asked Oliver, interested but sceptical. 'Days, weeks, months, years? Hours, maybe?'

'How can I know?' asked Chel. Lack of sleep made her sound irritable, but Oliver laughed.

'You are seriously weird, do you know that?' It was almost admiring. 'So tell me, what was that thing last night?'

The question was so unexpected that it made Chel jump. She shuddered at the recollection.

'I'm not sure. I don't know much about it, but I think it might have been an elemental. Whatever it was, it was foul.' She put her hands to her face and shivered, in spite of the fire. Oliver said,

'And are you going to tell me how it came to be there?'

'Judy and I had been experimenting with an Ouija board. We wanted to see if we could get in touch with Matt Sutton.'

'What on earth for?' If Oliver sounded angry, it was because he, too, had been scared to his soul, and talking about it brought the feeling back.

'Because he wants something. We thought he might tell us if we could find a way to communicate.'

'You kept on saying he'd gone,' said Oliver, accusingly.

'After we met Nonie, I thought he had... but he hadn't.'

'So was your experiment successful?'

'Don't sound like that,' Chel begged him. 'I don't think we even reached him, as a matter of fact. We thought that we had... but... well, he can't have been like that... not evil. Nonie loved him, and I know that she's gone down in your estimation, but she could never have loved a man who became... *that*. Anyway, I'm not certain elementals were ever actual people at all.' She got to her feet and sat on the arm of his chair, close to him for comfort with her arms round his neck and her face hidden against him. 'It was horrible. I can't tell you... I thought it was going to swallow me up, and I wouldn't *be* any more.' She was shivering with distress. Oliver got an arm round her and hugged her.

'It's all right, sweetheart. It's over, it's gone. Try not to think about it.' Stupid thing to say, he told himself. The Thing had been utterly vile.

'If you hadn't come...' said Chel, shuddering. He felt her shaking with the bare thought of it, but since he felt the same way could only hug her tighter, wordless. After a while the shakes stilled and she stopped half-strangling him and sat up, pushing her hair back from her face and trying to smile.'

'You were wonderful,' she said. The shakes were still in her voice, she was ashamed to hear. 'How did you know... how to get rid of it, I mean?'

'I didn't,' said Oliver. 'I was winging it. It just seemed to me that if you admitted the power of evil, which right then I wasn't in a position to deny, you had to admit the power of good, and it was a good moment to test the theory out.'

'But you claim you aren't a Christian.'

237

'I don't claim, or not claim, to be anything. And I don't think that it matters what you call yourself anyway, it's the intention that matters not how you classify it. If you believe in a God, or even in a simple good, any religion's consecrated words that carry the seeds of that belief will do to defend you from evil, or any prayer from the heart would have done as well. There is no god but God, if there's one at all.'

Chel was silent, contemplating what, to someone of her upbringing, sounded like a heresy, and Oliver lifted her thought from the air and answered it.

'If men had been content with God and not invented religion, there wouldn't be any heresies, no religious persecution, no bigotry, and there'd be a lot less wars, too, and we should all be much closer to the truth - whatever that is.'

'What do you think it is?'

'I have no idea. And I'm very sure you won't find it by playing around with Ouija boards and spiritualism, there's too many open doors that way.'

'What do you mean, too many open doors?'

'Last night, something came through one of them,' Oliver reminded her. He still had his arm around her, now he drew her close against him. 'Listen, Cheryl. Whatever you think, or whatever you want to know, promise me you'll never do that again? It's dangerous. I think that, last night, we were very lucky indeed.'

The use of her full name showed how seriously he was speaking.

'Matthew Sutton keeps trying to use me,' said Chel, troubled. 'He wants something. He wants it desperately. I want him to go away to wherever he should be now - I wanted to tell him he couldn't have it, and he must move on.'

Oliver looked startled, but interested.

'Why, what does he want, do you think?'

Chel shook her head. After last night she was no longer sure that she knew. She said so.

'I can't imagine. I thought I knew, but after last night... well, I don't. But whatever it is, he needs it so badly that he can't finish dying without it, and he's asking for our help. I know he is.'

'Come on, Chel!'

'He cries all the time. Can't you hear him in the wind, these cold nights? You heard him once.'

It was Oliver's turn to be silent, neither admitting nor denying the accusation, and Chel waited. After a few minutes, Oliver said, slowly,

'If you genuinely believe that, then you're being stupid.'

Chel sat upright, indignant.

'Oh, thanks a bunch!'

'No no, I didn't mean it like that.' He turned to look at her seriously. 'Listen, Chel. If any man had something that was so important to him that it kept him, or any part of him, here when he was dead, is it likely that he never mentioned it in his lifetime?'

'I - ' began Chel.

'If it drove him that hard, it would be clear to all the world, and clearer still to anyone close to him, anyone who loved him, for instance. Nonie has to know where the bodies are buried - ask her, and use your alarming Ouija board for firewood.'

It was so obvious that Chel wondered why she had never thought of it. It was also a road beset with thorns, for not only would it feel like an impertinence to ask any such thing, but since Dot's revelations, their relationship with Nonie had changed. No longer so much a friend, more a teacher, a gulf had opened between them. Oliver's doing, if not exactly his fault. So she just stared at him, mentally backing off from the proposal.

'Think about it,' Oliver advised her. 'If you really think it's that important - and I'm not going to question what I in no way understand - give it a fair hearing. And no more Ouija boards - promise me.'

'I promise,' said Chel fervently, relieved that something in his proposal was easy, and seized swiftly on her own gambit for changing the subject. 'The coffee's getting cold.'

She went upstairs later and stood outside the door of her room, oddly reluctant and hesitant. The door was firmly shut now, and one day she would have to open it, but... today?

No point in postponing it, much better get it over. She took hold of the handle and firmly flung the door back. It banged against a chair that Judy had left behind it, and swung gently back towards her. Chel reached out a hand and stopped it.

Beyond, the little room looked ordinary and innocent. The worktable, and the canvases stacked around the walls and on the sofa bed, a pile of abandoned boards in the corner, the long lengths of assorted framing, all looked as they always did. Harmless. Everyday. Chel felt silly and over-dramatic, but she made the sign of the cross before she stepped over the threshold.

It had gone into the corner behind Oliver's early pictures, she recalled. She didn't want to touch it again, but she couldn't bear the thought that it was there. She crossed the room and moved the pile of boards cautiously to one side with her foot.

It lay there in the dust behind the pictures, innocent as the room. A small, eggcup-like object of clear plastic, that last night had pulsed with a life of its own, and filled the whole house with black, horrible thoughts... and worse. Chel had to make herself pick it up with the very tips of her fingers, and held it at arm's length.

You couldn't crush evil with a hammer, just as you couldn't really burn it to ashes in a saucer, and it was absurd to think that you could. It wasn't even the cup itself that had been evil, but whatever had possessed it, and for that she didn't think Oliver could disclaim all responsibility, whatever he chose to think himself. If she and Judy had opened the door and asked the Thing in, the original invitation had been written - drawn, rather, by Oliver. Even so, even though she knew it was irrational, she smashed the cup to fragments, swept them all carefully onto a sheet of cardboard, and tossed them, as she had tossed the ashes of Oliver's drawing, through the window to the wind.

She stood in the middle of the room. Decision time.

'Matthew Sutton?'

The wind sighed past the house, and the room was very still. If there were any spirits here now, they weren't evil ones.

'It's all right,' whispered Chel. 'We'll help you, if we can. We'll talk to Nonie, and if she knows, and if it's something we can do, we'll do it. I promise you. But if we can't, you must understand and go. Is it a deal?'

Was it her imagination, or was the sigh that she heard then more than the wind? The sigh of someone who was weary with waiting, and who at last saw an end of it...?

'I promise,' repeated Chel, and left the room, shutting the door very gently behind her.

XV

Chel had never breathed a word to Maggie about Matthew Sutton's continuing presence, partly because, however she fought against it, she always was made to feel that she was in competition with her over Oliver. She didn't want to confide to Maggie anything that might make Maggie feel too involved with them, however childish this reluctance made her look. She wouldn't have mentioned the experience with the Ouija board either, but Oliver had no such inhibitions. Maggie had professed both interest in, and knowledge of, the paranormal, even if she didn't claim to be psychic herself, and the unpleasant experience that he and Chel had had on the landing had upset him considerably. He wasn't prepared to let it rest without knowing more about it.

'You're interested in phenomena,' he said, when she dropped by a few days later, complaining she hadn't seen them for ages. 'Chel and Judy conjured a demon from the vasty depths the other night, messing around with an Ouija board. What are your views on that?'

Maggie was enthralled. Chel realised she hadn't got the picture at all, and thought Oliver was joking.

'We tried that once when I was at college,'she confessed. 'You don't have to be a medium to get results, you see, although I suppose it would make it easier if somebody was. We got all sorts of messages, it was fascinating.'

'Were any of them verifiably correct?' asked Oliver, with interest.

'Oh yes.' Maggie sounded as if it was the most ordinary thing in the world. 'Some of them were amazing. It really does work, you know - but you do need to be very careful. It doesn't do to make a habit of it, or get too involved. It's like reading tarot cards, some people get dependent on it. And it's supposed to be possible to invite possession if you use it too often, although it never happened to any of us. It's like any other drug, I suppose, dangerous to exceed the stated dose.'

'Chel and Judy were trying to get in touch with our resident ghost,' Oliver told her. 'Apparently he's still here. They've both seen him.'

Maggie didn't know whether to be reproachful or shocked.

'You never told me,' she said accusingly, and Chel felt as silly as she maybe deserved, and looked sheepish.

'The subject never seemed to come up,' she said lamely. A lame sheep - how pathetic! Maggie had this gift for setting her at a disadvantage in front of Oliver.

'Oh well.' Maggie brushed her own disappointment aside in order to impart knowledge. 'It wouldn't have worked anyway - at least, I don't think so. If your ghost - did he have a name?'

'Matthew Sutton,' said Chel, who thought Maggie almost certainly knew already, given what she was and who Matthew Sutton had been.

'If Matthew Sutton hasn't passed on, you wouldn't reach him. The Ouija board communicates with the spirit world, and Matthew Sutton is still on the fringes of this one. You shouldn't really have tried, anything might have happened.'

'As it did,' commented Oliver, and Chel asked,

'Like what, for instance?'

'Well,' said Maggie, considering. 'I'm not absolutely certain, but I think if you were trying to communicate with a spirit who wasn't actually there, you might get some bad vibes back. Something else, trying to get in on the act. It might even be dangerous - they can be, you know. Not all spirits are good, not by any means.'

'Now, she tells us!' said Oliver. 'Chel, why didn't you ask your friend here before you and Judy did your conjuring trick? It would have saved a load of grief.'

'But if they sell them for children to play with...,' Chel defended herself.

'They don't any more that I know of, and they never would've, if people weren't so sceptical,' Maggie told her firmly. 'Anyway, how many children would go into it with the serious intention of calling up a real spirit? How many children see ghosts, if it comes to that?'

'More than you might expect, maybe,' suggested Oliver.

'But,' said Chel, 'we got messages that really seemed to relate to Matthew Sutton, and to what I was thinking about - '

'Ah!' cried Maggie, quickly. '*To what you were thinking about.* Spirits can be very mischievous, you know. It was probably teasing you.'

'*Teasing*!' exclaimed Chel. It was hardly the word she would have chosen herself. She thought about it. 'You mean, it was just reading my mind, and didn't really *know* anything?' She found the idea comforting.

'Of course. What else could it do, if it wanted to convince you? You were awfully lucky that that's all that happened, if you ask me.'

Chel would have left it there, but Oliver said,

'That wasn't all that happened,' with such significance that Maggie stared at him in astonishment.

'What, then?'

He told her about the horrible thing on the landing, and she was duly horrified.

'But that's awful! Are you sure it's gone? Elementals are the most terrible things imaginable, not real people at all, and they're terribly difficult to get rid of! They feed on the spirit of blood and excrement, and foul things like that.'

Chel remembered the spectral drip of blood from the roof that had preceded the manifestation, and the awful stink, and felt her flesh crawl on her bones. She never went upstairs after dark since that night unless all the lights were on.

'But it did go,' she said, almost pleadingly. 'Oliver got rid of it.'

Maggie was staring at them both as if she expected them to sprout horns at any moment.

'You were lucky then.' She hesitated. 'Are you going to try again?'

'No!' said Chel, with such force that Maggie laughed, but then, she hadn't been on the landing.

'I don't blame you,' she said, and looked pensive, almost, Chel thought, as if she was half-disappointed and would have liked to be asked to join in. As if in confirmation of this, Maggie went on, 'I wish I could see a ghost, though. They never seem to appear to me.'

'You can see them for me, and welcome,' said Chel.

Discussing it with Nonie was less simple. For one thing, she came less often these days, not only because the happy relationship she had with Oliver had been tarnished by the intervention of the Dreaded Dot but because he needed her less. He worked much more confidently now, and a lot more slowly, with far more attention to detail, his own very definite style crystallising into a form that Nonie didn't wish to influence with her own. They talked rather than worked when she was there, always now about painting and technique, and sometimes experimented, and if Oliver needed her advice he asked for it, and she gave it. As a method of instruction it appeared to work admirably, although to Chel it seemed impersonal. Nonie said, dispassionately, that Oliver's pictures were good, and getting better all the time, and he might produce quite a presentable exhibition if he worked at it, matching the detachment, almost the coldness, that started with him. This cool appraisement, if it was intended to disguise her pride in her pupil, signally failed in its object. She confided to Chel, in a rare moment of expansiveness, that one day he would probably paint her off the map.

'He has enormous talent, and the will and the time to learn,' she said. 'Already, I don't think I know of any other living painter who has the same feeling for water - when the skill catches up with the eye, he's going to be the best.'

243

'Matthew Sutton was a very good painter, too, wasn't he?' asked Chel, as if casually, feeling her way.

'He didn't paint the sea,' said Nonie, taking this remark at face value. 'Or very seldom - he loved town and country scenes, trees and fields, houses and people - people in the abstract, that is, not portraits. He never painted those. But yes, he was good. If he had lived - ' She broke off. 'Do you know, even after all this time I find it dreadfully hard to accept that he's dead and will never paint another picture. He had everything to live for, it seems so unjust.'

They were in the kitchen, washing up after lunch, and hot suds and teatowels made an unlikely, if vaguely comforting, background for the discussion of the supernatural that Chel hoped to introduce, but there would never be a better opening line than that, she told herself, and tried to screw her courage to the sticking point.

'What sort of a person was he? Do you mind talking about him?' she asked, as idly as she could.

'No.' Nonie paused, thoughtfully drying a mug. 'No. I haven't talked of him for a very long time. At first it hurt too much - when something like that happens, right out of the blue, you know yourself that you find ways of blaming yourself. In the beginning, I thought that it was because we had... well, not quarrelled exactly, but disagreed, that he was killed - thinking about it, you know, as he got nearer home, instead of concentrating on what he was doing. By the time his friend Mac had finally convinced me that it was denigrating Matt to think he would ever be so stupid, and I was needing to talk, everything had moved on. Nobody was interested any more, only in his pictures. So I never have talked about him much after the first shock.'

'Tell me then. So he was a good flyer,' prompted Chel.

'The best. He was a lot older than me, but no doubt the scandalmongers have already told you that - nobody really remembers now what they knew, or didn't know, but mud sticks. He flew in the RAF, Bomber Command, all through the Battle of Britain and right up to the end of the war and in the Berlin Airlift too. He was Wing Commander by then, although he was young for it, you grew up quickly in those days and there were plenty of vacancies for promotion. He had the DSO and the DFC, and a list of commendations as long as your arm. A brave man, but a very troubled one.' She put down the mug and picked up another one, but made no attempt to dry it. 'We met at college. He was a lecturer, I was a second year student. He had used to be a serious painter but... I think he had a mental block, actually. He couldn't paint any more, he'd lost it. Oh, the ability was still there... but the light had gone out. He taught to eat, he made no secret of it. Helen -

Oliver's mother, that is - said that he hated it, she was probably right. He certainly wasn't very good at it.'

'So what was his problem? The war? It must have been over a good few years by then.'

It was surprisingly easy to talk to Chel, Nonie found. She had the quality of understanding, for all she was so young - perhaps just because she was so young and had already been through so much. And a lot of water had passed under the bridge since those days of the fifties and early sixties, someone of Chel's generation wouldn't think Matt soft for his beliefs. Only someone like Peachey could ever think that, when he had fought so hard and so long in spite of them. That wasn't softness, that was - so Nonie believed - misguided courage, but courage of a high order. Courage for which he had almost destroyed himself. People didn't do that nowadays, they were most of them too streetwise, or had counselling instead. A different world, even if the jury was still out as to whether it was any better.

'That war stopped, but others didn't. There was Korea, for one, people seem to forget about that these days, but he grieved over it almost as if it was personal. I don't think he ever forgave himself for what he did - he jumped straight in when the war started - World War II - full of ideals of patriotism and found out very early that it wasn't a simple matter of fighting for what was right. He was a bomber pilot, I told you that. Indiscriminate killing of civilian people who maybe didn't even want war in the first place, that's how he came to see it... it broke him right up. And what had it all been for, if there it was, still going on? Vietnam - that was on the go before he died, others too... the Cold War, all that, it all ate into him. At heart, he was a very gentle man. He used to say...' She broke off. 'Sorry, you aren't interested in all this. You should tell me to shut up.' She began to dry the mug.

'No, please. I am interested. I'd like to know about him.'

Nonie laughed.

'I don't think anyone knew *that*,' she said. 'Do you know, it wasn't until his funeral that I even knew anything personal about him, about his family for instance? And I think that I was probably closer to him than anybody.'

'So, what did he use to say?' prompted Chel. She was interested now for Matt's own sake as well as their own. A picture was beginning to emerge that fitted in so neatly with the things that she had suspected about him that she almost felt that she had known him. Perhaps this came over to Nonie, for where she had been going to shrug off the query and change the subject, she suddenly decided to go on. It had, after all, been waiting to be aired for a long, long time. She said, feeling her way, anxious not to let Matt be misunderstood,

'You'll maybe think this silly, I don't know. He used to say that the only thing that kept him sane was the belief that this life wasn't all that we had - that if he had to believe that it was, he couldn't live with himself knowing what he had done. Young men like himself, women and even children, all with their lives ahead of them and all their ambition unfulfilled - he had killed them, crippled them, he had seen his friends die and suffer the same way, and come out unscathed himself. He felt guilty. As if he hadn't paid.... Some of those people that he killed could have been his friends if the world had been different. He needed to believe - and I believe with him - that they had gone on. That they lived somewhere else, and they weren't dead or crippled any more, and whatever they had failed to do because of him they could go on and do it.'

'Surely that's standard religious belief?' ventured Chel, but Nonie shook her head.

'Yes, maybe it is, but more personal - he felt he owed them, he hated himself, and that's an awful thing, so in a way he had to rationalise it. He hated himself for the same mindless cruelty that disabled Oliver, but it wasn't the same at all; the men who did that were sick with the sickness of your time, not ours. I used to tell him that he should go into the church and get it all out of his system, but he could only communicate through his painting, except with me. He was a very shy person - not a bit like Oliver, for instance.'

No, shy Oliver was not, but he had his own attitude problem.

'Oliver just can't be bothered with people.'

'And he knows - has probably always known - exactly where he's going and how he intends to get there. He might have been made to change the destination, but his path is sure. Matt was always terribly unsure, at least when I knew him... but perhaps he was a different person before war changed him. It turned his values upside-down, and he never turned them back up again. He felt so strongly that what he believed was true. I'll tell you how he put it.' Nonie tilted her head, remembering, trying to get it right. 'He used to say that childhood was the time for hayfields and sunshine, flowers and innocence, the time when we're closest to God, and it lasts so short a time - I hate to think what he would have made of today's precocious little brats, turned into tiny adults before they've had any simple fun! We live in a time that sneers at innocence.' She paused, thinking about what she had just said, before continuing. 'Then, when we grow up and we have to live in the world that others have made - then, all the flowers of innocence are dead, and all that's left is a hard, barren, cratered wasteland that will last until we die, and it's up to us to help each other across it as best we may. Some of us never see beyond it - but if we can only keep faith, if we do our best, then one day we'll find a divine justice beyond that black horizon, and it won't matter what other people have done to us or made us do - what will count then is what we've done ourselves and the reasons for it, and with whatever chances we've been given, good or bad.'

It all came back to her so clearly, Matt's stumbling vision of glory, described all those years ago for her inner eye to see. Her voice softened at the memory.

'He saw it as a golden dawn with the rising sun shining through a mist... it was uncanny that it was in a mist that he died. He did paint the land that he thought would lie over the last horizon - the one he fought for, I suppose. A dream world, where we found all the things that we considered to be good. Only, his picture was his own dream - other people's might have been horribly different.'

'I've seen it, haven't I?' said Chel.

Nonie looked at her quickly, and away again.

'A reproduction, anyway. It was the best thing he'd ever done. He gave it to me, before he died, and I could never bear to sell it. While I have it, it's as if he's still with me - part of him, anyway.'

'It's a wonderful picture,' Chel agreed. She hesitated, for now came the hard bit. 'Nonie - if he believed so strongly in life after death, can you think of anything that would have kept him here - kept him earthbound?'

'What?' Nonie stared at her.

'I think he's here, in this house. I feel him, strongly. And he desperately wants something. He's wanted it since the day he died. I don't think he can move on without it.'

Nonie could have said that Chel was imagining things, and if it hadn't been for the strange experience at the studio she would have done, and would have been both deeply angry and most bitterly resentful, as much on Matt's behalf as on her own. She felt the first seeds of that anger and resentment before she remembered, and, reading Chel's expression, swallowed them. She spoke unevenly.

'People have always said that this place was haunted, but I never believed it was more than just stories. There was never anything here for me.'

'I think it was true,' said Chel. 'He would have been here, you know - for you more than anyone. But you can't hear him, or see him. Most people can't.'

'Is it silly to feel cheated?' asked Nonie, trying to keep satire from

247

her voice. She was white to the lips, resentful, excluded, hurting. Chel said, offering consolation,

'I thought - that day we met - that it had been you he wanted. To comfort you... and I still think that I was right. There was something he needed to say to you - ' She broke off. Something flickered on the edge of her consciousness and was gone. The greater need pushed back in. 'It wasn't just that, though,' she said. 'He went for a while, but then... he came back...' She became aware that she was twisting the dishcloth into a knot between her hands, and dropped it back into the water. 'All the time - it's not me he's been calling for, or even you. It's been Oliver. I thought at first - and I know it's stupid now - that he wanted to take over - to possess, not Oliver particularly, but any artist. To go on living. But I don't think that can be right. Not if what you say is true. He wouldn't be like that.'

'No,' said Nonie, slowly. 'No, he wouldn't be like that.'

Chel hesitated. Before she went any further, there was something it was imperative to know. The wrong answer, and it was time to go, that was very clear.

'Nonie, this is going to sound really silly - but did you ever call him by any pet name? Like... well, *Bobo* for instance?'

'I beg your pardon?' Nonie looked so obviously startled, not to say offended, that Chel's heart lightened immediately. 'Good God, no! Nobody ever called him anything but Matt, me included. He'd've died of embarrassment if I'd called him Bobo!'

Sheer relief made Chel's knees go wobbly. She leaned on the sink for support.

'Then what? I wanted to ask him, but he can't tell me - he can't explain. I don't know how to find out, unless you can tell me. I think he must have it, whatever it is, or he'll never progress. He can't.'

Nonie was silent for so long that Chel thought she wasn't going to be able to answer. Her first thought, that Matt needed an answer that she had never been able to give him, and that she still didn't know herself for sure, she dismissed. Once he was dead, that would no longer have been important. So what would have been? And she knew the answer this time.

She thought she did, at least. If she was right, if this was for real - and half of her believed it had to be, even while the other half poured scorn - then it was the most wonderful thing she had ever imagined. It held such promise, such unbelievable joy. If she could trust Chel.

'I don't believe in all this spiritualist crap,' she said, half-apologetically. Fighting it, Chel discerned, and felt the anger too.

'Neither do I,' she said. 'I know that sounds silly. I never asked for it, I don't want it. I'm not a medium or anything, it just happens. I can't go into a trance or produce ectoplasm or whatever it is... I'm not a spoof.' She repeated, helplessly, 'It just happens.'

Nonie said nothing. She realised that Chel had no idea what had happened in her studio, and so didn't argue with her assertion that she wasn't a medium and couldn't go into a trance. It seemed to her that she had two choices. To turn her back and walk away was one, and that would have to mean, turn her back on everything. Not just Matt, but Oliver and Chel too, because this would mean it was some kind of unforgivable scam. Or she could go along with Chel, weird as it all sounded, and really rather repugnant as it would be.

Which?

The answer came, simple and unarguable. To go along with Chel, if she was, as she termed it, a spoof, couldn't hurt Matt. To turn her back and walk away without finding out, perhaps could.

She made her decision.

'All right, I'll buy it.' She paused. 'I can't believe I said that.'

'So what, then?' asked Chel. She looked tired, Nonie thought, not triumphant or even relieved, but like someone toting a burden of which she very much wished to be rid. She said,

'Chel... Matt painted his land over the horizon, but he never painted the way there. He meant to - he wanted to. He had it all in his head, he had even prepared the canvas for it, he was nearly ready to begin. He meant it to be the best thing he'd ever done. His masterpiece - something he thought he owed the people he had killed. Comfort... restitution... something like that. A way to earn his place in the hereafter maybe. He was going to do it soon.' She paused, and said abruptly, 'But he died instead.'

In the silence, the sound of the kitchen clock ticking on the wall sounded as loud as a grandfather clock. Chel said uncertainly,

'Then he's been looking for someone to paint it for him, you think?'

'I can't think of anything else.'

'But that would mean he knew Oliver could paint like he does before Oliver even knew it himself. That's impossible, Nonie.'

Nonie felt herself on firmer ground, thankfully.

'What makes you so sure that Oliver didn't know?' She added, as if it answered everything, which she knew very well it didn't, 'Anyway, Matt never met him - it wouldn't make any difference, I suppose. Oliver wasn't born when Matt died.'

Chel seemed to be arguing against herself, something Nonie found reassuring. She still couldn't quite get out of her mind the idea that this was some kind of put-up job.

'Oliver paints the sea, not countryside things. He doesn't paint a bit like Matthew Sutton.' She pulled the plug and took Nonie by the arm. 'Let's go and tell him. We have to do something, so let's go with what you feel Matt Sutton wants himself.'

'If I'm right,' muttered Nonie. 'If we're not all away with the fairies.' But she allowed herself to be urged into the conservatory, where Oliver was half listening to the radio, half dreaming into space. Chel practically dragged Nonie in and switched off the sound.

'Oliver, Nonie thinks Matt Sutton wants you to paint his masterpiece.' It sounded seriously weird, put into words like that. Oliver, understandably, looked astonished, but he didn't laugh.

'Why?' he asked.

For the second time, Nonie tried to explain Matt's philosophy, more difficult to Oliver, between whom and herself there had arisen friction. She spoke with an urgency that sprang from the certainty, growing by the minute, that Chel's story, on the face of it incredible, was totally reconcilable with what she remembered of Matt. Matt... who had always had such a terrible compulsion to absolve what he saw as his guilt.

'He saw it as a landscape,' she said, and just describing it brought Matt so close that she had trouble now in holding her voice steady. Matt, who had apparently gone, unfulfilled to cry in the night... Matt who had loved her, whom she had loved. She continued with an effort. 'First the flowers,' she continued more firmly. 'And standing hay, because he was brought up in the country, you know, and to him it was the symbol of a perfect childhood. Sliding down haystacks, and things like that. Innocent things... not like today, when you can't say the simplest thing without someone bursting into a lewd laugh. And then, beyond it - '

'A huge expanse of bare earth,' said Oliver, interrupting. 'With deep cracks where it hasn't rained for ages, and great polluted puddles in other places, and bomb craters and nothing growing... and people walking across it like shadows, finding their way to whatever lies ahead of them - helping each other. It was a mystic number of them, I think - thirteen. And just a few stunted trees on an empty horizon. And the dawn beyond, gold and rose coloured, with clouds blowing across it and mist, low down. Among other things, it's a picture of the futility of war and the resilience of the human race.'

Nonie and Chel stared at him, Chel in amazement and Nonie in something close to shock.

'How could you know that?' asked Nonie, blankly.

'I've seen it,' said Oliver.

The incredible statement hung in the air between them.

'You can't have,' said Nonie.

'When? Where?' asked Chel, more practically, but with equal scepticism.

'The night we spent on the landing. I dreamed it.'

The only occasion on which he had ever been upstairs. Chel swallowed nervously.

'Would you do it? Could you do it?'

Oliver said nothing.

'Not because of bloody Dorothy!' said Nonie, before she could stop herself. Shock, that Oliver should have recited the pattern of Matt's vision so accurately out of nowhere, despair that Matt's spirit, that should have been freed, should be earthbound still by old political games that mattered not a toss, old resentment against Dot, all coloured her voice. Oliver shook his head.

'You must know that's not so,' he said. 'Whatever's going on here - and I have no more idea than you what it is - has nothing to do with bloody Dorothy.'

'Then what?' asked Nonie. 'I've still got the canvas he planned to use. I never used it myself, I don't know why, it didn't seem right... but it's in good condition still. It might need re-stretching - it's a big one. But that's not a problem.' She heard her own voice, pleading, and was amazed at herself. *All that spiritualist crap*, she had said it herself. Now listen to her!

'It's nothing like that,' said Oliver. He looked at her, with a certain speculation that made her feel uneasy. 'It's this. It seems to me, with all due respect to Chel and Judy, that some people would be asking what we were all on at this moment. If you allow that it's really happening - and although I know it is, something in me refuses to believe it - then I want to know the answer to a question.'

'How will it help us, whatever it is?' asked Chel. It was no good blaming either Nonie or Oliver, they only had her word for what she saw or heard or experienced. She wouldn't believe herself, if she was honest.

'Because if there *is* a sensible answer, and that can be added to what happened the other night, then I *think* I may accept that it isn't the mushrooms we had for breakfast.'

'What did happen the other night?' asked Nonie, wondering if it would help her own problem with belief, just as Chel said,

'So what's the question?'

'Just this.' He turned to Nonie. 'If he wanted to get someone to paint this picture, surely you were the obvious person to go to, rather

251

than a complete stranger. So, why didn't he?'

'I don't hear him,' said Nonie. Her face had taken on a shut look. Oliver's speculative look deepened.

'No more do I. It apparently hasn't stopped him. So?'

Her own voice echoed down the passage of the years. Shouting at poor Matt, asserting herself, asserting her independence. *I want it to be my name that people remember for its own sake, not for yours! I can't use you for a stepping stone, and if I never did, people would still say that I had if we were married. I can't marry you - I won't do it - I'll give you my heart, my life, my soul, but never, never, my art.* But her name had been associated with his anyway, and she had still made a name for herself nearly as well-known and well-respected as his had been, that girl obsessed with her own identity. And the price of that was that Matt, whom she had loved more than anyone in the world and never realised quite how much until she had lost him - Matt must go to a stranger and beg for help when he most needed it. If Oliver was truly a stranger. They were part of the same charmed circle, had overlapped in time although Oliver had still been in the womb. She said, slowly and with difficulty,

'He wouldn't - there were reasons - '

Instinctively, Chel reached out to comfort her, not understanding in a literal sense but sensing hurt there.

'Then Oliver will give it a go,' she said.

'Hold on a minute,' said Oliver. 'I've never seen one of his paintings. I have no idea how he worked, and if I did, I couldn't - wouldn't, in fact - copy.'

It was such an unexpected - and at the same time, paradoxically, to be expected - echo of her own attitude that Nonie was taken aback. But Matt, who had never been a stupid man, must have learned something from her intransigence, surely.

'Perhaps that doesn't matter,' she said. 'Perhaps it's better that way. You paint what he's put into your head, but you do it your own way. What matters is what he wanted to say.'

'A picture of hope,' said Oliver, meditatively. 'Maybe that's appropriate.'

'So you'll do it,' said Nonie, more a statement than a question. It was disconcerting, and unexpectedly undermining, to find out how close Matt, who had been dead for more than thirty years, still was to her heart. The day he died suddenly felt like yesterday. Her voice cracked shamefully, she was twenty-four again, and heartbroken. Perhaps it was this display of vulnerability that melted the barrier that Dot had so deviously built, or perhaps it was only insubstantial in the first place. Oliver looked at her from under his eyelashes, a watchful, almost calculating look, and with a dexterity completely unlike himself, changed the dangerous subject..

'That now being understood,' he said, 'what are you planning for Christmas? Chel's arranged a tribal celebration, fancy coming to join us, or do you have a programme of debauchery already planned?'

Nonie had been looking for excuses not to join her brother and his family: her niece, Shona the Juggernaut, had long since married and by this time headed up a tribe of children as determined as herself. Even had Nonie been a family person, they were hard work. Even so, she treated the query with caution. There were too many overfalls and tide-rips around Oliver to lose concentration, and too much at stake.

'Oh... I shall have a quiet day on my own in the cottage, and go out for a drink with friends in the evening, I expect.'

'Have a noisy day here instead,' invited Chel. 'You can still nip back for the drink in the evening if you want to. And we'd love to have you with us. You know that.'

Christmas with Matt. How sentimental. How foolish. How tempting.

'You don't want an elderly maiden-auntly stranger, not if you've got family coming,' said Nonie, and Oliver said,

'Chel's family, not mine. You'd be safe. And they'll like you.'

'Do come,' coaxed Chel. 'Elderly is a state of mind, and anyway, you aren't.'

'And maidenly, we already know about,' put in Oliver, with a grin.

Nonie laughed, reluctantly.

'Do you really want me?'

'Yes,' they said, in unison.

'Then thank you. I'd love to.'

She left soon after, with much on her mind, and when she had gone, Chel left Oliver staring into the fire lost in thought, and went upstairs. She had no idea, even now, whether she could call Matt Sutton at will, and no real intention of trying - once was enough to cure her forever of trying to communicate with the spirit world - but she thought that if she sat for a while close to the spot where he had left this life in body, and refused to leave it entirely in spirit, she might be able to leave some message that would be understood.

She sat down at her worktable and leaned her chin on her hands. It was quiet, another still, misty, late November day. Matt Sutton, of course, had died in a summer mist, widespread over the whole county, not what the locals called a Trelewan Special like today's.

She thought about him for a while, that gentle man who had the courage to fight for what he believed, yet hated himself for doing it, torn against his inclinations but prepared to pay the price. As he had paid, trying to console himself with the conviction of an after-life of which he was, perhaps, unintentionally himself the proof. It was interesting that he, like Oliver, had discarded traditional thinking, almost as if the need to explore new worlds of the mind, as well as the physical world, was inherent in their natures. He must have been like Oliver in other ways, too. She wondered if he had held onto his past life because of an urgent need to pass his message on in the only way he knew, or if it was a deliberate wish to reach the crowning pinnacle of his career before he left. Either way it had kept him - or something of him - tied to this world.

If there was another life - if Matt Sutton hadn't simply been rationalising to still his own conscience - if he had been right, it really did make the principle of forgiving those that despitefully used you at least theoretically possible to live up to. Armed with such a belief, she might even be able to forgive the vicious attack that had ruined Oliver's life. It would, she found suddenly, be a great relief now to be able to forgive it and consign it to the past.

Perhaps that was why man had invented himself gods in the first place. To ease his own grief and guilt, and assuage his fear of the unknown. To blame when things went wrong, to remove the ultimate responsibility.

The powers of good and evil were real enough.

It was specious beyond reason to accept the freedom of choice between the two and then grumble because being good wasn't the easy option. To dismiss the possibility of God because so many people had freely chosen his opposite. It had to be what you chose yourself that counted in the end. You had to struggle across your own wasteland, you had to help others across theirs, and you had to have standards, and morals, and all the other things that sounded so stuffy and boring, and they had to come from the very heart of you, or you would end up a hollow sham like the Dreaded Dot. What would be her level in Matt Sutton's heaven? God would read her motives, as those around her certainly couldn't.

What had he seen as the ultimate end for mankind?

The sudden realisation that she wasn't ready to accept all these new ideas, that she wanted to go on being ordinary and imperfect as she had always been, came as a shock that effectively swept away the enlightenment that she had felt almost within her grasp. She remembered why she had come up here.

Talking to Matt Sutton as if he was there was becoming a habit. She didn't realise she shared it with Nonie.

'It's the picture, isn't it?' she said. 'The picture that you didn't have time to paint? Oliver will paint it, if he can. Is that what you want?'

The words were just words, they sounded silly and pretentious in the quiet room. There was no answer to her questions, nothing but silence. She knew, quite suddenly, that there would be no more manifestations, no more cries for help. Just the picture that was a gift to Oliver, no longer Matt Sutton's, and the memories that Nonie carried in her heart.

So, a picture of hope, painted by a disabled adventurer fighting his way back to a full and hopefully satisfying life. Not bad, Matthew Sutton, not bad at all.

It was probably sillier even than asking her questions, but Chel said goodbye.

XVI

The day before Christmas Eve, Nonie was still deliberating as to whether she should take Matt's painting of the autumn woodland, that had been her godson's christening present, from the bank's strongroom and give it to Oliver for the second time, but finally she decided against it. Oliver had never seen one of Matt's paintings, maybe it would be wrong to show one to him at this point. It should be valued too, before she handed it over, she had seen enough of Chel and Oliver to get the message that they were impractical about such things.

It had been a long time, she realised as she trawled through the St. Ives shops for alternative gifts, since she had looked forward to a family-style Christmas, sad that it couldn't be her own family, with whom, these days, she found little in common. She chose books to parcel up for the two unknown children and raided her own craft gallery for a handsome pot for Chel's sister and her husband, but Oliver and Chel themselves were more difficult. It had to be exactly the right gift. She had never given them anything before, and she wanted them to remember it all their lives, but nothing she looked at seemed to fill the bill.

The trouble was, they weren't people who attached a lot of importance to possessions. Chel, she had noticed, didn't even have an engagement ring, or if she did, she never wore it. They seemed quite happy to drift through life with one mediocre picture and a few books to their names, plus the clothes they stood up in. What did you give to people like that? What would they choose, if they were asked? And possibly even more pertinent, were they really like that or had circumstances simply made them that way? It felt as if she had known them both for ever, but she still couldn't answer that.

Perhaps Chel wasn't. Oliver certainly was, and it was Oliver that she particularly wanted to please, she realised. She felt, unreasonably surely, that she owed Oliver. So, what was the perfect gift for him, that would also give pleasure to Chel?

And phrased like that, it was easy.

Chel's sister Tracy and her husband Tom, together with Micky and Candy, descended on Moor House that same afternoon. Chel, who hadn't really expected them to come at such short notice, had looked forward to their arrival with about equal parts of pleasure and apprehension, half-fearing, even while knowing the fear was probably unreasonable, that her sister had been despatched to Cornwall not so much as a peace-maker as a spy in the enemy camp. Family Christmases were almost a sacred institution in their own right in Chel's family; for Tracy, and even more the beloved grandchildren, to be released from attendance was more deeply significant than Oliver appreciated. She didn't try to explain it to him, he would never have understood. As far as family matters went, he came from a different planet. The complications sometimes made her feel tired just thinking about them.

It was therefore a great relief when Tracy hurtled out of the car on their arrival, straight into her little sister's waiting arms and hugged her until she could hardly breathe.

'How lovely to see you! We could hardly believe it when we got your invite!'

'Did they understand?' asked Chel, hugging her back with all her strength, her immediate preoccupation leaping to the fore.

'Understand?' Tracy stood back, holding her at arm's length to look at her, Chel thought, critically. 'They could hardly wait to get us packed and on the road! We come as a kind of family MI5, I should warn you. You look marvellous, I must say!'

'Oh shit!' said Chel, brokenly, and hugged her again. 'I'm crying, I'm sorry.'

'And there was us thinking you wanted us,' said Tracy. 'Here - have a tissue. And don't sniff, it's bad for your sinuses.' They looked at each other and laughed, Chel scrubbing at her cheek with a crumpled tissue. Micky and Candy slid out of the back seat of the car and stood, hovering, by the door, unsure of themselves. Chel stared at them in amazement, a fresh wave of compunction sweeping over her. How they'd grown! She couldn't believe it.

How long was it? They had gone to Suffolk for Christmas the year they got married, then there was the year they spent in Greece, then she had been poorly when she was pregnant and they hadn't gone anywhere... then the accident, or whatever you liked to call it, and her miscarriage, then the awful Christmas in the bungalow with her parents... then this year. That made it - oh God, surely not? - three years, since she had seen her nephew and niece! Tracy looked at her sympathetically.

'Doesn't time fly when you're having fun?' she said. Chel turned back to her, her mouth open.

'I hadn't realised...' she said.

'We gathered that. And don't start crying again, *please*! Come and say hullo to your auntie, you two, before she washes us all away!'

Micky and Candy came forward shyly. Candy had been five when they last met, she must barely remember her aunt. Chel was swept with a fresh wave of remorse, how had she ever come to let such a thing happen?

Candy, recovering rapidly from her initial shyness, was as ever equal to the social occasion. Submitting to a kiss from her aunt, she said,

'Is Uncle Oliver here? Gran said he was poorly, and we had to be good.' She sounded as if she took this as a personal affront - which, remembering the last meeting between the two of them, was understandable, given Candy. Oliver was surprisingly good with small children. Her mother had said, rather cuttingly she remembered, that he was mentally about their level. But that was before... Chel stopped her thoughts there, before they galloped out of hand.

'I think you'll find he can hold his own,' she said. 'He's around somewhere. Tom!'

Her brother-in-law came round the back of the car, a box full of coloured parcels in his arms. He stooped sideways to kiss her.

'Hi, Cheryl. Where would you like these?'

'Bring them in. All of you - come in, out of the cold.' Chel turned towards the door.

'But don't go empty-handed,' Tom interrupted swiftly. 'Kids grab some of those bags. Trace, can you bring that other box?'

Tracy went round to the rear of the car, marshalling the children ahead of her.

'You'll never believe what Mum sent,' she said. 'Come on Candy, you can carry more than that - take that one too - that one *there*, thank you!' She heaved a large box into her arms and turned round, laughing. 'I think she thinks Cornwall is the end of the world, she's packed you half the shop!'

Laden, they staggered merrily into the house, dumping bags and boxes around the dining area and on the breakfast bar. The visitors looked around curiously, the children immediately running to the fat green tree in the corner.

'There's a proper tree!' cried Candy, in delight. 'Just smell the Christmas!' She gave a deep, regrettably juicy sniff which must have given her sinuses a blasting, her face radiant.

'You haven't decorated it,' said Micky, critically. The box of decorations, a few their own but most of them Nonie's, stood untouched on the worktop.

'No, I thought you two would like to do that this evening,' said Chel, and they whooped with delight. Tracy made a face.

'I hope you know what you're doing,' she said.

Attracted by the noise, Oliver emerged from the conservatory.

'I see the Martians have landed,' he observed. His arrival on the scene, Chel thought, was like turning the barrel of a kaleidoscope, the colours shifted and the pattern changed. The children, who had been rapidly adapting, became shy again. Tracy's mouth opened in amazement, the last time she had seen him, creeping with trepidation into a hospital ward, he had been half dead, flat on his back with people shaking their heads over him. Now, in spite of the sticks, he looked cheerful, healthy and just like anybody else. But there was a change... She described it in her head. *Grown up.*

'My goodness!' she said. 'I don't believe it! You look like a different man! The last time we met...'

'I feel like a different man,' said Oliver, swiftly cutting short any uncomfortable reminders.

'So do I, often,' said Chel feelingly, and they all laughed. But behind the laughter, she was uncomfortably aware that Tracy's amazement was her fault, she had underplayed all the news she had relayed to home, largely, she realised with shame, to keep them all away. She wondered, uneasily, what else she had underplayed and thought with misgiving of Oliver's paintings and his coming exhibition - an exhibition which she was not even certain she had ever mentioned. She shifted her feet, uncomfortably. Nobody seemed to notice. Tom came in with the last of the luggage and she said, with relief, 'Let's get some of this stuff upstairs, shall we?'

There was a stampede for the stairs from the children, anxious to explore this unusual house, peremptorily called back by Tracy.

'Don't go empty handed,' she ordered, and they came reluctantly down again.

'Can we go and explore the garden?' asked Candy hopefully, her eye caught by the open conservatory door.

'When you've helped with the luggage,' chorused everyone but Oliver, who gave her a sympathetic grin. She returned it saucily and picked up the two smallest bags she could see. The stampede upstairs was repeated in a more orderly fashion, Chel leading the way, Tom bringing up the rear. Oliver, left alone below, listened to the excited squeals and the laughter and the opening and shutting of doors and wondered, for the first time in his life, if he had missed out on something during his childhood and more, if he was still missing out on it to this day. After all, he had two sisters, he had a brother-in-law, he too had a nephew and a niece. It was an unfamiliar thought, and not a wholly pleasant one. But too late now, surely. The presently fashionable word *dysfunctional*, once used by Chel, drifted into his mind and out again. He shrugged his shoulders and returned to the conservatory where, with unusual forethought, he decided that it might be a good idea to tidy up a bit.

Upstairs, there were a few minutes of racing around exploring. Candy had to sample the bathroom, and Micky made a face when he found he had to share a room with her.

'Well, I don't want to share with *you* either!' she retorted, re-emerging onto the landing in time to retaliate. 'There's this other room, can't he have that?' and she flung open the door to the small bedroom before Chel could stop her - if she had been going to. There was a pause, while Candy's eyes grew rounder and rounder and speech appeared to have deserted her. Then,

'Oh, wow!' she exclaimed.

'Candy!' Tracy caught her hand. 'You don't just go opening doors in other people's houses, do you mind!' She went to shut the door again, and of course, also saw the stacked pictures. Unlike Candy, she said nothing for a moment. Then she turned and looked her sister firmly in the eye. Chel, guiltily recalling a casual mention of *Oliver is doing a bit of painting*, a long time ago before it had become serious, found herself looking away.

But Tracy said nothing - not then. She gave the protesting Candy a shove and pulled the door to behind them.

'But Mummy!' Candy objected, 'Mummy, they're *boo*tiful.'

'You've been eating too many turkey drummers,' said Tracy, firmly. 'Tom, take these two down into the garden and let them run off some steam. Chel and I will get this mess sorted.'

'That's right, keep the plum job for yourself,' Tom complained, rounding up his children.

'And don't let them annoy Oliver,' Tracy shouted after them. Then she turned and viewed the muddle on the floor of the best bedroom. 'Right, that's got rid of them. Come on Sis, to work! Those bags belong to the kids, if you do those, I'll unpack our stuff.'

Chel carried the bags into the second bedroom and flung them onto one of the twin beds. She felt like the lowest kind of worm, and decided that she probably deserved to. After all that she had said to Oliver about his treatment of his, admittedly rather awful, family, what had she done to her own? Shut them out, cut them off, lied to them by omission? All of that. And in return, her parents had disrupted their own precious Christmas and sent Tracy and Tom and the children helter-skelter to Cornwall. To spy? No. To make sure that all was well with her, and that was the biggest indictment of all. They should have known already.

Tracy came into the room a few minutes later to find her sister sitting on the edge of a bed, deep in uncomfortable thought. She sat down beside her.

'Those pictures,' she said. 'I only caught a glimpse, but Candy's right. They *are* beautiful.'

Chel reached a decision. There was, after all, only one that was remotely logical. She got to her feet.

'Come on. I'll show you.'

She led the way back along the landing. Tracy looked at the pictures in silence for several minutes. Then she said,

'Oliver, of course. Why did you never say?'

'Because...' said Chel, and stopped. Tracy perched on the arm of the sofa bed.

'So is there a purpose in all this?' She gestured around the room. 'Are we allowed to know?' There was an edge to her voice, familiar from many confrontations over the years. Tracy was about to come the big sister.

'Please...,' said Chel. 'If it helps, Oliver's family only know because they came here. Uninvited,' she added.

'Unlike us, who waited - an awful long time - for an invitation,' said Tracy. There was a silence while the two of them tried to stare each other out. An old game. Chel looked away first.

'It's so hard to explain,' she said. Tracy tossed her head.

'I would think it might be. Do you *know* how upset Mum was, when you just upped and left without a word? That awful Nankervis woman thought that she was behind it. There was hell to pay! A real row.'

'Who won?' asked Chel, with a glimmer of interest. Tracy grinned.

'I think Mum did, actually.' Then she frowned. 'But that doesn't excuse what you did.'

'How? How did Mum win?'

'*How?*' Tracy stared at her. 'What does it matter *how*? Because she thought you had done the right thing.' She paused, realising what she had just said. 'But in the wrong way, of course. You should have taken her into your confidence. She would have helped.'

Chel hesitated.

'And would she have managed not to tell Oliver's family? In the heat of the row, or afterwards... would she, Tracy? If Jerry had begged her, for instance?'

Tracy knew, from years of experience as a member of a normal, cheerfully quarrelsome family, when she had painted herself into a corner. She made an impatient gesture.

'But that doesn't matter now,' she said, and Chel, regrettably, giggled. She put her hand over her mouth. Their eyes met. 'Oh - *you!*' said Tracy, and gave a reluctant grin. 'But seriously Cheryl, you hurt them. You hurt us all, come to that. Did we deserve that?'

Chel spoke slowly.

'I don't think that you - any of you - understand. The state that we were in - Oliver and me - wasn't just because he was hurt and ill - and you know how ill he was, you came and saw for yourself. It was a lot of things. You don't realise, if you come from a family like ours - if you're lucky enough - how it can be for other people. The Nankervises - her anyway, never wanted us to get married. She tried everything she knew to break us up... we had to run to escape her. Her and Susan.'

'They wouldn't have *followed* you,' Tracy objected.

'Oh, wouldn't they? *Her* and his father - they were here almost the instant they knew, making trouble. She was making trouble,' she added, fairly. 'He wasn't. At least Mum and Dad left us in peace.'

'They didn't think you wanted them,' said Tracy.

'That shows how wise they are, because I didn't,' said Chel. 'Not then.' She sat down at last, on the sofa bed beside her sister. Tracy laid a hand on her shoulder, unexpectedly gentle.

'You're right in one way,' she said. 'They don't understand. Not about Oliver's family. But they do understand that you've changed. You changed before you even got married.'

'And now I'm changing again,' said Chel, wryly. 'How can I help it, after all that's happened to us?'

'Oliver looks well,' said Tracy, unexpectedly changing the subject. She gave her sister's shoulder a squeeze. 'After what Mum said back in March, I didn't expect that. Nor did she, she's been imagining you looking after a complete invalid, all on your own, that's been half the trouble. Some invalid!'

'I told you all he was much better.'

'She thought you were just being brave, Cheryl. She didn't want us to bring the kids, she said it would be too much and they wouldn't enjoy themselves.'

'The kids were the whole point,' said Chel. 'And it was Oliver's idea, not mine. Oh Trace, I'm sorry! What more can I say? I didn't deliberately keep things from you all. It was just so difficult, talking to Mum and Dad and knowing... it wasn't just the Nankervises that didn't want us to marry, you know.'

'Are you happy?' The question was so unexpected that Chel looked up at her sister in astonishment.

'Happy?' she echoed. 'Of course I am!'

'Only Mum thought, perhaps, that you weren't, and that was why.'

'We went through a bad patch. I think we're over it now. But only because we were left on our own, Trace. We needed the space.'

Tracy nodded.

'Yes, I can see that. I don't know if Mum and Dad will.'

'But you'll try and make them?'

'Of course I will.' One final squeeze, and Tracy removed her hand. 'Now, tell me about these pictures. Even a moron like me can see they're not just occupational therapy, so give.'

'They're for an exhibition. He's been having lessons from a famous artist. She lives in St. Ives.' Chel hesitated, but Tracy would meet Nonie on Christmas Day. 'Actually, she's his godmother, although he hadn't seen her for years.' Or even known she existed. She crossed her fingers behind Tracy's back, but to her relief Tracy took the statement at face value. She knew, after all, that Oliver's natural mother was artistic, although she had never met her, and St. Ives was just the place to find another artist.

'Is that where the exhibition will be, St. Ives? Maybe we can get down to see it. Spend a week and let the kids play on the beach.'

'Actually, it's going to be in the West End,' said Chel, and closed her eyes.

'Now, why doesn't that surprise me?' asked Tracy, dryly.

Before Chel could rise to this challenge, the sound of hurtling footsteps on the stairs was followed by the arrival of Candy in the doorway, right on cue.

'Auntie Cheryl, where's the beach? Daddy said there'd be seaside, and there isn't!'

Chel got to her feet, relieved at the reprieve.

'Of course there is, this is Cornwall, but it isn't right here, and anyway, it'll be dark very soon. Daddy can take you there tomorrow morning, while Mummy and me stuff the turkey and make mince pies, how about that?'

'You're sure there is one?' Candy demanded suspiciously.

'Cross my heart and hope to die,' said Chel. She took her niece's hand. 'Come on, baggage. Let's go decorate that old tree!'

Decorating the tree successfully distracted Candy's one-track mind from paddling and sandcastles, and provided a riotous half hour that went a long way towards dispelling any lingering discomfort that Chel and Tracy might have felt after their talk and allowed Chel to prepare the supper for everyone without missing out on the fun.

'I don't actually like open-plan that much,' she confessed to her sister over the vegetable peeling. 'But it's convenient on occasions like this.'

'Do you always sleep in the living room?' asked Tracy, who had been wondering about it. 'We didn't dispossess you, did we?'

'Oliver doesn't do stairs very well yet,' said Chel. 'Or only the first few. But he's getting there.' She glanced at Tracy and away again. 'I never thought that he would.'

'Nor did anyone else,' said Tracy, soberly. 'I can't believe - ' She broke off, and finished briskly, 'Anyway, that's all in the past, you can see that a mile off. What are your plans? I suppose you won't stay here, if you don't really like it.'

'It does for now,' said Chel, slowly. She thought, did they *have* any plans? 'I think, really, we're just going with the flow until something breaks. The bungalow sells, or our landlord evicts us, or Oliver makes a fortune painting.'

'And what do you do?' asked Tracy, pertinently. 'While he paints with this artist, you must have a lot of time.'

'I've got friends,' said Chel, and wished she hadn't sounded so defensive.

'Get a job,' Tracy advised, briskly. 'It's obvious that Oliver doesn't need any looking after. There must be hundreds of hotels round here. You could go back to your own career.'

'I could, of course,' said Chel, and was about to say that hotel management seemed to have lost its charm, when Candy came rushing into the kitchen area, apparently in distress.

'Auntie Cheryl, there's no fairy! There's got to be a fairy for the top!'

'She means an angel,' said Micky, in a superior tone. Tracy raised her eyes to heaven.

'Whatever she means, if there isn't one, there isn't one.'

'I'm afraid we just put a star on the top,' said Chel, apologetically. Candy's lip stuck out.

'It's not the same.'

'Candy, don't start making a fuss,' said Tracy. She looked apologetically at Chel. 'It's been a long journey, and they're very over-excited. Sorry.'

'I want a fairy,' said Candy, scowling. To Chel's surprise, there were tears running down her cheeks. She went to put an arm round the child.

'Come on, it's not that important is it?'

But Chel had become a stranger to Candy. She pulled away.

'Gran has a fairy. There's *always* a fairy. It's the last thing to go on the tree, always!'

'Come on Candy, don't make a silly scene,' said Tracy. She looked

264

at Tom. 'Do something, can't you?'

'What do you suggest, wave a magic wand? *I'm* no fairy, thank you.'

The situation trembled on the verge of disaster. Chel understood that Candy was feeling bereft of familiar things, but Tracy was simply tired and had had enough. Any moment, and there was going to be a family row, and what a good start to Christmas that would be! The atmosphere crackled.

Into this potential dynamite factory, Oliver strolled with all the armour generated by having lived with dynamite all his life. Candy, recognising the only person who wasn't - yet - cross with her, ran to him and flung her arms round his waist. Oliver grabbed at the worktop.

"Hey, hey, what's all this about?'

Everybody answered him at once.

'She's just making a stupid fuss,' said Micky.

'Take no notice, it's just Candy,' said Tom.

'She's tired, and it's well past bedtime,' said Tracy, firmly.

'Just a storm in a teacup,' said Chel.

'There's no fairy,' sobbed Candy, rendered inconsolable by this united front against her.

'Good gracious, isn't there really?' asked Oliver. 'Well, we're very sorry - aren't we, Chel? We haven't had much practice at Christmas, you're very right to tell us.'

'Why do you call Auntie Cheryl, Chel?' asked Micky.

'Because I'm lazy,' Oliver answered. He took Candy's hand. 'Don't cry, we'll fix it.'

'We can buy one tomorrow,' said Tracy, belatedly finding a solution.

'What's all this about tomorrow? Got any baking foil, Chel? And maybe some card.'

'Baking foil, certainly. Card - why would I have card?'

'Empty a cereal packet,' said Micky, practically. 'You can put it in a freezer bag.'

'You've obviously played this scene before,' said Chel, opening the cupboard, and Tracy laughed.

'*Blue Peter* is still an institution.'

Chel found the required items and gave them to Candy, together with the kitchen scissors, the latter with reluctance.

'You'll make them blunt,' she said. 'And leave enough foil for the turkey, please.'

Oliver had already seated himself at the dining-room table and set the children spreading newspaper. He took no notice of this carping.

'Have we got any glue?'

'In the kitchen drawer - that one, Candy love, get it for me, there's a dear.' Chel tipped the peeled potatoes into a pan and carried it to the stove. 'And don't take all night, Oliver, whatever you're doing. We need to eat sometime.'

Candy pulled the drawer open. It was full of interesting junk, she immediately saw. Elastic bands and odd spoons, paper bun cases, old pencils, pens without tops and tops without pens that didn't match them, and an odd-shaped lump wrapped in kitchen paper with Winnie the Pooh on it. There was a drawer just like it at home, but that didn't stop her from saying,

'Goodness Auntie Cheryl, what a muddle!'

'Just find the glue and skip the lecture,' Tracy begged. Candy picked up the paper-wrapped lump and held it in her hand.

'What's this, Auntie Cheryl?' she asked, but nobody was taking any notice: she dropped it quickly back in the drawer and picked up the tube of glue, suddenly afraid that she was missing something.

Oliver was already busy with card and scissors, cutting half-circles of foil and card and then a full circle of foil, while the children watched in fascination. The half-circles he glued together and fastened into a cone with the aid of two paperclips and more glue, the full circle went over the top, gently pushed down to form folds. Candy jumped in delight.

'It's a robe!' she cried.

'It is indeed.' Oliver set his cone aside. 'Now, you make a ball with these bits round the top of this...' A thin tube of left-over card appeared as if by magic. 'Put some glue on to hold it - that's it, don't get it all over yourself. Nice and round, now.'

Micky came abruptly down from his big-brotherly high horse.

'What can I do?'

'You can ask Chel for some thin string and a button,' said Oliver, busy with the scissors.

'Thanks a million, I've got things to do,' said Chel, but this new slant on Oliver had her fascinated. 'The drawer, Trace. There's all sorts in there.'

Tracy pulled it open again. String, she saw immediately, in an untidy coil.

'Are you sure there's a button in here?'

'There should be several. I throw them in there when they come off in the wash.'

'Don't you ever sew them back?' asked Tracy, amused.

'Sometimes.'

Tracy scrabbled about among the oddments, pushing the paper-wrapped lump to one side, unregarded. There was a button lying there on the bottom of the drawer. 'You were right, here's one.'

'One is enough,' said Oliver, abstractedly. 'All right Micky - take that felt-tip, draw an angel's face on that piece, and wrap it round Candy's ball...carefully, mind.'

By this time, even Tom, Tracy and Chel had gathered round. Under his hands, the silver angel took shape. Smooth silver face with eyes turned up to heaven and round mouth open in song, silver strands of hair in a fringe and falling to her shoulders, flat silver arms with hands folded in prayer, fronded silver wings spread wide.

'And a halo,' cried Candy, thrilled. 'Make a halo, Uncle Oliver.'

'Fuse wire,' said Tracy. 'There was some in the drawer.' Micky, this time, ran to get it.

Twisted silver round fine wire circled the round silver head. Then, last of all, a careful hole between the soaring wings, string threaded through the buttonholes, then drawn carefully through, and there was the angel, ready to tie on the top of the tree. Candy took her gently on her palm and looked at her in wonder.

'Uncle Oliver, you're really, really clever,' she said. 'This is the *best* fairy!'

'Angel,' said Micky, automatically.

'Let Daddy tie her on the tree,' said Oliver, sweeping the debris together.

'And then bath, while Cheryl finishes the supper,' said Tracy. 'You can eat in your pi-jams for once, both of you. Come along, chop chop!'

Chel went back to her cooking, very thoughtful. Not for the first time lately, her ideas had shifted, formed new patterns, told a different story from the accepted text. How old had Oliver been when his mother left? About four or five, she thought. How much did you remember before you were five? Not a great deal that was specific, although those years were important in the making of the final adult, so people said. So Oliver's happy handling of children, he hadn't learned from Helen. Who, then? It was surely unlikely to be Dot, although of course, you never knew. Not Nonie, either, he didn't remember her. That left Jerry. There was nobody else.

Jerry, who thought the world of his heedless son with his hardened attitudes.

Bloody Dot!

And then she thought of Oliver creating a Christmas angel out of nothing, and the absorbed faces of the children, and the tears rolled down her cheeks for the second time that day, so that when Tracy came back into the kitchen, leaving Tom supervising towels and pyjamas, she found Chel weeping into a teatowel.

'Hey, hey, what's all this? You've done nothing but cry since we got here!'

Chel simply walked into her arms, and instinctively Tracy held her tight.

'I was just thinking,'Chel said, through her tears. 'What a great father he would have made.'

'Ah...' said Tracy.

She had pulled herself together by the time the children came downstairs, and set them laying the table while she and Tracy dished up supper, and even by that time she still hadn't worked out whether she had cried for their lost child, the only one they were ever going to have, or for Jerry who had blown it with such finality.

Just as they were falling to sleep that night, Oliver unexpectedly gave a smothered laugh.

'What's the matter?' Chel demanded, hovering on the edge of slumber.

'I was just thinking,' said Oliver. 'What will you do if young Candy comes rushing downstairs complaining that there's a strange man in their bedroom? She's your niece, after all.'

'He's never been in that room,' said Chel, indignantly.

'Only because you haven't. He's been everywhere else up there, including the bathroom if we believe Judy.'

'He wouldn't frighten a child!' said Chel. She was, she realised, talking about Matt Sutton as if he was still a real person. 'Anyway, he's gone. He's got what he needed. He won't come again.'

'Hope you're right,' said Oliver, sleepily.

XVII

But there were no disturbances during the night, and in the morning the family gathered for breakfast with no ghost stories to relate, a little to Chel's relief for she knew, somewhere at the back of her mind, that to credit Matt Sutton's desperate spirit with any finer feelings towards children was probably unreasonable. If he existed at all as a spirit, it was because of his dedicated self-interest. Looked at in that light, he and Candy would probably be highly compatible.

'This morning,' said Candy, as if to illustrate this point, 'we're going to the *beach*, Daddy.' She sat down firmly at the breakfast table.

'Whoa, hold on a minute! Maybe Auntie Chel wants some help,' said Tom, without, apparently, realising just what he had said. Candy looked him in the eye.

'Daddy, you *promised!*'

'Never,' said Tom, with an uneasy feeling that somebody *had* said something like that, but was it him?

'Auntie Chel won't mind,' said Candy. This time, Tracy picked up on it.

'Auntie Cheryl to you, madam, and perhaps you should ask her before you answer for her?'

'Auntie Chel will do fine, thank you,' murmured Chel. 'I think it's a very good idea, get them out of the house for a while and you and I can get some work done without them underfoot - that is, unless you want to go with them, of course. Only stuffing the turkey, and things like that. Nothing major, like housework, I did all that before you got here.'

'What a waste of time,' said Tom. 'Well, if you're sure, I'll take them both out of the way and let them blow off steam. Can we walk, or do we have to take that dreary car?'

'I thought it looked rather a nice car, what I saw of it,' said Chel. 'New, isn't it?'

'It's Grandad's, and Dad hates it,' said Micky.

'Grandma said our car wouldn't even make it to Exeter,' said Candy. 'She made us borrow it, and Grandad was cross. *He* said our car wouldn't make it to Lowestoft, and he had to go in for his teeth.'

'So, what's the matter with it?' asked Chel, curiously. She had almost forgotten what family life was like, and felt swamped in nostalgia.

'Just old age,' said Tom. 'Otherwise, it's a perfectly good car.'

'Give or take a dodgy gearbox, unreliable brakes, and wonky steering,' remarked Tracy.

'It's an automatic,' said Micky, answering the question that Chel had intended. 'Dad says it's an old man's car.'

'Well, it is,' said Candy. 'It's Grandad's car, and he's old.'

'Whatever, you'll need it to get to the beach,' put in Oliver, and added unexpectedly, 'I might come with you - show you the way.' He said this so airily that Chel looked at him in immediate suspicion, but his face was blank and innocent.

'That doesn't mean you two spend all morning in The Old Success and leave the children to drown,' she told him.

'Perish the thought!'

'Do we trust them?' Chel asked Tracy.

'Oh, please! Let's have a morning off.'

A lingering suspicion that Oliver had more than child-care in mind remained at the back of Chel's mind, but she knew it would be useless to probe any deeper. The children, in any case, were delighted that Uncle Oliver was going to join them and, as Tracy remarked, anything for a quiet life.

'Candy doesn't change, does she?' commented Chel, when at last the beach party had gone and the house was quiet again.

'Unfortunately, no. She simply gets more articulate - as I daresay you noticed.'

'You need to watch her,' said Chel. 'I've noticed already, she overshadows Micky. He's very quiet.'

'But deadly,' commented Tracy. 'Don't waste pity on him. He more than holds his own, believe me.'

Chel thought of the years she had lost of the children growing up, and sighed.

'I wish - ' She broke off.

'So do we all,' said Tracy, briskly. 'No good crying over spilt milk, Cheryl. What's done is done, and all that crap.'

'It wasn't an easy choice, you know. And it wasn't meant to be forever.' She sounded defensive, and was sorry for it. Tracy looked at her, considering.

'Come on, Cheryl, it isn't the end of the world. I'm sorry if, last night, I made you think it was too important, I was tired. We shall all survive, and anyway, you and Oliver have every right to live your lives however you choose.'

'However that is,' said Chel, opening the fridge to remove the turkey.

'And how is it?' asked Tracy.

Chel put the dish with the turkey down on the worktop and stood for a moment looking down on it. The Million Pound Question, here it was again.

'I wish I knew,' she said.

Tracy said,

'Suppose, for instance, that your bungalow sold tomorrow. It will one tomorrow, some time. It's no good being so negative, you know. You must plan ahead.'

'I can't *see* ahead,' said Chel. She realised as soon as she had spoken that she had half hoped for a quick mental flash into the future, as had happened to her once or twice, but there was none. So much for learning to use clairvoyance.

'Well, what if *this* place sells tomorrow. You must surely have thought about that. What does Oliver say?'

'Oliver just paints,' said Chel, and shrugged her shoulders.

Tracy gave her an elder-sisterly look.

'Come on Cheryl, pull yourself together!' She reached for the kettle. 'Forget that turkey for the minute, let's have some coffee, and talk this thing through.'

'There's nothing to talk about,' said Chel.

'Oh yes, there most certainly is! Is Oliver planning on art, or painting or whatever you like to call it, as a new career?'

That brought Chel up short. She hadn't thought of anything as positive as that, but now the idea was presented to her, she saw that it was obvious.

'Yes, I suppose he is.' He had drifted into it, but now he was ensnared. He would never go back to the sea, whatever the future held. Even if, she suddenly realised, he could. It was as simple, and as definitive as that, but it had taken Tracy to make her see it.

'You *suppose*!' Tracy rolled her eyes to heaven.

'Yes, then,' said Chel.

'Does it make a living - art?' asked Tracy, curiously, knowing nothing about it. Chel thought of Helen, and of Nonie, and of Gifford Thomas. None of them looked to be on the breadline.

'I think it must - if you're good enough.'

'Is Oliver good enough?' asked Tracy, directly.

'People seem to think so. And of course, he is who he is. People have heard of him.'

'Well, that's a start. Capital and income, and your earning potential too. If he's going to paint, he must have a studio, of course.'

'Of course...' Now I know where Candy gets it from, Chel thought. She reached for the coffee jar and spooned coffee into two mugs. It

271

gave her an excuse for not looking at Tracy.

'It means you can think constructively,' said Tracy. '*Do* it, Cheryl, for God's sake! All Oliver has *ever* done is to drift with the tide, you can't expect any help from him.'

'That's not true,' denied Chel, wondering suddenly if it was. Oliver had always seemed very much in control, but had he actually been going anywhere? Helen, she thought treacherously, had never thought so. On their first meeting, she had said as much. She had said *he works hard, but sticks with nothing, and he's always searching for something that he never finds.* She took refuge in sarcasm. 'I'm sure that you're full of suggestions, however.'

Sarcasm was wasted on Tracy, who had known her all her life.

'Start by asking yourself a few questions. You don't want to live here, or in your bungalow in Embridge, so where do you want to live? That has to be the first one.'

'I do want to live here - not exactly *here,* but here. In Cornwall. So does Oliver.'

'Cornwall's a big place,' Tracy commented.

'We've made friends here,' said Chel, defensively. 'And there's Nonie - Oliver's godmother. He needs her. He's learning from her all the time.' She looked at Tracy defiantly, but should have known better.

'OK, that narrows it down. Within commuting distance of St. Ives, then. Town or country? Village - this village, for instance?'

'Trace, will you stop interrogating me like this! You'll shine a lamp in my face in a minute! All right, sea, then. Beside the sea.'

'Not this village, then. You see, you *do* know, if you think about it!' said Tracy, triumphantly.

Cheryl finished her coffee and stood up.

'I do know that if we don't do that turkey and the mince pies, the kids'll be back, and nothing finished.' And she stalked off to the kitchen.

Tracy, having sowed the seed, was satisfied. She strolled after her sister and tipped her mug into the sink.

'OK, what do you want me to do?'

By lunchtime, the turkey was well and truly stuffed, the mince pies cooling on a rack, and the vegetables peeled for next day, so that by the time the rest of the family party returned from Sennen, the sisters were sitting with their feet up, discussing their siblings - two brothers whom Chel hadn't seen for as many years, plus a sister-in-law and a new little nephew, the last of whom she had never seen at all, although she had been sent photos. Chel was just learning all about brother Mike's new girlfriend, a potential front-runner according to Tracy, when the front door crashed open and a breath of cold air and a wave of sound engulfed them. Micky and Candy were full of themselves, sandy and happy and brimming with news.

'The beach is *wicked*!' cried Candy, flinging herself onto her mother's lap. 'It goes on for *miles and miles and miles* and Uncle Ollie drove Grandad's car round and round the car park!'

'What?' said Chel, sitting up abruptly.

'*Who*?' said Tracy, at the same moment, pushing Candy off onto the floor. 'Uncle Oliver, my child, where does this *Uncle Ollie* come from?'

'He doesn't mind, he said we could,' said Micky.

'But who said *he* could?' asked Chel.

'Dad,' said Micky.

Chel didn't know whether to be shocked or delighted, and before she had made up her mind, Tom and Oliver came in, looking pleased with themselves. One look at Oliver's face, alight with his achievement, put all thoughts of *owner's permission* and *insurance* and *Shouldn't you have checked it was all right for you to do it first?* out of her head. He had pushed open the door to freedom, and she knew that she couldn't spoil it, whatever she privately thought, although her first, shuddering reaction had inevitably been *Oh God, suppose he had found he couldn't stop it?*

But being Oliver, he had probably made sure that he could before he started. He did have some sense. Not a lot, just some.

Tracy was right. It was more than time to think ahead.

'What on earth is your consultant going to say when you see him?' she said, and getting to her feet, put her arms round him. 'You *idiot*, Oliver! What will Tom's father say?' She couldn't help that, it slipped out. Oliver laughed, hugging her, pleased with himself.

'What he doesn't know won't hurt him. It was too good a chance to pass up, Chel, and I didn't hurt it. There's not a scratch on it, I promise.'

'One or two startled surfers,' said Tom. 'We didn't take it on the road.'

'I should hope not!'

'But I could,' said Oliver, and smiled.

'What's there to eat?' asked Candy.

The children were far too excited for a quiet afternoon to be on the cards, so after lunch, Chel and Tracy put them into Chel's car and took them to Penzance for some shopping, giving the men an afternoon off.

'Although it hardly seems fair,' said Tracy, as she climbed into the passenger seat. 'They may have had them all morning, but we weren't exactly doing nothing - and what are they going to do, I ask you? Sleep in front of sport on the telly!'

'Which would you rather do?' asked Chel. 'Look after Micky and Candy or make mince pies? Or sleep in front of the telly, come to that. Oliver will probably paint, anyway.'

'Daddy will sleep in front of the telly,' said Candy, hanging over the back of the seat.

'Do up your seat belt, please,' said Tracy, automatically.

In Causewayhead, to Chel's horror, they ran slam into Maggie and Jack, with a full complement of children. Candy was charmed, of course. There was only a matter of months between her and Amy, the eldest of the five, and they hit it off immediately.

'We've been doing some last-minute shopping, and now we're on our way to Land's End so the children can play on the pirate ship,' said Maggie, after introductions had been made and greetings exchanged. 'Why don't you come too?'

'Oh *please*, Mummy!' cried Candy, bouncing up and down.

'We've got shopping to do,' said Chel - mendaciously as it happened, for they were only here for the children to spend their pocket money. Maggie looked disappointed and Candy let out a wail.

'But *Mummy*, there's a real pirate ship!'

Tracy hesitated. The attraction of a pirate ship was undeniable, but she sensed reluctance in her sister.

'Maybe we could go another day,' she said. Candy sulked.

'I want to go with Amy.'

'Well, why not?' said Maggie, expansively. 'Would you trust us with her, Tracy? We've got the minibus, there's plenty of room for one more, or even two more. If you two have shopping to do? We'd be only too pleased.'

'What d'you think, Trace?' asked Chel. 'They'd be safe with Maggie and Jack, I promise you. We've known each other for years.' Only a slight exaggeration there, she told herself, and the important bit was true.

'*Please,* Mummy!'

'It seems a dreadful imposition,' said Tracy.

'Rubbish, we'd be delighted,' said Jack. 'When you have as many as we do, a couple more makes no difference! And I'm sure they don't want to be dragged around the shops, do you kids?'

Since this whole expedition was undertaken to please the children, Chel was interested to see what they would reply, but Woolworth's had no hope against a pirate ship. In no time at all, Tracy and Chel found themselves blessedly alone. They headed unanimously for the nearest tea shop.

'You really didn't want to go with her, did you?' said Tracy, as they waited for their order. 'What's the matter, don't you like her? She seemed OK to me.'

Chel sighed.

'Oh, she is OK. I think it's her fecundity.'

'Gracious, what's that? You do know some breakteeth words since you married Oliver!'

'It isn't Oliver so much,' said Chel, absently. 'It was living with a journalist before him... and it isn't just that. She fancies Oliver, and it's a bit wearing.'

That, Tracy could understand. She looked sympathetic.

'Well, I can see that. But as he isn't here...?'

'I just didn't feel like her today,' said Chel, hoping to close the subject. 'Now, on Boxing Day we're invited to some cousins of Oliver's, and they're real friends. Judy's mum and dad have the farm where we lived when we first came down here, and that's where we're going to go. Candy and Micky will love it.' And no doubt Tracy would learn about the motor home, but she no longer cared about that. Just having her sister here was therapeutic, she felt as if she was walking out of fog into clear sunlight. Being herself, the person that she had always been, and if Oliver could drive and be independent, she could stay that way, her needs no longer, of necessity, subordinate to his. It felt as if a weight had rolled off her, that she had not really been conscious was there. It might even be possible to plan ahead after all. Together, even.

Later on, as they browsed around W.H. Smith's, laughing at the cards, Tracy found a chance to peep into a dictionary and look up "fecundity". Having done so, she returned the book to the shelf and gave her sister's back a considering look. She thought that passing on the insight thus gleaned to those at home would be treachery, but she filed it for her own information.

Micky and Candy were returned home tired, quarrelsome and hungry, having spent an exhausting afternoon keeping their end up with Amy and her brothers and sisters. Chel, who had made sure that tea was on the table to obviate any infiltration by Maggie & Co., wasn't required to use this subterfuge, Maggie handed them over at the door.

'Must dash, the baby's howling and the kids are all clamouring for food! See you over the holiday, Cheryl, you must bring your family over so the kids can play again!'

Candy's mutinous face seemed to say *over my dead body*, and Chel had to smother a smile. She said,

'Thanks Maggie, we'll see how it goes. Say thank you, children, for a lovely afternoon.'

To Candy's credit, she did so, politely, and Micky mumbled something, but as soon as the door was closed on Maggie, Candy burst out,

'That Amy is the *pits!*'

'I beg your pardon, miss?' said Tracy, from the kitchen.

'She *is*, she wants her own way *all the time*, and she pulled my hair when I wanted the slide first, and it was *my turn!*'

'Oh dear,' said Tracy, unsuccessfully hiding a grin. 'Case of the biter, bit, was it? Never mind, upstairs and get into the bath, there's angel cake for tea.'

'Angel cake like on top of the tree?'

'Not exactly, it's pink and white, now *up those stairs!*' She pushed them towards the stairs. Micky reared back like a startled horse.

'Not me too, Mum! I'm *two years older!*'

'And just as mucky,' said Tracy. 'Up!'

There was a stampede up the stairs and the sound of feet thumping across the ceiling and doors banging. Tom folded the evening paper, which he had been hiding behind, and sighed.

'Tears before bed,' he prophesied, and sure enough, before long the sound of outraged crying floated down.

'There's some red wine opened ready in the kitchen,' remarked Oliver, and Chel went to fetch it. After a few minutes, Tracy came down, looking hot and bothered, and Chel mutely handed her a glass. She pushed her fingers through her hair, making it stand on end, and took a swig.

'Thoroughly wound up and over-excited,' she said. 'There'll be going to bed without tea in a minute, if there's much more!'

'Oh come on, it's Christmas Eve,' said Oliver, with a tolerance derived from the fact that it wasn't his responsibility.

'Really!' said Tracy, and made an expressive face. Tom got to his feet.

'I'll go and sort them out, shall I?' he said.

'You may try,' said Tracy, and flung herself into a chair. 'Something's up, but she won't tell me what, and Micky doesn't know. Oh God, who'd have children!'

'Have another glass,' said Chel.

Tracy remembered that her remark might have been construed as tactless, but then she decided that there was no point walking all the time on eggshells in case she said the wrong thing. She accepted the refill and sipped it more moderately.

But by the time Candy and Micky reappeared, Candy was all smiles again, cajoled out of her tantrum with some high jinks in the bathroom, and a late tea - or possibly an early supper - was eaten with no more than the usual amount of high spirits. After it, Chel and Tracy cleared the table and left Tom and Oliver with the washing up, taking their turn relaxing by the fire while the children sat under the Christmas tree trying to guess the contents of the various parcels. It was all suddenly very peaceful.

''*twas the night before Christmas, and all through the house, not a creature was stirring, not even* Candy,' remarked Tracy, stretching out her legs luxuriously. 'Are we going to the midnight service tonight, Cheryl? Is the church in the village a nice one?'

Chel, who had never attended a service there, although of course she had seen it from the outside, was about to say so when Candy shot like a bullet through from the dining area and flung herself on Tracy.

'No Mummy, no, you can't go out, you mustn't!'

'Excuse me,' said Tracy, fighting her off. 'What's all this *can't*?'

'Please Mummy, don't go and leave us!'

'Why, what do you think is going to happen to you? You won't be left on your own. I don't suppose Uncle Ollie will want to come.'

'No, no, *no*!'

Tracy took her by the shoulders and pushed her away so that she could look at her. Candy's face was pink and her eyes were full of tears. She was so close to hysteria that it was obvious that there was more to this than mere cussedness, and Chel, looking at her, had a sudden horrible idea as to what it might be. She bit her lip, but Tracy wasn't looking at her.

'Come on Candy, what's the problem here? We always go to the midnight service, you know we do.'

Candy's mouth set mutinously.

'If you go, then I want to come too.'

'Candy, you're shattered! You'd be bored stiff and fall asleep. Don't be silly, now.'

'I want to come. I don't want to be left here!' Candy wailed, on a rising note.

By this time, the men had come from the kitchen to see who was being murdered, and Micky had left the tree to follow them, afraid of missing something. Candy was sobbing openly, stamping her foot and screaming incoherently, and Tracy was beginning to get angry. Chel moved forward and put her arm around the distressed child.

'What's the matter, Candy?' she asked. 'Has Amy been telling you stories?'

Candy sobbed.

'She said there was a ghost in our bedroom. She said this was a haunted house.'

Chel muttered under her breath,

'I'll bloody *kill* Maggie!' She pulled Candy towards her, held her close.

'Come on sweetheart, you know that's nonsense. You didn't see one last night, did you?'

Candy reluctantly admitted that no, she hadn't.

'But Mummy and Daddy were there last night. Amy said you hear it first, howling and shrieking in the roof, and then it grabs you with its bloody hands and eats your heart out!'

'It sounds to me as if Amy has an over-active imagination,' said Tracy. 'I never heard such rubbish in my life!'

Oliver sat carefully down in his chair and leaned his stick against the fireplace.

'Candy, we've lived here for months now and nobody has eaten our hearts out,' he said.

'You sleep down here!' cried Candy, unanswerably.

'Ah. Bit like me is it, then? Doesn't do stairs.'

Candy almost giggled, then remembered the point at issue and stuck her lip out again.

'I tell you what,' said Chel, with more accuracy than her hearers realised. 'Uncle Ollie is pretty good at dealing with ghosts, so why don't you snuggle down on the sofa here when we go out, and he'll watch over you until we come back?'

'I suppose it doesn't matter if something eats *my* heart out,' observed Micky.

'Nothing is going to eat anybody's heart out,' said Tracy, exasperated.

'You can both of you kip on our bed,' said Chel. 'Then if anybody has nightmares, Oliver is right here. But *don't* then wake us all up at dawn to open presents. That's the deal. Done?'

'I don't want - ' began Candy, but Tom interrupted her.

'*Done*, Candy? Or do you want Mummy to get really cross with you?'

'Couldn't you not go?' pleaded Candy, but she was calming down now, and Tracy resisted.

'Done?'

'Oh, all right then. But - '

'No buts. We're all going to play a game now,' said Tom. Micky grinned.

'How about *Haunted House*?' he asked, and Tracy clipped his ear.

'Shut up, you!'

'Murder, then?'

'Consequences will do nicely,' said Chel hurriedly, and got up to find paper and pencils.

Later on, as they drove to the village for the midnight service, leaving both children fast asleep downstairs, Tracy remarked,

'So what was all that about? Was it just Amy being mischievous, or is there some tale about your house?'

'You know how it is,' said Chel. 'It was derelict for ages, and stories began.' There was no point in denying it, she realised. Tracy only had to ask almost anyone in the church tonight to hear one version or another of the story. 'It's never hurt us,' she said, with truth.

'Ah, but have you ever seen it?' asked Tom. The corners of his eyes crinkled as he smiled, and Chel felt unreasonably patronised.

'Get away! If I said I had, you'd think I was loopy!'

'But all the same, you were very quick to tell the children they needn't go to bed until we got back - without any reference to us, as their parents,' Tracy pointed out. But Chel was on firm ground here, and answered without guile.

'It just seemed sensible. If Candy had a nightmare, there's no way Oliver could get up to her in a hurry, it's one disadvantage of leaving him to babysit. And the chances of her having one looked pretty high to me. I'll have Maggie's guts for garters when I see her next! How *could* she be so stupid as to talk about things like that in front of her children?'

'Bit progressive, your friend Maggie,' commented Tom, but they had reached the village now and he said no more, being preoccupied with finding a parking space.

The candlelit church and the midnight mass with its familiar carols was soothing, and afterwards there were friends to greet in the moonlit churchyard, wishes of *Happy Christmas* to exchange. Chel took a certain satisfaction in these greetings, they showed Tracy, if nothing else, that she and Oliver were not sad people living half a life, but had a wide circle of friends and acquaintances, news which she was anxious should find its way home to Suffolk. They drove home afterwards in a restful silence, to Chel's relief, and found the children fast asleep on the bed, and Oliver ditto by the fire. The only light in the house was from the winking coloured lights of the tree and from the fire.

'What a sweet sight,' whispered Tracy. 'Tom, can you carry them up without waking them? I'll go and turn the duvets back.' She yawned, and kissed her sister. 'Happy Christmas, Cheryl. We'll leave you to put Oliver to bed.' She giggled, and so did Chel.

'Happy Christmas, Trace. Happy Christmas, Tom.' She reached up to him and kissed his cheek. 'Sleep well in *Amityville*, all of you. See you in the morning.'

Tracy was halfway up the stairs. She grinned down at her sister.

'You certainly live interesting lives,' she remarked, and turning, ran lightly up the rest of the flight.

And what, *exactly,* had she meant by that? Chel wondered, but was far too tired to ask.

Nonie arrived the next morning while Tracy and Tom and the children were out at the Family Service, loaded with parcels and two bottles of wine. She found Chel sitting all alone at the foot of the Christmas tree, with tears running down her face.

'Chel?' She put the parcels down on the table, uncertain what to say. 'Chel, what's the matter?'

For a moment, Chel didn't answer. She put up a hand and brushed the tears from her cheek.

'Just being silly, I suppose. I was having a quiet moment while they'd all gone to church.'

Nonie hesitated. She knew Oliver better than she knew Chel, the ties going back a long way into the past. To Chel, she was an older friend; no less, but no more either.

'Where's Oliver? Don't tell me he's gone to church, because I shan't believe you.'

'He's gone for a walk. Up the lane. He drove a car yesterday.'

'Well, bully for him.' Still feeling out of her depth, Nonie said, 'D'you want to talk about it, or is it a private thing?'

'Oh, it's private all right,' said Chel. 'I'll tell you though - you must think I'm a real party pooper, sitting here howling on Christmas Day.'

'Christmas can be a funny time,' said Nonie, wisely. 'I have problems with it myself. Come on - get up and wash your face, and we'll hit a bottle of wine together.'

Chel got to her feet. She spoke half to herself, half to Nonie.

'I feel desolate.'

'About what, exactly?' asked Nonie gently.

'About Jeremy,' said Chel. She saw the question in Nonie's eyes and said, 'He was our baby... poor little thing, he didn't have a chance and I know I shouldn't dwell on it... but it seems as if, if I don't, he never even existed... and sometimes, like today, *I just can't bear it.*'

Nonie put her arms round her, drawing her head to rest on her shoulder.

'Why shouldn't you think about him? I think you have every right, and maybe *particularly* on a day that's so much a children's day.'

'People say it's morbid,' Chel mumbled, her face hidden. 'But he was our son - I cuddled him in my arms, Nonie, and then he was gone... how *can* I just carry on as if it never happened? Last Christmas was so awful, I suppose it just got lost in the awfulness, but this time... he would have been eighteen months old, into everything and loving it all... and instead, he's just a lonely little boy in the cold ground.'

Nonie felt tears prick behind her own eyes, but knew if she gave into them they would both be discovered howling when Oliver or Chel's family came back, which wouldn't do at all. She pulled herself together.

'Come on Chel, it isn't like that, and you know it. If he's anywhere at all, he's moved on to another place. My mother always used to say that there were special angels who looked after the babies, and maybe there are.'

'That's a lovely thought,' sobbed Chel. 'I wish I could believe it.'

'Why shouldn't you believe it? You know of your own knowledge that the spirit can go on.'

Chel was silent for so long, her face hidden, that Nonie began to wonder if she had said the wrong thing, but at last she lifted her head and sniffed, wiping her hand across her eyes.

'I'm sorry, Nonie. That was a really cheerful greeting for you, and on Christmas Day too! Don't take any notice of me, I'm just being self-indulgent.'

'No you aren't, and don't let anyone try to tell you that you are,' said Nonie, briskly. 'You have every right to grieve, and if people have been telling you to put it behind you, it's no wonder you feel desolate now. Maybe, even, it's because until now you didn't have the time to grieve properly. It's a funny thing, grief, you can't bottle it up. It needs to find its way out. Believe me, I'm an expert.'

'Like a boil,' said Chel, wryly.

'Just like a boil, if you must be so disgusting! Now let's get at this wine and pull ourselves together. You nearly had me going there!'

Chel washed her face while Nonie wielded the corkscrew, and they went to sit together by the fire. The house was full of the smell of roasting turkey and with the tree twinkling away in its corner, Chel began to feel better. She also, in some strange way, felt closer to Nonie than she had ever felt: she was Oliver's godmother, Oliver's mentor, and Chel had just gone along for the ride. That had subtly changed this morning and it was a good feeling.

Nonie leaned back in the corner of the sofa with a sigh.

'This is good. Now, tell me more about this car Oliver drove. It sounds to me as if he's getting above himself.'

'Oh, miles above,' agreed Chel. 'It's Tom's father's car, and it's an automatic. He found it easy, so there'll be no stopping him now. And a very good thing too,' she added, after a moment's reflection.

'Yes,' agreed Nonie. She hesitated. 'It's nearly time to move on, Chel. Have you any ideas?'

'Tracy asked me that, too,' said Chel. 'The answer is no... not definite ideas. I think I feel that we need to get to grips with reality again first... we've been living in a bubble this last year. Just the two of us. Healing.'

'And now you feel that you're healed?'

'It certainly begins to look like it.'

'Then here's to you both!' Nonie raised her glass and drank. 'Take your time but not too much of it. Something may turn up tomorrow.'

'I feel that, too. In fact I think it will, though probably not tomorrow, although I have no idea what.'

'With you two, I dread to think.'

'I think it's time we did something a bit... sensible, although I dread the word.'

'Sensible needn't be dreadful, you know. But yes, you need some sort of life plan. You, more than Oliver. His path is probably set now.'

'Is he really that good?' asked Chel, wanting to know.

'I think so. Giff Thomas thinks so, and Matt used to say he was never wrong.'

'He's a bit of an oddball, isn't he - Gifford Thomas?'

'He's a rampant old queen, to be fair, but as shrewd as they come, and with a heart of pure gold. His partner died of AIDS, you know, about ten years ago now.' Nonie paused, thinking of kind Donald and his death and all its implications. 'They were together for years, but they had a break by mutual agreement and Donald... well anyway, Giff nursed him devotedly until nearly the very end.' She added, without quite intending it. 'He isn't even HIV positive himself. So...'

'Poor man,' said Chel. 'Has there been anyone else?'

'I wouldn't know. So nothing serious anyway. But... oh well. He just works harder.'

Before Chel could find a response to this sad comment, the phone rang and she got up to answer it. It was Susan.

'Just rang to wish you a happy Christmas,' she said, stiffly.

As always, Susan made Chel feel all fingers and thumbs.

'Thank you, and the same to all of you. I'm afraid Oliver is out, but

I'll tell him you rang.'

'Good. Thanks.'

Pause.

'Are you going to your parents?' asked Chel, to fill it. 'Do give them our best wishes.'

'I will.'

'And Deb? Will she be home?'

'She will be today. She's spending tomorrow with her friends that are going to run this sailing school. I told her, don't let them talk you into putting money into it. It sounds like a recipe for disaster to me, they know nothing at all about it.'

'Oh well, I expect they'll sort something out.'

Another pause. This time Susan broke it.

'I took flowers to Jeremy this morning when we went to church. I thought you'd like him to be remembered today.'

Chel swallowed. Not for the first time, Susan's thoughtfulness, both unexpected and on the face of it, uncharacteristic, took her breath away. She found her voice.

'That was good of you. Thank you.'

'I thought that *someone* should remember him.' That was more like Susan. Tactless and abrasive.

'I remember him,' said Chel, and Susan replied with unexpected gentleness.

'I know you do.'

She rang off, and Chel turned helplessly to Nonie.

'That was Susan. She always manages to take the wind out of my sails. She took flowers to Jeremy.' Her voice wobbled. 'That was so sweet of her.'

'Susan was a dear child,' said Nonie. 'Henry, her father, he was a lamb. She's got to be a little bit his daughter, hasn't she? Dot only brought her up, she wasn't the sole progenitor. You shouldn't be so surprised.'

Chel had never given a moment's thought to Susan's unknown father, but now she did.

'Tell me about him. What happened to him?'

Since Henry was yet another person who had died, Nonie hesitated, feeling that there had been enough death and desolation for one Christmas morning, and while she did so, the front door opened and banged shut, and Oliver limped through into the room. He walked everwhere now with only the sticks, dismissing Chel's - rather tepid - suggestion that he wait until he had seen the consultant again with the comment that he intended to live now, not later. He looked windblown and disgustingly healthy, smiling at them in mock horror.

'Just look at you two topers, and the day's hardly begun! You should be ashamed. Hullo Nonie, Happy Christmas.'

'Happy Christmas. Here - have one on me,' said Nonie, pouring. She handed him the glass and they exchanged a demure kiss as he took it. 'Chel's been telling me about your exploit with the car. Get the stairs licked, and you can come to my studio. Here's to it!' The glasses clinked. Chel placed hers on the mantelshelf.

'Time to put the spuds in. The mob will be back from church any second, no holier than when they left, and we can do the presents.'

Right on cue, the front door banged open again, and Candy and Micky careered through, Candy singing at the top of her voice,

> *'While shepherds washed their socks by night,*
> *All seated round the tub,*
> *A bar of Sunlight soap came down*
> *And they began to scrub!'*

Tracy arrived hard on their heels, saying,

'Shut up, Candy, please! What will Oliver's godmother think?'

Nonie was already laughing.

'She'll think that the old ones are still the good ones,' she said. 'I sang that at school, Candy. Do you know the next verse?'

'No, and please, she doesn't want to!' said Tracy. 'Hullo, you must be Oliver's godmother.'

'Yes, I do!'cried Candy, indignantly.

'No, you *don't!'*

'Have a drink, Tracy,' said Oliver, sympathetically. 'Nonie, this is Chel's sister, as if you couldn't guess, and the bloke over there, trying to pretend he's nothing to do with them, is Tom, her brother-in-law.'

Hands were taken and shaken, while Candy sat mutinously down, muttering. The phone rang, and she grabbed it.

'Hullo, this is Candy - hullo Gran! Yes, we're having a lovely time, but Mummy won't - '

At this point, Tracy grabbed the phone, hissing,

'Grandma Harrison or Nanny Wainwright?'

'Nanny Wainwright,' said Candy, resuming her sulk.

'Cheryl!' called Tracy. 'It's Mum! Hullo Mum... yes, lovely, the kids have been on the beach and we took them to the Family Service but it hasn't had any effect... yes, he's here. Hang on.' She handed the phone to Oliver. 'She wants to speak to you. Yes, *and* you, Micky. To *all* of us, just wait your turn!'

Nonie sat back in her chair watching and listening to them all. After a minute or two, Oliver came and sat near to her. She glanced at him, seeing that he, too, was watching the surge of family togetherness around the phone.

'You're a lucky man, you know, did you but realise it,' she remarked. Oliver made a face.

'I'm beginning to. And I'm beginning to wonder how much of my own family life I was responsible for wrecking.'

'There's no point in thinking like that,' said Nonie. 'You did what you did, you can't undo it even if you want. And you weren't the choreographer, you simply danced to the tune... believe me. I know that woman.'

'That's what Helen calls her,' said Oliver, with a small smile. '*That Woman*. The emphasis is all.'

'I can imagine.' Nonie hesitated. 'She hurt your mother, Oliver. Unspeakably, and deliberately, because she selfishly thought she was entitled. You mustn't go on blaming Helen, she hadn't a hope. Outclassed, outgunned and outmanoeuvred. She cared, you see. It makes you horribly vulnerable.'

Oliver made no reply to this, and as Tom had just put the phone down there was no further opportunity for talk - had the conversation been going to continue. Nonie thought it probably hadn't.

'Time for the tree,' said Tom, clapping his hands to gather everybody's attention. 'Before the kids burst. How's the turkey, Chel?'

'Handsome,' said Chel. 'I've just taken him out to rest.'

'Should've thought he was a bit past that.'

'Oh, funny, funny!'

Tom played Father Christmas, although Micky said it should have been Oliver, because it was his house. Candy caused an awkward moment by saying that no, it was a Daddy's job, but it was swept under the carpet by the combined efforts of Tracy and Nonie, the one in squashing mode, the other swiftly changing the subject.

'Thanks,' muttered Tracy, when she was able to do so under cover of delighted squeals and rustling paper. 'I never realised Christmas was such a minefield!'

The distribution of presents continued. Nonie kept an eye on her own small package for Oliver and Chel, anxious to see their reaction, and as it happened, it was almost the last one to be opened. Chel had it in her pile, she picked it up and then shook it, cautiously.

'It rattles.'

'Hope it's not broken then,' said Tracy. 'The way these two rampage around, nothing would surprise me.'

'No, it's meant to rattle,' said Nonie. Chel tipped it from side to side.

'There's something sliding around,' she said. 'Whatever is it?'

'Open it and see,' ordered Candy, bouncing up and down, and as it seemed a sensible suggestion, Chel did so. The paper removed, a small box was revealed. She lifted the lid and, everyone's eyes now on her, peered in. She looked up, and met Nonie's eyes.

'What...?'

'What is it, what is it, Auntie Chel?' cried Micky.

Chel picked a bunch of keys out of the box and studied them. There was a label attached to them, she read it and then passed it to Oliver.

'*Villa Achaea,*' he read, aloud. He looked at Nonie, eyebrows raised.

'It's my villa down in the Saronic Gulf,' she explained. 'I couldn't think what to give you, then I thought you'd like the freedom of it. Go when you like. I'm usually out there in spring and autumn, often for several months. Join me, you'd be welcome, or go on your own. I want you to share it.' She hesitated. 'Was I right?'

Oliver and Chel exchanged a look. Oliver looked down at the keys in his hand.

'Oh yes, you were right.' It was almost a sigh. 'Where is it, exactly?'

'A place called Ayios Giorgos, it's - now what have I said?' For Oliver had burst out laughing. 'Do you know it?'

'Oh God, yes! Ayios Giorgos, and half the people in it! Nonie, it's a wonderful present!'

'*How* do you know it?' demanded Candy. 'It's foreign!'

'Yes, how *do* you know it?' asked Tracy. 'Did you go there when you were delivering yachts, or whatever it was you did?'

'Not exactly, but I knew it, and then one year I skippered a flotilla that was based there. I think you could fairly say that I now know it inside out.'

'I know that flotilla,' said Nonie. 'Panther Sailing, or something. They've got a big base out there, yachts, dinghies, you name it. They have options on a lot of the holiday accommodation.'

Chel wasn't listening. She had probed deeper into the box and pulled out an envelope. It had half a dozen photographs in it, she shuffled through them, and her heart seemed to stop.

A headland that rose towards the land, clouded with olives and spiky with dark cypress. A curving shingle beach, a Greek village tumbling downhill to a little harbour, a white villa set apart... almost, she saw the curve of dark-blue, broken glass from an antique float behind it. She swallowed, forcing her pulse to steady.

'It's gorgeous! Look, Oliver.' She passed over pictures of a square white house with faded blue shutters, and a balcony hung with

286

bougainvillæa. A vine-twined pergola to the side shaded a stone patio with tables and chairs, and there was a superb view of a sea of unbelievable blue. Candy hung over Oliver's shoulder.

'Can we go there too?' she asked.

'Candy!' said Tracy, automatically.

'Of course you can, if Chel and Oliver want you,' said Nonie.

'They do!'

'Don't you be so sure, madam,' said Tracy, smiling. 'Now, pack up some of this paper into a bin bag, both of you, and make sure you don't sweep up anything important with it.'

Christmas Day proceeded on its usual merry way. The turkey was eaten, the crackers pulled, the mottoes read and giggled over, the phone rang a further twice - Tom's family, and Debbie. No contact from Dot or Jerry. No surprises there, thought Chel, on a discordant, disgruntled note.

'We need to play a game now,' said Candy, firmly, when the last bit of washing-up had been put away. 'What proper games have you got, Auntie Chel? Not that old Consequences!'

'Well... none, actually,' Chel had to confess, and at Candy's disbelieving look felt constrained to add, 'Most of our things are still in our old house.' But no games, that was a dead cert. She and Oliver hadn't been great on playing games - not that kind, anyway.

'There's *Cluedo* in your bookcase,' said Micky, accusingly.

'Is there? I had no idea.' Chel had been vaguely aware of a few battered boxes of wet-day board games left over from the owner's holiday-letting attempts. She counted round the circle. 'But only six can play that. There's seven of us.'

'Candy's too young for it, anyway,' said Tracy. 'She wouldn't have a clue... oh, sorry about the pun!'

'I would so!' exclaimed Candy.

'I tell you what,' said Oliver. '*I* wouldn't have a clue, so why don't you help me? I'm sure that would be allowed.'

'You being such a poor old invalid, I suppose!' said Tracy, silencing Micky's immediate protest that it wouldn't be fair. Candy ran to get the box.

'We need pencils.'

'Try the kitchen drawer.'

'I know, in the one with the funny stone,' cried Candy, running to the kitchen.

'The what?' asked Chel, but Micky already had the lid off the box and was officiously checking that the pieces were there and she forgot about her question almost immediately.

Four rounds of *Cluedo* proved that being the mother of Candy and Micky qualified Tracy for a career at Scotland Yard, and then it was time to watch a film on television and allow the adults to collapse into chairs and the children to wind down.

'At least it's not *The Wizard of Oz*,' said Tracy, and Tom remarked that he rather missed the old Wizard and would like to see him reinstated.

'Sssh!' said Candy. 'We can't hear if you chatter, Daddy!'

Tom opened his mouth and then closed it again with a shake of his head. He closed his eyes.

'Dad's gone,' said Micky, a few minutes later, and so he had. A gentle, purring snore made a soothing background to mayhem on the screen. Tracy and Chel slipped off to the kitchen after a while to fetch sausage rolls and glasses of coke for the children.

'Bed, when this is over,' said Tracy, when Candy protested. 'It's been a long day, and it's nearly eight o'clock.'

'But Mummy - '

Tom mumbled, without opening his eyes,

'We can't hear if you chatter, Candy.'

Both children were too full of chocolate to be really hungry, and too tired, and went off to bed in the end with the minimum of fuss. There were no protests about ghosts tonight. Candy, coming down in her dressing gown to say goodnight, flung her arms round Chel and hugged her.

'This was the best Christmas *ever*, Auntie Chel!'

When the two of them had disappeared up the stairs for the last time, Chel yawned, stretched and got to her feet.

'Who's for a turkey sandwich and a slice of cake with a glass of wine?'

'Make that coffee,' said Nonie. 'I've got to drive home, remember.'

She followed Chel into the kitchen.

'Candy was right,' she said, as she helped Chel to slice up the cold turkey. 'It's been a wonderful Christmas. I can't remember when I've enjoyed one more.'

'And that was a wonderful present you gave us,' Chel said. 'Like giving Oliver the keys to the kingdom. Do you really want to share your lovely villa with us?'

'I never had anyone to share it with before,' Nonie pointed out.

'You've got friends.'

'Friends are not family. Surely today has shown even Oliver that there's a difference? People need both.'

Chel turned and leaned her back against the worktop.

'Well, we're glad to be your family, if that's how you feel about us. Nonie... don't think I'm being impertinent, will you, but... wasn't there ever anyone else?'

Nonie shook her head.

'Maybe there might have been... but there's unfinished business between Matt and me, that won't ever be resolved now. It holds me back, somehow.'

'So there *is* someone.'

'I'm too old for romance, Chel. And people get tired of half a loaf and want the whole bakery. Talking of which, are you going to butter that bread or shall we eat these sandwiches dry?'

There was something nudging at the edge of her thoughts, but for the second time now, Chel couldn't pin it down. She took the hint and changed the subject.

'I'm glad, anyway, that you've enjoyed my mad family. I shall miss them when they go.'

Nonie repeated something that she had said earlier in the day to Oliver.

'You're very lucky.'

'I know,' said Chel.

The children were loaded into the back of the car, the luggage was all aboard, Tom, goodbyes said, was belting himself into the driving seat. Tracy, standing beside the open front passenger door, gave her sister a last hug.

'It's been great, Chel, it really has.' The shortened name slipped out without her realising. 'I shall be sure to tell Mum and Dad that you aren't swamped in doom and despair.'

'Tell them to come and visit.' Chel hugged her back, already choked with the realisation that she was going to miss them all dreadfully during the long, cold days of January.

'I will. And Chel... tell me one thing, will you?'

'What's that?' asked Chel.

'*Is* this a haunted house?'

'What do you think?' asked Chel.

XVIII

Chel and Oliver went to a party on New Year's Eve, something that Chel had at one time feared they might never do again. It took place at Nonie's cottage on the cliffs outside St. Ives, and was attended by a motley assortment of painters, craftsmen and fishermen, with all of whom Nonie appeared to be on the best of terms. Oliver blended seamlessly with the crowd, as he always did, but Chel felt herself uncharacteristically fading into the background. It wasn't, she knew, that she didn't like the people, or that they didn't like her. It was something to do with the fact that while Oliver, in spite of his disability, was a doer, she herself had found nothing to do. She had nothing to say for herself. On a night traditionally devoted to resolutions for the year ahead, perhaps she should resolve to pull herself together. If she did not, she was well aware, the past two years would end up having damaged her far more than they had Oliver.

A woman was making her way towards her through the crowd, two full wineglasses in her hands. She was around Nonie's age but still dressed as she had been in the seventies, long Indian cotton skirt, loose peasant blouse, curly brown hair, now streaked with grey, falling on her shoulders, Annie would never change. She was still the same eager, idealistic hippie that she had always been, Maggie without the brains. The cord that tied the waist of her skirt was adorned with bunches of tiny silver bells that tinkled as she moved. Her round, rosy, ingenuous face was smiling

'Here - I saw your glass was empty. Isn't this fun?' She handed over one glass, and took a sip from the other. 'Your husband is Nonie's godson, isn't he? I remember when he was born! It was all so tragic, but he took her mind off it a bit, it helped, I think.'

'What was tragic about it?' asked Chel, feeling that she had picked up a book and started reading it in the middle. Annie had always tended to have that effect on people.

'Oh - darling Matt being killed like that coming back from Scotland, and everything. You must *know* about it!'

It was the chronology that had beaten her. Chel frowned.

'Were the two events so close?'

'A month or so. Helen came down here when it happened, *enormously* pregnant, poor darling. She was wonderful. Without her, I think Nonie would have gone under, she was desperate. Quite desperate!'

Well, Chel knew that feeling. She had a feeling, though, that Annie shouldn't be discussing this, it felt like an invasion of Nonie's privacy.

'Well, that was good, then,' she said lamely. But Annie was irrepressible.

'So wonderful that the son turns out to be so talented,' she said. 'But then, his mother is brilliant, isn't she? Such a shame that it all went wrong for them, they were such friends.' Her eyes were bright with curiosity. 'Do you know what happened? Nonie would never tell us.'

'No, I don't,' said Chel, although she could by now have made a good guess. 'These things do, don't they? How many of your college friends do you still keep in touch with, after all? I know there's none of mine.' Although that, she admitted, had only been secretarial school, and hardly the same, but there was no need to say that to Annie.

Before Annie could reply to this, a grizzled fisherman clutching a pint had edged her from Chel's side and she drifted away, still smiling.

'You don't want to take no heed of her,' he said. 'All chatter and nothing upstairs, her. I'm Jimmy.' He held out an enormous hand, and Chel took it and was engulfed. 'Good to meet you. It's what the girl needed, someone of her own. Has done for years.' He spoke gruffly, and to Chel's relief, didn't pursue the subject. A thin woman with faded blonde hair and a friendly grin came to join them.

'Hullo, you're Chel. I'm Lisa. Pleased to meet you!' More hand-shakings. 'We've known Nonie for ever, I expect Jimmy's told you. She keeps her friends - bar the one, of course.'

'That'll do, Leez. It ain't no business of our'n.' said Jimmy. It had been enough, though, to show Chel that even after all these years, there was speculation among her old friends as to what had come between Nonie and Helen. They must have been really close for the question still to be absorbing after so long. Dear Dot, thought Chel. Boiling oil would be too good for her.

'Bit of a sailor, your man, so I understand,' said Jimmy, changing the subject. It was, Chel thought, a typically Cornish understatement. 'Painting'll be a bit of a change, then.'

'Yes, well, he had to do something,' said Chel, and Jimmy nodded.

'Yes, the girl said there'd been a bit of unpleasantness,' he said, now making, Chel thought but did not say, the understatement of the year. The oddity of hearing Nonie called *the girl* enchanted her. But Jimmy was older, perhaps she had been a girl to him when they first met. On impulse, she asked him,

'I suppose you knew Matt Sutton, didn't you?'

Jimmy's face clouded.

'Aye. We was mates, you could say.'

Lisa said,

'Jimmy and his Dad kept their gear under the loft - where the craft shop is now, 'til Dad died, and Jimmy went on the trawlers, then Nonie cleared it out and started the business. I run it for her now the kids are grown. A bit of a memorial, I reckon it is, though she doesn't say. He helped her, you know, so she helps others. Handing it on. You know?'

Chel decided that Lisa must be very fond of Nonie and close to her to have thought that out, and liked her for it. She said, out of politeness more than anything,

'Is it successful? I mean, is it a real help to the craftsmen?'

'You could say that. Come summer, I'm run off my feet. Could do with someone sensible to help me then, not these girls just filling in the time 'til they can be off with their boyfriends.' She looked at Chel sideways, slyly. 'What d'you do with yourself while hubby's busy with his paints?'

'Not a lot,' Chel had to admit, and then defended herself by adding, 'Up until fairly recently he needed me there, but lately I've been thinking I needed a job of some kind, just to keep my hand in until we know where we're going.'

'Well then,' said Lisa.

'It wouldn't be permanent,' said Chel. 'Maybe just for this summer... you see, we don't know. What's going to happen?'

'Suits me,' said Lisa.

The offer having been made and accepted, with no actual proposal being made, Lisa gave a brisk nod and moved on.

'I'll be in touch, then.'

Jimmy looked at Chel with a secret smile on his face.

'Bit of a steamroller, my Leez,' he remarked. 'Don't let her roll over *you,* girl.'

'It suits me fine,' said Chel, realising that it was true. If Oliver was going to be working in Nonie's studio, she wanted to be part of the fun, not a sit-at-home little housewife.

'That's all right, then.'

Chel decided that she wasn't going to ask if it had been a put-up job. As she had told Jimmy, it suited her, after all, and she thought that she would find it interesting. And better people than Lisa had tried to roll over her in the past. Some of them, she admitted to herself, had succeeded too. But not Lisa. She felt she could work with Lisa.

Nonie found her later.

'Having a good time?' She held out a plate of smoked salmon canapés. 'Here, have one before they all go. I hear you're going to

292

work with Lisa next season?'

'So it seems,' said Chel, accepting the canapé, and reflecting that news travelled fast.

'Great. You'll find it interesting.'

'I believe you.'

'Educational, too.' Nonie looked at her warily. 'You must lead different lives, but not live in different worlds - but you already know that. Anyway,' she laughed at herself. 'Who am I to give out advice on making relationships work? Must be the last person on earth, when you think about it! Have you got a drink, it's almost midnight?'

Eating her canapé as she joined in the circle of friends now forming, Chel realised, as the clock began to strike, that she still had no idea if she had been manipulated or not. Moreover, she didn't care. It worked for her.

Oliver was beside her, smiling.

'Having a good time?'

'Terrific. I think I've got myself a job.' Before he could query this, Big Ben began to strike from the television set buried in a corner of the room, almost unregarded until now, and *Auld Lang Syne* reverberated from the rafters. Withdrawing from the energetically narrowing circle with Chel in his arms, Oliver kissed her soundly.

'And a Happy New Year to you, Mrs. Nankervis!'

'It's going to be a goodie. I feel it.' She kissed him back. 'We're on our way at last, can't you feel the tide under us? I love you.'

'Happy New Year!' chorused everyone, and glasses clinked.

Soon after the New Year celebrations were over, it became necessary to return to Embridge for Oliver to see the consultant at the Spinal Injuries Unit there, where most of his treatment had been carried out. Declining a not-very-pressing invitation to stay with Susan and her husband - one from Jerry and Dot was not forthcoming - they stayed at the Queens Hotel, where Chel had once worked as trainee manageress. It felt strange to be there as a guest, almost uncomfortable in a way, but they got a substantial discount and a room with a view of the sea, which helped.

'Do you ever feel that you want to go back into catering?' Oliver asked, over dinner on their first night. Chel shook her head.

'I don't really know what I want. I'm hoping that working with Lisa for the summer may help to clear my mind.'

'You were good at it. You loved it once.'

'I know.' She looked around her at the lofty Victorian dining-room with its flock wallpaper and thick velvet curtains, it's heavy, respectable furniture. Period stuff, making a statement. *This is a solid, traditionally-run hotel.* She thought of it as stuffy now, she found, although once she had found it impressive.

'I've changed, I think. If I still want to be in catering, it isn't this kind.' She twiddled her fork, thinking. 'It's no good, Oliver. After all that's happened - is still happening - I honestly don't know any more.'

'You need to think about it. Things aren't going to stay as they are for ever.'

'I know, don't tell me, I keep telling myself. *Life isn't a rehearsal, you know.*'

'It's true. Truisms are. This is all we get.'

Impulsively, Chel reached across the table and touched his hand.

'We're going to make the most of it, don't worry. Your exhibition, holidays in Greece, planning for the future, even working in the craft shop. We're making a bridge, Oliver. It will lead somewhere, I know.'

'What, more clairvoyance?' He was laughing at her, his eyebrows tilted mockingly but with affection in his voice.

'Don't knock it,' said Chel, firmly. 'It scares me silly sometimes.'

'I'm not surprised, if what you conjured up on the landing is a sample!'

'Don't laugh at it - please.'

'Believe me, I don't laugh at it. Only at you. You look so serious.'

'I *am* serious.' But she laughed with him. He leaned back in his chair.

'So, the winds of change are blowing, are they?'

'Logically, they have to be, don't they?'

It was an answer of sorts - half an answer, perhaps. Since the New Year's party at Nonie's Chel had felt... not a wind, exactly. A gentle turn in the tide, as she had said at the time. Soon, maybe, it would gather power and begin to rush them ahead. She liked the thought, turning it over in her head. Then the waitress brought their starters, and the moment passed.

But the next day it returned, wind or tide, very much on the move.

Chel picked Oliver up at four o'clock, after his day of assessment at the Spinal Injuries Unit, and found him ablaze. Not since the day he had chanced on the *Hesperides* under the sea had she seen him so lit up.

'I'm a walking miracle, me,' he told her proudly. 'And I can drive, so long as it's an automatic, in fact, do any damn thing except weightlifting. And I don't have to haul back here again, I can go to Plymouth for my next assessment and *drive myself* there!'

'First we'll have to change the car,' said Chel.

'Change it, nothing! We'll buy a second one. It's time you were set free, too.'

'Money,' said Chel, half-carried away with him.

'We'll earn some. Or steal some. Or sell some shares. I don't care. This one is your car.'

That was only the start. Back at the hotel, two messages awaited them. One was a phone message from Susan, asking one of them to ring her, the other a note to Oliver from Bill Rowlands, who was directing the salvage operations on the *Hesperides.*

Heard you were in town. Can you find time to call round this evening? Give me a ring if not, or I'll expect you.

'We'll go after dinner,' said Oliver. He was sprawled on the bed watching rugby on the television. Chel thought he looked tired, but then he had not had an easy day, but even so there was a once-familiar vitality about him that warmed her heart.

'I'll ring Susan, shall I?' said Chel, knowing that he wouldn't. She took their mobile into the bathroom so that she could hear over the shouting and cheering.

'There's some people want see over your bungalow for a second time,' Susan said. 'They can't make an offer until they've sold their own place, but they're definitely interested. They're retiring or something, and want to be near their son. Just thought you'd be glad to know that there's movement there at last.'

'Better if they made an offer, but at least it's a start,' said Chel.

'They seem pretty keen, actually.'

These were the first people who had even bothered to take a second look, let alone make an offer. The bungalow needed exorcising in Chel's view, but she could hardly say that to Susan.

'Well, thank you for keeping us posted.'

'Don't mention it.'

End of conversation. Chel switched off with a small sigh and went to rejoin Oliver. After the happy Christmas with her own family, talking to Susan and being back in Embridge left a sad, bad taste behind.

Bill Rowlands was an entirely different case. He and his wife welcomed them with warmth and exclaimed over how well and happy they both looked.

'Being in Cornwall obviously suits you both,' said Bill, approvingly. 'Oliver, I would never have believed it, you look as if you might survive after all!' He hugged Chel and gave her a kiss on the cheek. 'It looks as if your kidnapping stunt paid off in spades, well done!'

'Does everyone know about that?' asked Chel.

'Local folklore, the redoubtable Mrs. Nankervis saw to that.'

'Ugh!' said Chel, knowing what slant would have been put on it.

'Don't worry pet, everyone who knows you knows what to believe,' Anne, Bill's wife, comforted her. 'And you're not coming back - are you? - so why think about it!'

'God forbid!' said Oliver, and Bill grinned.

'Come on through, and we'll open a can or two. I've things I think you'd like to see.'

They went through into Bill's office, where various small finds from the *Hesperides,* and pictures of the larger items were spread on his desk for inspection.

'We had a good season last year,' Bill said, turning a concreted lump of coins over in his hand. 'Slow - we had to wait on the archaeologists, it's an important site, but when this lot goes to auction, it's going to make a splash - pardon the pun. Oh - and there's another cheque for you, Oliver, remind me to give it to you before you go.'

'Enough to buy a car?' wondered Chel, half to herself.

'Two or three cars, I should think, if you're not into Jaguars.' Bill grinned at her. 'Why, need a new one?'

'Oliver does,' said Chel, with satisfaction, and watched Bill's grin widen.

'We must drink to that!'

Anne was already opening cans and pouring into glasses. She passed them round. Bill raised his glass.

'Here's to all of us, and here's to your future, both of you!'

'To the future,' chorused Chel and Anne.

'To independence,' said Oliver.

'We'll drink to that,' said Bill, and did so, deeply. 'Now, come and have a look at these.'

Chel had the greatest difficulty, the next morning, in restraining Oliver from going straight out to buy a car.

'Cool it, you!' she said. 'We're going home, remember? We don't want to drive two cars back, and anyway, you should walk before you run, it's a long way to the other end of Cornwall.'

Oliver, who felt that he had just received parole from a life sentence, reluctantly agreed to this.

'But if we pass any likely garages when we get near home, we'll stop,' he conceded.

'All right, we will,' Chel agreed.

The hall porter, an old sparring partner of Chel's from her working days, knocked on the door at this point.

'Take the luggage down for you,' he said, without preamble. The whole town knew what had happened to Oliver.

'That's sweet of you, Charlie, thanks.'

'And don't you dare bother to tip,' added Charlie, loading himself with their two small bags, that Chel could quite well have managed on her own. He went out, and Oliver picked up the room key from the dressing table.

'Come on then, sweetheart. Home.' The word sounded strange on his lips, like a foreign language.

Neither of them had made any suggestion that a visit to his parents, before they left the town, might be in order. They tipped Charlie anyway, said goodbye to those of Chel's old workmates who were still there, and drove away without a backward look. There were things to do in Cornwall, friends to see, plans to make, a car to buy, a picture to paint. A life.

Chel had thought that psychic manifestations had gone from Vellanzoe, and it was true that over Christmas there had been nothing, and nor did Matthew Sutton ever appear there again. But in January, when Nonie brought the big canvas, originally prepared by Matt, across to them, and Oliver began working on the picture, a very strange thing happened.

It was Maggie who first pointed it out, without fully understanding its significance, for the history behind the picture had remained a secret between Chel, Oliver, Nonie and Judy, and would so remain. Maggie came round one afternoon to see what was going on, and stood for some time looking at the roughed-out sketch on the canvas, and the area on which Oliver had already worked, studying a red-gold sky with dawn-bright streaks of radiance fanning from the mist-softened, empty curve of a dark horizon, and she said,

'I don't know if it's the subject, or if it's just me, but this doesn't look like your work at all, Oliver.'

'You don't think so?' asked Oliver, who was uneasily aware of it himself.

'You usually work in a much more... *loose* sort of way, I suppose. Easier... less - if I say *controlled*, you'll misunderstand me. This is going to be brilliant. But it isn't you.' She hesitated. 'I suppose what I mean is, an artist's brushwork is as good as a signature, and this - well, it just isn't your signature.'

'It's a bit of an experiment,' offered Oliver, not wholly dishonestly.

'I like your own style,' said Maggie. 'This looks as if it's been painted by someone else - someone quite different. You aren't going to change your style are you? It would be a pity if you did. This isn't you.'

It was the third time she had said that, in various ways. Oliver

297

nibbled the end of his brush.

'You don't like this?'

'Oh yes, I like it very much. But it's somehow derivative, and your work is always so distinctive.'

Oliver laughed at that, but when Maggie had gone away again, Chel went over to look at the canvas over his shoulder and studied it more carefully than hitherto. She had thought that it was her own lack of knowledge and the unfamiliar subject that had made it seem unlike him. With Maggie's more informed opinion to back her own, she found that it was indeed derivative. The discovery gave her the strangest sinking feeling in her stomach.

'What's the matter?' asked Oliver, but she wouldn't tell him. Her refusal didn't make him feel any easier.

The painting grew only slowly. Oliver didn't work on it all the time, sometimes he wouldn't touch it for days, partly because it was large, and therefore tiring to work on. Moreover, he knew that he was approaching it with a compulsive energy that belonged to a stronger, fitter man than he could claim to be these days, and without putting it into words, even to himself, he recognised that Matt Sutton understood only that he was working with a talent that he could use, he hadn't realised that the body through which he was working was recovering from injury. The good thing was that he would come and go at Oliver's own will, as if time no longer mattered to him, just so long as Chel was around to be the channel, for her willingness to accept him at last seemed to have given him the longed-for freedom of the house. If Chel wasn't there for any reason, the picture was dead. Oliver did try once, for his own interest, and was disconcerted when he saw the contrast between his morning's work and yesterday's, even though something in him had half-expected it. He scrubbed it out with a turpentiny rag and didn't mention it when Chel returned, and it was some time before he touched the painting again.

Nonie must have seen what was going on, but she made no comment. She hardly looked at the picture when she came over, finding it deeply disturbing on many levels. But she did see, and indirectly point out, a side-effect that Oliver himself had dismissed as his own - probably conceited - imagination.

Matt Sutton had been an artist of considerable standing, a Royal Academician, with great experience and knowledge and with outstanding talent.

'Your brushwork is beginning to come together at last,' said Nonie, looking critically at Oliver's current piece of his own work. She was always nagging him about technique, although he was worlds away from those early paintings that gathered dust upstairs, constantly dinning it into him that to be even exceptionally gifted was not enough; like any other trade, painting needed to be learned from the bottom up.

'And particularly in your case,' she told him. 'You're already famous as a record-breaking round-the-world yachtsman, and your mother is equally well-known in her field. Unless you have everything bang to rights, and probably even then, there will always be people who will tell you that you should have been content with the one, or are cashing in on the other. And however talented you are, and however hard you work, nothing will give you technique but time and experience.'

What she hadn't added, because obviously it didn't occur to her, was *or being taken over by a master who already has it.* Matt Sutton, taking Oliver's eyes and hands to fulfil his own need, inadvertently bequeathed knowledge. He left behind him nothing of his own style or vision, but Oliver could no more help learning from him than he could have helped breathing. His hands retained the master touch and turned it to his own use. Matt Sutton could have said no clearer *Thank you.*

All through a January liberally dashed with rain and occasionally lightly powdered with snow, Matthew Sutton's vision took shape until it was finished, all except for the flowers. The green and gold hayfield blazed against the black earth, Oliver - or Matt Sutton - had even painted the wind that blew through it. Chel looked at it now, her face sober.

'I don't think he was altogether right - Matt Sutton. Being grown-up isn't all bomb craters and dust and ashes. There are other things too. Look at us, we've had our share of mud, but the flowers have gone on growing too.'

'Very picturesque,' Oliver commented.

'You know what I mean.'

'He lived through a world war, remember,' said Oliver. 'You can gauge his reaction to it by the strength of his need to paint this picture. He was a sensitive man - unduly sensitive, I suspect. And Bomber Command were responsible for a lot of mindless mass destruction, he was probably clever enough to work that out long before history did it for him. Maybe he never saw things quite straight after that. To be honest, I don't think even Nonie knows - although Gifford Thomas may.' He paused, frowning. 'Anyway, I don't think that's what he means, exactly. It isn't the world itself that he's trying to portray, it's our knowledge of it. You grow up, and you don't forget what you learned, even in the good times, and knowledge needs to be used. Will you ever forget the last couple of years, for instance?'

Chel shuddered.

'No.' She studied the picture thoughtfully. 'It isn't a comfortable picture, is it? I don't think I could live with it. It's not... not *homey* enough. Those people are travelling a hard road.'

'Don't we all?' asked Oliver, suddenly flippant, and Chel didn't reply.

In the middle of February, the weather unexpectedly stopped playing with the pretty snowflakes and dumped a load of trouble onto Bodmin Moor. Local radio spoke of roads blocked by drifting snow, abandoned cars and fallen power lines. In the far west, a thin skim of icy snow covered everything and the birds shivered in the trees. The local news on television that evening showed graphic pictures of vast expanses of unbroken white as far as the eye could see, and the crawling line of the A30 cluttered with cars that had skidded into the side of the road or into each other, or simply been abandoned where they had ploughed into drifts, and gritting lorries ploughing through the chaos in the dark with their lights gleaming onto ice.

'It all looks very dramatic,' said Oliver, ever the cynic. 'I can't help thinking that some of these images are a bit selective, though.'

'Just the same, I'm glad I'm not driving in it,' said Chel, with a shiver. 'And if you're honest, so are you - particularly in that flash wagon of yours!' Oliver, predictably, had gone for a nearly new sporty convertible with some grunt under the bonnet - fresh air and fear, said Chel, shuddering, and do make sure you can stop the thing if you have to, won't you?

'It wouldn't bother me,' said Oliver, now. The phone rang. 'There you are, I said they were exaggerating, didn't I? The phone lines aren't down.'

Chel picked it up.

'Hullo?'

'Cheryl!' She recognised the voice at once, and made a face at Oliver.

'It's your father,' she hissed.

'I'm out,' he mouthed back.

Jerry sounded less urbane than usual.

'Cheryl, I'm sorry to bother you, but is the weather as bad down your way as they say?'

'It's not bad here,' said Chel. 'The Moor is pretty bad, I think.' She paused. There had been something in Jerry's voice that required it. 'Is anything the matter?'

Oliver raised his head and looked at her curiously. At the other end of the phone, Jerry cleared his throat.

'Probably not. It's just that we've lost contact with Debbie. She's supposed to be driving down to the Helford today to see her friends, and she hasn't arrived.'

'Bugger,' said Chel, and immediately wished she hadn't. 'I'm sure she's all right. It's pretty chaotic, but there haven't been any serious accidents that we've heard.'

'Who?' asked Oliver. 'Who's all right?'

'Debbie,' replied Chel. 'She's on her way to St. Erbyn but she hasn't arrived.'

'Give me the phone.' Oliver reached out his hand.

'Hang on - here's Oliver.' She handed it over.

'Dad? What's this about Deb? When did she leave?'

'She said she was starting out this morning. She would have run into it about mid-day, I suppose, if she left when she said - just when it started coming in really bad.'

'She's pretty sensible. I expect she got off the road smartish.'

'She would have rung. The lines aren't down.'

The crackle on the line as he spoke made Oliver think that it wouldn't be long before they were. He tried to be positive, alert to the anxiety in his father's voice.

'They may be in some places. If she got to St. Erbyn, it's pretty much out in the boondocks.'

'I rang Tim and Lesley when we didn't hear from her. They said she hadn't arrived.'

'When was that? The weather would have slowed her down, remember, even if she decided to give the A30 a miss because of it.'

'She was mad even to start!' Jerry sounded angry.

'That's Deb for you,' said Oliver, knowing that he would probably have done the same.

'Is it still snowing down there?' asked Jerry, hopelessly, knowing there was nothing to be done.

'Not here, but it is higher up, according to the radio. The side roads are blocked, but she would be on a main road whichever way she came. Don't worry, Dad, until you have to. Perhaps she went through Plymouth, it isn't so bad when you're off the ridge of the moor. And there are lots of places she could stop and take shelter.'

He rang off, having offered what comfort he could, and looked at Chel.

'What do you think?'

Chel was silent. Thinking about Debbie, and where she might be, brought a white wall of snow into her mind, impenetrable and cold.

Wherever Deb was, it wasn't on the A30, but oddly, she had no feeling of danger. Rather, a surge of power pushing forwards. Deb, she found herself thinking, was changing lanes. Changing gear too, moving up and onward. She tried to feel her way through the cold wall and got nothing she could identify.

'I think she's all right,' she said, when her silence became noticeable.

'Logically, there's no reason why she shouldn't be, but why do *you* think so?' The emphasis on the pronoun was slight but unmistakable. Chel shook her head.

'If I knew that I could set up shop in a fairground,' she said. 'I just think she is, that's all. If anything is wrong - and I think it may be - it isn't with her.'

'And that's all? Just that she's all right?'

'That's what matters, isn't it?'

But Oliver persisted.

'This clairvoyance thing - would you know, do you think, if she *wasn't* all right?'

'I don't know, do I? I don't know if it works like that. I think it's only possible to invade other people's privacy if they want you to - or maybe if they need you to. I don't think you can use it to *spy* on them.'

'I wasn't suggesting you did spy on her. Only it's a filthy night, and...'

'Go on, say it,' urged Chel. 'You love her. Admit it.'

'She's my sister,' said Oliver, defensively.

'So is Susan.'

Oliver said, reluctantly,

'And I suppose I'm fond of her, too, in a twisted, backhanded kind of way. But Susan isn't possibly in danger.'

'Well, there's a step forward!'

'Don't try and pick a quarrel with me, please. I'm worried about Deb.'

'I told you, she's all right. She's simply leading her own life - like you did.'

'I didn't worry about me,' said Oliver.

'No, but other people did.'

The discussion might have foundered there, but because Chel realised that Oliver, possibly for the first time in his hitherto selfish existence, was genuinely concerned about another person, and a member of his family at that, she made a further effort to explain.

'I'm sorry. It's all I can tell you, and I have no idea if it's simply subjective, because I want her to be and to be fair, it's the most likely option, or if I *know*. Deb is OK, wherever she is. And if you want to know something else, clairvoyance isn't a gift. It's a burden.'

'Isn't there something called psychometry - you know, where you take something belonging to someone and read them from it?'

'If there is,' said Chel, with conviction, 'it's something I don't want to know about.'

And of course, Debbie turned up a couple of days later, with a tale of having taken a wrong turning in the blizzard and found herself down the original long lane that hath no turning.

'But I found a cottage,' she said, cheerfully, when she rang to say she was safe. 'And I'm sorry, if everyone was worried sick like Dad says you were, but I was fine. Being heroic, if you must know.'

'Why, what have you been up to?' asked Oliver, refusing to admit how relieved he was to hear her voice, even to himself.

'Rescuing people. Writing messages in the snow with logs to guide rescue helicopters, stuff like that. I'm a heroine, me!'

She didn't explain further, but Chel, when Oliver repeated this to her, thought that the resourcefulness of both Debbie and her brother must come from Jerry, since he was the common factor, so how come he had made such a monumental mess of his own life? She didn't say this to Oliver.

'Funny, isn't it?' she observed, instead. 'There you are, living your own life and it feels like the centre of the world, but all around you there's other people with their own lives too - each of them a story of its own, but intertwined, like a great big living saga.'

'Come on, let's not get too deep in here!' said Oliver, laughing at her, but the feeling that Debbie had embarked on a story of her own, and that it would have far-reaching consequences, remained with Chel and made her wonder.

The flowers on Matt Sutton's canvas grew and blew in the wind, the last tiny, doomed insect buzzed among the grass stalks.

'You haven't signed it,' said Chel.

'I can't sign it,' said Oliver. 'I didn't really paint it.' It gave him a strange feeling to put it into words, and a stranger feeling seeing the picture there in front of him. It was utterly unlike anything he had ever done before, or would ever do again. It bore so little resemblance to his own work that he felt curiously detached from it, as if he had had nothing to do with it at all. Chel gave him an odd look, but as always, resisted the temptation to pursue her conviction that Oliver, too, wasn't immune to seeing things, or feeling them at least. Nonie however, when the problem came to her attention, was more forthright.

'But you must sign it, if you're going to exhibit it,' she told him, firmly.

'But I'm not going to exhibit it.'

'You must,' Nonie repeated urgently. 'That's been the whole point, don't you see? If you don't, you might just as well never have painted it.'

The picture, which she knew to be indisputably Matt's unpainted masterpiece, was something that she would never explain to herself until the end of her life, she almost thought that she was afraid of it, and certainly it made her feel very strangely towards Oliver, but at least she had it clear in her mind what Matt would have wanted now.

Oliver said, his voice sounding cool,

'If I sign it with his name, it's a forgery. If I sign it with mine, it's a lie. Which do you suggest?'

'You painted it. We all saw you,' said Chel. Oliver shook his head and said nothing. The picture, propped against the back of the sofa with the light from the window falling across it, glowed mute and unsigned, waiting for a decision. Nonie said, slowly, stating the obvious,

'It's no use to Matt hanging on your wall, or mine. It has to be seen for its message to be given a chance to be understood. Without its proper provenance it will never see the light of day. You must sign it. He meant you to have it - he must have done. If he doesn't, there's been no point to anything.'

'Just sign it,' urged Chel. 'He's come with you this far. Just sign it with whichever name comes into your head. His or your own, leave it to him.'

Nonie fetched a brush and she and Chel held the big picture steady between them. For a second, Oliver hesitated, still unwilling to make a decision, but suddenly it seemed as if the decision wasn't his at all. It must have been imagination that he felt the touch of another man's hand guiding his own, and that he knew no more than Chel or Nonie what he would write, but there the name appeared.

Nankervis, and beneath it, very small, the year.

XIX

The owner of Moor House, so Hedge & Hollow had written to inform Oliver and Chel, had taken his property off the market when they had first signed the lease, in accordance with the agents' expert advice. A property began to look as if there might be a problem with it by remaining on the market for too long, they went on to explain, and while there was money coming in from the lease and the house was being lived in and looked after, they had advised on a temporary withdrawal. Now, with the new season on its way, it was to go on the market again, and would they please be ready to allow prospective purchasers to view the place. The letter, they were glad to see, hadn't been signed by the unspeakable Mr. Gittings, but by Mr. Hollow himself.

'Do I ring them and say that's OK?' asked Chel, doubtfully, of Oliver.

'Do we have a choice?' he sounded interested, and Chel laughed.

'I suppose we don't. What do we do if someone buys it? After all, it hasn't got a problem any more, has it?'

'Hasn't it? The stories haven't gone away.'

There had been no further news from Susan. Chel heaved a sigh.

'Oh well... I suppose we have to go on going with the flow. I'll ring them, shall I?'

Ringing them felt a bit like sitting down at the top of a helter-skelter, there was no knowing what might happen next except that it might well be fast and uncomfortable. Useless to expect Oliver to take an intelligent interest, he was in another world half the time, these days. An unsuspected artistic temperament had reared its ugly head under the influence of an aim in life, and a lot of the time she thought that he didn't even listen if he considered the subject of conversation was boring. Or perhaps he had always been like that, on reflection. She sighed, as she picked up the phone, wondering where they would be this time next year, and if it would be in any way permanent.

'I'm so glad you rang,' said the girl at Hedge & Hollow. 'There's some people in here now who want to have a look at it, how's that for coincidence?'

'Amazing,' said Chel, with a hurried look around the room. Apart from Oliver's painting gear in the conservatory, it didn't look too bad. 'When do they want to come?'

There were murmurs in the background, and then the girl said, 'Would this afternoon be all right? About two? We can send someone to show them round, if you prefer.'

'I don't mind doing it,' said Chel. 'This afternoon is fine.'

'That's lovely. It's a Mr. and Mrs. Lacey.'

'Fine. We'll expect them at two.'

When she switched off the phone, Oliver had vanished into the conservatory and she knew from experience that it would be useless to try to talk to him now. Feeling unexpectedly at a loss, for of course they hadn't expected to stay here, nor had they even wished to, she wandered into the kitchen and leaned her arms on the worktop, wishing that there was someone, even a neighbour, to discuss it with. She could phone someone, of course, but it wouldn't be the same, and even as she thought this she heard barking outside the front door, as if she had summoned it. Smiling at the ridiculous picture this idea made, of herself dancing round the cookpots chanting incantations, she went to open the door, just as Judy raised her hand to knock.

'Judy! I was just thinking I wanted someone to talk to, and there you were as if I'd just conjured you.'

'Oh please, no more conjuring!' said Judy, with deep feeling. 'Can I come in, now I've answered the mystic call? It may not be snowing any more, but it's cold out here!'

'Sorry.' Chel stood back, dragging Sheba with her out of the hall. 'Please. Coffee?'

'Thought you'd never ask,' Judy came in and slipped off her jacket, hanging it over a chair. 'So what did you particularly want to talk about, or were you just lonely?'

'Come into the kitchen, and I'll tell you.'

'I've wondered sometimes why nobody came to view this place,' observed Judy, when she had been brought up to speed on events. 'Nice of the git Gittings to tell you.'

'Probably thought it would give us ideas,' said Chel, picking up the two mugs and heading for the woodburner. 'I wondered if it was something to do with the reputation of the place, myself.'

'Why should it be?' asked Judy. Sheba was already stretched out luxuriously in front of the warmth, Judy gave her a push with her toe so that she had room to put her feet when she sat down. 'After all, they aren't exactly going to put it on the details they hand out, are they? *This property comes complete with resident spook.* I don't think so!'

'The only thing is...' said Chel, curling her feet up on the sofa with her mug between her hands. She watched the thin curl of steam rising from her coffee for a few seconds, then, seeing Judy's enquiring face, went on. 'The only thing is, what do *I* do?'

'Keep shtum?' suggested Judy, reasonably.

'That's what I'm wondering. You see... well, *someone* will tell them, the instant the village knows they've made an offer - if they do, that is. And we know that there is no ghost, not any more. He's gone. So...'

'Are you sure of that?'

'As sure as I can be. So, if I'm acting in Mr. Williams's best interests - and he's not been a bad landlord, all things considered - well, shouldn't I say something?'

'Tricky one, that,' said Judy, thinking.

'Of course, some people don't mind the idea of a ghost.'

'True. You didn't.'

'We were pretty desperate. And Matt Sutton needed us, he wanted us here. And then there's the problem, if they do buy it, where do we go? Perhaps we should have stuck to the motor home after all.'

Judy wrinkled her nose.

'You could be homeless, then, any time from Easter on? Bad time for one of Dad's vans, but I suppose you could have one like you did before, just for a few weeks. But it would hardly help you in the long term.'

'We need to make a big effort to find somewhere of our own. Only we still have the same old problem.'

'Money tied up in the bungalow.' Judy nodded sympathetically. 'How about a bridging loan?'

'Risky - there's a nibble on the bungalow, but nothing definite. To be honest, I've given up hope. The thing is like an incubus, just squatting there, leering at us.'

'There's a few things different from last year, though,' said Judy, thinking.

'There is? Do tell! It all looks like a dreary repeat to me.'

'Everyone knows you now,' said Judy. 'And Oliver is going to make money - probably, anyway. You aren't restricted any more as to *where*. And you can go out to work if you have to so you can think higher rent. Come on, Chel, be positive here!'

'It just came as a shock,' said Chel, reflecting. 'I don't know why, it's always been on the cards. Provident people would have thought ahead.'

'Yes, well, that's never been Oliver, for a start.'

'I thought it was me, though. I seem to have lost my way completely this last year.'

'Time for a few new year resolutions, then.'

'But it's March tomorrow.'

307

'It's never too late,' said Judy, sententiously. 'It's like your sister said at Christmas - you've just let go of the reins - or in your case, probably the tiller - and let things run away with you.'

'Oh, did she indeed!' said Chel, indignantly. 'She had no right!'

'Well, you can't leave Mr. & Mrs. Whosit to the mercy of wind and tide, so what are you going to tell them?'

'God knows,' said Chel.

'There you go again!' said Judy, with a wicked grin. 'Leave it to God - well, one day the Big G may get tired of carrying the can, you know. Take control - for God's sake!'

'All right then,' said Chel, unconsciously throwing back her shoulders and sticking out her chin. 'I'll tell them.'

'Wow!' said Judy, admiringly. 'Can I stay and listen?' And they both dissolved into laughter.

But in the end, it proved unnecessary, which Chel considered rather a waste of the first firm decision she seemed to have made in years. Mr. Lacey was ordinary enough, but his wife was a complete ditz, as Chel lost no time in telling Oliver when she next saw him - Oliver had taken advantage - *mean* advantage, so said Chel - of his new-found freedom and shot off in his car to Nonie's studio in St. Ives, where the steps up to her door no longer posed a serious problem, and left Chel to hold the fort, saying,

'I'm no good at things like that, you know I'm not,' as he vanished through the door. Chel, who to be frank had no experience of Oliver showing people round houses to draw on, watched him go with a certain amount of relief, if the Laceys had invaded the conservatory - as they would - while he was painting, his reaction was open to speculation. As soon as she saw Mrs. Lacey, she was doubly relieved.

'I just *love* old houses,' she told Chel, as she swept through the front door with her husband, smiling indulgently, in her wake. 'You can just *feel* the atmosphere, don't you think? All those lives, soaked into the walls as the years go by!' She paused to take a deep breath, and spread her hands, while Chel's ill-regulated imagination created a bloody massacre on the living-room carpet. 'This is a happy house, I can sense it!' She adopted a listening pose. 'I always know things like that, I'm a bit psychic, you know - aren't I, Graham?' She appealed to her husband, who gave Chel a sheepish look.

'Of course you are, darling,' he murmured.

If she was, Chel thought - although she doubted it herself - her reaction to the upstairs bedroom was going to be interesting confirmation of what she herself knew to be so, Matt Sutton was gone. More probably though the woman simply had an over-active imagination and a desire to attract attention.

Is that me? she suddenly thought, and wished that she could agree that it was. On the list of Top Ten Unwanted Talents, clairvoyance must come pretty high.

It was obvious, however that ghosts were a good selling point here.

'Oh, how *lovely!*' cried Mrs. Lacey, when Chel opened the doors into the conservatory. She tripped up to Oliver's easel and stood entranced. 'I paint, too, you know.' Her eyes roved around the room. 'This will make a *wonderful* studio for me! Won't it, Graham?'

'Of course, darling,' murmured the patient Graham. He looked at Oliver's current, only half-finished painting with interest. 'Nice work. Do you sell them? I wouldn't mind owning that.'

Oh, wonderful! Oliver would have really loved this! Chel smiled.

'It's my husband's work, actually. He's putting on an exhibition.'

'Oh, *I* did that,' cried Mrs. Lacey, predictably, clasping her hands. 'I and my friend Martha Saunders, have you heard of her? She's quite well thought of in Chippenham - we put on this exhibition together, *so* exciting! Of course, I don't do seascapes. I paint animals and birds, I just *love* Mother Nature's creatures!'

She would, thought, Chel, and I can just imagine what they'll be like. She turned away from the easel hurriedly.

'That's all of downstairs, would you like to see upstairs?'

Mrs. Lacey thought the bedrooms were delightful.

'So big, for a cottage, you know!' she cried.

'It was two cottages, actually,' Chel felt constrained to point out, but she wasn't listening. Hands clasped once more, she was walking round the big bedroom, where Chel had first made the acquaintance of Matt, with her head on one side.

'Just feel the vibes, Graham! This house is blessed with good fortune, you can feel it in the very air! The spirit of it....' She allowed her voice to tail away into a telling silence, as she lifted her head as if she could smell something on the *very air.* Aviation fuel? Chel wondered. Blood? But no.

'People have been happy here,' breathed Mrs. Lacey.

With a prize pillock like this, why bother to mention the all too real history of the place? She would only rationalise it into hearts and flowers, Chel decided.

'I'm so glad you like it,' she said. 'We've been very happy here.' True.

'Oh *yes!*' breathed the prize pillock, rapturously. '*Don't* we, Graham?'

Graham looked at Chel through narrowed eyes.

'I understand you're the tenants,' he said. 'No problem there, I hope? We would get vacant possession?'

Bringing it with you, if I don't mistake the case, thought Chel unkindly, and smiled.

'No, no problem. Our lease runs out next month, and Mr. Williams has the option not to renew it. So long as we know in plenty of time to make alternative arrangements.'

'You're sure? We don't want any trouble with sitting tenants.'

'I can guarantee it.'

They were all headed for the front door now, Mrs. Lacey still in raptures, Mr. giving Chel the third degree.

'So long as there's no problems there, we may be interested.' He looked at her in a gimletty sort of way. 'Have you anything in mind?'

'We only knew it was back on the market this morning,' Chel pointed out, which was misleading since they hadn't known it was off in the first place. Nobody here needed to know that. She opened the front door and smiled.

'It's been nice meeting you. Maybe we'll see you again?'

Mr. Lacey grunted, but Mrs. Lacey clasped Chel's hand this time, in preference to her own, and looked deep into her eyes.

'Oh, you *will*! I know these things.'

And maybe she did and maybe she didn't, thought Chel, closing the door on them in relief, but it was obvious that Mr. Lacey knew a thing or two, poor bloke.

Oliver returned in a thoughtful mood.

'So, what did they think of the place?' he asked.

'Oh, she *lerved* it, such wonderful vibes!' said Chel, rolling her eyes.

'Good God!' He stared at her. 'But were they interested, do you think?'

'Hard to tell, really. You know what people are like - full of something one minute, and forgotten it the next. He asked if we were prepared to get out without a fuss.'

'Ah. Well, that was reasonable, I suppose.' Oliver looked at her. 'We are, aren't we?'

'Oh yes, we don't want to cause any trouble - not even to Mr. G. But God only knows what we'll do with all our stuff, it isn't like when we first came down. We've got worldly goods with us.' She didn't expect Oliver to consider this a problem, more to wave it away as an irrelevance, but to her surprise he said,

'Yes, I've been talking about that with Nonie. She says we can store our things in her studio until we find a place, if necessary. There's a bedroom nobody uses where it can all be put.'

'That's something. Did she have any bright ideas as to where *we* could be put?'

'She said she'd work on it.' Oliver grinned at her. 'Come on, Chel, we've always landed on our feet before.'

'I think I'm losing the spirit of adventure,' said Chel. 'Where would you paint, for instance?'

'Oh, anywhere... Nonie's place?' He dismissed it as unimportant. He *would* paint, that was certain, it didn't matter to him where. Somewhere would turn up as it always had. Chel, who wished she shared his confidence, sighed.

'They may not want to buy it of course. If she finds herself confronted with a real ghost story, she may change her mind about the *vibes*.'

But once Mrs. Lacey had entered their lives, things could only get weirder. Three days later, there was another telephone call.

'This is Veronica, from Hedge & Hollow,' said a girl's voice. 'Those people... the Laceys. You won't have forgotten them.' She spoke with conviction. Oliver, to whom she was speaking, remarked,

'I didn't actually meet them myself, but my wife said that she was memorable.'

'Nice description.' There was a pause, while the unseen Veronica rolled the idea of the memorable Mrs. Lacey around her rebellious mind. She had been asked to make some difficult phone calls in the course of her working life, but this one was surely the worst. 'Look, I don't know how to say this. Will you believe, I'm only following the client's instructions?'

'Me, I'll believe anything,' said Oliver. 'Six impossible things before breakfast? No problem!'

'Wait until you hear before you start boasting. *She*'s set her heart on the house, and he's prepared to make an offer, but... well, they had a stroll round the village when they left you, and a cup of tea at the pub... and....'

'They heard stories?' asked Oliver, already knowing the answer. 'So what? She said the place had wonderful vibes, I understand.'

'She's changed her tune a bit,' said Veronica. 'Oh, she still wants the place - but she's saying now, she just *knew* there was something, she *felt* it *here* - and I'm not sure if it was her heart or her stomach she was clutching, to be honest.' She paused. Oliver was beginning to enjoy this conversation.

'We've not had a problem,' he said, not altogether accurately.

'She said that Mrs. Nankervis - your wife - wasn't a sensitive,' said Veronica, on a note of despair. 'She said that there was a lost soul trapped in the loft that only she could feel... she's *raving!*'

'Oh dear,' said Oliver, sympathetically. 'So are they going to make an offer, or aren't they? We really need to know.'

'I know, I know, and I really feel for you! But she says she wants to perform a Spirit Rescue, whatever that is, and he says he'll only make an offer if she's allowed to. And Mr. Williams says, let's just get shut of the place, shall we? So - '

'We allow her in to perform it? No problem,' said Oliver, cheerfully. 'When does she want to come?'

'I'll be in touch,' said the unhappy Veronica.

'She wants to do *what?*' asked Chel, when this conversation was recounted to her.

'Perform a Spirit Rescue, whatever that may be.'

'No!' said Chel, immediately. She remembered the elemental on the landing and shuddered. 'No, definitely not.'

'Come on Chel, what harm can it do? And if it shifts the house...?'

'No. Remember what happened last time someone messed about up there.'

'I'm not sure we can actually refuse,' said Oliver.

'Then we get out first.' Chel spoke with decision.

'OK,' said Oliver. 'Where shall we go?' He sounded genuinely interested.

'I don't care. Anywhere. One of Jeff's vans. A barn. Under a hedge. Does it matter?'

'How about Greece?' said Oliver. Chel stared at him.

'Greece?' she echoed, stupidly.

'Ayios Giorgos. Nonie's villa. We can book a flight, store our things, and leave Mr. Williams to look after his own problems. What's to stop us?'

'Finding somewhere permanent to live?' suggested Chel, making a bid for common sense.

'Plenty of time when we get back. We'll ask Judy and Keith to keep an eye out.'

Outside the window, a March wind blustered, throwing spatters of hail against the glass. In the Saronic Gulf, the spring would be already coming, the sun would be getting some warmth into it. If Nonie was happy to store their things, they could travel light, be free again.

'Oh, what the hell?' said Chel. 'Let's do it! Phone Hedge & Hollow before we change our minds, say the silly woman can do what she likes once we've gone. Everyone will think we've gone mad, but who cares about that?' She paused, not unpleased with the idea of universal consternation. A small reservation slipped unbidden into her mind. 'But check with Nonie first.'

Oliver was counting on his fingers.

'December, January, February, March... what was that you said last year?'

Chel remembered.

'*Four*!' Her eyes widened. 'No, it's a coincidence. It must be.'

'Well, I do have it on good authority that you aren't sensitive.'

'I'm sorry?'

Oliver had picked up the mobile and was pressing buttons. His eyes laughed at her.

'*Oh ye of little faith*! Nonie! Listen, something's come up.'

The instant Chel went into the shop and asked for any large boxes that might be going spare, the news that they were leaving travelled like wildfire round the village. Judy, who after Nonie had been the first to know, told Chel to take this as a compliment.

'If they didn't like you, nobody would care,' she said. 'So, is pillock-lady buying the place?'

'Who knows? Who cares? It's not our problem, but she's kick-started our lives again.'

'I thought you were going to work at that place in St. Ives, what happened to that?'

'Lisa doesn't mind. We shall be back before the schools break up, it doesn't get really busy until then.'

'You're going for as long as that?' Judy was round-eyed.

'We've nowhere else we need to be. So why not?'

'I shall miss you.'

'Come out for a holiday. Nonie won't mind.'

'I didn't mean that... although, we would love to, of course. I meant...' She frowned. 'I just get a feeling, I don't know why, that you won't be coming back. Not to Trelewan. It's never been your kind of place, has it?'

'We've been happy here.'

'Only because it suited you at the time.' Judy shook her head. 'No, I don't see you settling here. Be honest, do you?'

Chel sat back on her heels in front of the box she was packing with their china, and thought, for the first time, about a future that was more than a mirage, that was going to happen whether they wished it or not. Trelewan had been kind to them, but... no, Judy had a point. There was no water, no boats, no action here. Oliver, healed, was going to start looking for all of those. This quiet place would never be his choice. Wherever they looked for a permanent home, it wouldn't be here, and it

313

didn't take a crystal ball to see it.

'I see what you mean,' she said, slowly. 'But we may not be far away. I don't think we shall leave Cornwall.'

'That's something. You don't think you'll want to stay out in Greece, then?'

'If we can go there whenever we want? No. We have too many roots in this country.'

'*You* have,' said Judy.

'So does Oliver. He just doesn't admit to it.'

Judy pulled out one of the kitchen drawers without comment. 'How much of this is yours? Do you know any more?'

'That one?' Chel glanced up. 'Most of it, but a lot of it's rubbish. Just use your discretion.'

'Lot of old pens from charity envelopes,' said Judy, scrabbling. 'String... kebab skewers... how do these things accumulate?' She picked up a small knobbly parcel wrapped in kitchen paper. 'What's this?'

'Don't know. Don't care. We'll sort it out when we finally move. Just sling it in for now.'

Judy duly slung it, into a plastic container in which she had been stashing small oddments, and put the lid on. She opened the next drawer. Beside her, the mobile phone began to ring.

'Answer it, will you?' said Chel, wrapping plates in newspaper, and Judy did so. She spoke for a moment, then held it out.

'She says she's your sister-in-law from Embridge. She wants Oliver.'

'Oh,' said Chel, without enthusiasm. She took the phone, squatting back on her heels again.

'Susan, hello. How are you? I'm sorry, Oliver's out.'

'It doesn't matter, you'll do. There's been an offer on your bungalow. Not a brilliant one, but the agent advises taking it. He would, of course, he's sick of having it on his books.' Susan mentioned a figure. It would, Chel swiftly calculated, pay off the mortgage and repay Oliver's father. Without that debt to bind them, they were free to do what they liked with disposable income, capital, their lives. The word *free* was like a starburst inside her head, filling it with light.

'Oh Susan, that's marvellous news! Of course we'll take it.'

'You should try for a bit more,' said Susan.

'No. Grab it while the iron is hot.'

'You burn your fingers that way,' said Susan, dryly. 'Shouldn't you consult Oliver first?'

'He'll say the same. Take the money and run.'

'If you're sure about that, you'd better phone and tell them yourselves.' Susan recited a number, and Chel wrote it down on the flap of the box she was packing. 'In the meantime, do you want me to make arrangements to store the rest of your stuff?'

Chel had forgotten that there was still some of their furniture in the bungalow. She had thought, when she left, that she never wanted to see any of it again, but if they were now moving back into a place of their own, she maybe ought to have second thoughts. There was a rather nice three-piece suite there, a dining room table and chairs, bedroom wardrobes and drawers, a double bed, electrical equipment - fridge-freezer, microwave, that kind of thing. Rugs too, and curtains. She mustn't be too hasty here.

'Would you mind? It would be a great help if you did.'

'It's no skin off my nose,' said Susan. 'I'm not going to pack it personally - I shall simply ring someone who makes it their business.'

No surprises there, then. Even so, Chel knew that she ought to be grateful.

'That would be great. Thanks, Susan. And I'll be in touch.'

She switched off the phone, and Judy looked at her curiously.

'You didn't tell her you were moving out, then.'

'She doesn't need to know.' Chel waved the mobile. 'This will ring, even if we're out in Greece.' She bounced to her feet, and grabbing Judy, waltzed her round the kitchen. 'It's sold, it's sold, the bugger's as good as sold!'

Four. Four months, as it now turned out. And then, *October.* Maybe.

Judy struggled free.

'But won't it stop you going abroad? If you have to sign contracts and things?'

'Oliver's father can deal with it and send us things to sign,' said Chel, refusing to be brought back to earth. 'Greece isn't the ends of the earth, they have a postal service. Anyway, we're off in a couple of days. Oliver's collecting the tickets now. Exeter to Athens, and that horrible bungalow *isn't going to stop us!*'

'My goodness, this is a change from cautious, worry-about-everything Chel!'

Chel threw her arms wide.

'Then look closely! This is the real me!'

'And very happy I am to meet her!' said Judy, cordially, and they both started laughing, Chel's euphoria rubbing off on Judy, so that Oliver, returning from Penzance, walked in on a scene of such hilarity that it was some moments before he found out what had caused it.

There was nothing left to do but finally to clear out Moor House and leave it as they had found it in accordance with the contract, to say goodbye to Maggie and Jack, to Charlie and his girlfriend Kate, to their other new friends.. Their last night in Trelewan was spent with Judy and Keith, in the morning, Judy drove them to Exeter together with Oliver's painting gear and a couple of bags of clothes. She hugged them both as they said goodbye.

'Have a lovely time. And come back soon.'

'We will,' said Chel, although they all knew that they wouldn't. 'Take care. We'll send postcards, and you've got the mobile number.'

'We'll try and come out to see you.' Judy was almost crying, knowing that it was silly but unable to help it.

'Mind you do.' Oliver kissed her cheek. 'Cheer up, we'll be back before you know it.'

They were gone into the airport building. Judy walked back to the car. It was going to be very strange without them around, but she had better get used to it fast.

The first morning they spent in Ayios Giorgos, Chel woke early and lay for a while, watching the stripes of sunlight that squeezed through the shutters to lie across the foot of the bed. A feeling of deep wellbeing possessed her and she stretched like a cat beneath the duvet. Greece! Here they were again, with what seemed like a lifetime behind them and another lifetime, against all odds, ahead of them. It was impossible to stay in bed. She sat up cautiously.

Beside her, Oliver slept on. The flight and the long drive from Athens had been hard going, although he hadn't admitted it, and their arrival in the early evening had been followed only by a quiet supper and an early night. The caretaker had left milk, bread, eggs, tomatoes and fruit, and they had eaten simply, omelettes and oranges, which was all very well when you were tired, Chel thought now, but between that and an airline lunch, she was now ravenously hungry. Oliver, no doubt, would be the same. Time to get up and explore the possibilities of the village. Quietly, she slipped out of bed. The tiled floor was cool against her feet as she slipped into the shower room adjoining to get dressed.

Downstairs, she wrote a quick note to Oliver and propped it against the kettle. *Gone to find something for breakfast. Back soon. Good morning!* before slipping out into the fresh morning air.

In spite of the sun, it was cool and windy outside and there were clouds in the sky. March. Well, you couldn't expect miracles, even in the Mediterranean. Chel opened the gate in the low, white wall and stepped out onto a footpath which, Nonie had told them, led one way to

316

the little bay that could be seen from the garden, and the other way to the village. She turned left, towards the village, the illusion that she walked the curve of the blue glass sherd whispering at her ear. The village dispelled the fancy, it turned out to be a delightful place.

The path, rough and stony, led downhill along the curve of a low cliff, and came out on the quayside. Here, bright coloured caiques and white yachts lined the harbour wall, even this early in the year, and opposite, a line of tavernas, mostly shuttered and quiet, sat sleeping behind their vine-hung forecourts. Only one seemed to be open, its chairs and tables already set out and a seductive smell of coffee hanging on the air outside. Chel hesitated, and as she did so, a man came out and began to set salt and pepper grinders on the checked cloths. That decided her. She turned onto the forecourt.

'Am I too early for coffee?' she asked.

'Certainly not, *kyria*.' He pulled out a chair. 'Sit here, and I will bring you some. Would you like bread with that, or a croissant perhaps?'

Chel, who was very hungry by this time, opted for bread, it sounded more solid than a croissant. It came in a basket, crisp and warm from the oven, with a pat of cool, white butter and a tiny pot of apricot jam, and flanked by a pot of steaming coffee. The waiter, who could quite easily have been the proprietor, she decided, seemed inclined to stop and talk.

'You will be the friend of Nona, from the Villa Achaea,' he said. 'She tells us you are coming. If there is anything you want, you ask me, I am Yianni and my wife, that is Maria, she cares for the villa through the winter. We can do anything.'

Chel sank her teeth into the fresh white bread, and spoke, regrettably, through a mouthful of crumbs.

'You can tell me where this bakery is. This is wonderful!'

Yianni was charmed to tell her. He also pointed out the supermarket, the pharmacy, and the man who sold the freshest fruit and vegetables for miles around.

'And if you want fish, you ask Dimitrios. His taverna is not open for the season yet, but he is fishing when the weather is good. That is his boat, the big caique on the end.' He pointed. Big, Chel thought, was the right word. 'He is friend of your Nona, he will be happy to help. Dimitrios, he knows everyone in Ayios Giorgos.'

'I suppose there isn't that much trade for the tavernas out of season,' Chel speculated.

'One moment.' Yianni vanished into the taverna and re-emerged carrying his own cup of coffee. He sat down opposite Chel. 'You permit? In one week, two, the flotillas will begin again, the people will come, all the shops will open. Now, we have our village to ourselves. My friend Dimitrios, he is all fisherman in the wintertime, his taverna is good one, but for the holiday trade and he has other business interests. The local people come to Yianni, we divide the trade thus and everyone prospers. It is good, no?'

'Sounds very sensible to me,' said Chel. She sipped her coffee, hot, strong, and comforting. 'And the others?' For there were several more tavernas along the harbour.

'They will open in the evenings, maybe, or at the weekends. Some for coffee in the day. When the people come, all will be different.'

'Are there many visitors?' Chel enquired.

'Many, many. The flotilla company, they have their own clubhouse - ' He gestured to a big white building on the other side of the bay. 'But there are many apartments, and when the boats come in, there is much jollity and dancing. You must come. You will like.'

'I'm beginning to think I will.' Chel drained her cup and poured more coffee. Two young men, wearing shorts, and sweatshirts bearing the Panther Sailing logo, familiar to her from her own season with the company, came walking briskly down the quay, laden with tools and sailbags. Yianni nodded, contented.

'Not so long now. We will awake and the dancing will begin.' He smiled and got to his feet, his own cup empty. 'Enjoy your breakfast, *kyria*. We meet again, you must come here and eat under the stars.'

Chel sat for a while, watching the two young men as they busied themselves on the deck of one of the boats. She had experienced one season herself as hostess on Panther Sailing's Ionian flotilla, and she had enjoyed working with Oliver, at that time the skipper. But you outgrew things like that, she thought now. Maybe she and Oliver had outgrown them unduly fast, but it would have happened anyway. She wondered if there was anyone here whom he had known and thought, probably not. Five, six years was a long time in the flotilla business, people moved on. As she should now. She went into the taverna to pay for her coffee and then, armed with Yianni's advice, set out in search of the bakery, which wasn't hard to find. The moment she began to climb the shallow steps of the main village street she smelt it, fragrant and tempting. She climbed right through the village back onto the coast road, and approached the villa with her shopping from the front, where they had parked their hired car last night. There was another car parked outside now, and a man going up to the door, a handsome, middle-aged Greek, casually dressed. He paused when he saw her.

'You are Chel.' He smiled at her. 'Nona ask I call. I am Dimitrios

318

Theodorakis, I am Nona's friend.'

Are you, indeed? Chel thought. She looked at him with interest. This must be the man who owned the taverna next to Yianni's, the man with the largest boat in the harbour. She hadn't expected him to be so prosperous-looking, more of a rough fisherman. The car was mouth-watering, sleek and sporty. He took her basket from her and opened the door for her, perfectly at home. A *good* friend of Nonie's then.

Not only of Nonie's, it then turned out. Oliver was behind the breakfast bar making coffee, all traces of yesterday's weariness gone. He looked up as Chel came in, saw Dimitrios Theodorakis, and put the *cafetière* down on the worktop.

'Theo!'

'Oliver!' Dimitrios Theodorakis was astounded, but obviously delighted. There was an interval of hugging and backslapping, accompanied by a flood of Greek, which Oliver spoke fluently but which went straight over Chel's head. Finally, Oliver remembered her.

'Chel, I'm sorry! Theo, this is my wife, Theo is an old friend, Chel.'

Chel would have shaken hands, but Dimitrios/Theo forestalled her, taking her in a gentle embrace and kissing her on both cheeks.

'The wife of Oliver, now this is something I never thought to see. I am happy to make your acquaintance. Today is a day for happy surprises.'

Oliver had now gathered coffee, milk and mugs onto a tray.

'Let's take this outside in the sunshine.'

Chel carried the tray, Oliver still needed a stick and Theo was Greek. She returned for a basket of rolls still warm from the bakery, balancing plates and knives precariously on the top. The three of them sat in the strengthening warmth and talked, and as they talked, Chel caught herself wondering if there wasn't a new twist to the story of Matt and Nonie.

'She is a lovely woman, your godmother,' Theo said at one point, soberly. 'It is a tragedy that she should have shut herself away from marriage, and from children. The life that she lives on her own is a waste of a beautiful person.' He had refused the rolls, saying that he had already had breakfast, but sat with his mug cupped between his hands, watching the liquid as he swirled it about.

'It was her own choice,' Oliver remarked, breaking into a croissant.

'It is not a choice that she should have made.' Theo sounded severe. 'One should take hold of life with both hands, it is the most precious gift we will ever receive.' He raised his head to smile at Chel. 'Your husband, here, is an expert in these matters. Do others than myself know that you are here?'

'That *we're* here, yes. That Oliver is here, I don't think so. Nonie didn't know, you see, that people knew him as well as they seem to.' And neither did I, she thought, but I suppose I should have expected it.

'Ah. Well, this should be interesting.' He set his mug aside. 'I thank you for the coffee, *kyria* Chel, but now I must be going, I have work that I must see to. But we shall meet again.'

He left, seeing himself out with the ease of one who knew the house well, and Chel looked at Oliver. He met her eyes with a smile in his own.

'Well?'

'Who is he - Theo? From what I was told this morning, I thought he would be a fisherman.'

'Oh... he's a bit of everything, really. An entrepreneur, I suppose you'd call him. Who told you about him?'

'Yianni, the man with a taverna on the harbour. I stopped for coffee. You were asleep.'

'Yianni,' Oliver mused. 'Yes, I know Yianni. He runs a great taverna, shall we eat there this evening? Give him a surprise?'

Chel agreed that would be a nice idea, but returned to Theo immediately.

'Did you get the impression that there was more to his admiration of Nonie than met the eye?'

But Oliver had noticed nothing.

'Now you're imagining things,' he said, indulgently, but Chel still thought that there had been something.

The next week or so passed pleasantly. Yianni was predictably overjoyed to see Oliver again, sorry, but blessedly philosophical about what had happened to him, and interested in his new career as a painter.

'Not that I am surprised,' he said. 'I remember you in the old days, Oliver my friend, always settling a debt with a picture, or sitting on the wall with your paints and your pencils. You were always happiest with a brush in your hand. Why, I believe Maria has one of your paintings to this day!'

'Hang on to it,' Oliver said. 'When I'm famous, that'll become the most valuable bowl of meatballs in the world.'

Yianni laughed, not taking him wholly seriously. He went away and came back with three small glasses of Metaxa on a tray.

'We drink to your approaching fame,' he said, handing them round. He raised his glass. 'To the most valuable *keftethes* in the world!'

They drank, laughing. Yianni left them with a nod to attend to other customers.

'I tell Maria, take care of that picture,' he promised.

Illuminating, Chel thought, but Nonie had said as much. Sad that Oliver had felt it necessary to keep it so quiet from his friends at home, and from his family.

They ate several evenings a week at Yianni's taverna, it was as cheap as eating at home and more fun. Oliver spent his days working, using the balcony outside the bedrooms as a studio, drawings and gouache mainly, and sketches to be worked up into oil paintings when they eventually got home again. As the weather got warmer, they swam together in the little bay below the villa, and Chel could see that this was a good thing to do, that he was getting stronger every day. The stick spent most of its time in the house now, he seemed to have forgotten he had ever needed it. Chel, tired of tripping over it, put it away in a cupboard. The act, she felt, was symbolic. Then Nonie flew out to spend a few weeks, and Chel's suspicions were immediately confirmed when Theo, whom they had met from time to time since his first visit, appeared magically on the doorstep before she had even unpacked, bearing two bottles of wine. Nonie greeted him as an old friend - she, too, called him Theo, but Chel, watching carefully, was even more certain that on Theo's side, at least, there was more than friendship.

'Tonight, my taverna opens for the summer,' he said, when greetings were over. 'There is big party, with Greek dancing and many happy people. You come, the three of you, as my special guests. Please.'

'How can we refuse an invitation like that?' said Nonie, smiling. She was obviously pleased to see him, but more than that? Chel put out a cautious feeler when he had gone.

'He's been very kind - your friend. He brought us fish and a bottle of brandy.'

'Yes, I asked him to look after you and see you settled in,' said Nonie, blithely. Nothing to work up into a romance in that, you might ask any friend such a favour, Chel reflected, but still she wondered.

The evening at the Taverna Astakos was memorable. Dimitrios Theodorakis, Chel realised, now, didn't run the taverna himself, he employed people, something that Oliver, of course, had already known. Nevertheless, he was very much in charge, seeing that everything ran on oiled wheels with a professionalism that Chel had to admire. A man of many parts he might be, but each of those parts would run like clockwork. And a real charmer, but she noticed that with Nonie he didn't try to charm. With Nonie, he was more... honest? When the evening ended, she was certain of at least one thing; whatever Nonie thought, Theo worshipped at her feet.

Interesting.

The Panther Sailing season was opening now, and Nonie, Oliver and Chel fell into the lazy habit of strolling down to the harbour at lunchtime for a drink and a snack at Yianni's, where Oliver and Chel enjoyed themselves in watching the flotilla boats manoeuvring in and out and offering criticisms on their skill and the competence of those in overall charge, the skippers, hostesses and engineers of the three flotillas based in Ayios Giorgos. There was nobody involved that they knew, but that was to be expected. In and around this pleasant lifestyle, Oliver sketched, painted and lay in the sun, his skin becoming as richly olive as when Chel had first met him, and Nonie painted him while he did so, putting a likeness onto canvas so acutely perceptive that it made Chel uncomfortable. Nobody should be able to see into another person's soul like that, she thought uneasily, although she could also see that the ability to do so was what made Nonie such a brilliant portraitist. She painted Oliver as she had long ago painted Matt: concentrated, absorbed in what he was doing. In the background, loosely defined, ships and boats, waves and lighthouses, icebergs and rocks and dolphins, filled the spaces around his head.

'And when I've finished this,' said Nonie, 'I want to paint you, too. Do you mind?'

Since they were staying in Nonie's villa, it was difficult to refuse. Chel did try, half-heartedly.

'My face wouldn't make much of a picture,' she said.

'You do yourself an injustice,' said Nonie.

Nothing more was said, but Chel had to assume that her consent had been deemed. In the meantime, she swam, explored the village, and became friendly with the Panther Sailing staff, who had become used to seeing her face around. Lotus eating, she thought, but the taste of lotus was seductive. She had even reached the stage when she only thought about the need to go home and look for somewhere to live about once a day. It was a Catch 22 situation anyway, how could they return when they had nowhere to live? And how could they find somewhere to live when they had nowhere to return to? Instead of worrying about it, she threw herself wholeheartedly into sunshine, warm sea, new friends and delightful boating picnics on Theo's boat - not the fishing caique, a smaller, more civilised one that didn't smell strongly of fish - and although she was unaware of it she, like Oliver, was recovering her bloom and her joy in life.

Oliver had painted a picture of Sounion that Nonie said made her heartstrings vibrate. It was an oil painting, one of only a few that he actually painted out there. The ruins stood out stark and huge in the foreground, blackly silhouetted against a stormy sunset and a flat, gleaming sea full of threat. Far away in the distance, the tiny outline of a lonely yacht broke the horizon, desperately heading for home before the storm broke, black against the fiery sky. It was a menacing picture, the presence of the sea-god Poseidon suggested in a twist in the clouds and a dark shadow on the water. Nobody looking at it, Chel thought, could wholly believe that the tiny ship would make it to harbour, but oh yes, they would hope so. It was a powerful picture, and very distinctive. For perhaps the first time, Chel realised of her own knowledge exactly how good a painter Oliver was going to be, and as she did so it occurred to her also for the first time that out here, she had had no flashes of foreknowledge, no strange intuitions. She had become in possession of herself again.

Whereas Oliver hadn't cared a toss if Nonie painted him just so long as it didn't interfere with what he was doing himself, Chel found it made her terribly self-conscious. She was a person who didn't even particularly like having her photo taken, and to sit for hours under close scrutiny, however impersonal she felt it to be, was an ordeal. It was this feeling of being forced into something that she didn't want, added to the strange rapport that seemed to grow between sitter and painter, that finally gave her the courage to say,

'Nonie, can I ask something?'

'Depends what it is,' said Nonie, indistinctly, for she had a habit of placing brushes between her teeth when she wasn't using them for a moment.

'You might think it impertinent,' said Chel.

'I think we know each other better than that.' None removed the brush and spoke clearly. 'Let me guess. Theo.'

'It's not really any of my business.'

'True.'

'But it's impossible not to wonder.'

Nonie sighed.

'I suppose I couldn't really hope to escape your perceptive eye. Well, in answer to the question that you didn't ask, yes, we have been lovers. And no, we aren't now.'

'Why not?' asked Chel, genuinely interested. 'He's lovely.'

'He is. But it began to get too important. And he deserves a lot better than a woman who can't commit.'

'Does he think so? After all, he's still around.'

'That's his choice. Nobody makes him.'

'But you ask favours of him - like looking after us, for instance. Isn't that a bit... dubious, if you won't...?'

'Go on sleeping with him? It isn't like that, Chel. Not that I don't care, I do. It's... something in me.'

'What in you?' asked Chel, wanting to know. Nonie laid down her brush. For a moment, she was silent. She had tried to explain, in the past, to one or two people who had pestered her about it - Helen and her own mother were just two on the list. Helen had come closest to understanding, but Helen had gone away. Theo was angry and exasperated by turns, and it hurt her to hurt him. Matters would come to a head one day and she would lose a dear friend, to put it at its lowest, and even to herself her reason sounded thin. But she lived it. She knew that if it was thin, it was also as strong as titanium and quite impervious to reason. Quite simply, what she hadn't been sure she could give to Matt, whom she had deeply loved, she couldn't feel right about bestowing on another man unless she could be sure that Matt had accepted why it couldn't be him. And she wasn't sure, could never be sure. Matt was long gone.

'It's not,' said Chel, cautiously, and unconsciously echoing her thought, 'terribly fair on Theo.'

'No.' Nonie picked up her brush again and painted for a few minutes without speaking. When she finally did speak, it was carefully,

'When Matt died,' she said, 'it was a dreadful shock. I was waiting for him to come home... I was going to tell him that I would marry him...' Her voice tailed off. After a moment or two, Chel said, with interest,

'And would you have?'

Nonie shrugged her shoulders, and went on painting with great attention.

'I don't know. I *do* know that he wanted me to, and just like Theo, couldn't understand why I wouldn't when he knew... he must have known that I loved him desperately. I'd spent two days agonising about it, and in the end I came to the conclusion that I was being unreasonable... and I would marry him. And then he didn't... I was waiting for him, and I heard footsteps on the steps outside and I thought, *here he is*... and in that few seconds, all the joy that I was going to give him was in my heart and in my head... but it was Mac. Come to tell me that he was dead. Bang - just like that. It was... I can't find a word for how it was. But something in me died with him in that moment and... it won't revive.'

'I expect you were traumatised,' said Chel, wisely. 'These days, they'd probably offer you counselling, for what good that might do... so what's the problem? Do you know?'

She spoke so calmly that for a second, Nonie stopped painting and stared at her.

324

'There is no problem. I just don't want commitment. It's as simple as that, but I don't know *why*. Just something in me.' Lie. She did know.

'It's never as simple as that,' said Chel. Nonie shrugged her shoulders, indicating as clearly as if she had spoken that the discussion was now over, but Chel, not certain now if the compulsion was from inside or outside of herself, felt impelled to continue, aware that she was walking a minefield but unable to resist.

'Who was Mac?' she asked, which seemed an uncontroversial enough way of keeping the conversation alive. 'Have we met him?'

'He was Matt's business partner,' said Nonie, shortly. 'I haven't seen or heard from him for years.' She painted a few strokes, then laid down her brush and looked at her watch. 'Half past eleven, time for a drink. Where did Oliver go?'

'Down to the harbour,' said Chel, giving up. She wouldn't try again, she decided, it would rightly be deemed intrusive, and she could feel that Nonie was on the verge of being very upset indeed.

'Ah. Up to no good, I wouldn't wonder. I was wondering how long it would be before he couldn't keep his hands off the boats.'

'Me too.' Chel stood up, stretching her cramped limbs luxuriously. 'I can't believe how improved he is: except for his walk, which is more of a lope these days, you'd never know anything had happened to him... just so long as he remembers that it did.'

'He will,' said Nonie. 'He's got too much at stake. Orange juice, or something stronger?'

'Something stronger,' said Chel, immediately. Nonie went in through the french windows, and Chel went to sit on the wall that edged the garden, where she could see down to the bay and the whole wide, blue expanse of the gulf. Distant islands shimmered in heat haze, yachts and dinghies played on the water. *La-la Land,* she thought. *This isn't real, not for us. Somewhere like this could have been our place, but not any more. We've got to go back.* Objective, or subjective?

Nonie spoke behind her, so unexpectedly close that, lost in her own thoughts, she nearly jumped out of her skin.

'Matt and Mac went shares in a small plane, they ran an air-taxi business. It all went to blazes when Matt crashed it. Mac hadn't the heart to carry on, even with the insurance money. He went to work for one of the big airlines, and just... drifted away. Lisa was once his girlfriend, but even she doesn't hear from him now.'

'I don't know about *even* she,' said Chel, trying to keep the conversation light. 'I don't keep in touch with *any* of my old boyfriends.'

Nonie came and sat beside her on the wall, handing her a glass of

325

white wine as she did so.

'Retsina I'm afraid, but it's well chilled.' She took a sip from her own glass. 'Why do I feel as if I can say things to you that I haven't even thought for years? You could be my daughter!'

'Maybe that's why.' Chel sipped too, and pulled a face. 'In spite of what you and Oliver say, I don't think I shall ever get used to retsina. I'd sooner drink turps!'

'You more or less are.'

For a while, they drank in companionable silence, enjoying the warmth of the sun on their faces and content and at ease with one another.

'Why *don't* you want commitment?' asked Chel, after a while. 'Was it just Matt, or anyone?'

Nonie thought for a while, and answered as honestly as she could.

'I think it was just Matt. Because he was an artist, and famous, and I was just starting. I didn't want people to say *oh well, she was his wife, of course* - like I've heard people say about Elizabeth Stanhope Forbes, although she was such a fine artist in her own right... it may sound self-centred, but it mattered to me.'

'I can understand that. I think, in a way, Oliver feels the same about Helen, as a matter of fact. But it doesn't apply to Theo.'

'Oh... Theo. Are we back to him?'

'You were lovers, you say so yourself. You're still good enough friends for him to move heaven and earth for you if you ask him. You even agree that he's a lovely man. So like I asked just now, where's the problem? Theo isn't an artist, is he?'

'God - no! Far too pragmatic.'

'Well, then? I'm sorry if I sound pushy, but I think this is important.'

If it had been anyone but Chel, Nonie knew that she would have given a very short answer - more, would have given it half an hour ago. But she knew things about Chel, things that she didn't pretend to understand, but knew were true. She couldn't, however much she wished to, dismiss her. And she suddenly realised that she didn't wish to, it was a dilemma that needed to be faced. Chel was probably as good a person as any to help her to make sense of it. It was time, Nonie realised, to make sense of it. She didn't want to lose Theo as a friend, regretted losing him as a lover. She did, she realised, love him. Not in the same way as she had loved Matt, but he was a different person, as was she herself. Matt was first love, young love, special. Theo... was fun, companionship, warmth, affection, contentment, all the things that although she had never thought of them as love, she knew made up the sum of its parts. One kind of love, and a good kind. Which, contrarily, was why she would no longer make love with him.

'I haven't lived like a nun over the years,' she said, now.

'I'm very glad to hear it.' Chel grinned at her, lightening the atmosphere between them.

'No - I mean, there have been other men. I didn't swear eternal faith or anything. But always, somehow... you see, I'm not sure even now that I *would* have married Matt, if he had lived. Helen thought I wouldn't have, maybe she was right. But the thing is, I never had the chance to find out. Nor to know if he would understand if that was the case... and because I loved him so much, which I did, and because the last time I saw him we were arguing about it and I hurt him... and because I've always wondered if it was because of that he crashed - not suicide, certainly not, but just not concentrating, you know?... well, it's sat there in the back of my mind, always - would I, or wouldn't I? So if I said, to Theo or anyone else, yes, I'll marry you... then that would be a betrayal.'

'He isn't here any more,' said Chel, gently.

'But I am,' said Nonie.

Into the silence, the sound of the cicadas flowed, hot and summery. It filled a long pause.

Chel had finished her wine, shuddering over the last drop.

'I hate the stuff but somehow, out here, it seems right to drink it.' She frowned into her empty glass. 'Stalemate, then?'

'It seems so.'

Chel privately thought that it was a terrible waste of two really great people who might have been happy together, but she was also starkly aware, somewhere deep down, that when someone had so persistently haunted the place where they had died, as Matt Sutton indisputably had, normal rules had to be suspended. Nonie probably didn't think of it quite like that, she just knew that there was something here that, for some reason, she couldn't do. Chel wished that there was something she could say to break the deadlock, but knew there wasn't. Matt Sutton and Nonie had created it between them, they needed to settle it between them, but his voice was stilled for ever.

XX

Chel's portrait was finished. Behind her head, as in Oliver's, vague representations of the things that Nonie felt defined her swirled in a cloudy background; a crystal ball, runes, a scattering of Tarot cards. Looking at her own face, she hardly recognised herself although the curly red-gold hair, the clear greeny-blue eyes, the broad cheekbones and the freckles were familiar enough. She looked at herself in amazement, wondering where Nonie had found the laughter, the generosity of her mouth, the elfin charm.

'Remember,' said Nonie, watching her. 'You never see yourself as others see you. Look at someone - not you - in a mirror, and study them. You'll be amazed at the differences.

'It's somehow not me,' said Chel.

'It's exactly you,' said Oliver. 'Fair and fey,' and Chel blushed.

Her work finished, Nonie said that she must go home, at least for a while.

'But you can stay here as long as you like. It's obviously doing you both the world of good.'

'We must go back soon,' said Oliver, reluctantly. Chel looked at him in surprise, she hadn't imagined he had given any thought at all to the future. 'We really need to think seriously about finding somewhere to live,' he went on. 'And there's work to be done that I can't do out here. But maybe a few weeks.'

'What will you do when you *do* come back?' Nonie asked. 'You won't walk straight into a place of your own.'

'Rent somewhere,' said Chel, hopelessly. She was sick of rented places. Moreover, she had a sinking feeling that a painter in - increasingly large - oils wouldn't fit comfortably into most of them. Nonie gave her a sympathetic look.

'If it helps at all, I suppose you could live in the studio for a while,' she said. 'I know the bedroom is full of your stuff, but there's still a bed in it. It won't be exactly four-star comfort, but you can cook, and there's a bathroom and somewhere to sit - even a plug for your telly. I lived there for years and survived very happily.'

'We can't do that - what about you?' said Chel.

'I have to be away anyway part of the time, a commission to do in London. And in the meantime, I've a small studio at the cottage I can use so long as it's only temporary. Think about it. It would be a bit primitive, but it wouldn't be for ever.'

'And think how convenient for work,' added Oliver, grinning at Chel.

Nonie left the next day, Theo driving her to Athens to the plane.

'See you in about a month - when it gets really hot,' said Chel, as they said goodbye, but it wasn't to be that long.

It was already June, the season in full swing. Oliver had somehow ended up working with one of the flotillas as a shore-based instructor, on a strictly unofficial basis. The skipper of the beginners' flotilla - one week ashore, one on a guided cruise - had weasled out of him his qualifications for the job and put in some powerful persuasion for him to lend a hand every now and then with the harder cases, and this had completed what Greece itself had begun. He was himself again, raring to go, and Chel's only worry now was that he would remember his limitations. She didn't voice it. She was herself happily involved with lending a hand too, here and there with this and that, amazed at the pleasure she found in being constructively occupied once more. The month they had left didn't seem long enough.

Then, one evening as they sat on the terrace after supper, dreaming over a glass of wine and putting-off the washing-up, the mobile rang. Chel went reluctantly back into the house to find it and answer it.

'Hi, Chel,' said a familiar but totally unexpected voice.

'Debbie!' exclaimed Chel. 'Hullo, this is a surprise!'

'A nice one, I hope,' said Debbie. 'Listen Chel - I won't run up a bill on this one, but are you still looking for a house?'

Chel's heart bumped - but then, it was natural, wasn't it?

'Why, do you know of one?'

'Actually, yes. It's not on the market yet, but it will be soon, and it looks like the sort of thing you might like - that is, if you don't mind living on my doorstep. Oliver might object, of course.'

'Oliver might surprise you, these days. Where is it? What's it like?'

'Well, I'd say it was perfect. Just down river from here, there's another creek, that wanders up into the woods. There's an old stone quay there, and a row of about five houses, and they've all got access to the water - although they use it mainly for winter lay-ups, because the creek dries out at low water. The house at the end nearest the river is the one that might be for sale, I only know because I asked our cleaner, but listen, it's perfect for you. It's quite old - they all are - three bedrooms - well, more like two-and-a-half - and all the rest of it, a terraced garden at the back, and a little patch of lawn opposite, on the creek side of the lane. But the crunch line is this, there's a garage and workshop adjoining, and up above it - guess what - is a studio! Quite big, according to Mrs. Tregear, with a balcony overlooking the creek. It used to belong to a real artist, although the present owners use it as a playroom for their grandchildren.'

'It sounds wonderful,' said Chel, wondering if it could possibly be as good as it sounded. 'Why are they selling, if it's so perfect?'

'Too much for them, they're going to live near their daughter in Surrey - they just want one more summer there for the grandchildren, and then there's vacant possession at the end of September - if you got in quick, they'd probably make a private sale to someone who was prepared to wait, and it could cost you less. I thought I'd let you know quickly in case you were interested...?' She tailed off on a questioning note, leaving Chel with her mind reeling.

After the end of September came October.

She was unfamiliar with the Helford River, but knew that it was beautiful. Half-remembered names spun through her head, *Frenchman's Creek, Helford Passage, Polwheveral, Port Navas...* romantic places, associated with Daphne du Maurier, that was about the sum of her knowledge. But it wasn't so very far from Trelewan and St. Ives, only twenty or so miles. Too perfect to be true?

'You'd better speak to Oliver,' she said.

While Oliver and Debbie talked, she went back out onto the terrace and resumed her wineglass, her thoughts in chaos. The bungalow had finally sold at last, the money - what was left of it after clearing the mortgage - was in the bank. The house that Debbie described would be expensive in that location, but they had the money from Oliver's accident insurance - indeed, they lived on the income. But they could both earn their way now. If not this house - although it sounded perfect - then something similar. She hadn't thought about spending quite so much, but she saw now that, for what they would need, she had probably been being naïve. But a quarter of a million? It would be at least that. They'd have to be barking mad!

Her heart began to beat faster, drumming in her ears. They couldn't - they *couldn't*. Only a Nankervis could think that they could.

October.

Oliver came back.

'What do you think?' he asked. 'Sound promising?'

'Woof!' said Chel, and bayed at the hanging moon. Oliver understood immediately.

'Quite - but then we always have been.'

'It sounds perfect,' said Chel. 'We'd have to go and see - but oh Oliver, think of the *money*!' She quailed. They had no hope of getting another mortgage, neither of them had any recent work history at all. It would be a capital sum. Quite possibly their entire capital sum.

'Having no money never bothered us before,' said Oliver, and grinned at her. 'And just think of the home we might have.'

'Nor it did.' She smiled back. 'Anyway, we might not like it.' Was that said hopefully? She wasn't certain. Oliver picked up the wine bottle and filled both their glasses. They clinked them together, grinning like idiots.

'Sounds like us for the studio, then,' said Oliver.

October...

The plane roared towards Exeter, eating up the miles between past and future. Chel leaned back against the headrest, nursing a faint hangover from Panther Sailing's riotous goodbye party the previous night, conscious of a rising excitement. Marking time was over, she knew it in her bones. Some of it had been fun - be honest, quite a lot of it had been - but nobody could live like that forever, in Never-never Land. You had to have more than that or you were hardly living at all.

Yianni had kissed them on both cheeks last night, and shed a few tears while his wife openly wept. This morning, Theo had come to the villa early to say goodbye, his face sad.

'But we shall be back,' Chel said, kissing him warmly. 'You can put money on it!'

'But will you?' asked Theo, sombre. 'I think that Nona may sell this villa, move on. I think that she is ready for a change.'

'She hasn't said so, has she?' asked Chel.

'No, but I think it is so. I think she will come to believe it. There is nothing now that she needs in Ayios Giorgos.'

Now, as with every second England came closer and closer, Chel wondered if Theo was right. Nonie had openly admitted to the winding down of her relationship with him, quite probably she did feel that it was time to move on. Ayios Giorgos was his place, if she had nothing to give him that he would want, perhaps it would be kinder to leave. But would it be the most sensible thing to do?

Maybe Nonie, like themselves, needed to come to terms with life as it was, rather than how it had been or how she wished it to be. Matt, like Oliver's total health and strength, was gone beyond recall. Shouldn't she now be making the most of what remained? Of the love of a good man like Theo?

Only, you couldn't live other people's lives for them. And whatever was blocking Nonie's way forward was at least as formidable as the block that had been in Oliver's way. More so, quite possibly. It depended how much had really been between her and Matt Sutton, and only Nonie, now, could answer that.

Poor Nonie. Chel, who had come very close to losing Oliver in a similar way, closed her eyes against imagined pain. No wonder it had left such a scar... she shuddered away from the idea of it, it was too close to home. And Oliver had lived to tell the tale. She stole a glance at him now, deep in a book, and felt a great wave of thankfulness sweep over her.

At Exeter, Nonie waited to greet them, and English summer rain poured down. The vibrant colours and glowing warmth of the Mediterranean seemed a whole world away.

'I've got everything straight for you,' she told them, as they loaded the car. 'There's food in the fridge, and I got one of the girls from the shop to clean round a bit and make up the bed. I unpacked all your sheets and things, I hope you don't mind, it's all in the airing cupboard in the bathroom. I hope you'll be all right there.'

'Don't see why we shouldn't be,' said Oliver, who set no great store on domestic comfort. Chel, who wasn't that bothered either, agreed.

'You lived there, you said - and you should have seen the flat we had when we first got married if you're worried about us now - one room in an attic, with the shower on the passage outside !'

'So why *am* I worrying?' Nonie asked herself, as they left the airport car park. She changed gear with a sigh. 'I've forgotten what it's like to be young and carefree, that's my trouble.'

The studio, when they arrived - via Church Farm, where their cars had been left - was quiet, warm with the residual warmth of the damp June day, and somehow welcoming. Nonie, or possibly Lisa, had done her best to make it homelike, there was a vase of flowers on the low table by the fire, and bright throws over the shabby sofa and chairs, a rug by the hearth, a dried flower arrangement filling the empty hearth, Oliver's upright armchair was placed to one side. Matt Sutton looked down at them from the wall almost as if he was glad to see them there, and beside him hung Oliver, dark and romantic by comparison, and equally absorbed in whatever it was he had been doing when Nonie painted him. Working, in both cases, Chel thought. Nonie's two artists. The husband she had never married and the son she had never borne. It was an uncomfortable thought, and she dismissed it hurriedly.

Oliver's few Greek oil paintings, that Nonie had brought back with her as air freight, had been unpacked and leaned against the wall, all except Sounion which was propped up on an easel. What he referred to as his heavy painting gear, which had been in the bedroom, was in its canvas bag on Nonie's painter's trolley, and the adjustable bed that took up so much space was against the wall now, covered in a bright

Indian blanket and a pile of cushions. The walls were still hung with Nonie's own pictures. There had seemed no point in removing them for, hopefully, such a short time, and Oliver wasn't planning to sell from here.

Oliver looked around him in satisfaction.

'Yes, we should be all right here for a bit, but I think, Chel, we shouldn't hang around. Nonie will be wanting it back.'

'We'll give Deb a ring tonight,' Chel agreed. 'Get things moving.'

There was a small pile of letters on the table by the flowers, they had given the Craft Shop address to their families when they arranged to come home, these had all come in the last week. Chel picked them up and sifted quickly through them. One from Tracy, she discovered, one from her brother Mike, serving with the Army for a second tour in Northern Ireland, one from her sister-in-law, one from her mother. Dear of them, all welcoming them back. And one for Oliver, from Susan. She would have recognised the formal handwriting and the thick, expensive paper anywhere. Her heart sank. Susan seldom wrote, and it never boded any good. She held it out.

'I doubt if it's *Welcome Home, Oliver and Chel, from all of us in Embridge,*' she said. 'But you'd better read it anyway.'

'You read it,' Oliver said, heading off in the direction of the bedroom. 'I'm going to have a shower.' He vanished through the door and Chel looked at the envelope in her hands with reluctance. Experience had taught her, however, that if she didn't open it, it would sit around unopened indefinitely. With a resigned sigh, she slid her finger under the flap.

You've got to go and sort Deb out, Susan had written, after some rather perfunctory preliminaries. No *please,* or anything conciliatory like that, Chel noticed. *It was never a good idea, her going to work with Tim Howells when they were so thick together not all that long ago. He's only just got married, you know that don't you? She was never much of a beauty, Lesley Salter, just a plump little domestic body, nobody knows what he saw in her, she doesn't even sail, the situation's dynamite. Someone like that can't hold a candle to Deb, and then there's the propinquity thing. Mummy is in a flat spin, there's no end of trouble brewing down there! She met Phyllis Salter in town last week, and apparently she was wringing her hands over some letter Lesley had written. You know how Mummy feels about the sanctity of marriage - a comment that would no doubt have astonished Helen - she couldn't bear for Deb to be responsible for breaking them up. I know Phyllis Salter isn't a great friend of hers, but these things get around, and if Tim and Deb find they can't keep their hands off each other, then she'll just have to come home.*

It's down to you, Oliver, you're on the spot. Go and see her and talk some sense into her, she might just listen to you.

And plump pink piggies might flap around the church tower, Chel thought - on both counts. She couldn't see Oliver preaching *or* Deb listening, why couldn't Susan do her own dirty work? And as for appealing to Oliver's respect for his stepmother's views, Susan must be out of her tree! She crumpled the letter in her hand and almost threw it in the bin, but restrained herself at the last moment and placed it carefully on the worktop. There was a bottle of Bardolino sitting there, she now noticed, with a corkscrew and two glasses beside it, and a card with the words *Welcome Back* written on it in Nonie's untidy writing. How apposite! Nonie might have guessed there'd be a need. She seized the corkscrew and set to work on the bottle.

Oliver re-emerged from the bedroom, freshly clothed and damp about the hair, to find Chel sitting down with two glasses of wine, one half-empty, and the bottle on the table.

'What did she have to say?' he asked, without curiosity. Chel made a face and pointed to his glass.

'Drink. You're going to need it. She wants you to go to St. Erbyn and lecture Deb on the evils of home-wrecking.'

'Why? Whose home is she trying to wreck?' Oliver picked up the glass and seated himself in his chair with the air of a man prepared to enjoy himself. 'I can't see Deb in the role somehow - or has that plonker Tim got the hots for her again?'

This was so close to the truth - the truth as represented by Susan at least - that Chel wondered for a second just who was supposed to be clairvoyant round here.

'Something along those lines. Anyway, your stepmother is having the vapours, and Susan wants you to sort it out.'

'No way.' Oliver took a sip of his wine. 'Mmm. That's good. Anyway, I don't believe it. If Deb wanted to make waves, she'd find a better way than that. Tim Howells is history.'

'Your family live such public lives,' said Chel. 'Apparently your stepmother has been accosted in the street by some woman... does *everyone* know your family's business?'

'Ah well, you know the answer to that.' Oliver gave her a suddenly cool look, and just for a moment a whole lot of things that should have been in the past were there in the room with them. Gossip in Embridge had nearly brought them to their knees, too. Chel said, hurriedly,

'Well, I agree that Deb's old enough to paddle her own canoe, but Susan will expect you to do *something*, you know.'

'Like what?' asked Oliver, with interest. 'Go and play the heavy brother? Deb wouldn't believe it, she'd fall about laughing.'

The moment, thankfully, seemed to have passed.

'We'll be seeing her anyway,' Chel said, catching at a straw. 'Maybe she'll say something... or....'

'Or the plonker Tim will follow her around with his tongue hanging out? I don't think so really, Chel, do you? There's nothing so dead as yesterday's romance.'

Chel's eyes flitted uncontrollably to Matt Sutton's portrait over the fireplace.

'Hopefully,' she said. There was no chance, she saw, that Oliver would say a thing to Debbie, and why should he, after all? She got to her feet.

'We've no dining table, so I'm going to warm up those pasties Millie gave us, and we can eat them round the telly,' she said. 'While they're warming, I'm going to have a shower too, so you can find the plates and things, OK? They're in a box marked *CHINA, etc.*'

Subject closed. But as she stood under the shower, feeling the aches and pains of the journey washing away under the warm water, she wondered about what Oliver had said. Yesterday's romance, she had to conclude, sometimes refused to lie down and die at all.

Deb had spoken to the people who owned the house, she said. They liked the idea of a private sale going through to their own timetable, and were quite happy for Chel and Oliver to go and look at their home. Sunday would be a good day.

'I don't really know them,' she said, on the phone that evening. 'They seem pleasant enough, though. Elderly. Not stupid. They're going to get a valuation.' She hesitated. 'I never thought about it, but riverside property is quite expensive. Would that be a problem? I really don't know how your affairs...' She tailed off. Chel, to whom she was speaking, really didn't know either. She said,

'Let's cross the bridges one at a time, shall we? Sunday suits us, any particular time?'

In the background, she could hear people talking, laughing. The sailing school must be doing good business, or possibly Deb was in a pub somewhere, it was that kind of sound.

'You say a time. I'll tell them - get *off*, Roger! Go take a running jump...' Laughter. 'Sorry Chel. My fellow instructor was spilling beer down my neck. He's a lunatic!'

'Sounds fun,' said Chel, recognising the note of affection in Deb's voice. Roger? That sounded a better bet than the plonker Tim -

although in Oliver's book, come to think of it, a lot of people were classed as plonkers, so Tim was probably perfectly normal. 'Shall we say Sunday afternoon then? About two-ish? Can we meet you for lunch somewhere, or are you working?'

'Might scrape a lunch hour off, that'd be nice. There's a good pub in the village.' She hesitated. 'I'll fix it with Tim. See you in the bar at half-twelve? Unless you hear from me - *Roger*! Give over, do you never learn?'

Something fishy there, Chel thought, as she switched off the mobile. Something in Deb's voice... No. She simply didn't see Deb as a home-wrecker, whatever Susan said. And the Dreaded Dot, who had brought her up after all, could take the credit - and by the same token, should see it for herself. Thoughtfully, she put the phone on the table.

'Lunch with Deb at the village pub on Sunday,' she said, to Oliver. 'Don't know what it's called, she didn't say, so presumably, there's only one. Look at the house afterwards, OK?'

'Works for me. What's the matter?'

'Don't know. But she seems to be fending off someone called Roger.'

'Told you,' said Oliver.

The pub was called the Fisherman's Arms. It sat squarely on the foreshore, on a section of the village street that was simply a causeway awash at high tides, its forecourt on a terrace raised above the watermark. Deb was waiting there when they arrived, seated under a sun umbrella with a glass of lager beside her, looking brown and very pretty. Beautiful, even. She had a glow on her that could have been the sunshine and the enjoyment of her job, or something else. Her hair, bleached now by the sun rather than her hairdresser, and fashionably shaggy, blew into her smiling eyes with the wind off the water. She waved as they walked onto the forecourt. Once again, Chel caught a tremor of... something. *Could* Susan possibly be right?

There were other people there too, students of the sailing school presumably, and a lean, brown-haired man who was introduced as Roger. Chel looked at him with interest, but could discern no chemistry between him and Oliver's wilful young sister. Good friends, she surmised, but on Deb's side anyway, no more. While everyone was being introduced, another man came out of the pub door carrying a tray of drinks, lanky and fair with floppy hair and glasses and a pleasant, good-natured face.

'And this is Tim,' said Deb. 'Oliver knows him already - Tim, this is my sister-in-law, Chel.'

'Hi Chel, Oliver. What are you drinking?'

There was going to be no opportunity for any private talk, which might be a good thing, Chel decided. None of the people whose names she had been told answered to *Lesley*, and Tim had positioned himself beside Debbie in a very proprietorial way. She found herself agreeing with Oliver, if there was anything going on here she really didn't want to know. One thing she was sure of, Susan was wrong in at least part of her surmise. Deb, it was perfectly plain, considered Tim only as a friend for whom she happened to work, and surely that was all that mattered? What Tim did was up to him and his wife.

'So, what do you think of the show so far?' Debbie asked. 'Nice place, isn't it?'

Chel, who was already in love with the steep, tumbling village street that wound up through the hanging woods, with the glint of sun on the river, with the familiar, pungent, riverside smell of mud and tar, with the moored yachts on their trots at the mouth of the creek and the rickety wooden jetty that ran out over the water, tried to keep her feet on the ground.

'Seems like a pleasant enough place,' she said, smiling. Tim gave her a lazy smile.

'Oh, it is - give or take the odd bastard.'

'Like it might be you, sweetheart?' asked Debbie, without animosity.

Chel felt her hackles prickle on the back of her neck, and didn't know why. Debbie was laughing, Tim smiling, Roger, she noticed, looking down his nose. Once again, she had the sensation that some undercurrent was running. Oh damn! It wasn't all coming back, was it? She had been free of it in Greece, why *here*? *I don't want to know things,* she raged against who-or-whatever had given her the gift. *Why can't I just be like everyone else? It's none of my business!* But it was going to be. She knew it as surely as she knew the sun would rise tomorrow. Whatever Deb was up to, and God knew what that was, was going to affect them all - herself, Oliver, Nonie, Jerry, even Dot, all of them. Deb was being spun into the pattern, and it wasn't going to make a blind bit of difference whether they bought the house here or not. It was already happening.

'Chel?' Oliver leaned across to murmur in her ear. 'You all right? Only you've gone a bit white. D'you want to move out of the sun?'

'No, I'm fine. Bit of a headache. Excitement, probably.' She grinned at him. He leaned closer and dropped his voice to an almost inaudible level.

'Told you he was a plonker, didn't I?'

The house, when they finally got round to seeing it, was a gem. Or possibly, Chel thought, quailing at the probable price-tag, not so much a gem as one of the crown jewels. Square and white, with a grey slate roof and two dormer windows peering out at the creek like bright little eyes, it was immediately friendly. The rough, unmade lane ran outside the front door, and as Debbie had told them, a tiny lawn took up the space between the lane and the creek. There was a high stone revetment that protected the bank and kept the water in its place, and steps that wound down to a tiny landing stage. Deb had omitted to mention the flagpole. At the back, a small patio became a tiny, terraced garden. There were white metal chairs and tables, and a wistaria climbing a pergola. Inside it was even better. Downstairs, two rooms had been knocked into one to make one big living-room overlooking both the creek and the garden, the light reflecting off the water dappled onto the ceiling.

'You're seeing it at its best, of course,' Mrs. Horsefall told them, deprecatingly. 'The tide is in and the sun shining. And this is the kitchen...' She opened a door and Chel almost fell down two steps onto a quarry tiled floor. The kitchen was a more recent extension, making the house L-shaped, it had bigger windows and plenty of light. There was a Rayburn, and limed oak cupboards with little yellow knobs and enough space for a table and chairs. Chel, already falling in love, lost her heart completely.   There was a downstairs cloakroom too, and upstairs, two double bedrooms overlooking the creek, and a tiny one with bunk-beds in it at the back, together with the bathroom, built over the kitchen extension.

'We had this done years ago to accommodate the grandchildren,' said Mrs. Horsefall, with a shy smile. 'But now, they don't come in big family groups any more, and we're getting old. It's too big for us.'

'It's lovely,' said Chel, feeling it to be the understatement of the year. Mr. Horsefall twinkled at her, smiling.

'And you haven't seen the best bit. I understand you're looking for a studio?'

'It's an essential part of the deal,' Oliver told him.

'No problem. Walk this way.'

They went outside. Wooden double doors gave onto the garage, with a workshop area to the side.

'Parking for a second car beside the house, if you need it or there's room outside here.' Mr. Horsefall had taken over the honours, Mrs. was in the kitchen, making tea. 'And now, up here...' He opened a gate beside the garage and led them up a narrow flight of stone steps tucked close under enclosing shrubs. At the top was a door, which he unlocked and threw open.

'Da-da-di-daaaa!' he sang, and stood aside to let them through.

The room, which was built of wood, was full of light. Skylights in the roof augmented the light that poured in through big french windows that opened to the deep balcony. They went out onto this and looked down at the little creek below. It was all so perfect that Chel was almost afraid to believe it was real. Oliver had gone quite silent, she could guess what he was thinking.

'I'll leave you to talk about it,' said Mr. Horsefall, happy with the impression he had made. 'Come down when you're ready, the wife is just brewing up.' He nodded to them and left them on their own. Chel took a deep breath.

'How can they bear to leave it?' she breathed.

The green, fertile river valley was quite unlike any part of Cornwall that she had yet seen. Here, there were no steep cliffs and nesting seabirds, no sea pinks blowing in the wind, no rocks and crashing waves. Here was shelter, calm, hanging woods and hidden creeks... *port after stormy seas...* the half-remembered phrase drifted into her head from nowhere. She leaned her arms on the balcony rail and drank it all in, knowing that the wilder, stronger Cornwall that she and Oliver both loved was only a short step away. She truly felt as if she had come home after a long and difficult voyage.

Oliver's step sounded on the boards behind her.

'What do you think?' he asked. Chel answered without turning her head.

'Head or heart?'

He came and leaned beside her.

'Good question. How about head for starters?'

Chel answered instantly,

'It'll cost an arm and a leg, and probably a second arm as well. We won't get a mortgage, and we have no idea yet whether your pictures will actually sell.'

There was a silence that went on for a long time. Finally, Oliver said,

'I'm not sure we should look at it quite like that.'

'How, then?' Chel asked, wishing to be convinced. Oliver said, slowly,

'Try this. The money we're talking about is what I got from my accident insurance, and we know they didn't pay out the full sum because, thank God, I'm not totally disabled, but even so, I paid a high price for the privilege of being master of a few hundred thousand pounds. I should like to turn it into something that would give us as much joy, even in a different way, as what I lost to gain it.'

'That works,' said Chel, after a pause. 'I'm not sure that your father will agree, but it works for me.'

'There's more. I never meant you to have grief and unhappiness and worry, or responsibility that bowed you down. I wanted you to have adventure and laughter and hard work that meant something, and the whole world to play in. I owe you, because it was my own arrogant stupidity that brought us down... and if you love this place as I think you do, then I want you to have it. And if the price of it is even the whole of my gain from that moment of stupidity... well then, you're entitled.'

'You've thought this out,' said Chel, unsteadily.

'Yes. But I've still got my eye on the ball, I promise you. We can work, both of us. We always had to in the past. We managed, we were content. The only difference here would be that the house we lived in would be our own, we'd have things like council tax and upkeep, but we wouldn't be paying rent. And even at its highest, I don't think this house would take all that we have. We'd have a safety net. And in the future, the option of taking out a part-mortgage if we needed to. If you really want it.'

For the first time since this conversation had begun, Chel turned to face him.

'Do *you* want it?'

Oliver turned round, resting his back against the rail so that he could see through into the studio, cluttered now with children's toys and discarded furniture, but full of potential.

'What do you think?'

'We could look at other places.'

'Why?'

Chel said,

'You've always run a mile from your family. Debbie would be just down the road.'

'If she stays. If it doesn't all go pear-shaped on her, it looked a bit dodgy to me. Silly twit!' He wasn't referring to Debbie. 'Anyway, of all my family, she's the best.'

'I don't think she'd consider that a particular compliment,' Chel tried to smile, but her heart was thumping so hard that she could hardly breathe, and she found it difficult.

Oliver reached out and drew her into his arms, holding her close.

'It's a way to go. I feel that it's a good way, even if it isn't quite what we had in mind at the start. So long as you'd be happy here. You like Deb, don't you?'

'I don't really know her,' said Chel. Her arms slipped round him, too, and they stood there for a moment or two, silent. Then Oliver broke the spell.

'In that case, it's time you did. Come on, let's go and have that tea - and don't be too enthusiastic, we don't want to end up paying over the odds and we haven't even had a survey yet. It may be falling apart for all we know.'

'It doesn't look like it.'

'You never know,' said Oliver, darkly, leading the way to the door. 'Let's not get carried away here. We're laying our heads on the block as it is. Let's not hand our families the axe.'

'So,' said Mr. Horsefall, when polite banalities had been exchanged and tea and biscuits were under way. 'What do you think of the place?'

'Edwin and I feel that we would like you to have it,' said Mrs. Horsefall, smiling sweetly at Chel. 'We've loved this house, and it needs young people. Do you sail at all? It's the perfect place.' She sighed. 'Our sailing days are long gone, alas, but we used to keep a boat on the river and lay her up here. So convenient for the winter maintenance.'

They had no idea, Chel realised, to whom they were speaking. So quickly did fame slip away. She saw Oliver warming to this little old lady who spoke so nostalgically of her sailing days, not in the least offended. Relieved, probably, knowing him.

'We've done a bit,' he said, now, and avoided Chel's eye.

'Oh, then you *must* get a boat! Doesn't your sister work at that new sailing school? They've moorings there, up in St. Erbyn Creek, I believe, isn't that so, Edwin?'

'Yes, they do, but aren't we getting away from the point a bit, Lucy? What do you think, young man, young lady? Is this the house for you?'

'We like it, yes,' said Oliver, temperately.

'And can you afford it? We've had a valuation, they reckon we can ask a quarter of a million.'

Spot on, thought Chel. Well, can we? How would Oliver answer that? With sums of money of that magnitude involved, she was keeping right out of it!

But Oliver had grown up with privilege, such sums didn't even make him blink. To him, anyway, the only use for money was to get what you needed out of life, that had become obvious only this afternoon. The big surprise had been that he saw any use for it at all.

'It needn't be a problem. We'd need a survey, of course, and then we can talk about it. How long do we have before you need to put it on the open market?'

Mr. Horsefall narrowed his eyes. No, he wasn't stupid.

'We can give you a couple of weeks. We need to be able to leave before the winter sets in. My wife's arthritis won't take another winter by the water.'

'So silly...' murmured Mrs. Horsefall. She doesn't want to leave, Chel suddenly thought. Poor lady, fancy having to abandon all this. Fancy having such pain that you felt you had to. She said, without quite intending to,

'Actually, we love it. And if we buy it, we'll pay cash.'

Oliver burst out laughing.

'Whose side are you on?' he asked. Mr. Horsefall was laughing too. Mrs. was smiling. Chel blushed.

'Well, I *know* you shouldn't say things like that when you want to strike a bargain, but what's the point of beating about the bush? We *do* love it, and let's face it, you know we do! And you won't take advantage and cheat us, will you?'

'Although,' said Oliver, later, as they drove back into the village, 'I wouldn't be so sure of that, if I was you. He's nobody's fool, that old bloke.'

'No,' said Chel. 'I trust him. The only problem may be if they don't think we really have the money.'

'You shouldn't be out without a keeper!' commented Oliver, with admiration.

But Chel had fallen for St. Erbyn, and looking around her, she saw plenty of opportunities for her future employment here. There was the pub, for instance, they might have a use for her training there, in the bar or the office. Or in the adjoining restaurant, or one of the several guest houses that they passed along the road out. Or if the plonker Tim did lose his head over Deb and wreck his tender marriage, maybe even running the residential side of the sailing school, but she did hope that would never happen. But whatever the outcome there, she knew that the wind was in their favour, and blowing hard. The feeling was a good one, if unfamiliar. She relaxed back into her seat with a little sigh of content.

Let it blow!

And in that lovely house, nothing would be living except themselves.

XXI

The summer flew past, there was so much to do. Chel began working in the craft shop almost before she had finished unpacking, and Oliver was kept fully occupied, working up his Greek sketches into full-scale oil paintings. Some of the more detailed drawings, Nonie advised, he should leave as they were and frame them up to fill in the corners, together with some of his other sketches. Not everyone, she pointed out, could afford Gifford Thomas's prices, but a lot of people, hopefully, would be wanting a piece of the action.

'And they're good,' she added. 'You've got plenty to play with here - you can work those up later if you want to.'

'Not if I've sold them, I can't,' Oliver pointed out.

'We'll put them through the fax machine downstairs. It's a photocopier as well, will that do?'

Oliver agreed that it would, and Chel spent a happy half-hour copying them off and putting the copies into a folder. The wonders of modern technology, she thought, as she did so; Van Gogh never did this.

'But perhaps he would have liked to be able to,' said Lisa, to whom she confided this fancy. 'When you've finished with that, can you get some more of that blue and white pottery out of the stockroom? It's walking out of the shop this week, must be something in the air.'

In the midst of all this activity, Debbie phoned once more. Oliver was away at the time, summoned up to London to do some advance publicity. He had gone, grumbling at the waste of time and invasion of space, with Nonie to see he didn't get away, so that it was Chel who answered the phone yet again.

'Well, maybe that's a good thing.' Debbie sounded doubtful. 'Only, I heard a bit of news, that I probably shouldn't have been told, and I'm wondering... well, it's been a bit on my mind.'

'If you shouldn't have been told, maybe you shouldn't tell me,' said Chel. She and Debbie, for one cause or another, were only the merest acquaintances after all.

'Probably, but I must tell *someone*. I did think of Oliver, but you'd be better, really. Oliver and Mum don't exactly see eye to eye, after all.' She went on, before Chel could prevent her - if she had been going to do so, she wasn't sure. 'Dad's bought a flat. Down on the harbour, in that new luxury apartment complex by the marina. He isn't living in it, but... I mean, if he isn't planning to, why would he buy it? And if he *is* planning to...'

The inference was obvious. Three cheers for Jerry, if so, Chel thought, but did not say. But maybe it was simpler.

'Perhaps it's on behalf of a client,' she suggested, reasonably.

'Well, I thought that, but my informant says not. It's the show flat, and he's bought it with all the furniture and things, and it's just sitting there... kind of empty, really. He never goes there. Just owns it.'

'So who told you?' asked Chel.

'Oh, I used to go out with the sales manager for the complex. I think he felt a bit awkward about being sworn to secrecy when he knew us all... so he passed the buck to me. Now, he sleeps at night and I don't. Typical man.'

Was there anyone in Embridge with whom Deb hadn't gone out? Chel wondered, perhaps unreasonably.

'So, what did you expect Oliver to do?' she asked.

'Good question. Listen to me, I suppose.'

'He wouldn't have. You ought to know that.'

'I know Mum can be a real pain sometimes,' said Debbie, apologetically. 'But she's tried to be a good Mum to us, she can't help being herself. It seems so unfair, if he's just going to... well, run out on her. Or maybe you don't think so?'

Oh yes, she can help it, thought Chel, and mentally added that it would serve the Dreaded Dot exactly right. She could hardly say that to Debbie, however, who had probably never been allowed to see the rough side of her mother. She temporised.

'If people are unhappy together to the point that one of them wants out, is it a good thing that they should be expected to stay together?' she asked, and then, because it seemed like the obvious question, 'Has he got a girlfriend, do you think?'

'I can't discover any trace of one, but then, people wouldn't tell me, would they? It's as if... as if he's just given up on everything and is planning to walk away.'

'But he hasn't done so yet.'

'No.'

For some reason, a reference to straws and camels' backs floated into Chel's mind, lingered a moment, and floated out again. She said,

'Then perhaps you're worrying unnecessarily. Maybe he thinks they should move somewhere smaller now you've all left home, maybe it's a surprise.' It sounded feeble, even to herself, and Debbie treated it with the contempt it no doubt deserved.

'And maybe the moon is made of blue cheese,' she said. 'Don't

344

patronise, Chel. I'm not a child.'

There was really no answer to that.

'Well, I'm sorry,' said Chel, wondering if she was. 'It's hard on you, and you shouldn't have been made to know, your friend needs a hard kick where it hurts, if you want my opinion. Have you mentioned it to Susan?'

'Are you joking?'

'Yes, I see what you mean.' Chel suppressed a sigh, she really didn't want to be dragged into Nankervis family politics, it wasn't her best subject. 'I don't know what to say, Deb, except I'm always here on the end of the phone if you need to talk.'

'I know,' said Debbie, unexpectedly. She hesitated. 'Chel...'

'What?' asked Chel, when she didn't go on.

'Oh, nothing. It doesn't matter. Thanks for listening.'

'Do you want me to tell Oliver when he gets back?'

'Better not. And Chel - I shouldn't have told you, really.' *And he shouldn't have told me*, hung unsaid in the air.

'Don't worry, your secret is safe with me.' She paused. 'I've always wanted to say that.'

'You're a star,' said Debbie, and they parted on a laugh.

When she had switched off the mobile, Chel sat for some moments without moving. There was an odd feeling up her arms, like caterpillars looping over her skin, she didn't like it. Debbie had almost told her something there, something she wasn't at all sure she wanted to know.

Other people's lives, she was fed to the teeth with them! And she had her own back now, and didn't need them either. Anxious to be rid of an uncomfortable aftertaste, she picked up the mobile again and dialled Judy's number. Time for a girlie chat to blow the shadows away.

Oliver arrived back the following day, in a foul mood. All the things that he would sooner have had forgotten had been dragged rattling out of the cupboard and had their bones exposed to the view of PR people whose ideas on publicity did not coincide in any way with his own. If they had owned a cat, he would undoubtedly have kicked it. As it was, Chel was the chief recipient of his attack of spleen. She bore it for a while, recognising that he needed to blow off steam, but when he reached the stage of slamming round the studio invading her precious day-off peace, something snapped. She leapt off the sofa, where she had been trying to read a particularly enjoyable book.

'If you didn't want those things dragged up and thrown in your face, then you shouldn't have done them in the first place!' she shouted at him. 'Stop being such a selfish bastard, and give me a bit of space!' She flung the book into the cushions and stomped off across the studio to the bedroom door. 'Just come off the walls, will you? I'm going to sort out some of those boxes if there's no peace and quiet to be had in here. You may have forgotten, but I haven't, that we've got a big move in a few weeks!' The bedroom door slammed behind her. It was the only place she could go to escape him.

Chel sat on the bed. She found that she was shaking, and was surprised. She had been looking forward to his return, and to hearing about London and the gallery, and what did she get? Unbridled artistic temperament slamming all over the place! She had missed him, it was a long time since they had been apart, and the studio was too small for the shenanigans - let's face it - of a spoiled brat! Oliver never had liked things going against him.

The truth was, she thought more calmly, Nonie's studio was too small for his wild personality, he needed a bigger arena. Once he had had the world, she found herself hoping that St. Erbyn would be big enough for him. At least he would have his own studio there. She sat for a few minutes thinking about it and feeling her mood softening. The house was as good as theirs, the deposit paid, everything under way. Oliver's father, managing the conveyancing for peanuts, had made no comment, surprisingly; maybe his own affairs were taking up his attention.

Would he really walk out on Dot? Chel found it difficult to imagine what might make him, when he had already put up with so much, but he was obviously up to something. Of course, there were other explanations for the flat, she had offered two of them herself, and there was at least one more - investment - but they all seemed thin in comparison to the obvious. Far more probably, he was just waiting until Deb was off his hands, along with Oliver and Susan, and his path free to walk. That had the ring of truth about it. If - *when* - that happened, it would really set the cat among the pigeons. Dot would go ballistic!

The thought was a pleasant one, and unkind as it might be, she owed no sympathy to Dot. Finding that she had stopped shaking, she got to her feet. No way was she going to go back into the studio until Oliver, too, had cooled off, so she might as well do what she had said she was going to do. In these boxes that were stacked around the walls and taking up space, there were a number of things that had no right to be there; searching for life's essentials, such as cutlery and plates, she had seen them lurking. Old magazines, she had certainly spotted, a chipped jug, a plastic box that she thought might contain the contents of the kitchen drawer - there had been several drawers in the kitchen, but Chel knew the one she meant. There had been nothing worth taking with them in *that*! Better get rid of it now. She began her task.

It was amazing, she found, what she and Judy seemed to have considered part of an essential life-support system. Old jam jars seemed to be favourite, she recalled that they had intended to go brambling in the autumn, and make loads of jam and jelly. The Rayburn would be perfect for it - but no. She would be far too busy moving in to bother with blackberries. She piled the jars on the bed, together with a bundle of clothes only fit for the jumble sale and the magazines that had started her off. What was it about moving house, she found herself wondering, that made you so insecure that you felt you had to hang on to each and every piece of might-be-useful rubbish that you owned? Tracy and Tom, she recalled, had done exactly the same. That had been jam jars too, Tracy maintained that they bred under the sink. She grinned at that thought, which led inexorably on to another. Unlike Jerry, her own parents had had a great deal to say on their proposed move, Creekside, as it was unimaginatively named, would cost more than the Wainwright family had ever seen in one place in their lives.

Perhaps it was improvident of them, she thought now. They would be living in an expensive waterside residence, which was really too big since there wouldn't ever be any children to fill it - she pressed tentatively on the sore spot, and winced - and they would, if Oliver's pictures failed to take off, be in a low income group. But by the same token, if there were to be no children, there was nothing to stop her going out and getting a job, even her mother must see that she would need to, on more grounds than one.

When the pile on the bed grew to be a small hill, Chel repacked the boxes and piled the junk into the one thus emptied and dragged it to the door. She was about to open it, braving Oliver's rampant ego, when she saw the plastic box had fallen to the floor and was trying to hide under the bed.

'Oh no, you don't!' She picked it up and was about to fling it on top of the jam jars when she paused. Judy had filled it, perhaps she ought to check it out before she slung it. Opening it, she tipped the contents out onto the bed.

The room seemed to go very still, time stretching out endlessly.

Slowly, with a strange reluctance, Chel reached out and touched the jumble on the bed. Old elastic bands, cocktail sticks, a squashed tube of glue, a small lump wrapped in kitchen paper... just the usual junk. Bin it, Chel, there's nothing of value here... nut she picked up the paper ball and unwrapped it, and the contents rolled out onto her palm.

A round shape, crusted with earth. She stared at it in surprise... and then she remembered. The day last year when she had found herself trapped in the field behind the house, the day Nonie had come over and altered their lives for ever... the day she had seen -

The day she had seen an old tree trunk lying on the ground, she told herself firmly. The rest was your fevered imagination, my girl, and you know it.

The wrapping paper had fallen to the floor. She put out a cautious finger and ran it across the thing in her palm. It wasn't a stone, it was metal of some kind under its earth crust, cylindrical in shape. Some old artefact, she remembered she had wondered if it might be valuable. It didn't look valuable. She wasn't even sure exactly what it was, but it might be a box.

Curiosity getting the better of her, Chel opened the bedroom door and ventured out into the studio. Oliver had disappeared, thank God. A quick look over the half-door showed that his car was still there, so he had probably gone for a walk to bring his blood pressure down, and a very good idea too. She went to the sink and turned on the tap, holding the cylindrical object under the stream of water, watching the surface earth washing away down the plug.

It was still pretty crusted even after that. She went back into the bedroom and rescued the chipped jug from the discard box and, filling it with warm water, dropped the object into it. It was definitely a box of some sort, she could see the join now, and a tiny hinge. How long had it been in the earth? It couldn't be all that long, surely.

Thirty years, said something in her head. Just over thirty years. Oliver's age, near enough, and -

'Oh, don't be ridiculous!' exclaimed Chel, and realised immediately afterwards that she had been talking to Matt Sutton's portrait on the wall. She blushed. Thank goodness nobody had seen *that*!

Leaving the jug on the draining board, she went back to her book, but it failed to hold her attention now. Before very long, she was back at the sink, reaching for a nailbrush, and working away at the little box, carefully so as not to damage it, cleaning the last of the earth away until it sat on the draining board as a recognisable object.

What she had, she found, was a small, round, pewter box, engraved on the lid with a thistle. The centre of the thistle was an oval orange stone, she thought it was what was called a cairngorm, a kind of rock-crystal much in vogue in the Highlands of Scotland.

Matt Sutton had been flying home from Scotland. She distinctly remembered somebody telling her so, although she couldn't recall whom. This thing was unmistakably Scottish.

After a few moments that seemed to go on for ever, she picked the box up and tried to open it, but it was stuck fast. All she achieved was a tiny grating noise.

'What on earth have you got there?' asked Oliver.

Chel jumped and swung round with a cry of surprise, to find him standing just behind her. His bad mood seemed to have evaporated, he was looking with interest at the box in her hand.

'Something I found in the earth,' she told him, wishing her heart would stop thumping, it made it hard to speak. 'Over the garden wall - ' She coughed. Oliver picked it out of her palm and examined it.

'Not an archaeological remain, that's for sure. Looks more like an example of tartan tourist tat. Whose garden wall?'

'Ours. Mr. Williams's. I was trying to open it.'

'It's corroded to hell,' said Oliver, peering at it. 'You need some WD40 on it. There's a can in that bag under the table.'

'I'll get it, shall I?' asked Chel, when he continued to study the box, and receiving no reply, went and hauled the old canvas bag, in which Oliver kept nearly as much rubbish as she had found in the bedroom, out from under the painter's trolley. She handed him the tin of WD40.

'I thought it was pretty,' she said, in defence of the box.

'If you like that sort of thing.' Oliver was working away, intent on what he was doing. He put the box down on the draining board, now oozing smelly oil.

'You could have put some paper under it,' grumbled Chel, doing so.

'Sorry. We need to leave it for a bit now.' He reached out, turning her round and drawing her against him. 'Sorry, Chel. It's just that I wanted to leave all that behind me, forget it.'

'You never will,' mumbled Chel, her face buried in his shirt.

'I'm beginning to realise that.' He rested his cheek against her hair. 'Oh Chel, I never meant it to be like this.'

'That's half the fun, isn't it?' Chel raised her head to look up at him. 'The surprises - they're not all bad, Oliver. Who cares that we never sailed round the world together? We'll do something else instead.'

Without consulting, they were edging towards the bedroom door. Oliver stumbled over the box that Chel had abandoned in the doorway.

'Ouch! What the hell is this?' The mood shattered, as Chel broke free and hurriedly pulled it out of the way.

'Sorry, sorry, load of old rubbish.'

'That sounds about right.' He caught her back into his arms and kissed her. There was a long, entirely satisfactory, interval. 'Funny about old rubbish,' he said, raising his head at last. 'It gets you every time.' And he kissed her again.

Some time later, Chel re-emerged from the bedroom, tousled and flushed and wrapped only in her dressing gown, to put the kettle on. While it was coming to the boil, she put teabags into two mugs and then picked up the box again, twisting it to and fro in her hands. This time, it seemed to give a little, and she found that by levering it with her fingernail, she could raise the lid a tiny bit, but not enough. She took it back into the bedroom with the tea, wrapped in its oily paper. Oliver, in a state of post-coital relaxation, couldn't work up any interest in it.

'It's only a box, Chel. If it's full of anything, it'll only be earth.'

'It's got a very tight-fitting lid,' Chel argued. 'If anything ever was in it, it's still in there.'

'Why should anything be in it?' He sipped his coffee, looking at her inquiringly over the rim of the mug.

'Well...' Chel was working at the lid, trying to prize it open with the end of the teaspoon. Oliver sighed, and took it from her.

'I can see we shall have no peace until you've seen inside your Pandora's box,' he said.

'Don't say that!' cried Chel. Oliver grinned at her, and placing his thumbs against the lid, pushed hard. It popped open and he handed the box back to her.'

'There you are, weakling. Christmas is here.'

Chel found that, now she could do so, she didn't really want to look inside. Perhaps it was Oliver's reference to Pandora's box, but she suddenly *knew* there was something there that was going to change the *status quo*, throw open doors, let in light on... well, what? The phrase *where the bodies are buried* leapt into her mind and shocked her.

'Well, aren't you going to open it after all that?' asked Oliver.

Chel took a deep breath. Silly to feel that she was on the edge of a great discovery, the little box wasn't big enough to hold anything that earth-shaking. Taking hold of the lid, she gently tried to lift it.

The tiny hinge was tight, in spite of the oil it resisted.

'Gently does it,' said Oliver, interested now in spite of himself. 'Don't force it, work the oil in a bit, work it up and down - that's it.'

Then finally it gave way. The lid opened up properly, and they looked inside the box.

A twist of rather grubby cotton-wool was the first thing they saw, and it was Oliver, not Chel, who put out a hand and gently removed it. Underneath it was a bed of crimson velvet, cleaner this time, and nestling in it, a tiny circle. A ring.

'Treasure trove,' said Oliver. Chel didn't answer. She put out a cautious finger and gently poked the ring, then lifted it out, turning it in her fingers.

'Oh, wow!' she said.

The cotton-wool and the tightness of the lid had protected the ring over the years, and it was of white gold and so hadn't tarnished. It lay on Chel's palm as clean and bright as the day it had been bought in an Edinburgh jeweller's shop, a simple half-circle of emeralds and sapphires, glinting like seawater and as deep.

'Wow...' she repeated, on a long breath.

So, what she had thought she had seen had been a true seeing, the little plane had lain there, broken and smashed and as dead as the man whose bloody corpse was lifted from it. And this... this had rolled, from his pocket or from some resting place within the plane, and fallen, unnoticed, to the ground, and no doubt some heavy-footed paramedic had placed his great boot on it and pushed it into the soft earth, and there it had stayed... ruining a life.

Theo came into her mind then, the sadness in his eyes when he had spoken of Nonie selling the villa, and the pain in his voice... and now, maybe it wasn't too late, if Nonie could only be made to understand.

'You're crying,' said Oliver, gently. 'Why're you crying?'

'For the waste,' said Chel, and wept openly.

Susan was on the phone this time, scorning the written word as inadequate and incoherent with misery. And this time, Chel was almost prepared. Thanks to their new friendship with the Horsefalls, what happened in St. Erbyn, however Debbie tried to brush it under the carpet, now found its way back to St. Ives, even had the news not already arrived via Embridge. The repercussions were going to be widespread.

'She's done it,' said Susan. 'The little tart's done it - she's just done what she's always done and walked in and taken what she wanted - yes, just like Oliver! - and poor Lesley's come home in *pieces*. She says Tim tried to kill her to get her out of the way - '

'Oh, come on Susan, you don't believe that!'

But Susan, like the unknown Lesley, was past reason.

'And now she's going to make this *dreadful* mistake and marry that awful man! And Mummy and Daddy have had the most dreadful row over it and he's walked out, and the worst of it is it turns out he's been planning it for ages, just like Deb, and - '

Chel interrupted again.

'He isn't an awful man, Susan. It was all accidental, and Lesley must know it. She's just over-reacting.' She sounded impatient because the fire at the sailing school, in which Lesley Howells had almost died, had shaken her badly. She had smelled burning talking to Deb months ago and the implications made her sick.

No! I don't want it!

'She's ruined everything!' said Susan, presumably meaning Debbie rather than Lesley Howells. 'What are my children going to think?' That sounded more like Susan, thank goodness. Chel said, with what even to herself was a distinct lack of sympathy,

'That'll depend on how you explain it to them. And let Deb alone. It wasn't her fault and she *didn't* make a play for Tim Howells, it was all his own work.'

'You would say that! I suppose you're going to say next that it was all too big for them!'

Outsize romance. Well, perhaps.

'Don't be so silly,' said Chel.

Jerry himself rang later, and spoke to Oliver, for the second time in two days.

'I understand Susan has already told you that Dorothy and I have agreed on a separation.' If *agreed* was exactly the word, he thought wryly. Dot certainly hadn't agreed.

Since the only comment that Oliver could think of was *oh, good!* he said nothing, and Jerry, who would dearly have liked a bit of help, was forced to go on.

'She's talking about disinheriting Debbie. Well, I'm not happy either, given the circumstances, but I can't condone that. I've moved into a flat on the seafront, I'm not sure if it will be permanent but it's convenient for now. I'll give you the address, if you care to write it down.' Oliver gestured to Chel for a pencil and paper, making scribbling gestures in the air, and while she searched for them, Jerry continued. 'I'm afraid it isn't going to be easy for the girls, I'm relying on your support. You know, if they don't, that it's been on the cards for years.'

Did he know that? Oliver wondered. Truth to tell, he hadn't been paying that much attention, but now was possibly not the time to say so.

'I'm sorry, if you are,' he said stiffly.

'I'm not.'

'What?' asked Oliver, startled. Jerry continued as if nothing out of the way had been said.

'There'll be no divorce, there's no chance I want to marry a third time, but we shan't live together from now on. So far as her cronies in the church are concerned, she can stay whiter than white. My back's broad, I'll take the flack.'

'That's hardly fair, when she's the one who's been the pain in the arse,' Oliver suggested, suddenly and unexpectedly angry for his father.

'Has she, Oliver? Who let the situation arise in the first place?'

'She did, from what Nonie says.'

'Ah... Nonie.' Jerry paused. 'Well, she always was partisan.' He said it dismissively, as if Nonie's view of things hardly mattered.

'And her behaviour when you were down here was unforgivable,' Oliver continued. 'Why not admit it Dad - she's a prize cow, always was, always will be! Although that's a terrible insult to cows.' He hesitated. 'What finally made you call time, anyway? Was it this business with Deb?'

Jerry sighed.

'That was the final straw, I suppose. I couldn't stand her bigotry and hypocrisy any longer. She sits in judgement on matters of which she knows nothing whatever, and taking up a stand of such intransigence is going to solve nothing. And she harmed *you* unspeakably.'

'The story of her life, though, isn't it? I know best, and bollocks to the rest of you! She's done enough damage to everyone in her time, no messing, I'm not the sole sufferer.'

'I can understand your resentment,' said Jerry, quietly.

'Well, good, because it leaves no room for sympathy for her.'

'I don't believe she'll ask for, or expect, any sympathy from you.'

If that was meant as a rebuke, it missed its mark.

'The only pity is, you didn't do it years ago,' said Oliver.

'I might have done, if I hadn't believed that would only compound the damage.' Jerry spoke bitterly. 'Having already messed up the childhood of you and of Susan, I thought I'd leave Debbie alone.'

Oliver, silenced for once, handed the mobile to Chel, who had come back with the pencil and paper.

'You speak to him. I only rile him.'

He walked away, back to his interrupted work, and picked up a brush, but didn't use it. When Chel finished her conversation with Jerry, she found him just staring at his unfinished picture with eyes that saw something much darker.

'What's the matter?'

'Something Dad said. That he messed up my childhood, and Susan's. But he didn't. I did.'

Chel rubbed her nose, thoughtfully.

'I think that depends on where you measure first causes from,' she said. '*She* began it, wrecking your mother's marriage. *She* did nothing to ease the jealousy between you and Susan. *She* created most of the problems with you, you were only a child. Other women manage to be

353

stepmothers without starting World War III. And your father did nothing sensible about it. How does that make it your fault?'

'Children grow up. I began to enjoy it - making waves. I was *horrible*, but I never saw it before.'

Chel said,

'You blame yourself, your father blames *him*self, I expect Helen blames *her*self, in fact I know that she does. But really, the blame lies fair and square exactly where you've placed it all these years, and don't you ever think otherwise. She ruined everything, and you know why? Because she wanted what Helen had, and it's exactly that simple.'

Oliver turned to look at her at last.

'You said that very vehemently.'

'Because it's true. And you're the very last person I'd expect to be making excuses for her.'

She hadn't expected Oliver to be so upset by the break-up of his father's second marriage, and neither had he. They looked at each other, each of them trying to work this one out.

'It's Deb, I think,' said Oliver, finding the answer without posing the question. 'It's because it's over Deb. She was the only one of the three of us who ever cared about us all as a family. It's all wrong that it should be her that finally blew it apart.'

'Whatever Deb's done, she's done with her eyes open, of that you may be certain,' said Chel, with decision. 'Oliver, what's got into you? Since when have you even cared?'

Oliver laughed then.

'It's an odd feeling... you wouldn't understand it, your family's never going to do it. But even with all be bad feeling between us we were... a unit, I suppose I mean, and now we're not. It's very unsettling.'

'Tough,' said Chel, and then, speaking without thinking, added, 'It's a time for new beginnings anyway. They're all around us.'

'Oh, really, Madame Arcati? And what makes you say that?'

Chel grinned at him, mischievous, lightening the suddenly heavy atmosphere.

'Oh, I took an augury when I gutted the herring last night, of course. Don't be ridiculous, Oliver! What do you think?'

'What do *I* think? God knows!' said Oliver, and looked uneasy.

'And if you really want to know,' said Chel, finishing the conversation, 'it's not Deb you should be sorry for; if you ask me, Deb is the ultimate survivor - after you, that's to say - it's Susan.'

'Good God,' said Oliver, outraged, and dipped his brush in the prepared paint without further comment.

That shut him up all right, Chel thought, as she resumed the book she had been reading. On the other hand it was comforting to know that he wasn't totally without family feeling. One problem, however, remained.

Nonie.

Between them, she and Oliver had already been very hard on poor Nonie, reopened old wounds and in all probability thoroughly cut up her peace and made her fairly miserable, and all she had given them in return was help and kindness. Love, even. Now, there was this other thing. The ring, sitting in its box on the bookcase, glowed in Chel's mind as if it was radioactive. Oliver, who of course knew nothing of the events that had led to her discovery of it, seemed to take a simplistic view of *finders, keepers*, but Chel knew that wasn't right. The ring was Nonie's, no question. The problem was, how to give it to her.

Sometimes, Chel had the feeling that events had gained such momentum that she could safely leave it to solve itself. At others, she felt responsible, as if Matt Sutton's eye was on her, reproachfully - which was unfair, since she had felt no breath of him since Oliver had painted his picture. No, he had moved on, but the unfinished business that he had left behind him was still here. Fairly and squarely in her hands, and she had this strange feeling that he had trusted her with it, so that to ignore it would be to let him down, which was silly when she had never even known him. Only here, living in his studio, she almost felt that she *had* known him, and that was the silliest thing of all.

All the time, the move to St. Erbyn was getting closer and closer. There was a lot to organise, Chel found, which had to be done around her working hours, and which meant liaising with Susan to arrange for their furniture and other goods in Embridge to be brought out of store and transported on the given date, making sure that all the documents relating to the sale of securities arrived on time and that Oliver signed them, checking whether the Horsefalls were planning to leave enough carpets and curtains for them to manage for a while when they did finally move in, and in and around all this, arranging transport and insurance for Oliver's pictures as they went, bit by bit, from Nonie's studio to the Ladbourne Gallery and answering an increasing number of telephone calls from Giff Thomas's assistant, with none of which did she get much help from Oliver. He was far too busy, working like a demon as time began to run out on him, exhausted by the time the light faded in the windows, only wanting to flop down in his chair and fall asleep in front of the television and certainly not wanting to be bothered with practicalities. It made it all too simple to put awkward problems that weren't really her own to the back of her mind. In the end, Pandora's box simply got packed with everything else, and the outcome postponed.

Much later, Chel found herself wondering if her feeling that things would sort themselves had been a true feeling, and if so, how was she meant to tell the difference between that and mere procrastination, for in fact, the problem did solve itself, the day that they moved into Creekside.

Once again, she didn't rely on much help from Oliver, knowing perfectly well that he would disappear into his new studio and do his own thing, and given the fact that his big one-man show was now only weeks away, that was fair enough. Fortunately, Judy offered her help at the St. Erbyn end, and Nonie helped with the clearing of her own studio. By eleven o'clock, Chel was ready to be on her way - Oliver had already gone on, his car loaded with the last of his painting gear, just in case the van from Embridge was early.

'You've been a star,' said Chel, hugging Nonie as she prepared to leave. 'I don't know how we would have managed, and I know it's been a bugger for you, having us here.'

'Well, I won't say I'm not glad to have my space back, but it hasn't been so bad, you know.' Nonie hugged her back. ' Would you like me to come over this evening, see how you're settling in and bring a takeaway and a couple of bottles to christen the place - give you a break, and some help if you still need it? May I?'

'That sounds a wonderful idea,' said Chel.

The thought that at least she wouldn't have to worry about an evening meal was the main thing to sustain her through the day that followed. Moving house is never easy, and even with both Judy and a rather subdued Debbie to help, today was no exception. By the time the furniture van from Embridge ground away on the road to Helston, everyone was hot, tired and more than ready to quit, and much as she had appreciated their help, Chel was relieved when her two helpers climbed aboard Judy's motorbike and, waving frantically, roared off up the lane in the wake of the van. They seemed to have hit it off, she thought reflectively. Perhaps not surprising, they had a certain amount in common. Heredity no doubt. How strange!

The roar died away and blessed peace settled around her. The tide was in and the water making soft bubbling and sucking noises against the retaining wall, a gull swept up the creek on wide white wings, it was so still she imagined she heard the rush of air as it passed. She gave a sigh of pure satisfaction, and turned away to go in search of Oliver, whom she had hardly seen all day.

Up in the studio, he hadn't been idling about either. The wooden walls glowed with colour from his pictures, now hung for the first time, and a new canvas waited on one easel, a half-finished one on the other. The smart painter's trolley that had been a studio-warming present from Nonie was neatly arranged with palette, brushes, knives and tubes of paint ready to start work, and all his boards, mouldings, canvases and paper were stacked around the walls or on the shelves.   Oliver himself was on the balcony, leaning on the rail watching the creek, and the sideways glimpse of the river. He looked, Chel thought, watching him undetected, utterly content. This was the first time she had seen his pictures hung like this; Nonie's studio was, of course, hung with her own. Seeing them all together she realised, what she hadn't realised before, how he had changed. The early ones were wild, angry, full of frustrations, but the ones he did now were strong, full of power. The common factor was light. Oliver, she saw, had from the start painted light, as if it was a tangible element. These were not necessarily the best of his work, but they were impressive even so.

'Hullo,' he said, when she came to lean beside him. 'All right?'

'Mmm. You?'

'Yeah. Fine.' If he was tired, he wouldn't admit to it, she knew. 'We must get a couple of chairs up here, so we can sit and enjoy this.'

'And a table, so you can draw out here.'

'Ours...' said Oliver, making it sound almost like a prayer. 'Feel good?'

'Yes, and Nonie'll be here soon,' said Chel.

'That's good.' He meant it, she saw, the resentment he had felt last summer finally exorcised.

'Shall we go down?' she asked, smiling.

Oliver took her hand without answering, and joined thus, they crossed the floor to the top of the stairs. The door to the studio closed with a click behind them.

Nonie arrived later, when Chel and Oliver were relaxing in comfort, getting the feel of their unfamiliar home. The furniture from the bungalow, which Chel had always rather despised because, she now realised, of its surroundings, looked really rather nice, she decided. Oliver's father had paid for it, after all, and Susan had chosen it because she herself hadn't had the heart at the time, so on both counts it was good stuff. Dining table and chairs, three piece suite, coffee table, a sideboard and Oliver's old bookcase. Not a lot in this big room, but *theirs*. She had never thought she would look on it with so much affection, or realised how sick and tired she was of other people's furnishings, even Nonie's. By the time they had unpacked the small personal items and put them around, and hung a few pictures - those, they weren't short of these days! - it was going to be a pleasant room.

'They were so good to us - your family. I never realised,' she said, and found to her surprise that she almost choked on the words. 'They must have thought I was such an ungrateful little cow.'

'They just didn't want you to let them down in front of the neighbours,' said Oliver, with a quizzical look.

'No - no, I won't let you say that. Your stepmother, maybe, but your father and Susan... and look how wonderful Debbie was today.'

'Your trouble is, you're tired and it makes you sentimental,' said Oliver, but he didn't say it nastily. 'Do you want to go down to the pub to eat? There doesn't seem to be much on offer here.'

'Nonie said she'd bring something over,' said Chel, and right on cue, Nonie arrived.

She came in surrounded by a haze of curry, loaded with fragrant brown paper bags, clinking bottles and a square parcel.

'This is going to need reheating, it's cooled off a bit on its journey - not that one, that's not edible, it's a housewarming present.' She let the square parcel fall onto the sofa. 'Lead me to the stove, let's get this stuff warming and uncork the wine, and then you can open it.' She looked around her. 'My word, you have been busy - it looks great!'

'We were fortunate in that we didn't really have that much furniture,' said Chel, taking the bags of Indian takeaway from her. 'Come through and see the kitchen - it's brilliant. Huge! I can't believe it's all really ours.'

'Actually,' said Nonie, when the house had been admired and Oliver's studio inspected and they were back in the living room, 'it isn't really so much a housewarming present.' She stood with the parcel in her hands, looking down at it, biting her lip. 'It's yours already, Oliver. It was your christening present.' And she dumped it into his lap without ceremony, and immediately turned aside.

Oliver tore away the paper. The picture was in his hands, an autumn wood bright as a jewel, crimson and bronze and gold. He saw the signature in the corner, *Sutton*, and knew at once that he was holding a small fortune. It took a lot to render him quite silent, but this did it. He simply stared at it, for such a long time that Chel asked,

'What is it?' simply to break the silence. Oliver looked up then.

'It seems a little late... for a christening present.'

Nonie, still with her back turned, said,

'She sent it back when she married your father.'

'But what is it?' Chel repeated, although by this time she had guessed. Oliver handed it over to her without taking his eyes off Nonie.

'Why would she do that? It must have been worth a bomb, even then.'

'She thought that he... that Matt was an unsuitable influence for a Christian household,' said Nonie, and swallowed, hard. She added, through a throat gone suddenly tight, 'And she hated me, I saw through her, you see. She was filled with spite. She wanted to get me out of your life... and she did.'

'You didn't stay out though, did you?' said Oliver, with sudden satisfaction. He scowled, darkly. 'Bloody woman! Burning at the stake would be too good for her!' He paused. 'I don't suppose you know - my father's left her.'

'He took his time,' said Nonie, choking: she hadn't meant to get emotional, and was angry with herself. There was a pause. Oliver stood up and went over to her, putting his arms around her, drawing her head into his shoulder. 'Don't cry. Please. It's water under the bridge.'

'No, it isn't,' said Chel, clearly. All this time she had been sitting with the first original Sutton she had seen on her lap, running her fingers round the frame, feeling... what? She said, slowly, not knowing quite where it came from, 'Nonie, did Matt Sutton suffer from blackouts? Dizzy spells?'

'No, of course he didn't,' said Nonie, raising her head and sniffing. 'They'd never have let him fly if he did.'

'Well, I think you're wrong,' said Chel. Her fingers ran across the textured paint on the canvas. Yes, she was sure now. 'There's something that should have come out at the autopsy... and didn't. Maybe it wasn't bad yet, maybe he didn't realise... but that's what killed him. Nothing to do with you.'

'He had a *blackout*?' said Nonie. She moved away from the comfort of Oliver's arms, needing space to absorb this new idea. 'How can you possibly tell?'

'I don't know,' said Chel. 'I just can.'

'I think it's called psychometry,' murmured Oliver, in the background. 'You said you couldn't do it.'

'I said I'd never tried,' Chel contradicted him. She set the picture aside. 'It's beautiful, Nonie. Are you certain you want to part with it?' She wanted to change the subject.

'It's been in the bank for years, waiting. Chel - '

'Don't - please,' said Chel. She got to her feet. 'There's something else. I'll get it, it's upstairs in the bedroom.' She almost ran from the room. Nonie and Oliver looked at each other.

'Did she really mean that? She's not just... well, guessing?' Nonie was hesitant.

'Why should she?' Oliver picked up the picture and balanced it on the empty mantelpiece. 'God, he was a good painter, Nonie. I've never seen his work before. It's amazing.' Disquieting too, when he recalled the picture he himself had painted.

Nonie was silent. Chel was right, if Matt had had a blackout, it was nothing to do with her. It absolved her of that guilt at least, and vindicated what Mac had always maintained. It was nobody's fault... just bad luck, and now, they would never know why it should have happened. They might guess, if they had enough medical knowledge, but where would be the point? It was all history now. She felt a sudden sense of relief, like the easing of a deep pain after years of suffering. Absolution...

Chel came back down the stairs, hesitantly. She held Pandora's box in her hand.

'I've no more grounds for this than I had for the other,' she said. 'I just feel... well, this is yours, Nonie. I think he was bringing it back to you and I think... I think it answers your last question. I can only tell you that I feel it so strongly... you don't have to believe me.' She held out the little box and dropped it into Nonie's hand. 'Open it. It doesn't bite.'

Nonie hesitated.

'Chel...'

'Don't *ask* me,' said Chel, suddenly urgent. 'I can't tell you, and I wish it wasn't so. I never asked for it.' She turned her head away. 'Just open it.'

Nonie exchanged a glance with Oliver, but he simply shrugged his shoulders. She lifted the lid. The ring lay gleaming on its bed of red velvet. She swallowed. Oh God - where had this come from?

Chel said,

'It isn't an engagement ring, or even a wedding ring. It's an eternity ring. It means, until death us do part... or for ever. He knew you didn't want to marry him. I think that this was his way of telling you it was all right, he understood why... and that he didn't care, he loved you anyway. But you only have my word for it.'

Nonie picked the ring from its velvet bed, her sight too blurred to see it properly. It was Oliver in the end who rescued it and slipped it onto her finger.

'Oh God,' she said. 'I'm going to howl my eyes out, I'm so sorry.'

'Howl then, be our guest,' said Oliver, adding prosaically, 'and when you've done, can we get at that curry? My stomach thinks my throat has been cut!'

Nonie choked.

'I suppose I should say at this point, *I want to be alone*, but I don't. And curry sounds wonderful.' She ended on a gasp, and then the tears came. Years of them, dammed up until they drowned the world. She cried for Matt, and for Jerry and Helen, for Oliver and for Susan and for poor Peachey with his twisted mind, who had set the whole chain of events in motion, for all the things that should be past grief, crying it all away. After a while, Chel got up and went into the kitchen, coming back with a roll of kitchen paper and another bottle.

'That'll do,' she said, and Nonie knew that she was right. She drew a shuddering breath, and dabbed at her eyes with a length torn from the roll, sniffing.

'God, that feels better. I feel... *cleansed,* I think is the word. And as if I've been on the funny stuff, which I haven't for years. Maybe I should have.'

Oliver poured the wine and handed her a glass.

'Drink that down you. And will you take some advice?'

'Depends what it is.' She took the wine, hiccuping on a sob. He looked down at her, serious, the bottle in his hand.

'When you've got used to it... go back to Greece. You don't owe Matt any more, and he wouldn't want you to feel that you did. He isn't the only unfinished business around, is he?'

'I'm not the marrying kind,' said Nonie, from habit.

'Then don't marry, it isn't obligatory. But don't waste your life any more - don't waste Theo's life. He's a good man, Nonie.'

Nonie looked at Chel.

'Should I?'

'Look, I'm not a crystal ball merchant.' Chel picked up her own glass. 'But I say, go for it. Give it a whirl. All the other clichés. After all, is there a good reason why not?'

Nonie looked at the ring, gleaming like a band of seawater on her finger. She thought about Greece and about Dimitrios Theodorakis, and she knew that they were right. She raised her glass.

'To Matt,' she said. 'Bless his dear memory.' Her voice shook. 'And to tomorrow.'

The three glasses clinked together.

'To tomorrow,' they all said, solemnly.

'And to dinner sometime tonight,' added Oliver, and broke the spell with laughter.

*

Nonie drove home later, in spite of Chel's pressing invitation to stay, feeling at last the need to be alone. Calmed a little by a curry supper and the new and surprising discovery that her godson and his wife

361

really loved her, she also suspected that she might be in shock. Life, she hoped, didn't come a lot weirder than this evening.

Almost, she was tempted to go to the studio, but knew that it would be a mistake. It would do no good to go and wallow in the past, now was the time to start looking to the future. The person that she had been then had long been gone, held back only by the gossamer threads spun by fear of her possible responsibility, and by the unfinished story of Matt. Both over tonight, tidied away into *then*. What she needed to confront was *now*.

Back in her cottage, which belonged very definitely to *now*, she found that, tired though she was, she was too hyped-up to sleep, and went, as was her habit, into the little studio that she had made of an old dairy, and tried to do some work to bring herself back to normal.

Tonight, it didn't work. The ring on her finger kept catching the light, and thus her eye, and after a while she put down her brushes and simply sat on a stool, letting her thoughts run free.

She believed Chel, she realised - whether simply because she wanted to do so or because the belief was genuine hardly mattered. On neither count, was it susceptible to proof. Matt might very easily have had, if not a physical, a mental problem, and Giff would be the first to confirm that. Chel had said later on that she had simply got the feeling of blackness, maybe a stroke or an aneurysm, it was a strange thought that, even if he had come home safely that day, there might have been no future for them. But they would never *know*. Which brought her to the ring.

She twisted it round her finger, watching the green and blue stones glitter under the light. Eternity... until death do us part, Chel had said. Or for ever. Well, death had done its work, certainly, and as for *for ever*... who knew about for ever, anyway?

Was Oliver right, she wondered. Should she go back to Greece, to Ayios Giorgos, to dear Theo? Was that the right way to go? Chel had refused to be drawn, if so be she had powers she had refused to put them to use, and Nonie didn't blame her. People could put too much faith in fortune-telling - if that's what it amounted to, but was it?

She remembered what Chel had actually said. *Is there a good reason why not?* Well, was there?

No, there wasn't. All through her relationship withTheo, Matt's shadow had blocked the sun. Maybe when she saw clearly, she wouldn't want to continue that relationship, but surely, she owed it to him to find out. Oliver was right, he was a good man, and she had used him badly.

Nonie lifted her left hand and held it against her face, feeling the hard little circle against her cheekbone. Matt. Darling Matt. Maybe we'll meet again, when *for ever* comes, but in the meantime I have to get on with living.

Lowering her hand, she took the ring from her finger and replaced it on her right hand.

XXII

Since the dissolution of their marriage, although Jerry and his first wife, Helen, had spoken to each other, and occasionally even met when Oliver's behaviour had made it necessary, they had kept out of each other's personal space in order to maintain the semblance of friendship, so that when Jerry drove up the drive to Helen's converted barn home one Friday afternoon in November, it was the first time that he had been there. Nor was he either invited or expected, and maybe it was that alone that had given him this prickling feeling of nervousness, or maybe it was something else. Nonie, for instance, would unhesitatingly have classified it as guilt.

He sat in his car for a minute or two, taking in the low, red-brick house with its latticed windows and beautiful garden, and knew, as on one level he had always known, that Helen had managed very well without him. Her confidence in her own future had been entirely justified, and he couldn't imagine now how he had ever felt he needed to denigrate it into a hobby. Except that he didn't need to imagine, he told himself, he knew. Dot. Dot had broken up his marriage, alienated his son, and now had tried to outlaw his daughter - he couldn't think of Debbie as Dot's in any way, not after the terrible things that she had said and, let's face up to it, done. As for her other daughter, Jerry was deeply sorry for her, she was adrift, feeling that she belonged nowhere. Her loyalties were torn in two directions, she felt herself to be welcome in neither camp. Dot's work again. How had he ever allowed her to do it?

Apathy, he answered himself, more honestly than he had done for many years. It was easier to go with Dot's manipulative but soothing domesticity than to handle Helen's temperamental individuality. It was easier to leave the children to the women than to take charge himself. It was easier to let the whole family thing look after itself and to take refuge in work and in the making of money to keep them all in luxury and to consider that the justification. Well, he had the money, plenty of it, and his son refused to touch a penny of it, even in dire need, so a lot of good it had achieved. A fat bank balance and a lonely flat, and an alienated family scattered to the four winds, that was what he had to show for his life. Not much, when you came to think about it.

As he sat there, Helen appeared under a rose-arch to the side of the house and paused, framed in the fading leaves, staring at him in astonishment. He hoped it was just astonishment. He opened the car door and got out onto the drive, they looked at each other for a long, long moment.

Helen. Lovely Helen, whom he had wantonly thrown away. She stood there straight and slim, dark hair just brushing her shoulders in an expensively-cut curve and falling in an unfamiliar feathery fringe across her forehead, dressed in jeans and a loose plaid shirt that, from this distance, made her look still in her twenties. There was a smear of clay across one cheek, and her dark blue eyes, even from where he stood, were angry.

'What are you doing here?' she demanded furiously, and strode forward to meet him - to see him off, if her expression was anything to go by. He held out his hands, palms out, as if to fend her off.

'No - hold your horses a minute. Listen first.'

Helen stopped, just out of reach. Seeing him there, in her sanctuary and after what she knew to have happened, made her feel immediately threatened, her hackles rose like an angry cat's, defensive.

'You have nothing to say that I want to listen to. Just because you've at last seen through that - that *tart*, throwing herself at you the way she did, and you a married man, don't think you can come wheedling your way back into my good graces! I've nothing to say to you, Jerry Nankervis, except that it serves you *bloody* right!'

'I don't want to wheedle myself back into your good graces,' said Jerry. 'And don't start on me, I've had it up to *here* already!' He made an expressive gesture. 'Moreover, it's hardly fair when you remember that every time she came near us we had a row over your behaviour - '

' - over *her* behaviour!' Helen riposted, quick as a flash.

There was a pause, giving Jerry time to remember that he wasn't here to quarrel.

'Listen,' he said, taking a deep breath. 'All I want is to make sure that you don't hurt our son any more by not going to his private view. Nothing more sinister, I promise you.'

Helen was still prickly. Her lip curled.

'Any more than I have? Or any more than *you* have?' she asked, viciously.

'All of us have,' said Jerry. The argument was taking him back down the years. He wanted to take her in his arms, to hold her, to calm her. Too late. Too late, like every other bloody thing. Two sad words. Too late.

'Except wonderful Anona Fingall,' said Helen, bitterly, and to her own surprise and Jerry's horror, burst into tears. She said, furiously, 'And don't think I'm crying over *you!*'

'The thought never entered my head,' said Jerry, virtuously. He took her elbow. 'Come on Helen, let's not brawl out here in the cold. Can we go inside?'

Helen shook off his hand and stalked towards the front door, her head high. She didn't exactly invite him in, but she stormed through the door without closing it behind her, and Jerry took this as permission to follow her. Closing it carefully behind him, he heard rattling and banging from another open door at the back of the house, and the gush of water from a tap. Ah, tea. The universal panacea. That sounded better. He waited a minute or two to give her time to pull herself together and then followed the sound.

Helen was standing with her back to him, staring angrily out of her kitchen window. Beside her on the worktop, the electric kettle hissed gently to itself. She didn't turn her head, but she did speak.

'Oh, you're still here, are you?'

Jerry stepped up behind her, putting his hands on her shoulders. He had been going to apologise for barging in on her, and was astonished to hear his own voice saying,

'You've cut your hair. I like it.'

She shrugged him off and turned round. Tearstains had further smudged the clay on her face, she looked a proper urchin, he thought, no, she looked beautiful, and felt his heart treacherously softening. Oh no - oh no! He'd as soon try to stroke a wildcat! He stepped back.

'That wasn't an object with me,' she said. Her voice was deeply sarcastic. 'When you get to a certain age, long hair simply makes you look stupid. Or old. A divorced woman in her fifties needs to watch her image, so my American friends tell me.' Jerry winced.

'Ouch, Helen, lay off will you? You didn't have to be divorced - you're the one who walked out, remember?'

'Oh, really? It was that simple?'

'Look, what do you want me to do, wave a white flag?'

'It wouldn't be inappropriate,' she said, and flounced away to take mugs from a cupboard. Two mugs, so maybe things were not so bad. Jerry decided not to push his luck and withdrew to the far side of the island cooker unit. Something solid between them seemed a good idea.

Helen made tea and, taking a mug in each hand, marched through into the next room, a living-room that faced over the garden. Jerry, again without invitation, followed her.

It was a beautiful room, he immediately realised: no resemblance to the austerely elegant drawing room to which he had become used over the years, without so much as a cushion out of line and not even a newspaper left lying around. This was a room for comfort, for living in,

366

people came here, not like his own house. He felt unexpectedly jealous of the unknown visitors. It was furnished with deep, soft chairs that looked squashed as if they were used to being sat in, pale wood bookcases jammed with books, and curtains to the floor in a soft turquoise framing french doors and a wonderful view. There was a beautiful modern seascape hanging over the fireplace, gouache in cool shades of blue and green and purple.

'Isn't this one of Oliver's?' Jerry stood in front of it, looking up, eyes narrowed.

'Since he's signed his name in the corner, it seems a fair guess,' said Helen. She put one of the mugs on a coffee table, and threw herself into an armchair with the other, spilling it onto her gaudy shirt. She looked like a disgruntled child - in fact, was behaving like one, Jerry decided. He was at a loss as to how to stop her without precipitating a major row, which he certainly didn't want.

It must have dawned on Helen at about the same moment that she was behaving irrationally. She sat up, hauling a cushion into place behind her and trying not to spill her tea again.

'Do sit down, Jerry. Oliver gave me that last Christmas. I think that Chel put him up to it, as a matter of fact, but I love it anyway.'

'He's very good,' said Jerry, sitting down.

'What would you know?' Residual bitterness sounded in her voice, but she immediately looked sorry. 'Jerry, forgive me, won't you? I'm behaving like a spoiled child. I'm sorry.'

This was so much what he had just thought for himself that Jerry couldn't deny it, even in the interests of peace. He made a comical face instead.

'More like a hellcat, actually. Look Helen, I don't blame you. You must understand that. I just don't want...' He broke off, dimly recognising that exquisite tact was needed here, and tact of any quality had never been his strong point. Helen took the ball out of his hands and ran with it.

'You don't want me taking what happened in the past out on Oliver? Well, I'm sorry Jerry - I'm sure you're right, but... I *can't.*'

'Can't what?' asked Jerry, quietly. Helen said, not looking at him,

'Go into a room full of strangers and acquaintances, and worse, journalists, and particularly with you, and then have to meet Nonie face to face.'

'But you were sent an invitation.' It wasn't a question. Helen gave a very slight shrug.

'Yes, of course I was. I suppose Chel put me on the list, and Gifford's secretary sent it out... but I can't go.'

367

'It was Oliver, not Chel, who put you there,' said Jerry, quietly. Helen stared at him.

'I don't believe you! Oliver wouldn't, he hates me.'

'Don't be so certain. And they want you to be there.'

'I still can't go.'

'Helen, it was all a very long time ago. I'm sure Nonie has forgotten by this time.'

Helen stared at him.

'Oh, come on, Jerry! Get real! We were best friends. She's my son's godmother, for God's sake! With Oliver in front of her every day, how can she have *forgotten*?'

Jerry said steadily,

'She probably thinks no worse of you than you think of her. You aren't still holding a grudge, are you? I don't think Nonie bears any malice.'

'I did,' said Helen. 'I was *horrible* to her.'

'Doesn't it make any difference that Oliver wants you to be there?'

'Does he? I'm on better terms with Oliver just lately than I've been since he was a child, but I don't think we shall ever reach the stage where what I do, or don't do, is an object with him.'

'Oh, Helen.'

'Any improvement in my relationship with him is entirely down to that amazing girl that he married - who you all tried to freeze out, I seem to remember. As if where she came from mattered, when what she *was,* was so self-evident.' Scorn in her voice now, not entirely deserved perhaps. Jerry rather liked his daughter-in-law, and sometimes did feel guilty about the treatment she had received before she and Oliver had run away. From Dot again, but again, it had been easier to go with Dot than to take a stand. He failed to meet Helen's eyes, and drank from his mug inadvisedly. It was sizzling hot. He gasped, and choked, reaching for his handkerchief. When he recovered his breath, he found that at some point in his paroxysm, that last accusation had re-worded itself.

Before she and Oliver were driven away.

Like Helen.

Like Nonie.

And now, if Dot had been allowed to have her way, like Debbie.

'God, I've been a fool,' he said, starkly.

'We are all fools, one way or another,' said Helen.

'Was that a philosophical remark, or an observation on the present situation?'

'I'm not absolutely sure.' Helen was calming now, recovering from the shock of seeing him so suddenly, even smiling at him in a way that was almost friendly.

'Then don't add to your share of foolishness. Go upstairs and get yourself clean, put on your glad rags and come with me to London. Please, Helen.'

'Is this a proposition?' Helen wondered, an edge to her voice.

'No. It's an offer of moral support, with no strings attached.' Jerry paused. 'Look, Helen, Nonie is very much a part of Oliver's life. You can't avoid her for always, unless you want to avoid him, too. Do you? Now you admit yourself that things are better between you?'

Helen didn't answer. She turned her face away, and surreptitiously put up a hand to rub under her eyes.

'If you want to be a part of his life again, you have to face it.' He leaned across, putting his hand under her chin and turning her head round. 'You look like a clown,' he said, gently. 'Go and wash your face. And while you do it, think about what I'm saying. I'll wait.' He wanted to kiss her. She would probably break his jaw, and who could blame her?

Without speaking, Helen set her half-empty mug aside and left the room. In the downstairs cloakroom, she looked at herself in the mirror.

'A clown,' she mused, aloud. 'Oh God....' She leaned her forehead on the cool glass. There was a pain under her ribs that she thought might be her heart breaking again. 'I can't do with this... after all that's happened, the bugger wants to be *friends?* He wants to turn the clock back, and have everything as it was before *her?*' She turned on the tap, splashing cold water into the sink, and looked at her smudged, unhappy face despairingly. Jerry didn't even *like* Nonie, for God's sake, he never had, really.

A rogue thought came into her head then. Jerry *had* liked Nonie at first, they had all been friends together, it was all that fuss about Matt Sutton that had changed things, and why?

Dot again, of course. Was there one area of their lives where she hadn't infiltrated and spilt poison? Jerry had barely bothered to come to Matt's funeral, he had whisked her away immediately afterwards when she had wanted to be with Nonie and her friends, part of their circle, accepted among fellow artists. He had muttered darkly about not getting mixed up in unpleasantness... and she... she had let him.

Unpleasantness, incidentally, that she was morally certain was down to Dot's account.

So where did responsibility lie, then? With Dot exclusively, or with all of them, for letting her get away with it until she became a monster?

Too difficult, that one. Too long ago. Too painful. Helen dashed water on her face, hiding it in her hands so that she need no longer look at herself. There remained today, to go, or not to go? She imagined Oliver's face if she walked in on his father's arm. Not just Oliver's, even the suave Gifford Thomas might miss a beat. It wouldn't escape the notice of the press, either, no chance. She leaned her hands on the edge of the sink, staring down at the plughole. She had that sinking feeling that you get just before you do something that you think you might live to regret. She raised her head and stared into her own eyes. She thought that she looked scared.

Putting all thoughts of Nonie, her dear, dear friend, recipient of her most private thoughts, whom she had treated so very badly, firmly out of her mind, Helen turned and went back out into the hall. She called through the living-room door.

'Just go on waiting will you, Jerry? I'll have a shower.'

To what end, Jerry wondered? Simple cleanliness, an escape from persecution, or an evening on the tiles with her ex-husband? The mood she was in, he wasn't placing any bets. But her instructions were clear, he picked up a newspaper from the coffee table and opened it. He would just wait here and see what developed.

She was so long, that he wondered if she had climbed out of the window and made a run for it, not realising that there was a precedent in her history. Once, she had come down and he heard her in the kitchen, talking to someone, then realised it must be an animal when he heard a sharp, demanding bark. She went upstairs again after that and he heard a door close, then nothing at all. Eventually, glancing at his watch, he laid aside the paper that he wasn't really reading and went out into the hall. It might be taking too much for granted, but he had to do it. He called up the stairs.

'Helen? Time's getting on.'

He heard her footsteps on the stairs before he saw her, standing on the half-landing looking down at him with a challenge in her eyes. She wore a long black skirt and black boots with a pale blue silk shirt that highlighted the colour of her wonderful eyes, and round her shoulders, a black pashmina shawl pinned on the shoulder with a big sapphire brooch of obviously Scottish origin. She looked stunning, individual and exotic. Ageless. There were no traces of tears.

'You look as if you're going to war,' said Jerry, before he could stop himself. There was admiration in his voice. She lifted her chin.

'I am,' she said, and swept down the stairs like a storm, past him to the door. 'Come on then, we'll be late.'

The Ladbourne Gallery was a long way removed from that first gallery that Giff had opened with his uncle's money. Geographically to the west, with all that that implied, it consisted of three big upstairs rooms opening off each other through elegant archways. The walls were plain white with just the faintest touch of cream to warm it, the floors covered in honey-coloured tiles that gave a Mediterranean feel to the place. In the first, and biggest, room, there were a few spindly modern chairs but the others were full of space. Oliver's vibrant pictures turned each room into an exquisite jewel-box, full of treasures. There were one or two tall stands tucked into the corners, on which Giff had artfully displayed, not art but artefacts - a ship's propeller crusted with barnacles, the jawbone of a big fish washed clean and white by the action of waves, a piece of old timber decorated with the whorls and casts of teredo worms, an enormous seashell, an anchor. The whole effect was dramatic in its sheer simplicity. Chel, who had never been into a big art gallery in her life, found it rather overwhelming. Giff had done Oliver proud.

Among the sophisticated London strangers who thronged the rooms, the press and the prospective buyers, were one or two more familiar faces.

'What do you wear to a private view?' Chel's mother had asked, despairingly, over the telephone. 'I've never been to such a thing in my life!'

'Something elegant,' said Chel. Marilyn snorted.

'Elegant, me! Among all those people dripping with designer labels! I wonder you won't feel ashamed of me!'

'Mum! Don't be silly. Make Trace take you into Ipswich and hit the shops, she'll tell you what to buy. And get Dad into his decent suit, will you?'

'Oh Cheryl, I don't know if I can even get him to leave the shop for that long.'

'Rubbish, Mum! Trace is looking after it, and he'll be back soon enough, what's going to happen?' She added shrewdly, 'You both came quick enough when you thought I was going to marry Oliver - '

'Which you did,' interrupted Marilyn.

'Yes, and look how well it's turned out! So come and cheer.'

Debbie had said that she would maybe come up on her own later in the week and skip the private view.

'I'm a bit *persona non grata* at the moment, though they've all been very kind,' she said, with a wry grimace. 'Let Susan and Tom do the honours for the family on opening night, and I'll keep my head down out of sniping range. I've seen most of the pictures anyway.'

Chel tried to persuade her, but half-heartedly, as she knew that

Debbie was right.

The Dreaded Dot had not received an invitation.

Nonie had made a tentative call to Greece.

'Ah, Nona,' had said Theo. 'Now why do I feel that you are going to tell me something I do not wish to hear?'

'Well, I hope you're going to wish to hear it,' Nonie said. 'I was going to ask you to come to London and come with me to Oliver's private view.'

There was a silence that sizzled with unspoken thoughts. When he spoke again, his voice sounded strange.

'Is this for friendship's sake, Nona? For Oliver?'

'And for me,' said Nonie. 'Theo, I've been thinking.'

'Is this good for me, or bad?'

'Whatever you want it to be,' said Nonie.

'I'm on the plane.'

Judy and Keith had come in the spirit of adventure.

'I see Maggie isn't here,' said Judy, looking around her with awed amazement. 'What do I say when I see her?'

'Give her our love,' said Chel.

'Ouch!'

Chel relented.

'We did send her and Jack an invitation, how could we not when you think how much we owe her? Only, the kids are down with chicken-pox or something.' She didn't add, but Judy understood, that she was on the whole relieved.

Keith cast a measuring eye around the crowded room.

'Oliver looks like a mafioso,' he observed. 'Couldn't you get him to wear a tie, girl?'

Chel cast a swift glance at Oliver, elegant and handsome in a dark designer suit and a sparkling white shirt, open at the neck. The whiteness of the shirt made his skin olive. He looked stunning.

'You'd be amazed how hard it was to get him to go that far,' she said.

'But you...,' said Keith, looking at her admiringly. 'You look gorgeous!'

The little black dress - *little* being the operative word - had been a present from Nonie, and had cost enough to feed a large family for a week. Chel felt degenerate in it, but sleek and mysterious like a cat, albeit a ginger one. She smiled. Judy took Keith's arm, pretending to hold him back.

'Stop slavering, you!' They all laughed.

Notably absent were either of Oliver's parents. Chel felt sorry. She hadn't really expected Helen, but Jerry, she thought, would have made the effort.

Waitresses picked their way through the expensive throng, carrying trays of glasses and little canapés. When Judy and Keith moved on to look at the pictures, Chel felt suddenly a little lost and out of her element. Giff came towards her, lifting two glasses from a passing tray as he came. He handed one of them to her.

'Are you pleased, dear girl?' He lifted an eyebrow. 'We have attracted a lot of attention, you know. Everyone who should be here, is here.'

'Ah, but will it be a success?' asked Chel. He smiled.

'You're nobody's fool, are you, dear girl? Now tell me, just how did Oliver come to paint the picture he has called *The Way Home*. It's a strange anomaly, that one.'

'Oh...' said Chel. They had discussed this, she and Nonie and Oliver, knowing the question would be asked. 'Well... with Nonie giving him such help, and us living in the house... it was a sort of tribute to Matthew Sutton, I suppose.'

'A tribute.' Giff looked at her through narrowed eyes. 'Now, I have to tell you, dear girl, that I have seen a few forgeries in my time.' Chel started. 'No no, I'm not saying this is a forgery, of course it isn't. But people who imitate the style of others, for whatever reason, leave their own mark for those who know. It's hard to deceive a real expert, whatever you may think.'

'So?' asked Chel, when he didn't seem to want to continue. Giff looked pensive.

'So, dear girl, you must remember that I knew Matt better than most. His work, too. I have to say that I would never identify that painting as simply a tribute had Oliver not signed it, except for it's age. The canvas is contemporary, the paint, not. A mystery.' He smiled at her. 'Excuse me, dear girl, I must circulate. Shall I introduce you to some people?'

'I think I'd better go and rescue my parents,' said Chel.

She headed across the room to where they were standing alone, studying pictures with untouched glasses of wine in their hands, but was cut off along the way by Susan and her husband, Tom Casson.

'I was going to speak to Mum and Dad - ' Chel started to explain. Susan gave Tom a push in their direction.

'Go on Tom - look after them. I want to speak to Cheryl.'

'If it's about Deb - ' Chel began, when he had obediently left on his mission. Susan made an impatient gesture.

'No, it isn't about Deb. She's caused enough fuss! Tell me, did you and Oliver know about Daddy? About the flat?' She looked angry,

Chel thought. She temporised.

'Why should we?'

'He seems to take you into his confidence these days,' said Susan, with, so far as Chel could see, no grounds for her assertion. '*I*, of course, was the last to know!'

'He never said anything to us,' said Chel, relieved to slide out of the dilemma so speciously.

'I can't believe that he could do such a thing to Mummy,' said Susan. 'He must know she'll have to come round over Deb eventually, and she's always been so good, so strong for him...' She looked genuinely bewildered. Good for Jerry, or good generally? Chel wondered. For herself, she would deny either. She said,

'Well, these things happen. There's been a lot of pressure.'

'Mostly from you and Oliver,' said Susan, with a toss of her head, ignoring now her sister's present, not-insignificant contribution. 'I think - '

But Chel didn't want to hear what Susan thought, not here and now, she could sense that she was seriously upset.

'What do you think of the show?' she asked.

Out of the corner of her eye, she could see that Tom had exchanged her parents' wineglasses for tumblers of orange juice and was leading them towards herself and Susan. Good old Tom! A nonentity in his own house he might seem, but he was at least socially competent.

'Never mind the show,' said Susan, and was about to continue when her attention was caught by something behind Chel's shoulder. Her eyes widened, and she drew in her breath with a little hiss. 'Well!'

Chel turned. She was in time to see Jerry, holding the door open, and Helen walking past him with the air of a queen. Her jaw dropped. Out of the corner of her eye, she saw Tom hand his glass to her mother and take his wife's arm.

'Steady, Suse. Remember where we are.'

Susan, to her credit, restrained herself. She drew a deep breath.

'Now, I've seen it all!'

'What goes around, comes around,' Chel murmured, but not loud enough for Susan to hear her. She was startled herself. Giff had moved smoothly forward to greet the newcomers, she followed after him. Oliver was nowhere to be seen, which was typical of him, she thought unjustly.

'Chel, darling!' Helen greeted her with a warm kiss on the cheek. 'How lovely.' She was tense as a trip wire. Jerry had moved past them to greet Marilyn and Bob. They had never met Oliver's mother, of course, and looked as if they thought Jerry a suspiciously fast worker.

In Suffolk, the inference was, people had more finesse. Doubtful...
Helen lowered her voice and whispered in Chel's ear,
   '*And the crowd said to the lions, "Bite Daniel, bite him, bite him!"*'
   'But they didn't, if you remember,' said Chel. She linked her arm
through Helen's. 'Come and meet my parents. I'm so glad you came.'
   'Just don't leave me, in case the lions change their minds.'
   Helen's eyes roved swiftly round the room, but if Nonie was there,
she didn't recognise her. Twenty-five years was a long time, but
nobody changed that much, surely? There were several people that she
did know, however. She wasn't sure if that made her feel better, or
worse. She spoke a few words with Chel's parents, then an
acquaintance claimed her and she was swept off into the crowd.
   'What a beautiful woman,' said Marilyn, watching her retreating
back. 'You can see where Oliver gets it from. Is...?' She left the
question unspoken. Chel shook her head.
   'Don't ask me, you could have knocked me down with a ten ton
truck when they walked in together.' She caught sight of Theo, moving
towards them and beckoned to him. Theo knew nobody either, but she
had enough faith in his social graces to trust her mother and father to
him. He would see they enjoyed themselves and didn't retreat into a
corner.
   'Theo! Lovely to see you, what have you done with Nonie?'
   'She is talking shop to a lot of very noisy people. I search for
someone more congenial.' He bowed to her father when Chel
introduced him, and kissed her mother's hand. Marilyn melted visibly.
   'Look after them, Theo, there's a dear,' said Chel. 'I need to find
Oliver, if you'll excuse me.' And warn him, but she didn't add that.
Jerry and Helen had vanished into the crowd, they might be together
now or they might not, but someone would be sure to mention their
arrival together.
   Nonie was in the far room when Helen finally found her. She was
standing in front of the picture she always thought of as *Matt's picture*,
and fortuitously she was alone for a moment. There were other people
in the room of whom she was peripherally aware, but nobody that she
knew or who knew her. Lost in thought, she never heard Helen come
up beside her until she spoke.
   'I shall never be able to thank you adequately for what you've done
for Oliver.'
   Nonie turned, slowly, her thoughts still half in the past, so that it
almost seemed natural to find Helen standing at her elbow. Almost.
   'Thanks aren't necessary. It's been great fun.'
   Helen had been startled when she recognised her, indeed, had she

not been looking she thought she mightn't have known her. Nonie's dark curly hair showed a lot of white, although she was only, like Helen herself, in her mid-fifties, her face was thin, brown and lived in. Only the bright brown eyes sparkled as they used to do. Have I aged like that? she asked herself, startled, she's really let herself go, and she's skinny as a broom handle! Then Nonie smiled, and she realised her mistake. The warmth and sensitivity that had ensnared Matt Sutton was still there, and Nonie had never been a beauty anyway. She had grown older naturally and on the whole, gracefully - unlike me, thought Helen, I've fought every inch of the way. The unexpected friendliness of that smile touched her. A silly lump came into her throat.

'That isn't all I have to say,' she managed to say, past it.

'Don't - ' Nonie reached out a hand. 'That isn't necessary, either.'

'Yes it is. I've had years to think about it. I don't honestly think I would have done anything different if I had been you... and I threw away years of the best friendship I ever had.' She stopped.

'You were under great stress. She was gunning for you, she meant to get you. Believe me, I've thought too, and I worked it out. She got us all.'

'With just the one bullet, too. Remarkable, when you think about it.' Helen was relaxing. Nonie, who for a moment there had feared she was going to create a scene, was relieved. The years rolled back, and she grinned at her friend, unselfconsciously.

'So tell me, what do you think of your son's show? Clever bastard, isn't he?'

Helen revolved on her heels, looking about her properly, possibly for the first time.

'It's frightening in a way. All this sea, all these ships and storms and rocks, harbours and oceans. It's frightening, because he hasn't changed, has he? He's still some wild, seafaring maverick and I still feel... I feel that he'll never really come home.' The feeling was disturbingly strong. It left her bereft.

'And what do you think of this one?' asked Nonie, gesturing to the one behind them. She hadn't intended to broach that subject to anyone, but Helen's perceptive comments on Oliver had disarmed her. Immediately she had spoken, she wished she hadn't. They weren't friends any more, they were papering over the cracks merely. Or to put it another way, a gulf opened between you, you might fill it in or build a bridge, but it would never be the strong ground underfoot that it had been before. It opened communication, that was all.

Helen was silent for several minutes, studying the picture as if she hadn't noticed it before. Maybe she hadn't. The pause had gone on for too long before she spoke.

"It takes me right back,' she said softly. 'Where did it come from? And don't say, Oliver painted it. I can see he did, and that wasn't the question.'

'Giff didn't want to hang it,' said Nonie.

'I can see why he wouldn't.'

'I told him he had to. That it was a link from Matt to me to Oliver, and belonged here with the rest. That it was a tribute piece, even if it was a curiosity.'

'It's more than a curiosity,' said Helen. 'I mean... it's a complete throw-back. Oliver doesn't paint like this, nothing like. It's pure sixties.'

'One day, I'll tell you about it. Here and now isn't the time.'

The inference that there would be another time hung in the air between them. It was shattered by the entrance of Jerry through the arch.

'I came with Jerry,' said Helen, abruptly, seeing no help for it, and catching the look on Nonie's face, added swiftly and fiercely, 'And no, it isn't a grand reconciliation, it was more of a kidnapping. So don't read anything into it.'

'I wouldn't dream of it.' Nonie spread her hands. 'Hullo Jerry, how good to see you.'

Jerry felt himself equal to the occasion.

'*When shall we three meet again, in thunder, lightning or in rain?*' he quoted, and then wished that he hadn't as the memory of the last time they had all been together silenced all three of them. 'Sorry,' he said, when he had got his breath back. 'Social *gaffe*. Let's start again, shall I? You've done a grand job on the boy, Nonie. No wonder he never made a solicitor.'

'Good God, did he even think about it?' Nonie was astounded.

'Well, no. He didn't. All the thinking was on my side - only son, you know. To be fair, the only one of the three of them who might have been interested was Susan, and she got married instead.'

'There's a lot of Henry in Susan,' commented Helen. All three of them wondered, they couldn't help it, how much Dot had influenced Susan's life, too, and whether she would have made a good solicitor if she hadn't been married off. But presumably she had some say in the matter, Nonie thought. Because none of the things they were thinking could be said aloud, Helen's comment had almost as smothering an effect on the conversation as Jerry's had done, and it was a relief to be approached by Giff, accompanied by Theo looking for Nonie.

People were beginning to leave now, off to continue their evening elsewhere, leaving behind them a satisfactorily thick sprinkling of red dots indicating sales, and a warm atmosphere of approval.

'I've booked a table for dinner down the road,' said Giff, and named a restaurant that even Chel had heard of. 'You'll join us, Jerry, Helen? A little celebration, children, on the house. We've had a splendid evening!'

'I'm bound by whatever Helen wants to do,' said Jerry. He turned to her. 'We could find a hotel and stay up for the night. What do you think?'

Helen smiled, making her rejection graceful.

'I have to get home to feed my cat, and let the dogs out - but thank you Gifford, all the same. It would have been nice.'

'I'm sorry, but I understand.' He took her hand between both his own and held it. 'It's been good to see you again, Helen. The next time you want to exhibit in London, remember me. You don't have to feel bound to Goldstein, I'm sure, dear girl. He'd understand.'

'He certainly would, and probably murder us both!' Helen grinned at him, feeling herself on firm ground for the first time that evening. 'No, darling Giff, but thank you for the offer.' She leaned forward to kiss his cheek. Drawing back, she met Theo's eye, and noted immediately his protective proximity to her erstwhile friend.

'You haven't introduced us, Nonie,' she said.

'Dimitrios Theodorakis,' said Nonie, immediately. 'My old friend, Helen Macken, Theo - Oliver's mother, as if you couldn't guess.'

'Charmed,' said Theo, bending over her hand. Over his bent head, Helen's eyes met Nonie's, they were sparkling.

'Nice one, Nonie,' she said, so softly that only the two of them heard, like the whispering ghost of their old friendship. Her eyes flicked past Nonie to the picture behind her, and back again. 'I'm really pleased,' she said, more loudly. The phrase could have referred to the introduction or to the inferences that could be drawn from it. Nonie thought she knew which way it was intended.

'Thank you,' she said demurely. Helen turned to Jerry.

'Are you ready, Jerry? My poor darlings will have their back legs crossed by the time we get back as it is, and the cat will never meow to me again.' Her warm smile included them all. Helen at her classy best, Nonie thought wryly. She had changed, but not changed. She wasn't sure if this evening could ever be called reconciliation. Armed truce, more probably.

On their way out, Jerry and Helen said goodbye to Chel's parents, collapsed on two of the spindly chairs, and found Chel and Oliver talking to two young people whom they didn't recognise. Susan and

Tom were long gone, in who-knew-what state of misinformed confusion. The waitresses were collecting glasses. In the emptying rooms, the pictures hung against the walls, a presence in themselves. Noting the number of red dots, and calculating probabilities, Helen wondered if Oliver might find himself with a sell-out on his hands before the end. What would the critics say? she was curious to know.

'Well, we're off now,' Jerry said, with a joviality that rang falsely. Oliver looked cool, Helen thought, he must be finding this hard to take, and she didn't altogether blame him. She tried to make it better.

'Jerry was kind enough to give me a lift,' she explained. 'I hate driving in London, and he passed my door. Wonderful show, darling.' Oliver's valedictory kiss on her cheek was a step forward, but still impersonal. Chel was smiling though, she was a darling girl. They passed through the glass doors of the gallery and out into the cold reality of the street. The doors abruptly swinging together behind them cut off the sound of talk and laughter.

In the car, once they were clear of the London streets, and bowling down the M4 Jerry stole a cautious look at his companion. She was leaning back with her eyes closed, but he didn't think she was sleeping.

'Would you like to stop somewhere, and eat?' he asked her.

'No thank you, Jerry. I'm not into motorway food.'

'We could get off into the hinterland. There must be a pub.'

'Still no thank you, thank you.' She settled more firmly into her seat.

'It was good to see you able to talk to Nonie. It wasn't so bad, was it?'

'We're both grown up,' said Helen, dismissively. Jerry persevered.

'Good to see her with a man along, too. Do you think there's anything in it? She's mourned Sutton for long enough.'

'What would you know?' Helen asked. 'Women can function without a man, I have to tell you.' She sounded bitter, and Jerry, silenced, drove for a few miles in silence.

'Helen...'

'Sssh. I'm asleep.'

The next time he spoke to her, she didn't answer at all. She may, or may not, have been asleep. Jerry drove on towards Surrey and her home without trying again.

As he turned into her drive, security lights came on and in the house, dogs began barking. Helen yawned elaborately and sat up.

'Are we here already?'

'You know damn well we are. Look Helen, we've got to talk

sometime, you and I. Why not now?'

'No we haven't.' Helen opened the car door and swung her booted feet round to get out. 'We have nothing whatever that needs saying.'

'You can't mean that.'

'Yes I can.' She turned so that her chin rested on her shoulder and she could look at him. 'Just because you've finally seen the light over that woman, doesn't mean that anything's changed between you and me. For me, I still remember being constantly humiliated by you both. I still remember being alienated from my only child. And I still have to live with the knowledge that if he has any parents at all, which I doubt, they're Anona Fingall and Dimitrios Theodorakis, not you and me, and if you didn't do that yourself, you let *her* do it, which comes to the same thing in my book. So what they hell is there to say?' She got out of the car and slammed the door. By the time she had walked round the bonnet, Jerry was standing on the drive.

'At least invite me in and give me a cup of coffee. I've got to get home yet, remember.'

'You'll find somewhere open, I've no doubt.' She marched past him towards the house. He caught up with her as she was struggling to fit her key into the lock, her cat winding and purring around her feet.

'Here, let me.' He took it from her and fitted it into the keyhole. The door swung open onto the dimly lit hall. The barking was louder now, accompanied by scrabbling claws.

'Shit!' said Helen. 'Oh all right - you go and let them out while I put the kettle on, they're through in the utility room.' She stalked into the kitchen and opened a door on the far side. Two border terriers poured through, leaping and barking. The kitchen seemed full of them.

'The back door is that way.' She pointed through the utility room. Jerry said,

'Here, dogs,' and to his surprise, they flowed back through the door ahead of him.

It was dark in the garden, and quiet except for the rustling of the dogs in the bushes as they went about their business. Jerry leaned against the wall of the house trying to gather his thoughts, which were in confusion. When he had come here today, it was with no thought in his head but to prevent Helen from damaging her still-precarious relationship with Oliver. Seeing her, listening to her, watching her, had taken him straight back to that awful period of their lives when their marriage was crumbling under their feet and he had been able to do nothing to please her. Too late to realise now that he should have listened to her wishes and not to Dot's interfering advice. Too late by far to apologise.

The only trouble was, that at that time in their lives, he had loved her. Seeing her had brought the emotion back. Seeing her home had reminded him of the cottage they had shared, and her gift for home-making, for laughter, for fun, even her animals took him back. It had made him see, in one blinding flash, what he had given up so easily. Whether that meant that he still loved her now, he couldn't be sure.

The dogs came pounding back up the lawn into the light that spilled from the open back door and vanished indoors. Jerry didn't move.

He hadn't known how to handle Helen then, but did he know any better now? She hadn't always been so intractable; he remembered when they had first met, how tender and gentle, how loving she had been, how she had filled his whole horizon and blanked out everything but herself. How she had encompassed the world and made it sweet.

'Shit!' said Jerry.

'No doubt, somewhere on the lawn,' said Helen's voice, close to his ear. 'I'll clear it up in the morning, I usually take them all the way down to the field. Are you coming in, or are you going to spend all night out there?'

'I was just thinking,' said Jerry, slowly, 'how great a fool I've been.'

Helen said nothing, but she remained in the doorway, hugging her shawl to her against the cold night. She had kicked off her boots and stood in her stockinged feet. She waited.

'You must really dislike me,' he said, at last.

'No.' She sounded as if it was something she had given real consideration. 'No, I don't dislike you. But that doesn't mean you can wind the tape back and pretend nothing happened. For instance, how could I ever trust you again after what you did?'

Jerry stopped leaning against the wall and stood up straight.

'You're getting cold,' he said. 'Look, you've no shoes on. Let's go inside.'

'The thing is,' said Helen, pouring water from the kettle into a *cafetière*, 'life isn't so simple. Just as Nonie and I will never be the friends we once were, so you and I will never be lovers. Nonie and I might be on speaking terms - we probably will - but we can never be really close. And you and I can't even be that, realistically.'

'Why not?' asked Jerry, wanting to know.

'Because....' said Helen. She stood for a minute, staring unseeing at the dark square of the window. 'Because we can't, that's all.'

'Realistically,' said Jerry, borrowing her own word, 'give me one good reason.'

'I once said to Chel,' said Helen, without looking at him, 'that the trouble with the Nankervis men was that you don't stop loving them. Is that good enough?'

'It sounds to me like an argument on my side. *Do* you still love me?' She didn't answer him directly.

'If you loved someone, and they let you down so badly that you felt you could never trust them again... then could you be near them? See them? Be friends with them?'

'If they loved you - '

'You don't, Jerry. Don't kid yourself. You're lonely, that's all, and your nice comfortable marriage has broken up, you're back to the single life and it isn't all it's cracked up to be.'

'Marriage wasn't all it was cracked up to be,' said Jerry. 'Certainly not *nice* or *comfortable.*'

'So are you going to divorce her? Susan doesn't seem to think so.'

'No.'

'Then what can you offer me, anyway? It sounds to me as if she still comes first - no, don't answer that.' She rattled mugs and the *cafetière* onto a tray, and added a bottle of milk. 'Come into the other room. You can have your coffee, and then I think you'd better go.'

She led him back into her beautiful living-room, set the tray in front of him and curled up in an armchair, snug as the cat that leapt onto her knee, purring. They had more than one thing in common, Helen and her cat, Jerry thought as he poured his coffee. Soft and elegant and beguiling, with lethally sharp claws and teeth. The dogs had settled on the hearthrug, they raised their heads and wagged their tails, but didn't move.

'I don't think I'll bother, after all,' Helen said. 'It will only keep me awake - I made it pretty strong, to keep *you* awake.' She sounded almost as if she wished she hadn't bothered. Jerry sipped at his mug. The coffee was strong enough to blow his eyeballs out. It cleared his mind like tidewater across a cluttered beach. He felt like a man who had been bewitched, waking after a hundred years - or a prisoner, unexpectedly released from penal servitude for life, suddenly seeing the outside world again.

'The thing is,' Helen was saying, very softly, as if she had read his mind, 'Happy Ever After is a myth, it doesn't exist. It's like *Tir nan Og*, or Valhalla, or the Never-never Land. It would be wonderful to think it would be so, but Nonie will never marry this Theodorakis, any more than she married any of the others - including Matthew Sutton. Oliver is still to some extent disabled. He and Chel will never have children. Dot will always be Debbie's mother however hard she tries to disown her, and you and I, Jerry, have no future together. The End.'

Jerry heard himself saying, outrageously,

'When I said that marriage wasn't all it was cracked up to be, I meant marriage to *either* of you. Couldn't we try *not* being married?'

'We've been doing that for twenty-five years,' Helen pointed out. There was a spark in her eyes, but it died. 'No Jerry. Stop trying to turn the clock back.'

'I don't want to turn it back,' said Jerry, quietly. 'I want... I think I want... to fast-forward to a new age.'

'Old age,' said Helen. 'That's all it'll be, Jerry. And now, if you've finished your coffee, I think you'd better go.' She pushed the cat off her knee and stood up. 'If you don't, we shall *both* end up saying something regrettable.' Her eyes looked a defiant challenge.

Jerry had only half-finished, but he put the mug down and stood up too.

'But I may see you again? You'll lunch with me sometimes? If you're in Embridge?'

'Why?' asked Helen. 'Oliver's no problem any more, he's on his way. Or do you want to show me this flat that's so upset everyone?' She bared her teeth in a feline smile. 'You're a devious bugger, Jerry Nankervis, and the answer is *No.*'

'Oh well, it was worth a try.' Jerry shrugged fatalistically, and could have sworn that Helen was taken aback. She covered it quickly, but his heart missed a beat. He turned for the door. 'I'll say goodbye then.'

Helen padded after him into the hall and pulled back the catch on the front door. The cat ran out into the night, tail up, and vanished under the bushes, and the dogs made for the kitchen. Wise cat. Wise dogs.

'Am I allowed to kiss you goodnight?' asked Jerry.

'If you must.' She stood unresisting, proffering her cheek, but Jerry took her face in his hands, turned it, and kissed her squarely on the mouth.

'Mmmf!' mumbled Helen, and wriggled, without success, to get away. Jerry let the kiss go on and on, a hard kiss, full of... passion? Anger? He wasn't certain. Helen relaxed suddenly, her lips warm and soft, kissing him back - and then twisted away in a flame of anger. 'You *bastard*, Jerry! Get out, get out of my life!' She had clasped her hands tightly behind her back, as if she was afraid of hitting him... maybe.

'I'm going,' said Jerry, equably. 'I'll see you around, Helen Macken. Be sure of it.'

'*Goodbye!*' snapped Helen. The door slammed behind him. She stood with her back leaning against it, breathing hard, until she heard the sound of his engine fading down the drive.

POSTSCRIPT

My dear Nonie,

I thought you might be interested in the enclosed cutting, which is from this month's Arts *magazine. Ben Hyams, as you know well yourself, can be a bitterly scathing bastard of a critic, but he seems to have treated your all-too-well-known pupil very fairly. I was afraid that he might be lacking in sympathy, there is no doubt that the media have had a lot to do with Oliver's runaway success, but as the saying goes, the beast is a just beast and hasn't allowed the petty jealousies of lesser men to influence what he writes. Curious, what he has to say at the end though, don't you think? Is there something here, I wonder, that you failed to tell me, Nonie? I think this very unkind of you, if so. After all, I gave you every chance.*

On the other hand, fair is fair. There is something that I didn't tell you, too. The photographer who did the artwork for the catalogue had a lot of problems with that picture, indeed, the final choice had been computer-edited to make it possible to use. The problem seemed to lie in the curious fact that that picture, more than any, seemed to catch the light and reflect it back, sometimes in very bizarre ways. I enclose one of the more uncanny effects for you to see, and perhaps when you have seen it, you will give me a full tale? I should appreciate that, very much. Remember, Matt was my friend too, and long before he was yours.

Please pass on the Compliments of the Season to those two pleasant young people when you see them, and I look forward to seeing you all in the coming year. I hope that you are all fully recovered from the excitement of your visit to the Great City, and that Oliver has come to terms with success! It never happened to me, alas, but it must be an amazing experience to retire to one's bed many thousands of pounds richer than when you rose in the morning! I shall treasure the memory of his face when he heard the total for the rest of my life.

Sincerely,

Gifford

Nonie laid the letter aside with a smile for the final paragraph, and unfolded the enclosures. A photograph that fell out and fluttered to the floor, she ignored for now, being far more immediately interested in the press cutting. Ben Hyams wrote for one of the more reputable journals that dealt exclusively with the arts, and his comments were treated with respect. There had been many reviews, of course, in newspapers and magazines, most of them very positive, one or two spiteful, but what Benjamin Hyams had to say would carry enormous weight. He could make or break, and did so without compunction.

One views with both suspicion and scepticism the transition from blue-water yachtsman to marine artist, but it has been triumphantly achieved, he had written. *Oliver Nankervis has a lot still to learn, although one can watch his skills developing throughout this impressive first exhibition, but there seems to be little that one could teach him about his subject. His knowledge of the sea is obviously both deep and personal, and conceals, or even to some extent excuses, the shortcomings in his craftsmanship. In time, when he is as experienced as a painter as he is perceptive as an observer we may expect truly great things from this young man.* She let her eye run quickly over a critique of Oliver's colour sense, style and brushwork, most of which she could have written herself in almost the same words, until she came to the paragraph to which Giff had referred.

But there is one notable exception to all these comments, and it is a strange one indeed. In this exhibition there is only one picture which is not a seascape, coincidentally it is also by far the largest and thus draws the eye irresistibly. The technique here is completely different, indeed, if it was not signed with the artist's name, and people not present that are able to speak to its authenticity, one would give it quite a different provenance. Perhaps some of you who read this will never have heard of Matthew Sutton, if so, I advise you to seek out his work and study it. He was a singularly talented landscape painter some thirty years ago, tragically killed in a plane crash at what should have been the peak of a brilliant career. This one picture, and only this one picture, bears all the hallmarks of Sutton's very distinctive style, something which becomes all the more intriguing when one realises that Oliver Nankervis is the pupil of Anona Fingall, who, of course, is well-known as a painter herself, but who also, it is less widely remembered, was Sutton's "significant other" at the time of his death. Add to this that Oliver Nankervis lived, atthe time when he painted this picture, in the house into which Sutton crashed his light aircraft on that misty night so many years ago, and you have the makings of a fascinating little mystery.

Nonie sat for some time, the page in her hand, just thinking, very still. So Matt had achieved some sort of recognition for his own masterpiece, that would please Oliver as it pleased her. She hoped that he would be at peace now, and that the stories about Vellanzoe would be forgotten. Dear Matt... but he had been dead a long time, and there were no tears for him now. He wouldn't want them anyway. He would be pleased if he knew about Theo, he had always said she should have someone of her own age. Ironic, when you considered that Theo was ten years older than he had been when he said it. Nonie laughed, a genuinely amused laugh. Then she bent down and picked up the photograph.

The laughter died. Her mouth went dry with pure shock and her heart bumped once, and began to race.

There was the hayfield, the wasteland, the struggling pilgrims and the glowing sky.

And there too, outlined in shining light, was Matt Sutton's smiling face.